PROMISES
and Other
Broken Things

J.S. EADES

Website: www.jseades.com
Twitter: @JS_Eades
Facebook: AuthorJSEades
Instagram: @jseadesauthor

Editorial Assistance: Colleen Ferrier, Lara Krebs, and Lauren White
Cover Design: Heather D. Murray

Edition: Amazon Paperback September 2018

ISBN: 978-0-9939582-0-5

Massive thanks to: Heather, Lara, Colleen Lauren, Eva, Laura, D'Ann, Craig, Mara, Amy, and not least of all, my husband, Peter. All their help and support over the course of the two years it took to bring this thing together has been invaluable

Chapter 1

Amelia

Let me make one thing clear right off the bat. This is not a story about two people who met and fell in love, and of course had hurdles to overcome, but they loved each other enough that nothing was insurmountable. You know the ones—the kind where in the end true love always conquers all. This is a story about real life, and real love, and it may not be a fairytale, but it is ours.

Some people will tell you that, looking back, they can pinpoint the precise moment when their entire world changed, when their lives were suddenly and abruptly shifted down a different path. I'd heard stories like this before of course, lots of times, but I hadn't really understood just what having a moment like that meant. Most of these same people will also tell you that you don't know it when it happens, you only realize the incredible impact that moment had when you look back later.

I knew the instant it happened to me.

It was just after eleven on my first day of work at Baker, Wright and Kavanaugh. My new boss, Diana Sharpe, was finishing up giving me an office tour and, though it was still morning, I'd already reached information overload. Fatigue had settled over my mind.

I glanced up over her shoulder and saw a man walking down the hallway toward us. He was about medium height, with broad shoulders and unkempt dark brown hair. He wore a black button-up dress shirt with the top couple of buttons undone, and black dress pants that clung to his slim hips like they were custom tailored.

He saw me and held my gaze with the most intense pale blue eyes, and something happened deep inside me, something that almost physically hurt as I looked at him. I forgot everything Diana had just told me. I forgot who I was. I forgot how to breathe. And I know it sounds ridiculous, but I swear we both froze for what felt like an eternity, although it was probably only a second or two.

Then Ryan Kavanaugh, to whom I'd just been introduced, popped his head out of his office and said something to the dark-haired guy. He startled, breaking our strange connection and disappearing inside.

You know the phrase 'my heart dropped'? I'd never experienced that feeling before. But at that moment? When he vanished from my sight? I swear it felt like my heart actually fell a few inches.

Closing my eyes for a second, I took a much-needed breath, desperately hoping neither Diana nor anyone else had noticed my strange reaction. What the heck was that about? I wasn't a schoolgirl anymore. So a good-looking guy caught my eye? So what?

Well for starters, *good-looking* didn't even begin to cover it. He'd caused me to react in a way I didn't think was even possible in real life. I'd turned into some embarrassing romance novel cliché for a moment there. And, second, I firmly didn't believe in the silly myth of love at first sight that popular culture and some of my more naïve friends spouted. I was married. And this was my new workplace. So it didn't matter. Couldn't matter.

Except deep down in the pit of my stomach, I knew it did.

I started off the day—the day that would change everything, though I didn't know it yet—by showing up early.

It was silly of me, in hindsight. Just as my husband, Scott, had predicted as I'd rushed around our house that morning, all being early accomplished was gaining me more time sitting and waiting.

So I sat, and I waited. The red second hand of the retro-style clock on the wall behind the reception desk seemed to be defective. I was sure it was moving far too slowly. Pushing a stray lock of hair behind one ear, I glanced up at it again

I took a deep breath, smoothed down the fabric of my skirt and tried to relax. I was bound and determined to make a good first impression. Just like I always did.

I was a Good Girl. It was the category I'd been slotted into from an early age, bestowed upon me by my parents, teachers, and nearly every other adult who'd ever met me. Because of this, I had always seen myself through their filters: The Good Girl, The Smart Girl, The Girl Who Did the Right Thing.

When I walked into the office to start my first day at Baker, Wright and Kavanaugh, I was nervous, but confident. They had approached *me* with the job offer, after all, so I knew they had high expectations. I'd worked at Bellmore & Sons Advertising since graduating from college with my accounting diploma proudly in hand. After seven years and my chances of advancement looking slimmer and slimmer at the large firm, I started exploring other opportunities. When BWK began wooing me, I knew it was the right time to spread my proverbial wings and leave the bosom of Known and Comfortable.

In her most recent e-mail, my new boss had requested I arrive at nine o'clock instead of the earlier eight I would have preferred. Of course, I showed up at 8:45 and not a minute later. So there I sat on a very sleek, modern, and therefore predictably hard chair in the reception area checking messages on my phone and glancing frequently toward the large glass doors which swung inward into the office proper.

At 9:04, I began to fidget and tap my toe against the gleaming hardwood.

At 9:08, I couldn't sit on that uncomfortable chair a moment longer, and got up to peruse the company's framed awards bragging audaciously from an otherwise stark white wall. The receptionist cast a disinterested glance my way before returning her attention to her monitor.

At 9:12, one of the glass doors opened, and the most stunning woman I'd ever seen stepped into the lobby.

"Amelia York?" she asked politely. Her voice was kind of raspy—
it brought to mind images of long nights spent drinking whiskey in
smoky dive bars. Tall and shapely, she had shoulder-length black
hair, a flawless complexion and full plum-stained lips. Thick lashes
framed almond-shaped dark eyes. She imparted an immediate sense
of charisma that I couldn't help admiring.

I smiled, sticking out my hand. "I'm Amelia."

She gave me a quick once-over. Her face was carefully composed,
betraying no hint of what her initial impression of me was.

It seemed like she looked down at the neatly trimmed nails of my
outstretched hand for just a beat too long before taking it and shaking
it firmly, once. I got a fleeting sense she hadn't really wanted to
touch me, but forced herself to anyway.

"Diana Sharpe. Right this way." She turned and went back through
the door without waiting to see if I would follow, her pointy-toed
stilettos clicking along the floor.

I walked a few steps behind Diana along a hall lined with opaque
glass-doored offices, then turned left and found myself staring at
rows of beige cubicles. A small black sign stating we'd reached the
Accounting department was affixed to the side of one padded half-
wall. This cubicle-farm in front of me housed my new workspace.
My new co-workers. My new life.

A few people looked up from their monitors as I followed Diana
down the center aisle, no doubt anxious for their first glimpse of the
New Girl. Conscious of their curious stares, I returned the smile of a
pretty dark-haired young woman as we passed.

Diana stopped abruptly at an empty cubicle about halfway down
the row and waved a hand toward the desk. "This one's yours. You
can leave your personal belongings here, and we'll go into my office
to discuss your role."

I draped my jacket over the back of the chair and resumed
following her. Once inside Diana's office, I took a seat across from a
large and messy desk. A print of one of Degas' ballerinas adorned the
wall behind her chair, but no personal photos were displayed.
Wasting no time, she launched into a description of what the
company did, the corporate structure, and what would be expected of
me.

The three partners, Robert Baker, Lucas Wright and Patrick Kavanaugh, founded this advertising agency thirty-two years ago. The department I'd be working most closely with was Sales, as it would be my job to price out advertising for new business, suggestions for add-ons, and any changes the clients decided to make down the line. I would have regular contact with the Account Managers and their administrative assistants. Diana began listing names and roles of some of the people I'd be working with, both here and in their satellite offices across the country, while I jotted notes in the back of my day planner.

I was surprised to find myself feeling a little intimidated by my new boss. Women didn't usually intimidate me. Actually, I'd found that other women were often intimidated *by* me. Diana Sharpe, however, was not intimidated by me in the slightest. In fact, I was willing to hedge a guess that Diana Sharpe was *never* intimidated. By anyone.

Declan

Goddamn it!

I was running late. Again. I'd had an early morning client meeting in Richmond, and ended up stuck in rush-hour traffic trying to escape the city to get back to the office. Christ, I'd be lucky if I got into work by *eleven*. Too much to do and too little fucking time to do it in. As usual.

I sped down the highway toward Lynchburg, hoping like hell I wouldn't pass any cops along the way. Impatiently, I punched buttons on the radio until loud rock music filled my Mustang, but the throbbing beat only incited me to hit the pedal harder. The aforementioned client, The Happy Tomato restaurant, was proving to be a pain in my ass. They wanted to advertise, sure; they just didn't really want to pay for it. Everybody wanted everything for damn-near free these days. Which meant more meetings, more wooing, more cajoling, more of my precious time spent holding their hands and coddling them, when what I really should've be spending my valuable time on was seducing bigger, richer, higher-profile clients. I had my own bills to pay, after all.

Running a hand through my hair, I sighed in frustration. I'd always been able to sweet talk my clients, turn on the charm and make the sale. It's what I excelled at. But to be honest, lately I'd been feeling a little off my game. My mind just wasn't as focused as it used to be. Other things insisted on vying for my attention. Work things. Home things. My brother's crap. My ability to compartmentalize all these aspects of my life and just focus on the task at hand had been wavering lately, and all these different worries had begun bleeding through. Sometimes at the most inopportune times.

Which pissed me off, because I was *always* focused, always in control, always got shit done.

Fucking Ryan. Keeping my brother's secrets while trying to rein him in and clean up his messes was what had been throwing me off the most lately. And the little shit didn't even appreciate it. Hell, he wouldn't even admit he *had* a problem. And it wasn't like I could go to Daddy Dearest for any help in the matter. First of all, Ryan would deny it, and then probably kill me for ratting him out. Second, Patrick Kavanaugh would never believe his youngest son could have an addiction problem. Even if I did manage to convince him, he'd somehow find a way to make it all *my* fault, like he'd been doing for the past twenty-nine years. In his eyes, Ryan could do no wrong. I was the one who always fucked everything up. So, no, telling our father was not an option. I had to deal with Ryan myself.

The simple truth was no matter how much it bit me in the ass some days, I loved my baby brother, and wanted more for him than the hell he was currently creating for himself. It might be a thankless task, helping family, but you just do it anyway. Cause they're *family*. Enough said.

When I pulled into the BWK parking lot at 11:04, I sighed again. My day had started out shitty, and I couldn't help but imagine the ways in which it might invariably get worse. What further torments awaited me inside? Another argument with Ryan? A dressing down from my father? A confrontation with the Bitch From Hell, Diana? All of the above?

Most days I loved being out on the road, meeting my clients, addressing their concerns, and making them happy. I enjoyed it, and I was damn good at it. Being in the office, however, was a different story. A lot of my co-workers didn't like me very much. They still judged me for my past, and refused to consider the possibility that I might have changed. Eventually I just stopped caring or bothering even attempting to be anything beyond civil to most of them.

There were a few notable exceptions. My admin assistant, Colleen, was a godsend. Somehow, she managed to put up with all my demands and fluctuating moods. I didn't know what I'd do if she ever decided to leave BWK.

And then there was Josh in Accounting. While hiding out at the bar during the fresh hell known as our Corporate Christmas Party a few years back, I'd discovered that Joshua Marshall not only preferred the same brand of whiskey I did, but that he was also sort of a kindred spirit. And those were few and far between in my life. Josh was more than just a co-worker—I respected the hell out of him and considered him my closest friend.

But most of the people in the office thought I was an ass, only still employed not because I was skilled at my job, but because my father was a partner. So the chances of the remainder of my day passing without further annoyance were pretty damned unlikely. It was just a matter of how much shit I'd have to endure before it was over.

Then the cherubic face of my sweet little girl, Alexis, popped into my head. I imagined how happy she'd be when I walked in the door later and swung her up into my arms. How her huge blue eyes would light up, and how she would smile her gap-toothed grin just for me. With that thought, most of my tension drained away.

Taking a deep breath, I squared my shoulders and walked into the office.

If I'd known then what I know now, would I have done anything different? Would I have turned around, gotten back into my car and left? I've wondered that hundreds of times, and ultimately I still don't think I'd have changed a thing. Everything happens for a reason, and you just never know when change is going to grab you by the balls and squeeze.

Plus, how the hell was I to know that in a few minutes my life was about to be forever altered?

Amelia

A low headache had started to creep its tendrils up from the base of my skull to wrap around my brain. I'd tossed and turned much of the previous night in anticipation of starting my new job in the morning, and so far had been running mostly on adrenaline. But now my mind was overloaded with so much information that the inevitable exhaustion had begun to set in. How would I ever remember my way around this maze of a building? How could I possibly recall which name belonged with each of these new faces?

Diana's voice interrupted my thoughts. The undertone of boredom that had subtly infiltrated all her comments and introductions during the office tour was suddenly gone. "This is the Sales department. As I mentioned earlier, you'll be working closely with everyone here, as they rely on Accounting to get them the figures they need to present to our clients."

We stopped beside a cubicle where a pretty blonde woman was chattering into a headset as she frantically typed away. She looked up and saw Diana, widened her hazel eyes, and began to end her phone call. Tugging off the headset, she swung her chair around to face us.

"You must be Amelia, the new accountant," she chirped with a wide grin as she stuck out a hand. "I'm Sam Upshaw, administrative assistant to Ryan Kavanaugh."

Kavanaugh? As in one of the partners, Kavanaugh? I made a mental note to ask later. Taking Sam's outstretched hand, I returned her smile. The other woman's bubbly personality was contagious, and I felt my spirits perk up a bit. "Yes, I am. Great to meet you."

"Sam will be your main liaison with Ryan's block of business," Diana explained. "Most of his requests for pricing will come directly from her. She's worked here for five years and should be able to help you with any questions you have about either Ryan's clients or this department in general." Sam nodded in agreement.

"Great!" I said, trying my best to appear enthusiastic. "I'm sure I'm going to need to take you up on that."

"I remember how overwhelming it can be at the start. Don't worry—you'll be up to speed in no time. Hey, if you don't already have lunch plans, would you like to join Kaitlyn and me?"

Kaitlyn? I recalled Diana introducing me to someone named Kaitlyn earlier. Lunch with a couple of co-workers around my own age sounded like a perfect opportunity to begin making friends here. I smiled at Sam gratefully. "Kaitlyn from my department? That'd be great. Thank you."

Diana wore an impatient look. Brusquely, she asked Sam, "Is Ryan in his office?"

"You're in luck," she replied. "He got in about twenty minutes ago."

I frowned in confusion. Only twenty minutes ago? He got to work at 10:30 in the morning? Diana must have noticed my expression because she clarified, "Ryan is an Account Manager, so he has to meet with clients a lot outside the office. Come on, I want you to meet him." She started walking toward an office with the door slightly ajar. The nameplate on the wall beside it read, *Ryan Kavanaugh*.

"Talk to you later, Sam. Thanks again," I said as I followed after my boss.

"See you at lunch!"

Diana knocked once on the door, then pushed it open and stepped inside. I heard a sigh and an irritated male voice say, "What do you w-" It cut off sharply when I came into the office behind her.

A man of around thirty sat behind another large cluttered desk. He was handsome in an athletic kind of way, with a thick jawline and short brown hair that curled above a broad forehead. When he stood to greet us, I realized he had to be over to six feet tall. "Oh," he said, flushing. "I didn't realize you had someone with you."

"I've brought Amelia York, my new accountant. I told you she was starting today, remember?" Diana turned back to me. "Amelia, this is Ryan Kavanaugh."

Ryan gave me an appraising scan, and seemed impressed by what he saw. Sticking out a hand, he said, "Pleased to meet you, Amelia. Welcome to Baker, Wright and Kavanaugh." He smiled brightly, and his eyes smiled along with him.

"Thank you, Mr. Kavanaugh. If you don't mind me asking, would you happen to be related to the Kavanaugh whose name is on the side of the building?" His face seemed open enough, so I figured I might as well get the question out of the way.

"My father, Patrick. Nepotism has not gone out of style around here, as you'll see," he said with a wry grin. "You'll likely meet him soon enough, although he's semi-retired now and spends as much time as he can on the golf course. And please call me Ryan. Did you meet my assistant, Sam, on your way in?"

"She did," Diana replied for me, and he glanced over at her almost as if he'd forgotten she was standing there. "They're having lunch together today. I'm sure she'll fill Amelia in on all the goings-on around here," she added pointedly.

Ryan frowned for a split second, but looked back at me and quickly replaced it with a smile. "Good. She's pretty much my right arm. I'd be lost without her." I noticed Diana's eyes narrow a little at that. "Well, if you need anything, Amelia, don't hesitate to ask Sam or myself. We'll be happy to help you out."

"Thank you. Everyone seems so nice so far. I can't wait to get settled in."

"We won't take up any more of your valuable time this morning, Ryan," Diana interjected. "I *would* like to speak with you about the Tuscan Airlines campaign later though if you can spare a few minutes." She seemed just a little strained, although she was clearly trying hard to hide it. I heard the miniscule quaver in her voice on the last few words, and it surprised me. I wondered if the two had some sort of history. Sam would likely know. I guessed if there was a back-story, before long I'd hear about it. Not that I was really one for office gossip, but I'd found in the past that understanding the personal relationships between people in my direct working circle could sometimes be helpful in knowing how to react to situations.

"Come on, Amelia, there are more people to meet in this department," Diana said as she guided me out of Ryan's office.

"There are two other Account Managers who work out of this office. I know Marilyn Silver isn't in this week—she's in New York—but Declan might be around." We walked down the hallway to another office. The nameplate outside the open door read, *Declan Kavanaugh.*

Diana saw me eyeing it. "Ryan's brother," she explained. "I see he's not in. Well, maybe that's for the best today. You'll meet him soon enough." She turned up a row of cubicles.

I couldn't help but steal a glance inside the other Kavanaugh's office as I passed. It was impeccably neat: chair pushed into the desk, file folders and mail stacked in a tray in one corner, even the man's pens were lined up neatly beside his keyboard. Beside the computer monitor sat a hinged photo frame displaying a wedding photo on the left, and a portrait of a smiling child on the right.

Diana's voice interrupted my perusal. "His wife is Laura Logan, from the evening news in Swann's Landing," she said. "Small town minor celebrity. You probably know of her?"

My eyes widened as I clicked in. I knew exactly who Laura Logan was. Scott watched the local news almost every night over dinner, and he'd admitted a few times that he thought she was hot. Laura had gone to Swann's Landing High with us years ago.

"Oh yes, we actually went to the same high school." Though we'd never run in the same social circles, I seemed to recall that we'd had a few classes together at one point. How weird that now I would soon be working with Laura's husband.

A woman with curly dark hair stood to greet us, and Diana led me over to her. "This is Colleen Talbot, Declan's admin assistant," she explained. I smiled graciously, faking alertness, and shook her hand.

So many faces. So many names. They all seemed very nice, and I was sure after a few days I'd remember most of them. But right now, all this information and all these people were beginning to blur together. We'd gone through five departments before this one. All I could think about was that this tour was nearly over, and I couldn't wait to get back to my desk and take a few moments to regroup.

Seconds later, although the extent wasn't fully grasped at the time, the universe threw me a gigantic curveball. It wasn't until late that night as I tossed and turned in my bed, unable to sleep, unable to get the face of the blue-eyed man out of my head, that I got some idea how much potential this had to become a problem if I wasn't careful.

Chapter 2

Amelia

I'd just finished sitting with our department's lone senior accountant, Josh Marshall, taking notes as he showed me how to process certain billings Accounting was responsible for at the end of each month. So far, Josh seemed like a pretty cool guy. He was pretty laid back, more so than anyone else I'd met so far. In some ways he reminded me a bit of Scott.

Josh had been handling the bulk of my training for the past three days, and with spending so much time together we'd started to get to know one another. We both commuted into Lynchburg from Swann's Landing every day, and he warned me how icy the roads sometimes got in the winter. We discovered we had the same favorite waitress at Finnegan's, and we both had Pizza Palace on speed dial. I told him I'd married my high-school sweetheart four years ago. He confessed to me how smitten he was with his new girlfriend, Holly.

Between training with Josh, and lunch every day with Sam and Kaitlyn, I'd made some friends and was already beginning to feel more comfortable at BWK.

As I walked out Josh's door, I heard Diana call my name.

"Amelia, come into my office for moment." I noticed she rarely used the words *please* or *thank you*.

Changing direction, I went to her door. Where I promptly stopped breathing. I vaguely heard Diana say, "I don't believe you've had a chance to meet my new accountant yet. This is Amelia York." She lifted a hand my way, but I couldn't stop staring at the man standing in front of me.

"Amelia, this is Declan Kavanaugh. As you know, he's one of our Account Managers."

Declan Kavanaugh. The man I'd locked eyes with—and felt my gut plummet to the floor over—on my first day had been Declan Kavanaugh. The same Declan Kavanaugh who was married to Laura Logan. The same Declan who was Ryan's older brother. The same Declan Sam and Kaitlyn pretty much despised.

Crap.

With a start, I realized they were both waiting for me to react somehow—say something, shake his hand, do anything really. Not just stand there like some blushing, slack-jawed buffoon.

"Pleased to, uh, meet you, um, Declan," I faltered.

Wow. Could I make a worse first impression? Red-faced—check. Stammering—check. Maybe I could trip over my own feet and fall into his arms next? Then this whole thing would seem like a perfect meet-cute from one of those chick-flicks my friend Liv sometimes made me watch. Except in those, the awkward girl and the gorgeous guy always end up falling in love and living happily ever after by the time the credits roll. And neither one of them are ever married to other people.

Declan reached for my hand. It lifted as if it had a mind of its own and slipped into his. I prayed he didn't notice how damp my palm was. The corners of his eyes crinkled adorably as he smiled at me, and I couldn't help but smile back. When his fingers closed around mine and politely shook my hand, I swear I felt a low thrum of electricity shoot up my arm and fly straight down to my lower belly.

"I look forward to working with you. Amelia," he said in a low, smooth tone. There was a definite gap before he added my name to the end. It sounded like he'd rolled it around on his tongue for a second, like he'd tasted it to see how it felt on his lips.

I reluctantly pulled my hand out of his grasp and dragged my eyes from his. Diana was giving us a curious look. Not good. I flashed Declan an apologetic smile, mumbled something about having to get back to my training, and then got the heck out of there. It was an inelegant exit, but by that point I just had to escape.

Sitting down in my cubicle, I dropped my forehead into my hands and heaved a frustrated sigh. I needed to get a handle on this little crush I seemed to be developing and fast, before it ended up causing me difficulties I *really* didn't want.

"So, how's your first week been?" Scott asked as we were getting ready for bed on Friday. "You haven't said much."

He also hadn't been around much. Scott taught auto shop at Swann's Landing High, and between the end-of-year after school project help his students needed, and coaching the football team two nights a week and on Saturday mornings, he was a busy guy.

"Good," I replied nonchalantly. "They do things a bit different than Bellmore, but my training's going well."

He climbed into bed and pulled the covers back on my side. "Meet any cool people?"

My mind flashed to Declan, but I shoved the memory of those piercing blue eyes away. Sliding under the sheets, I replied, "Yes, actually. Several. I told you about Kaitlyn and Sam the other day."

Scott nodded. "Oh, yeah. The office gossip, right?"

"Sam's not...okay, well, yeah. Sorta." I laughed. "They're both great, though. Their stories are hilarious. And remember I mentioned the guy who's been training me? The one who lives here in town?"

"What was his name again?"

"Josh. He's great! I really think you'd like him. Maybe I'll set up a date for us to meet him and his girlfriend at Finnegan's for drinks. It'd be fun." I smiled at the thought. I'd have to ask Josh next week about planning an outing sometime. I was pretty sure he'd be into it.

"Sounds good. What about your boss? Diana? She decent?"

I paused to think about that. "She's...hmm. I'm not exactly sure what I think about her yet. She's a no-nonsense kind of person who expects a lot from me, but I can respect that. She always looks so perfect and in control, yet her office is a mess. And I honestly can't tell if she likes me or not."

Scott trailed his hand up my forearm. "Of course she likes you, Ames. Everybody likes you." He smiled at me reassuringly.

"Not everyone. Not that girl who had such a huge crush on you in college. Remember her?" I asked with a teasing grin.

He chuckled. "How could I forget? Yeah, she *hated* you. I never understood how anyone could ever hate you."

"She hated me 'cause I was your girlfriend. She couldn't get her claws into you, and it was my fault you wouldn't even look her way. I kinda get that."

"Even twelve years in, I still only have eyes for you," he said, shuffling closer to me as he continued to stroke my arm.

"You're sweet." I suddenly realized where this was headed.

Sliding his hand up to my shoulder and around the back of my neck, he brought his face close to mine. "It's been a while," he whispered as he began to plant soft kisses along my jaw.

To be honest, I wasn't really in the mood. But he was right—it *had* been a while. And there was no real reason why I should want to push him away.

So I didn't. But I'd be lying if I said the face I pictured when I closed my eyes and kissed my husband, the hands I imagined as Scott touched my body, belonged to him.

It was a beautiful, sunny morning. I sat at the kitchen table in my pajamas, sipping coffee and typing away at my laptop. I was sorting through all the notes I'd taken over my first week at work, attempting to organize them for easy retrieval. I was definitely not distracted with thoughts about a certain Account Manager. That wasn't happening at *all*.

The phone rang, startling me out of my reverie. It was my mom with a last minute invitation to come over for lunch. I glanced at the clock on the microwave and frowned. It was already 11:15. Where had my morning gone?

"Scott's coaching this morning. Not sure he'll be back in time for lunch," I responded doubtfully.

"Well, you come on over then. He's welcome to meet us here later if he likes."

Hmm. Spending time with my mom was not exactly how I'd imagined filling my Saturday afternoon. She had definite ideas about how she thought I should be living my life, and I often ended up feeling like I was letting her down somehow. On the other hand, I was eager to see my dad and find out how he was doing. I loved hanging out with my father. No one could send me into fits of hysterical laughter quite like he could.

"Okay, I'll let him know. Need me to pick up anything on my way?"

She didn't, and I disconnected. Sighing, I saved the document I was editing. I hadn't been focusing very well anyway.

Twenty minutes later, I was showered and dressed. Since it was a warm early summer day, I decided to walk, figuring the fresh air might help clear my head a bit.

Swann's Landing's so pretty in June. The huge oak trees that lined my street draped their luscious green arms over the road, each stretching to reach across and touch the branches opposite. A virtual rainbow of vibrant flowers bloomed in everyone's front gardens. Birdsong intermingled with the constant drone of busy lawn mowers. I couldn't have picked a more perfect day if I'd tried.

When I arrived at the home I'd grown up in, I paused on the sidewalk and smiled fondly as I admired the two-story white colonial with dark green shutters. Its wide front porch was a great place to sit unnoticed and watch the world go by. So many memories lingered there. Sometimes my heart ached with longing for a return to the simplicities of my childhood.

The door opened and my dad stood framed within, beckoning me to come inside. He was tall and stocky, with a shock of thick auburn hair laced with fissures of steel. I had inherited my dark locks and brown eyes from his side of the family.

Still grinning, I bounded up the porch steps to throw my arms around him. "How're you feeling, Daddy?"

"Better, sweetie. Better," he replied, stepping back from me. "More importantly, how are you? Settling in at the new job?"

"Don't change the subject," I admonished. "Are you still doing the exercises your doctor told you to do? When do you go back to see the specialist again?"

My dad had suffered a small heart attack a few months earlier that had given us all a bad scare. He was back to work now and claiming he was fine, but I still worried about him. He was only five years shy of retirement, and both my mother and I wished he'd cut back on the long hours he put in at the automotive plant. His doctor had advised the same. But Bill York was a stubborn man; he wasn't about to be told how to live his life by any doctors.

"Not for a few weeks. Stop worrying, Amy. You're as bad as your mother sometimes. Now come sit down and tell us all about your new job."

I examined his profile carefully as he stepped into the kitchen to finish setting the table. In this light, he seemed a little pale for June. Frowning, I wondered if I was just imagining things. I made a mental note to ask my mom when Dad was out of earshot. Then I joined my parents in the kitchen and updated them on all my news.

Declan

I stood unnoticed in the doorway of Josh's office, watching him absentmindedly sip black coffee while he studied rows of numbers scrolling past on his monitor. His face held a frustrated look I'd seen before, and I understood the columns weren't calculating out quite right. Somewhere in there lurked a tiny error and he was determined to find it.

I let him glare at the screen for a few more seconds before announcing my presence with a quick rap on his door. Irritation flared across his face as he looked up to see which asshole was disturbing his concentration. Then he broke into a relaxed smile at the sight of this particular asshole leaning against the doorframe.

"Mornin', Declan."

"Morning. Mind if I interrupt you for a moment?" I asked, stepping inside. Thick file folders were piled on the corner of his desk and on the floor along one wall. At least three of them were open, stacked up on his blotter with various multi-colored sticky notes scattered across the pages.

"No problem, buddy. Have a seat." He gestured to the chair opposite his desk. "What can I do for you?"

I sat down and leaned back, resting my right ankle over my left knee. "Any chance you have the pricing I need for Virginia TeleComm yet?"

With a surprised look, he shook his head. "Nope. Didn't you just e-mail me about that yesterday afternoon?" He chuckled. "Your rush is in queue behind the other three rushes that came before it."

"What if a bottle of Glenfiddich mysteriously appeared on your desk tomorrow morning? Would that help my request mysteriously appear on the top of your pile today?"

Josh raised an incredulous eyebrow. "No."

"Two bottles?"

He gave me a pointed stare. Then he sighed. "Make it three," he conceded. "Long weekend's coming up." He was clearly struggling to restrain a smile.

My lips curled into a self-satisfied smirk. "I knew you could be persuaded."

"Don't be a dick. And don't even consider leaving anything in here." Shuffling a few folders around on his desk, he found the one marked *Virginia TeleComm* and dropped the thick file beside his keyboard with a thud. "The things I do for you sometimes. I'm *so* gonna get an earful of shit from Diana if she finds out I reprioritized you over your brother. You know that, right?"

Yep, I sure did. I was fully aware of how Diana would react, and it wouldn't just be Josh who would get verbally ripped to shreds. Not that I cared if the bitch tore me a new one—hell, I actually relished having a good excuse to tell her off. But, though I knew Josh could handle himself, I didn't really want to cause him any additional hassles.

"If she does, you can blame it all on me."

The grin he was holding back broke out in full force. "Dude, you *know* I will."

Deciding to change the subject, I prodded, "So, the new girl…"

He looked up sharply. "Amelia?"

"Yeah, Amelia. Thoughts?" I tried my best to appear casual. She had been popping into my head far too often since I'd first laid eyes on her over a week ago. I'd be thinking about something mundane, like when my next meeting was, or stopping to fill up my car, or what book I was planning to read to Alexis that night, and suddenly random images of her big brown eyes or her shy smile would just dash across my mind. I didn't really understand it. Yes, she was hot, but so was Laura. Hell, so were lots of women. I had no idea why this particular one kept sneaking into my thoughts.

Josh cleared his throat. "I don't know her all that well yet. But first impressions? She's smart as a whip. Knows her stuff. A fast learner. A bit reserved. I like her." The expression on his face attested to that. "Why?"

With a cynical grin, I said, "She sounds perfect. Wonder how long before she gets bored of this place and moves on?" Pausing, I shot him a pointed look. "Nothing else to add?"

His brows narrowed. "Not sure what you want from me, Declan. No doubt, she's pretty, but she's married. And I've been with Holly for three months now, so it's not like I'm looking. If I were single, it'd maybe be a different story. But I'm not."

And neither was I. I needed to remember that. If I were single, these fantasies of Amelia pressed against the back of my office door with one long leg hooked over my hip as I did nasty, sinful things to her would be decidedly less unsettling.

"Cool. I was just curious." I rose to my feet. "Thanks. Always a pleasure. And you should check the backseat of your car before you leave for the weekend. You just never know who might leave you a little gift for the Fourth."

Josh shook his head, chuckling as I walked away.

Chapter 3

Amelia

 I'm walking down a hallway at work trying to keep up with Diana, who moves far faster than seems practical in her leopard-print stilettos. The relentless click, click, click of her heels on the linoleum fills my ears. Faceless people try to get her attention, but she ignores them all.

 The doors that line the left side of the corridor are closed. My heart-rate picks up. I start to feel anxious, but I'm not sure why. Diana stops abruptly in front of one of the doors and turns to it. It opens and Ryan appears, taking a step into the hall. He looks straight at her, not even noticing me. For a split second he seems confused, but then he grabs the sides of her face and drags her to him. Kissing passionately, they back into his office and slam the door.

 I'm shocked by what I've just witnessed, and look around to see if anyone else noticed this inappropriate display in the workplace. Narrowing my eyes in confusion, I realize I'm now all alone. The building is eerily silent. Not even sounds of Ryan and Diana from behind the door reach my ears.

 Moving further along the hallway, I realize that I'm looking for his office. More specifically, looking for him. *At last I stop in front of a closed door and focus on the nameplate beside it. Kavanaugh. An old Irish name. The metal of the doorknob feels cold. That's weird. I hadn't even meant to put my hand on it. I know I can't go inside. It wouldn't be right. What if he's in there? What if I get caught? No, I'm definitely not going in. My fingers don't listen to my brain though; they twist the knob and push open the door.*

His office is empty, and I feel a wave of mixed relief and disappointment. I slip inside. Walking over to his desk, I pick up the dual photo frame and examine the pictures. Laura, in her wedding dress, has a wide smile. She looks radiant and beautiful. Both her arms are wrapped around Declan's waist, and her head is tilted into his. I turn my attention to him. He's wearing a black suit with a light blue tie that matches his eyes. One arm is around his new bride. He's smiling, too. As usual, his hair looks like he's just run his fingers through it. Or maybe Laura did right before the shot was taken. He looks so happy. A knot of jealousy tightens inside me.

The curly-haired child in the other photo appears to be maybe two or three years old. I study her features looking for signs of Declan. She has dark hair like her daddy, and his blue eyes, but her wide smile is all her mother's. She's adorable. Looking at this photo makes me wonder what kind of a dad he is.

I set it back on the desk and turn toward the door with the intention to continue searching for him. My eyes flare as I see Declan standing with one hand braced on the doorframe, silently watching me.

"Amelia..." he starts and trails off.

He's staring at me and a rush of heat floods my body. I find I'm unable to speak, unable to move, snared in his serious gaze like some kind of frightened rabbit. My heart beats faster, pounding so loud against my ribcage that I swear he must be able to hear it. I can feel my pulse throbbing in my temples. Are my fingers shaking? I think my whole body is. But I'm not a rabbit, and this reaction is not out of fear. Well. Maybe it is. A little. Yes, okay, fear and excitement and lust and, and...

With one hand, he closes the door behind him and approaches me slowly, cautiously, like he's afraid I'll spook and run away. He's right to be cautious. But though I should run away, really, really should, I'm not going to. I'm not going anywhere. Because I want this. Bad. Maybe more than I've ever wanted anything.

He whispers my name again, and long-forgotten emotions well up from deep within me and gush to the surface. I wish he'd just touch me. I'm trembling with anticipation. Please, God, let him touch me.

Then he does.

His hand caresses my cheek, and his hypnotizing eyes are now only inches from my own. I can't help it; I flutter my lashes closed and part my lips in anticipation. His fingers slip around to stroke the back of my neck and tug my head forward. And then he's kissing me. And it's gentle and soft and sweet…and oh, I know we shouldn't be doing this. I know it's wrong—really, I do. But it doesn't feel wrong. *And right now I don't care about things like right and wrong. I don't care about anything but this. Us.*

His other hand grips my waist and pulls me to him as he deepens our kiss. Our tongues dance. His body feels rock hard against mine. I stroke up and down his back, and my other hand dives into his thick tangle of hair.

I am lost in him. All I want is him.

With a gasp I woke up, fingers knotted in the sheets and thighs clenched tight. My heart was racing. In an attempt to calm myself, I took a few deep breaths before rolling over to look at the clock on the nightstand. It was 3:42 in the morning. With a sigh, I plucked my sweat-soaked pajama top away from my chest. *Lovely.*

I slid out of bed carefully, so I wouldn't disturb Scott, and retrieved a clean nightgown from my dresser drawer before tip-toeing down the dark hallway to the bathroom. Squinting in the sudden glare of the overhead light, I stripped off my damp pajamas.

When I saw my face in the mirror, I blushed, remembering what had woken me. I'd been dreaming about Declan Kavanaugh—dreaming about *kissing* Declan Kavanaugh. It had been so *vivid*. I pressed a finger against my lips, swearing I could still feel his touch.

Oh God. What if I thought about that dream when I next saw him? The last thing I wanted was to look like some crushing grade-school girl. Not only would it be incredibly awkward, it would also be unprofessional, something that was just unacceptable to me.

Sam and Kaitlyn had filled me in about Declan. Oh yes, they had told me plenty.

He was not very well liked at BWK. That fact had become evident before I'd even completed my first week. According to Kaitlyn, he used to have a serious drinking problem, back before he started dating Laura. He'd even lost his driver's license for a while after being charged with a DUI, which was a pretty major handicap if you had clients you needed to visit across much of Virginia. But he was a partner's son, so of course he didn't lose his job, and they had found ways around it for him.

I also knew he apparently had anger management issues. The girls spoke of abrasive e-mails they'd received, and verbal spats they'd either overheard or been involved in. The general opinion seemed to be that he was an arrogant jerk who had no respect for his co-workers, and who always had to have his way.

There was a lot of history between Declan, Ryan, and Diana to consider, too. Sam told me Ryan had left Diana because she'd been having an affair with his big brother, but both Declan and Diana always denied it. Kaitlyn refused to opine on that particular issue, but Sam was convinced it was all true. She claimed there had been rumors of Declan and Diana secretly hooking up since before Ryan had even married her.

I filed each nugget of information away in my mind, but I was a woman who preferred to form my own opinions about people. Since I barely knew Declan, I decided I needed to keep an open mind, and try my best not to prejudge. There were always two sides to every story, and I had no idea what his was.

Sighing, I resolved not to stress myself out thinking about this anymore tonight. I had a drink of water and, though I suspected any further sleep would be elusive, crawled back into bed beside my snoring husband.

Declan

As I was leaving Alexis' room after tucking her in, I heard the front door open and I sighed. Yet again, Laura had missed out on spending time with our daughter before she went to bed. I understood how important my wife's job was to her, but sometimes it seemed to me like she forgot she had a much more important role that also needed her attention. Alexis was definitely a daddy's girl, but I knew better than anyone how much she missed her mother on evenings like these. Don't get me wrong—I loved our father-daughter time, but lately there'd been too many nights where the single parent routine was starting to get a bit frustrating for us all.

I trotted down the stairs to greet Laura.

She looked exhausted. Slumping her shoulders, she shrugged her jacket carelessly to the floor. Her usually perfect red curls were disheveled and limp. Her dark eyeliner was smeared, and the green eyes framed within were drained of their usual vitality.

Giving her a quick kiss, I said, "If you hurry upstairs, you might be able to still get in a cuddle before she's totally out." I'd thought the idea of seeing Alexis before she fell asleep might brighten my wife's spirits. It seemed I was wrong.

Laura shot me an irritated look. "I'm aware I'm late. No need for the guilt trip." With her heels dangling from her fingers, she began to trudge up the steps.

I contemplated not replying, but I just couldn't resist. "It's not me making you feel guilty, you know. I'll warm up your dinner."

She didn't reply, but she did turn in the direction of Alexis' bedroom.

When Laura joined me in the kitchen ten minutes later, she was already in her pajamas, though it was only 8:15.

"Shitty day?" I asked. My own afternoon hadn't exactly been a day at the fucking spa either, but I was good at burying all my frustrations the moment I walked in the front door and switched into Daddy Mode.

"Yeah. The new director seems to think I should be second anchor and playing off Adrian. I've been in this industry three years longer than him—I'm both more experienced and more professional. But he's a man, so they want him front and center. Idiots." She sighed and shoveled a bite of lasagna into her mouth. After swallowing, she looked up and held my gaze. "Sorry I missed eating with you guys again."

I shrugged. What could I say, really? We both had jobs that were important to us. We were lucky enough to have a very flexible babysitter who only lived a few houses down the street. Sometimes I had to be out of town on business, and if Laura was working late,

Alexis would either stay with Laura's parents or the sitter would come here and put her to bed for us. It wasn't an ideal situation by any stretch, but we'd been making it work as best we could.

"No apology necessary. We're getting used to it." Okay, yeah, that came out sounding a little pissy, but damn it, it really wasn't fair to Alexis to have to be apart from her mother so much.

"Declan," she sighed. "You know I can't help it. I thought you understood. You know I'd be home with you both every night if I could."

I just stared at her. Like fuck she would. These were her choices, and she was the one missing out on a big chunk of her daughter's life. Laura had much higher aspirations than anchoring small town nightly news. She craved the big time: NBC, or CNN, or hell, maybe even Fox News if she got desperate enough. Her career path would more than likely only take her further away from us, not bring her closer.

I thought about the times I'd brought up trying for a second child, and how she'd always balked at the idea. How she'd put me off with "now's not a good time, Declan," and "maybe in a few years, Declan." If she had her way, we'd be living in New York or Atlanta by then, and she'd be working even longer hours. Which meant a second baby wasn't going to be in the cards for her any time soon. If ever.

Part of me wanted to bring these things up to her, to shove in her face the fact that her only child was growing up without her goddamn mother around—a mother who was very much alive, just *choosing* not to be there—but I didn't. I knew my own childhood without my mom affected what I wanted Alexis' life to be like, what I thought she deserved. And Laura was frustrated, too. She was tired, and if I said that stuff, it would only end in yelling and tears and resentments, which would solve abso-fucking-lutely nothing.

So I just said, "I know, babe." Then I kissed the top of her head and went into the living room to turn on the baseball game and turn off my churning brain.

Amelia

After nearly three weeks, I was feeling a lot more confident and working independently most of the time. I still needed to bug Josh and Kaitlyn with occasional questions, but my understanding of how the processes in this Accounting department worked compared to my previous employer's became clearer each day.

I noticed it was almost noon and glanced over at Kaitlyn. Our eyes met across the aisle as she swiveled in her chair to look at me. We grinned at each other like we'd been doing this for years instead of only a few weeks, both grabbing our purses from our drawers to go meet Sam in the cafeteria.

When we walked into the large room, we saw she was sitting with Evan Silver, who was a junior accountant in our department. Evan was a couple of years younger than us, with spiky dark hair and a muscular build. He was single and Sam knew it. Apparently she'd been flirting with him off and on for months now, but he still hadn't asked her out. Since Sam was very accustomed to male attention, it was driving her crazy that Evan hadn't made a move yet.

Once we got our lunch, Kaitlyn and I joined them, and Sam began detailing the various frustrations of her morning. I ate quietly, as usual doing more listening than talking.

The metal chair beside me scraped the floor as it was pulled back, and I noticed Kaitlyn's eyes widen when she saw who was about to sit down. A plastic tray laden with food slid onto the table and I froze with deer-in-the-headlights surprise as I looked up into a pair of clear blue eyes.

"Mind if I join you guys?" Declan Kavanaugh asked.

A wave of heat washed over me, flooding my cheeks and dampening my palms. Overcome with unfamiliar shyness, I averted my gaze back down to my sandwich.

Kaitlyn offered a fake smile and cheerfully lied, "Not at all."

No longer very hungry, I surreptitiously watched Declan from the corner of my eye. He took a bite of his pizza, then, swallowing, turned to me.

"How are you settling in, Amelia?"

Crap. I'd really been hoping not to have to maintain my side of a conversation with him. I flashed Kaitlyn a 'please help me' look, took a breath, and glanced at him. "Great, so far. It's great. Everyone seems great."

I groaned internally. Had I really just said the word *great* three times? What happened to intelligent and eloquent Amelia? Oh, yeah, right. She was hiding, mortified.

"Glad to hear it."

He gave me an easy smile before turning his focus to Evan. "Plans this weekend, Silver?"

Wonderful. I was sure I'd made yet another moronic impression. There was no way Declan didn't think Diana had hired the village idiot now. The last thing I wanted was for him to decide I wasn't very bright. The girls had already told me stories of how he'd ripped into them if he didn't like their responses to his inquiries. If I was going to be working with this man, I needed him to respect me. I was an excellent accountant, and it was important to me he know that.

I needed to fix this. How could I fix this?

As I picked at my lunch and listened to everyone's chatter, I heard Evan ask Sam if she knew some song by a new band he'd just heard. I knew who he was talking about, but they weren't really my style— much too aggressive for me. The conversation around me then switched to talk of music, and I paid close attention, curious to discover if my tastes overlapped with anyone else's.

Declan mentioned Radiohead being on some all-time top albums list he'd read, and I perked up. I owned most of their stuff, and this was a band I was very capable of discussing.

Taking a deep breath, I said, "Everyone says *OK Computer* was their best one, but I prefer *The Bends* any day."

He turned to me with a grin, and this time I forced myself to hold his gaze more confidently, although my insides were still twisting.

"Oh yeah, *The Bends* is amazing, but I have a real soft spot for *In Rainbows*."

I smiled back and began to relax. Here was something we had in common that had nothing to do with work. "Yes, I love that one, too. What other bands do you like?" Before he could reply, on impulse I blurted, "Quick—top five desert island discs?"

His thick brows lifted in surprise. "Desert island discs? You mean which albums would I pick to have with me if I could only have five?"

"Exactly."

Declan's face turned reflective as he thought about it. Then he replied, "Subject to change at any time, but *In Rainbows*, of course. Coldplay's *A Rush of Blood to the Head*. Red Hot Chili Peppers' *Stadium Arcadium*. Pearl Jam's *Ten*. And Jim Coltrane's *Busker Blues*."

Hmm. I could agree with the first two, and I'd always had a soft spot for that Pearl Jam, since my parents had played that CD often when I was a kid. Chili Peppers I could take or leave, mostly leave if I was being honest. And I had no idea who that last guy was.

"Who's Jim...sorry? What was his name again? I don't know him," I admitted. "Good calls on the rest."

"Jim Coltrane. He's an American singer-songwriter. Kind of soulful folk-rocky. His lyrics really get to me. You should download *Busker Blues* and give it a listen, then tell me what you think."

I was flattered. Here I was, a near-complete stranger, and he wanted to know what I thought about some singer? Huh.

"So, what about you?"

What about me, what? Oh, right. My own desert island discs. How was I going to come up with five good ones off the top of my head?

"I'm going to preface mine with subject to change, too, 'cause I fluctuate often." My guts twisted tighter as he shared a knowing grin with me. "Okay, let's see. The Beatles' *Abbey Road*..."

"Excellent," Declan murmured, nodding with approval at my first selection.

"The Verve's *Urban Hymns*..."

"Is that the one with 'Bittersweet Symphony' on it?"

"Yes, although that's the song I tend to skip. Anyway, um, The Strokes' *Is This It?*"

"Don't know them."

"Really? How could you not know The Strokes?" I asked incredulously. I thought *everyone* had at least heard of them these days.

"That's three. Two more," he prodded, ignoring my outburst.

"Stop interrupting me, then," I told him with a smile. "Okay, last two. David Bowie's *Hunky Dory* and Arcade Fire's *The Suburbs*. But I could easily do ten, or maybe even twenty. Picking just five is totally subjective to my mood."

"Wow. I'm impressed, New Girl. You know your stuff."

I just nodded. Music was a huge passion of mine, but I knew I could sometimes come off as snob about it.

He took his last bite and glanced at his watch. "I gotta run, but it was great chatting music with you. I think I'll play *The Bends* in the car on the way to my next appointment." He got up, flashing me that dazzling smile that made my heart do little somersaults.

As I watched Declan leave the cafeteria, I tried to remember the musician he'd mentioned. Jim…something. I frowned. I had hoped to give him a listen so I'd have an opinion if the topic came up again, but I was blanking on the last name.

"Whoa. You just had an entire conversation with Declan Kavanaugh that was polite and friendly. Wonders will never cease," Sam said. "But just wait. You're still new. You haven't had the pleasure of meeting Declan the Dick yet."

I shrugged. "He seems okay so far."

"So did Voldemort at first, I bet."

"Samantha!" Kaitlyn admonished in a low voice, eyes wide. "That's not really fair. Declan's just a self-important ass. The world is full of them."

"Fine! Sorry. I've just had too many bad experiences with him." She turned to me. "Declan is *not* Voldemort." Lowering her voice, she muttered, "At least, not yet."

Chapter 4

Amelia

I pushed a stray lock of hair off my face with dusty fingers and grabbed another thick folder from the stack beside me. The name printed vertically down the tab read *Lynchburg Cable*, so I looked for a gap near the end of the long row of L's. I'd done a quote for this company just the other day with Josh, and knew it was one of Ryan's clients.

Our administrative assistant had left a few days ago for a new role in the Creative department, and the rest of us in Accounting were sharing her duties until someone new could be hired. I was taking my turn in the file room, sitting cross-legged on the carpet filing case folders into a lower shelf in the back, when I heard the door to the outer room open.

Diana's voice came from right around the wall behind me. "Something's going on with you, Ry. Something's off—I can tell. You weren't yourself on the phone last night." Her tone lowered. "You were high, weren't you? Tell me you weren't high." I heard uncharacteristic concern, and I froze, hoping she wouldn't peek into the back file room and discover me. My mind reeled with shock. Ryan, high? *Whoa.*

"Is *that* why you dragged me back here? To convince me to come clean to you? Never gonna happen. Even if I did have something to admit to—which I don't." Ryan's irritation was palpable.

"You can talk to me. We used to tell each other everything."

"Yeah, well. That was a long time ago. Back when I foolishly used to trust you."

"You can still trust me."

"Um, no."

"Why not? You seriously still blame me for everything?"

"I forgave you once, and look where it got me. You made a fool of me. You lied to me the whole time we were together!"

A sigh. "I'm getting pretty tired of always having to defend myself to you. As I've told you over and over—I didn't. It was just that one time, before we were even married. I kept my vows to you. I was faithful. Nothing happened ever again. I would *never* do that to you. I know you don't believe me, but it's the truth."

"Save it. You're both so full of shit you wouldn't know the truth if it bit you in the ass. Which it has. And I'm sure it will again. People like you and my brother never change. Don't think you can help me. Don't think you can be my friend. You and I may be forced to interact as co-workers, but that's all you are to me now." Footsteps.

Her voice took on a note of quiet desperation. "Talk to me, Ry. Who else have you got? Are you going to ask Sam for help? I don't think so. No matter what you believe, I still care about you."

"Go to hell."

The outer door slammed as he went back into the office area. I'd been sitting motionless since the moment I heard my boss's voice, and I hoped she'd follow him out of there as soon as possible. If she realized I was in the back and had obviously overheard, there'd be hell to pay.

I heard Diana inhale sharply, followed by a soft sniffle, and just knew she was fighting back tears. It seemed the Iron Lady had a weak spot in the form of her ex-husband. My heart went out to her a little. Could the things she'd said be true? Was Ryan really on drugs? Was she innocent of cheating on him with Declan? I knew Ryan and Sam were both convinced she had.

When the door opened and closed a second time, I released the breath I'd been holding in a rush. I'd just discovered a few more pieces of the complicated history of my boss and the Kavanaugh brothers, and, although I knew it was none of my business, the more I found out, the more I wondered what the whole story really was.

When I finished the filing, I stood with a yawn and stretched my arms high above my head. My muscles were all stiff and achy from sitting on the floor for so long.

Back at my cubicle, I checked my e-mail and saw I had a new message from Declan. The subject line indicated it was a response to a quote I'd done the day before. I hadn't had to do much work for him so far, but Josh was showing me quotes for pricing of advertising add-ons clients sometimes asked to see after their campaigns were already set up. He had given me this one to do on my own, and I'd worked out the cost for ConnectAssure's request carefully, triple checking my calculations and the wording of my accompanying e-mail before sending it off to Declan's admin assistant, Colleen.

I opened the message, both excited and nervous to see his response. As I read it, my face fell. A surge of irritation coursed through me as I scanned it over again. Sam and Kaitlyn had both warned me about the tone of his e-mails, and now it seemed I had a snarky message of my very own. It was cold and completely dismissive of what I had provided. He demanded a lower price. He did not say please. And he'd used *that* phrase, the phrase all accountants despise more than any other: 'sharpen your pencil'.

As in, 'why don't you sharpen your pencil and get some lower figures for me?' As in, 'obviously you didn't give as competitive a quote the first time around as you could have, so do it again, and do it better.'

The case file was still on the corner of my desk. I grabbed it and went over my calculations a few more times, but I found no errors. My quote was accurate, and there was no wiggle room I could see for further discounting.

Rising anger drowned out rational thought as I read Declan's message a third time. Did I mention how much I hate that phrase? I really, really hate that phrase.

Hitting Reply, I dashed out a response. I moved the mouse over Send and lingered there a moment with my finger resting on the button. Luckily I managed to retain enough presence of mind not to click it. I squeezed my eyes shut, took a deep breath, and then re-read my reply. While not unprofessional, it had definite bitchy undertones. As did his original message, but if I sent this answer back, from what I'd been told about Declan, it would probably start a heated battle over a minor issue. So I leaned back in my chair and clicked the little X in the upper right-hand corner of the open e-mail, stopping myself from giving as good as I'd got.

Instead, I decided it would be smart to forward it to Josh, and I took the file to his office to ask his advice. He was used to dealing with Declan—in fact, they seemed to have a pretty easy working relationship. Josh had Declan's respect; the rest of my co-workers clearly did not. And I was determined to earn it as well.

Josh was sympathetic to my annoyance. It was no surprise to learn he also hated that particular expression. He understood why my back got up at Declan's curt words, and together we re-did the calculations, found a way to provide a slightly improved figure, and formulated a polite but firm reply.

I returned to my desk still feeling edgy, but much more in control of my temper. There was just something about Declan's message— like he figured I was exactly the same as any of the other employees he sparred with—that had gotten under my skin. It was more than just that stupid phrase; it was his assumption that I was just like them.

At the end of the day, I still wasn't feeling much better about it. He hadn't replied a second time, which was probably for the best, but no matter what other cases I worked on, my mind kept drifting back to his e-mail.

Glancing at the clock in the bottom corner of my screen, I was relieved to note that it was almost time to leave. I just wanted the day to be over so I could go home and distract myself from obsessing over such a minor thing. It didn't deserve the attention I was giving it, and I knew it.

I was just about to reach for my purse when I heard a rap on the metal edge of the half-wall behind me. Swiveling in my chair, I found myself face to face with the very person who'd been inadvertently driving me to distraction all afternoon. My first thought was that Declan had come to argue with me some more over the pricing, and I mentally braced myself. Instead, he reached inside his jacket, pulled out a CD, and set it on my blotter.

"Nearly forgot to give you this before I left," he said with a smile. The light, fresh scent of his aftershave reached out and wrapped me in its embrace, immobilizing me.

Heat flared across my cheeks. My brows drew together as I glanced at the disc, then back up at him. "What?" That one confused word was all I could muster.

"You said you hadn't heard of him. Let me know what ya think."

I stared up at him, wide-eyed and dumbfounded. He had the cutest look on his face as he took in my perplexed expression.

Wait, wasn't I just ticked off at him a few moments ago? How could he flip my emotions around so thoroughly just by smiling at me? I couldn't decide if I thought this was a good or bad thing.

I think maybe I nodded.

"Have a good weekend, Amelia," he said as he turned to go.

"Thanks. You too," I mumbled.

I leaned forward in my chair and watched him walk away until he rounded the corner at the end of our aisle. Then I picked up the CD. It was a burned disc, and scrawled across the shiny metallic surface in black Sharpie were the words: *Jim Coltrane / Busker Blues*.

Declan Kavanaugh had been thinking enough about our conversation from four days ago that he took the time to make me a CD? And he wanted my opinion on it? I shook my head in disbelief.

Slipping it into my purse, I said my goodbyes and made a beeline for my car, excited to give this Jim Coltrane a listen on my drive home. It would give me an excellent excuse to either see Declan in person next week, or have a non-annoying e-mail conversation with him. Both ideas brought a little smile to my face.

Declan

I was still grinning as I got into my oven of a car and flicked on the A/C. Amelia's face when I'd dropped that CD onto her desk had been priceless. Something about the progression of her expressions— at first wary, then confused, then cautiously pleased—it was like no one had ever given her music before.

And that look she got just before I'd walked away? That was all because of me. Damned if I wasn't already trying to come up with new ways to evoke that amazing smile again.

Jesus. What the hell is wrong with me? I gave my head a shake to clear out those ideas. *Get a fucking grip on yourself, Kavanaugh. Married, married, married!*

I noticed Ryan's red Jaguar pulling out of the parking lot a few cars ahead of me. He'd been acting distracted and sort of shady when I'd popped into his office earlier, which had triggered my spidey-senses.

I wasn't an idiot. I knew he was using again, even if he denied it—which he'd been doing for the past few months. My brother had been a pretty good football player both in high school and college. He'd continued playing in a local pick-up league every autumn after graduating. Five years ago, around the time his marriage to Diana began to fall apart, he'd fucked up his knee during a game. Tore some cartilage. Must've hurt like a bitch, although frankly I'm sure being married to one did, too. He had surgery. They gave him painkillers. He got hooked. Not an uncommon story, right? Except this is Ryan I'm talking about—Mr. Addictive Personality.

He'd promised me the morning of my wedding day, standing there looking all dapper in his black suit, clutching Laura's ring in his fist as he swore, "No more pills, Declan. I'm done with that shit." And I'd been so full of happiness that day, so grateful he was my best man, and that we were acting like real brothers for the first time in ages, that I'd foolishly believed him.

Except Ryan's promises never amount to fuck-all. He'd finally dropped the idiocy of accusing me of sleeping with his wife, thank Christ, but without her in his life he became untethered. He drifted aimlessly, and it was only a matter of time before he started using again. I'd figured it out, dealt with him, and things went back to normal for a while. Until they weren't again, and we had to start the whole miserable process over. Every time was a bit different from the last, but I always managed to drag him back from the edge before he fell over. No one else found out, he never got arrested, and he never fucked up his career. Thanks to me.

I knew all the signs by now, and I knew how to handle him. He was a remarkably good actor when he needed to be. He had everyone else fooled. But he couldn't fool me.

As the cars between us turned onto Fifth Street, I drew closer. Maybe he saw me behind him, I don't know, but he suddenly put pedal to the metal and his little XFR took off. Shady, shady.

What the fuck are you up to, little brother? I thought, making a spur of the moment decision to follow. Hitting the gas, I raced forward just in time to catch sight of him making a left on Elm. Was the dumbass just going home? If so, why speed away from me like that? *Moron.*

Sighing, I slowed down and drove the speed limit the rest of the way to his place. It wasn't worth risking a ticket over. After the DUI I'd been slapped with six years ago, I tried to avoid police attention. My brain-dead brother should've been avoiding that, too, but I had an inkling logic was not commanding his brain right now.

Ryan lived in a small white bungalow at the back of a quiet cul-de-sac. I pulled onto the driveway beside him just as he was climbing out of his car. His look of surprise made me wonder if maybe he hadn't noticed me behind him after all.

"What are *you* doing here?" he grumbled, clearly not in the mood for any fraternal bonding. I eyed the sweat stains darkening the armpits of his gray button-up. *Nice.*

"Checking up on you," I replied. "What? You thought this was a social call?"

He went up the steps and unlocked the front door without answering. Rolling my eyes, I followed him inside. The place was a mess: clothes strewn everywhere, floors unswept, dirty mugs crowding the coffee table. I even spotted an overflowing ashtray precariously perched atop a throw pillow. My brother, who claimed to be a non-smoker, only ever bought cigarettes when he was stoned.

"You're high, aren't you?" I asked bluntly. As if I didn't know the answer already.

He fidgeted, avoiding looking at me. "Go home, Declan. I neither want nor need your company."

Grabbing him by both shoulders, I pulled him close, forcing him to look me in the eyes. His skin was flushed, and sure enough he had the telltale pinpoint pupils.

"You're a goddamned idiot, you know that, Ry? The fuck were you thinking? You took pills at work? And then drove home? Are you *trying* to get caught?"

He pulled away from me. "Leave me alone. I told you—I don't need your help. I'm fine. There is no problem." Denial had become second nature to him.

His eyes shifted rapidly around the room, still refusing to land on me. As he turned toward the kitchen, I took hold of his shoulders again and slammed him against the nearest wall, rattling the candleholders and books on the shelf nearby.

"Don't. Be. A. Fucking. Dumbass. You could lose your license, your job, even your motherfucking life!" I shook him once to emphasize my point. "I know you've fallen off the wagon again. Whether you admit it or not."

Ryan braced his palms against my chest and shoved me back a few feet. "Get the fuck off me. You're starting to sound just like Diana. The two of you talk about me today? Is that what happened? Is that why you're here?" He had a frantic, wild-eyed look about him, and his breathing was growing ragged.

I sighed and lowered my voice. "*No*, I haven't been talking to Diana. Why the hell would I talk to her about you? This stays between us."

Seizing his forearm, I dragged him to the kitchen and pushed him onto a barstool at the counter. The smell of dirty dishes moldering in the sink just about turned my stomach. Ryan needed someone to go all Dr. Phil on his ass in more ways than one or he'd soon have vermin infesting the place…if there weren't already. I shuddered at the thought.

He began to protest, but I interrupted him. "Sit down and shut up, brother. I'm gonna make some coffee, and you're gonna drink it. And you're gonna listen to me. You never fucking listen to me, and it's high time you started. You're gonna give me all your pills. All of them. I will search this entire goddamn house if I think you're holding out on me."

He glared at me. "They're all gone. I took the last two this afternoon."

"Bullshit!" I spat. "You think we just met yesterday? I *know* you. You've got them stashed away in various little hidey-holes all over the place, and you're gonna get them for me. Every last pill. Or I'll rip this house apart until I find them all. Your choice."

He looked like he was about ready to commit fratricide. Ryan might have been physically larger than me, but I was older and faster. He was also stoned, so even if he did try something, I was pretty sure I could take him.

Eventually he sighed. "Fine."

"Fine, what?"

Gritting his teeth, he shot me the Evil Eye. "Fine, I'll give you all the pills."

And he did. I forced him to gulp down three cups of coffee in rapid succession, which incidentally made him have to pee like a racehorse—also helpful—and then I followed him around while he dug out blister packs of pale yellow tablets from inside, under, and behind various things.

The bathroom was our last stop. As Ryan reached for the edge of the mirror above the sink, I looked at him incredulously. "*Really*?"

He glanced back at me, confused. "What?"

"The fucking medicine cabinet? You're a bigger dumbass than I thought."

He had the gall to actually grin and shrug before pulling out a half-empty pill bottle and tossing it into my waiting hands. My jacket pockets were nearly full at this point. I could have made a killing ridding myself of them to the pimps and pushers in some of the skeevy dives I knew of in Richmond, had I been so inclined. How the fuck had he gotten all these? Had he been secreting away this particular stash for years without my knowing? Maybe I was the one who'd been a dumbass. I clearly needed to start watching my brother like a hawk from now on. No one else would, if I didn't.

"That all?" I asked.

"That's all." Ryan walked into his bedroom and stretched out on the bed, staring at the ceiling. He yawned and threw an arm over his eyes. "Get the fuck out of my house, Declan."

"You're welcome," I replied.

And I left.

Chapter 5

Amelia

An e-mail appeared in my in-box one hot July morning announcing the annual company golf tournament. In two weeks the office would close early, and employees were all invited to participate in a round-robin tournament, with dinner in the clubhouse after. A sign-up sheet would be posted on the break-room door for twosome requests.

"Amelia?" I turned as Kaitlyn called my name from across the aisle. "Did you see the message about the tournament?"

"Just read it," I replied.

"You gonna go?"

"Are you?" I asked, wondering if I had the option of skipping out.

"Nope. I volunteer every Thursday right after work. Besides, I don't golf."

"Me, neither," I confessed. "I don't know. I'll think about it."

"You should go." She smiled at me. "You're new, and it'd be a great way for you to socialize with people here outside of work. Let them get to know you."

Declan's face flashed into my mind, as it so often did these days. "That's true. They can all mock the new girl when she makes a fool of herself," I laughed.

"Ask Sam at lunch. Maybe she'll pair with you. You guys would totally have fun."

"So it wouldn't matter that I don't know how to play?"

"Does Scott golf?" I shook my head. "Well, you could always take a lesson."

She was right. I should probably make the effort to attend the first corporate function since I'd started. But I knew nothing about golf, and didn't really want to look useless in front of my fellow employees. My dad used to play once in a while, back when I was a teenager, and I thought he still sometimes did. Maybe I'd ask him if he could show me how to hit the ball properly.

At lunch I was pleasantly surprised when Declan sat down across from me again. My face flushed as I returned his smile when our eyes connected.

We hadn't had any interactions since the afternoon he'd dropped off the Jim Coltrane CD. It had been in rotation in my car for the past week or so, but I was still trying to decide whether I liked it or not. It was definitely folksier than my usual tastes. Since I'd yet to form a definite opinion, I hadn't e-mailed him about it, figuring we'd discuss it in person at some point. And now here he was, sitting right in front of me. I kind of hoped he wouldn't mention it, selfishly wanting to save that conversation for when there weren't nosy ears around.

The talk around me soon turned to the upcoming tournament, and I listened with interest to stories about the various goings-on from previous years. It sounded like having a few beers on the course was pretty normal, and nobody took their scores too seriously. Good. If I decided to play, whoever got stuck golfing with me would need to keep their expectations low.

"Hey, do you have a partner yet?" I asked Sam when I could get a word in edgewise.

She smiled brightly. "Evan and I are teaming up this year—aren't we, Evan?"

He looked smug. "Yep. Double-trouble on the green. We're gonna kick some ass!"

Crap. There went that idea.

"Are you looking for a partner, Amelia?" Declan asked.

I'd assumed he was already paired up with Josh, or one of his other buddies. Maybe he could suggest someone he knew who still needed a second? "Yes. But I don't know how to play."

"I'll pair up with you," he offered. "If you want me."

If you want me. The words blared like a siren through my head.

I swallowed, my throat suddenly dry. The idea both excited and terrified me. My response flew from my mouth before I even thought it through. "That'd be great! As long as you don't mind me dragging you down."

He just laughed and made a joke about Evan's golfing skills, or lack thereof. His casual offer wasn't mentioned again, nor did any talk of music come up. By the time I returned to my desk, I wasn't sure if his invitation had really happened or not.

The next morning when I got in, I had an e-mail from Declan. The subject line simply read: *Golf.* He asked if I was still interested in partnering with him for the tournament.

I tried to keep my reply light. *Sure, but remember I have no clue how to golf. Want to teach me?*

He responded about a minute later: *Tomorrow after work?*

Whoa. Just me and Declan? Alone? I pictured myself standing in front of him on the grass, his arms wrapping around me from behind, guiding my hands into the correct position on the golf club, teaching me how to properly hold it, how to swing just right. I imagined the feel of his hard chest brushing against my back as he showed me how to move my arms.

Oh God.

I gulped. This was probably a terrible idea. I couldn't tell anyone here if we did—it might cause rumors to spread, and neither of us needed that. So it would have to be a secret meet-up. And there was no way *that* could be good. Could it?

No, it couldn't. Not with the crazy way he made me feel. Hanging out just the two of us was liable to be a bad, bad plan.

But if I was going to golf in the tournament, I *did* need to at least have a vague idea how to play. And it *would* give us a chance to get to know each other better, which could only be helpful for our working relationship. I would be less likely to be influenced by what others said once I'd formed an opinion about him myself—which I could only do if I learned more about him. When I saw first-hand that he really was the arrogant jerk everyone else said he was, well then this stupid little crush would sputter out all on its own. Which it *really* needed to. So, therefore, this would be a perfect opportunity to do just that, and I should take advantage of it. Right?

I rationalized and justified to myself that Declan giving me golf lessons tomorrow was a completely innocent—no, actually a *fabulous*—idea.

My heart was pounding. Before I could change my mind again, I typed my answer and hit Send.

Sounds good. See you then.

The next morning I felt like a teenager again, getting ready for my first big date with the hottest guy at school. I'd tossed and turned most of the night, unable to sleep, playing over in my mind dozens of different conversations I might have with Declan while on the driving range.

I debated ever-so-briefly not telling Scott about our after-work plans, but realized there was no reason not to. His reaction to hearing a male co-worker offered to give me golfing lessons to prepare me for a company tournament was relaxed indifference. Scott wasn't the jealous type, another one of the things I liked about him. He even told me he'd borrow his sister's clubs for me to use. So there was no problem there. The problem, or potential problem, all lay with me.

Scott had left early to drive his mother to a doctor's appointment, so I took extra-long to perfect my hair and make-up. I chose a pair of white capris to show off my tanned legs, and a teal capped-sleeve top with a scoop neck. My nerves were already kicking in and I hadn't even gotten to the office yet. How jacked-up would I be by the time four rolled around?

Those eight hours seemed to stretch on forever. I had no idea if I was supposed to meet Declan in his office and walk out with him, or in the parking lot and follow him to wherever we were going. Every once in a while, I'd open a new e-mail intending to message him and ask, but then I'd close it again. I didn't want to seem like I was pestering.

Around 3:45, just when I felt like my anxiety couldn't ratchet up any higher, a message from him arrived.

We still on? Do you know where Lynchburg Golf Club is?

I sighed with relief, and typed: *Yes. And no.*

His answer was just as fast.

Pop by my office on your way out. You can follow me over.

An irrepressible smile erupted across my face.

My heart pounded out a dancehall beat in my chest as I shut down my computer, said my goodnights, and headed for Declan's office. When I got to his door, I saw he was on the phone. He looked over and flashed me a crooked grin, holding up a finger to let me know he'd just be a moment. Today he wore a black golf shirt instead of a button-up. As usual, butterflies began doing pirouettes in my stomach. No matter how much my brain insisted it not, my body continued to react like this every time I laid eyes on him.

Hanging up, he turned to me. "Hey."

"Hey," I replied with a tight smile, trying to sound relaxed. And probably failing.

I walked with him out the back exit and into the employee parking lot. To my surprise, he went over to a sky blue Mustang sports car—not at all the kind of car I'd expected a salesman to drive. I'd just assumed it'd be an Acura, or an Audi, or a Lincoln, or something like that, probably in basic black. I don't even know why I'd guessed that. Maybe because at least a quarter of the cars in this lot were black? Maybe because Declan seemed to wear black almost exclusively? Seeing him standing beside that audaciously sleek car took my breath away. The vibrant blue brought out the very depths of color in his eyes.

He noted my surprise at his vehicle. "Yeah, I know. Pretty flashy. But it stands out. It's important to stand out to clients, to make a unique first impression. And it's a conversation starter, that's for sure."

I couldn't think of a good response to that, so I just nodded. It was inconceivable to me that Declan wouldn't make an impression on anyone who ever laid eyes on him.

"Which one's yours?"

Pointing out a dark blue Honda Accord, I confirmed I'd follow him and slid behind the wheel. My fingers were slick against the hard plastic as I drove. It was a hot day, but I was pretty sure the temperature had nothing to do with it. I prayed my extra-strength antiperspirant would hold out, at least until I was on my way home later. Sweat stains on my clothing were definitely not part of the impression I wanted to make.

I followed his car to the edge of town and along a rural two-lane paved highway I'd never been down before. Undulating fields of tall wheat bracketed the road, and here and there wooden barns with tall silos were interspersed like red islands among seas of pale green.

We turned off onto a narrow street lined by a few large homes. It dead-ended in the gravel parking lot of the golf course. If I hadn't seen the sign for Lynchburg Golf Club out on the main road, there's no way I'd have known it was back here. The white façade of the clubhouse rose up behind a manicured hedge, and I parked in front of it. Only a few other cars were in the lot.

Declan appeared at my door, pulling it open it for me before I'd even unbuckled my seatbelt.

"Thanks," I smiled. "Will I need to rent clubs?"

He reached for my hand to help me out. "Nope. We can both use mine today."

Swinging his golf bag over one shoulder, he led me around the large building.

I watched from the back of the pro shop as he procured a basket of balls for us, apparently complimentary because he was a member. Then I followed him out to the putting green. My nerves were already jacked up to eleven, and every time he glanced my way and flashed me that knee-weakening smile of his, they shot up another notch.

He demonstrated how to properly hit a golf ball, and I won't pretend I didn't appreciate the view from behind as I watched him swing. It wasn't like in the movies or my over-active imagination—he didn't once stand at my back and wrap his arms around me to show me how to hold the club. He was a perfect gentleman and didn't even touch me. Thank God.

He taught. We practiced. I paid attention and figured out some stuff. And we talked. And talked. And talked.

Declan wasn't arrogant or self-centered at all—far from it. He was genuinely curious about me. He wanted to know about my former job at Bellmore, what I'd loved about it, what I hadn't, and why I'd left. About my family, my life, and growing up in Swann's Landing.

He talked about his clients, his daughter, his wife. When I told him I'd gone to high school with Laura, he was surprised at first, then a bit disappointed when I didn't have any embarrassing stories about her to share. My nerves faded away more and more with every passing moment.

When it somehow came up that this past winter he'd gotten his first tattoo, I insisted he show me. He removed one shoe and tugged down the edge of his sock to reveal a small black fish swimming along the side of his foot.

"Alexis was born in February," he explained. "Piece of advice: don't ever get a tattoo on your foot. Too many small bones too close to the surface. Hurts like a bitch." We both laughed, and my anxiety subsided even further.

Walking back to our cars afterward, I realized I still hadn't told Declan what I thought about the Jim Coltrane CD. As he tossed his golf bag into his trunk, I blurted, "I like 'Wide Open Sky.'"

He turned to me wide-eyed as he closed the lid, then broke into a huge smile. "Yeah? It's my second favorite track on that album."

"'I'll lie here all night watching for a shooting star. Knowing you'll see it, wherever you are,'" I quoted. "The lyrics are beautiful. But your favorite is 'All Wrong For You', isn't it?"

His head tilted to one side. A slight breeze wafted his dark hair, and I felt the strangest urge to smooth down the flyaway strands. "Yes, it is," he replied with surprise. "How'd you know that?"

I shrugged. "I guessed." But that wasn't completely true. I'd just had a feeling. There was something about the words to that song. They were so sad, just so haunting and melancholy. It was the track that spoke to me the most, too. "The best songs in the world are the kind that move you and make you ache deep inside."

"You're like no one I've ever met, Amelia," he declared, still staring at me with a slightly bewildered expression.

I didn't know what to say to that. He wasn't like anyone I'd ever met either, but that wasn't a conversation I thought would be wise for us to get into.

"Thank you for the lesson," I said instead. "Hopefully I'll remember what you showed me when we have to do this for real next week."

"Don't worry, you'll do fine. It'll be fun." Then he flashed me another grin, got into his car, and I followed him as far as the highway that led back to Swann's Landing.

After I pulled into my driveway, I stayed in the car for a minute waiting for the current song to finish. I was giddy. There was no other word to describe it. I sat there thinking over all the things Declan and I had talked about, remembering his hair, his eyes, the tone of his voice, the shape of that small fish tattoo on his foot. I knew I shouldn't be indulging myself, knew it wasn't healthy to dwell on a man who was completely off-limits, but I couldn't seem to stop.

With a sigh, I shut off the engine and went into the house.

Scott wasn't home, so I sent him a text to let him know I was back. He walked in the door not five minutes later with take-out from Pizza Palace—my knight in shining armor, rescuing his damsel from slaving over a hot stove on a sticky summer evening.

He had a set of golf clubs over his other arm. "Borrowed these for you from Morgan," he told me, lowering the bulky pink bag to the floor in the front hallway. "She hardly ever uses them anyway."

"Thanks, hon. You're the best." I gave him a peck on the cheek before taking the pizza box from his hand.

"So, how was it?" he asked as he followed me into the kitchen and sat at our small table.

"The golf lesson?"

"Yeah. You like it? Do I need to learn?"

I laughed. "It's not too bad. I didn't suck as much as I thought I would, but I can't see myself taking it up as a regular hobby."

"Okay." He reached for a gooey slice. "Who gave you lessons again?"

I turned away from him to grab a plate from the cupboard for my own pizza. As casually as possible, I replied, "Declan Kavanaugh. He's an Account Manager who sits with us at lunch sometimes." I was on the verge of telling Scott a bunch of other stuff about Declan, but stopped myself. It probably wasn't a great idea to seem too interested in him.

It turned out I needn't have worried about sparking any suspicion. Scott began to tell me about his day with his mom and sister, and our conversation never did return to golf, or BWK, or Declan.

As we were getting ready for bed later, he offhandedly said, "My mom asked how much longer we're going to make her wait for grandkids again."

I froze at the mirror where I'd been slathering on night cream, and caught his eyes in the reflection. "What did you say?"

"The same thing I always do. I told her we'd let her know once we figured it out. But I doubt she's going to drop that subject anytime soon."

I sighed. "I know, Scotty. Sorry you keep getting pressured about it."

"I get why she asks. It's not like Morgan's going to have a baby anytime in the foreseeable future." His lips twitched with a suppressed smile, and I knew he was picturing his wild-child sister trying to take care of an infant. "Don't worry about it. Mom's just impatient for us to start a family. Give her a little one to spoil, you know?"

"I know. But I just started a new job. It wouldn't be right for me to show up pregnant right after they hire me. Not in the first year, for sure. You get that, don't you?" I turned to look at him.

"Yeah, I get it. I know you're not thinking about kids yet. But…Ames? I'd be lying if I told you I wasn't ready either." He slid off the bed and came over to me, putting his arms around me from behind. "I'm ready whenever you are."

The problem was I couldn't even imagine starting a family with Scott right now. And I had no idea when, or if, I'd ever want to.

Chapter 6

Declan

My mind was stuck on Amelia York as I drove home and walked over to the sitter's to pick up Alexis. Spending time with her this afternoon had been like a breath of fresh air to the stressful, often toxic, 'normal' that my life had evolved into most days. She didn't look at me with disdain, or annoyance, or—worst of all—pity. She was interested in my opinions and advice, and seemed to actually want to get to know me. Even though I knew full well that certain small-minded gossips in the office would have already filled her head with tales of what a massive douchebag I was—and hey, I'm not denying the truth behind some of that—she wouldn't have agreed to partner up with me, or go out alone with me today, if she believed what she'd undoubtedly heard. Amelia had obviously decided to make up her own mind, which already put her head and shoulders above most of her co-workers in my eyes. Absurdly I found myself hoping that as she got to know me, I wouldn't disappoint her.

When I walked through the neighbor's front door, the first thing I heard was Alexis' excited squeal of "Daddy!" Seconds later a bundle of energetic three-and-a-half year old flew into my waiting arms. I swung her in a circle and planted a big kiss on her forehead. Today was already a far better day than I'd had in weeks. More like months. Maybe longer.

Laura was working late again, so Alexis and I had another Daddy-Daughter night. I made spaghetti, and she made a mess. She was the only person on the planet whose messes didn't make me antsy. Not to say that I didn't clean them up as fast as she made them, but they didn't give me anxiety. And she was just so damn cute with spaghetti sauce all over her face, smiling at me proudly after she'd finger-painted a new Picasso on the tabletop.

Bath time came next, followed soon after by my favorite part of the night: story time. As I read *Fox In Socks*, she interrupted my garbled tongue twisters with peals of high-pitched giggles. By the time the book was finished, we were both laughing so hard we were in tears.

Throughout our fun I tried to keep one ear cocked in case I heard Laura come in before it was time for lights out. Of course, she didn't. It was yet another night of tucking our daughter in, kissing her goodnight and assuring her of how much her mother and I loved her. Tonight Alexis didn't even ask me where Mommy was. It saddened me beyond words that our child was getting so used to her mom not being there.

Laura texted saying she was stuck in a late meeting with her producers and didn't know what time she'd be home. I replied: *Whatever.* I was well aware my curt message would make her feel bad, but right now I really didn't give a fuck.

I did some work in my office for a while, but my ability to concentrate was marred by thoughts of Laura and Alexis, of Ryan, and in moments of weakness, Amelia. As I was getting ready for bed, I heard the front door open. A few minutes later Laura came into our bedroom.

"Don't start," she begged me as she dropped her purse on her dresser and walked to the en suite bathroom. "I know you're mad I didn't get home earlier, but please—I just can't fight with you tonight."

I sighed, my annoyance slipping away at the frustration in her voice. It was obvious neither one of us was very happy with the current status quo. "Another day from hell?" I asked gently when she returned.

She didn't answer right away, turning away from me to unzip and push down her blue pencil skirt and stockings. Normally watching Laura get undressed was a highlight of my day; a sexy tease of what I could look forward to after her clothes hit the floor. Tonight I just waited for her to change into her pajamas and get around to telling me what was stressing her out this time.

She climbed into bed and rolled over to face me with a grave expression. "You won't believe what I found out today."

"Tell me."

"My dad…" Her voice caught.

Oh, shit. I could tell this wasn't going to be good.

She exhaled the words in a rush. "My dad's been cheating on my mom."

What the fuck? I was so shocked I didn't even know what to say, so I just stared at her. My mouth may have even fallen open in surprise. At last I found my voice. "You're kidding? Does your mom know? How did you find out?"

"She told me over lunch today. It's apparently been going on for years."

"For *years*?" I repeated incredulously. "Why hasn't she left him already? Tell her we have a spare bedroom and plenty of space here."

"I did. She doesn't want to leave."

"What? Why the hell not?"

"I don't know. She's known about the affairs for a long time. And she decided to stay." Laura rolled onto her back and stared at the ceiling. "I just don't get it, Declan. Why would she choose to stay with a man who disrespects her and humiliates her like that?"

"I have no idea."

I thought about it, though. Laura and her brother were both adults. Their parents had a paid-for home, and weren't hurting for cash. There were no financial or familial reasons for her mother to feel obligated to remain in an unhappy marriage. Unless…could it be that she *wasn't* unhappy? Maybe for some unfathomable reason this worked for them both? But I wasn't about to suggest that possibility to my wife. She was too close to the situation to comprehend any reasons why two people might continue to maintain a marriage under those circumstances.

"Declan?" she whispered.

"Yeah?"

"I couldn't do it."

"Stick around?" I asked, though I knew what she meant.

"Yeah."

I reached over and squeezed her hand. "I know."

Amelia

A wide band of morning sun warmed a cozy path across the bed. Scott was over at the high school doing some upgrading to the auto shop that he'd planned to complete over the summer, and I was still being lazy after another restless night of patchy sleep. Curled up snug under my blankets, I was reading a novel and trying not to let my thoughts slip back to that dream I'd had a few weeks ago about Declan. Most of it had faded away—except for the kiss. That part I remembered all too well, and as I lay there, it stubbornly refused to stray far from my thoughts.

Between that dream and our interactions since, I had plenty to reminisce about, and I wasn't getting much reading done. When I happened to look at the clock, I realized it was 10:40. *Crap*! I was supposed to be over at my parents' place in twenty minutes! I'd promised my dad I'd help him go through the boxes in storage in the attic and take home the stuff I wanted so he could get rid of some of the clutter. My mom wasn't really strong enough to help with any heavy lifting, and I didn't want Dad to have to do it all himself. If I didn't show up soon, I knew he'd just start without me.

When I got there, we all sat in the kitchen and had coffee before getting into organizing mode. My father had just been to see his cardiologist to have some more tests done. According to the doctor, his health was looking much better, which was a huge relief.

As we chatted about some family friends who'd just announced they were expecting, I mentioned that Scott's mother kept bugging us about when we planned to have a baby.

Mom looked horrified. "Amelia! You just started a new job—the last thing you should be doing right now is telling them you need to go on maternity leave in nine months! It wouldn't be professional of you at *all*."

Rolling my eyes, I replied, "I have no intention of it. I'm not ready for kids yet. But good to know where you stand."

"Focus on your career first. Don't make the same mistake I made. You can start a family in a few years, once your position there is more settled." She stood and went to the sink to rinse out our mugs.

I sighed. *Right. Don't wreck my career like you did yours by getting pregnant with me. Got it.*

My dad and I climbed the ladder to the low-ceilinged attic. Plunking myself down on the wooden floorboards, I dragged the closest dust-covered box toward me. I'd brought up an empty carton to put any stuff in I wanted to keep, and a stack of plastic garbage bags to sort items for either a yard sale or the dump.

When I tore open the third box, I was surprised to find it filled to the brim with my old baby things. Small pink dresses, teddy bear-patterned blankets, bibs, little socks and the cutest pair of tiny white patent-leather Mary-Janes I'd ever seen. I held them up to my dad in amazement. "Wow, Daddy. Looks at these shoes! Was I ever really that small?"

My dad laughed. "Yes, Amy, you really were. Leave that box. Your mom wants to save all that for you if you have a daughter someday."

"She does?" I don't know why I was so surprised by that—it made sense, after all. I guess I just couldn't imagine my perfectly coiffed, immaculately dressed mother thinking about holding a baby. She hadn't ever dropped any hints to me about wanting grandchildren. Maybe she did; I wasn't sure, but if I were forced to guess I would've assumed she wasn't bothered either way. My mom had never made any secret of hoping I'd be very successful in my career. I was well aware she wanted me to be able to have the life she didn't get to.

"Yep. Here—I'll tuck that one into the back corner for when we need it someday. Can you write on the side of it what's inside?"

I scrawled 'Amelia's baby stuff' across the cardboard in black magic marker and pushed the box in his direction.

I sorted through a few more cartons, stuffing garbage bags as I went. One box was filled with yellowing school things of mine: report cards, essays, poems, and even my old diaries. I couldn't bear to part with that stuff yet, but didn't have the patience to sort through them, either. I set it aside into the Keep pile.

Man, it's hot up here! The air conditioning didn't seem to reach the attic at all. It would be time for a break for both of us pretty soon.

Pushing sticky strands of hair off my face, my thoughts returned to those little white shoes.

"Daddy?"

"Yes, hon?"

"Scott wants kids," I confessed.

He paused, turning to look at me with a concerned expression. "And you don't?"

I sighed. "No, it's not that. It's just…I'm just not sure. I might. But not right now." I scrunched up my face. "He'd make a great dad, I know he would, but…would it make me a horrible person if I said I really can't picture myself starting a family with him?"

"Oh, sweetie. You're not a horrible person. Have you told Scott you feel this way?"

I shook my head.

"Why not?"

"Because I'm only twenty-nine. I could still change my mind. Right?" I asked hopefully.

"Right. But could the problem maybe be that you just can't see yourself having kids with *Scott*?"

My throat grew tight at my father's words. He was always so astute when it came to me. No one got me the way my dad did. No one. Not my mother, not my friends, and definitely not my husband. Scott still saw the Amelia of Before; he didn't seem to really understand the Amelia of Now. Which I understood was at least partly my fault for not communicating well enough over the past few years.

"Maybe," I whispered.

My dad came over and, as we were both kneeling, gave me an awkward hug. "Amelia, you are a York. You are smart and strong, and you can do anything you set your mind to. But you have to stop living your life for other people. That means sometimes you're going to have to make hard choices. You need to do what's best for you. Not for your mother and me. Not for Scott. For you."

I sighed. "I know, Daddy."

"No matter what happens, no matter what decisions you make, or what path your life might lead you down, I will always support you. You know that, right?"

"I do." A single tear escaped the corner of my eye, trickling a dusty trail down the side of my nose. I dashed it away.

"Come on. It's stifling up here, and we've made a good dent in it for now. I think your mother has some fresh lemonade in the fridge." He held out his hand to help me up, and we headed for the steps.

Monday morning rolled around, and brought with it a new administrative assistant. Her name was Mandy Deschain. She was young—fresh out of high school by the looks of her—and petite, with shoulder-length brown hair and a cheerful smile. This meant I was no longer the New Girl, a title I was more than happy to hand off.

Just after ten, I got an e-mail from Declan asking me to grab the file for Blair and Sons Funeral Home and pop over when I had a chance to discuss the figures I'd sent to him last week. My heart-rate accelerated at the thought of sitting in his office with him, even if we would be discussing work.

Once I finished with the query I was working on, I retrieved the case file for Blair and Sons, refreshed my memory of what I'd done last week, and made my way to the Sales department with it clutched against my chest.

I tensed a little as I passed Sam's desk, not really wanting to explain where I was headed. Luckily she was on the phone. She caught my eye and flashed me a smile as I passed.

When I got to Declan's office, I paused to take a deep breath before knocking on the doorjamb and poking my head in. His face lit up with a grin when he saw me, and he beckoned me inside. He wore a blue button-up shirt that really brought out the color of his eyes. I had to remind myself to keep breathing.

"Have a seat, Amelia." He gestured to one of the guest chairs. I sat down and smoothed out my skirt, propping the case file on my lap.

He got straight to business, asking me to explain my reasoning behind only giving a limited discount to the price. This seemed like something pretty basic, something that he could have easily called or e-mailed me about instead of calling me over. After answering his question, I waited for him to get to the real reason for wanting to see me in person, assuming there had to be a more complicated issue to discuss.

To my surprise, he replied, "Okay. That makes sense." He made a notation in his own folder, closed it, and put it neatly to one side.

"So how was your weekend?"

"Good," I replied, a little confused by his sudden change of topic. "Yours?"

"Just good? Do anything worth mentioning?" Declan's smile made my mind hazy and slow to function, a reaction I hoped would diminish soon.

I clasped my hands together to prevent them from fidgeting. He wanted to chat? Really? Okay, I could do that. What had I done this weekend again? Oh, right. "Um, I went over to my parents' place to help my dad clean out the attic. Nothing too exciting."

"You close to your dad?" he wondered. The question was posed lightly, but I could sense an undercurrent of something more below the surface.

"Very much so—with my dad. Not so much with my mom. What about you?"

He looked uncomfortable. "My mother died when I was seven. Cancer. As for my father, well…let's just say it's complicated."

"I'm so sorry to hear that," I offered. I knew there wasn't any good way to reply to the news that someone had lost a parent.

"It was a long time ago. Ryan doesn't even really remember her." He shrugged in a 'what can you do?' kind of gesture. I wanted to ask him more about his mother. What was she like? What did he recall about her? How does a seven year-old boy cope with losing his mom like that? Did he have any female role models in his life after? But I didn't know Declan anywhere near well enough to ask such personal things. Maybe someday he'd tell me. Probably not. My heart ached for him. I wished I could reach out and take in my arms the little boy he used to be. Not to mention the grown man he was now.

Deciding it might be smart to change the subject to something less intense, I said, "Thanks again for making me that CD. It's starting to really grow on me."

His serious face flipped back to full-on smile. "Glad to hear it. Most of my buddies aren't into that kind of music. In fact, I don't think I know anyone else who appreciates Coltrane like I do. I've actually been trying to learn the guitar tabs to 'Georgia Girl'."

My eyes widened, insides tightening again. "You play guitar?" Oh, I was *so* screwed now. Wasn't the plan to stomp out this silly crush so we could be friendly co-workers without my wanting to lick him every time I laid eyes on him? *Crap.* He played guitar. Might as well dip himself in chocolate, too. This was even more of a disaster. An awesome, scary, incredible disaster.

"Not very well," he laughed. "But, yeah. I practice. Alexis loves listening to me play. She stops whatever she's doing and just watches my fingers move over the strings, totally mesmerized."

I bet she does, I thought. *I'd be mesmerized if you played for me, too.* "How old is Alexis?"

"Three and a half. And yes, before you ask, Laura was pregnant when we got married four years ago." He didn't seem embarrassed by it, but he definitely had a look on his face like he was expecting to be judged. And why wouldn't he? From what I could tell, everyone around here seemed to judge him harshly about everything.

I just smiled. "I got married four years ago, too."

He showed me the wedding photo and picture of his daughter that sat on his desk, and it was all very casual and relaxed, like new friends getting to know each other should be.

New friends. We were friends. Declan Kavanaugh and I. *Huh.* Who ever would have guessed?

When I left his office that giddy feeling came over me once again. I knew I was smiling, and hoped my co-workers wouldn't notice and ask why. I also decided that if we were going to treat each other like real friends, I should return his favor. I would make Declan a CD of some of *my* favorite songs. So instead of diving into the next case in my in-box, I opened an e-mail to send to myself at home and began to make a track listing. I hadn't been so excited about something so minor as picking out just the right songs in a very long time.

Chapter 7

Amelia

As I left my cool house on the morning of the BWK golf tournament, the persistent low drone of cicadas filled the already humid morning air, and I sighed. It was shaping up to be another Virginia summer scorcher. I swung my sister-in-law's golf bag into my trunk and jumped into the driver's seat to get the air conditioning flowing.

I'd taken my time picking out my outfit, but now suspected it would be damp and wilted before we even finished the first hole. Since the dress code today was casual, I chose a pair of knee-length blue shorts and a black sleeveless tunic that cinched at the waist. It showed off a little bit of cleavage—not that I had much to display—but not enough to be inappropriate. I'd ponytailed my hair, added a silver necklace, and finished off with mascara, lip-gloss and a spritz of peach body spray. I was as ready as I'd ever be to face work, and then a few hours with Declan in a golf cart—in other words, not in the slightest.

Employees attending the tournament were permitted to leave at two, but even with the shortened workday, every minute seemed to drag. I soon got caught up on my own stuff, so decided to pop into

Josh's office to see if I could take any work from him, since I knew he was swamped this week. As I expected, he was only too happy to hand over a few requests from his pile. With the files in my hands, I sat down across from him.

"I can't believe you're looking for extra work. Your efficiency is gonna make the rest us look bad," he teased. "So, did you manage to find a golf partner?"

I smiled. "Yes."

"Who'd you sucker into it?"

"Um, Declan, actually. He offered," I rushed to clarify.

"Did he?" Josh mused, one eyebrow rising. "You lucked out then. He's really good. He know you don't know how to play?" I hadn't told Josh—or anyone else at our office—about Declan giving me lessons a few days ago.

"Yes, and I made that clear *before* he asked me. Do you think he'll be annoyed about me dragging our team score down?" I'd been kind of concerned about that all week, although Declan had assured me it didn't matter.

Josh laughed. "Nah, I'm sure it'll be okay. He's not as bad as everyone around here says he is. I wouldn't worry."

"I'm not." But a part of me was. Not so much that Declan would be irritated, but that I'd make a fool of myself in front of him.

Josh held my gaze for a minute, narrowing his eyes as he studied me. The look on his face made me wish I had the power to read minds.

"Amelia…" he started, sighing. "Declan's a good guy at heart—he really is. Once you get to know him, anyway. I know he comes off like a dick a lot of the time, but…there are reasons for that. Just…try not to judge anyone by what other people tell you."

I smiled. "I never do, or I wouldn't have agreed to this. Thanks for the advice, though. *You* know him, don't you?"

Josh laughed. "I guess I do. As much as he lets anyone know him, anyway."

Biting my bottom lip, I considered his words. Declan had seemed pretty open with me at the driving range. He certainly hadn't been standoffish. Was that unusual? Did he treat me differently than most others? If so, why? And would he ever let me *truly* get to know him?

My mind was buzzing with questions. For reasons that I couldn't articulate to myself very well, I really wanted to know him.

I stood, but paused to look back at Josh as I reached the door. "So, who'd *you* end up getting paired with?" I asked, realizing he hadn't told me yet.

He rolled his eyes, chuckling. "Wanna take a guess? I'm clearly being punished for something."

My eyes widened with realization. "Oh, no," I groaned. "Diana?"

"Yep."

Although I had some more work to concentrate on, the next hour didn't seem to pass any faster. I checked my inbox often, hoping I might hear something from Declan about where to meet him, or if we'd drive there together. When it was approaching two and nearly time to head out, I asked Josh if I could follow him, since I'd never been to that course before. By then I'd assumed, with some disappointment, that I'd just find Declan when I arrived.

I trailed Josh's white Jeep as we hopped onto the Richmond Highway heading east. We got off about fifteen minutes later, took a few turns onto country roads, and at last pulled into the parking lot of the Falling River Country Club. It was filling up fast, and I ended up parking pretty far from the clubhouse. Tugging down the driver's side visor, I examined myself in the mirror and touched up my lip gloss. My heart raced with a combination of anticipation and anxiety at the thought of seeing Declan in a few minutes.

It was a scorching day, and I left the cool interior of my car with some reluctance. As I retrieved the clubs from my trunk, I paused to admire the view. I was surrounded by lush green: the close-cropped lawns, the majestic oak trees, the sculpted hedges. A pale gray clubhouse loomed in the middle of all of this verdant nature. The wooden siding was divided by a huge wrap-around deck, and there were staff in crisp white shirts setting tables along it.

Josh waved to me from beside his Jeep, and I hurried over to him, awkwardly hauling Morgan's pink golf bag over one shoulder. We walked along the side of the building and down a small hill. At the bottom I saw clusters of BWK people greeting each other as they milled around rows of white golf carts.

Josh clapped me on the shoulder and wished me luck before pasting on a fake smile and striding over to join Diana. I nervously scanned the crowd for Declan. At first I couldn't find him, and I grew even more apprehensive. Then suddenly his grinning face was in front of me, and I gasped, startled. He wore a dark red golf shirt and black cargo shorts. I'd never seen him in a bright color before, and was struck by how amazing the red looked against his tanned skin.

"There you are. Find the place okay?" He unburdened me of the clubs and took them over to prop up in the back of a cart with the number thirteen painted on the side.

"I followed Josh, actually," I replied, sliding onto the passenger side of the wide seat. It was upholstered in vinyl, and I was grateful my shorts were long enough that my thighs wouldn't get stuck to it. Two fresh bottles of water were waiting in the cup holders for us.

Declan sat down beside me, turned to meet my eyes, and I swear the temperature inside our little cart shot up a few degrees as he looked me over. "I would've offered to drive you, but I was out at a client's with Marilyn, so I'm without wheels."

"Oh, that's okay," I said, trying to keep my voice casual.

We were assigned to begin on the sixth hole for the round-robin tournament, and since Declan had played this course many times before, he knew where to go. We joined the line of carts and then turned to the right and took off down a narrow paved path.

When we found the tee-off spot, he parked the cart and went around to the back to choose our clubs. He selected a thick-based club from each bag, passing me the one with the pink pleather handle.

I thanked him and looked it over before smiling up at him. "This is a driver, right?" He nodded, apparently pleased I'd remembered. "My sister-in-law loaned me her clubs for the day. Have to say, hot pink is *really* not my color."

A perplexed expression crossed his face. "No? Huh," he remarked. Then he looked thoughtful. "I've never seen you wear pink, actually. You're not much of a girly-girl, are you?"

"Not really," I said, amazed he'd even noticed what I wore at all. Most guys didn't pay attention to stuff like that. Scott couldn't have told you what I wore the previous night or probably any other time, with the possible exception of our wedding day. Even then, if someone asked, I bet his reply would just be "white."

Declan brushed his fingers against the small of my back as he guided me toward the spot where we were supposed to tee off, and my train of thought evaporated All the muscles in my abdomen tightened. It felt like flames danced over my skin where he'd briefly touched me. *God*, this man did crazy things to my insides.

He knelt and pushed a red tee into the ground. Balancing a golf ball on it, he looked up at me with a smile. "Ladies first."

Well, here goes nothing, I thought as I approached the tee with hesitation.

I positioned myself at a ninety-degree angle to where I wanted the ball to go, and tried to recall all the things he'd taught me last week. Gripping the club with both hands, thumbs down, I bent my knees and took a few practice swings.

"You can do it. Just remember what I showed you." His voice came from only a few feet behind me, and I instinctively straightened back up as soon as I realized his proximity. Taking a deep breath, I resumed the position. My problem wasn't so much that I'd forgotten my lesson—it had a whole lot more to do with the man who was so closely watching me.

I psyched myself up, swung the club out behind me, and followed through with as much force as I could muster. I heard the sound of a low *foomp,* and something flew into the air in front of me. For a second I was excited, but then I looked down to see the ball still sitting serenely on the tee. Just beside it was a small hole in the grass where I'd taken out a divot.

My face grew hot. "Crap!" I muttered.

Declan chuckled before trotting down the lawn to retrieve the clump of earth I'd knocked out. He returned and pushed it firmly back into place.

"No big deal. Everyone does that sometimes. Just try it again," he said patiently.

Bending my knees, I got back into position, trying to concentrate solely on the ball and on where I wanted it to land, not on the eyes watching me.

I swung hard, and to my dismay another chunk of dirt went flying. *Double crap!* At this rate we were going to have little hollows all over the ground around the tee, not to mention a lineup of people cursing us as they waited to play this hole.

Declan brought the second lump of grass back and shoved it back into place. Straightening, he turned to face me. "Amelia, it's okay. Just try to relax."

I blew out a frustrated puff of air. "I'm trying to do what you showed me, I really am." I didn't want him to think I hadn't been paying attention during our lesson or that I'd already forgotten it.

"I know you are, but you're too stiff. You're stressing yourself out, and that's only going to make it harder. Believe me, I know. You should've seen me when I was learning to drive. My dad used to get *so* pissed off at me."

"Really?" I remembered him telling me that the two of them didn't see eye to-eye on much.

"Yep. And he'd yell at me, which only made me more tense." He put a hand on my shoulder. "This tournament today is just for fun, you know. No one cares how well you play."

"I care," I mumbled.

"I can see that." He smiled at me and, to my regret, dropped his hand back to his side. "Just…pretend it's just you and me here. No one else around for miles. And no pressure. Then focus on where the ball's gonna land once you knock it off that tee."

Turning around to face that little dimpled demon again, I reassumed the stance for the third time. I closed my eyes for a moment and imagined there was no one on the entire course but me. I didn't even include Declan, since his presence made me far more nervous than anyone else's could.

Then I opened my eyes, drew the club back behind me and, with a fast exhalation, followed through. This time, rather than a *foomp*, I heard a distinct *thwack*.

"Yes! You did it!" Declan exclaimed behind me.

Shielding my eyes with my palm, I scanned the expanse of clipped grass for the tiny white dot of my ball.

"Where did it go?" I asked when I couldn't locate it.

"Down there." He pointed to a dip just off to the side of the vibrant green fairway. "Don't worry about that, though. It'll be easy for you to get it back up where you want it. That was a great first drive!"

It was now his turn. When his back was to me, I pulled a tissue from the pocket of my shorts and wiped as much sweat off my face, neck and upper chest as I could.

The view of Declan Kavanaugh from behind as he teed off was impressive. Remembering that at any given moment we could have an audience, I raised my gaze to try to track where his golf ball would land. Once he noted its position, we jumped back into the cart and drove over to where my ball lay. Since mine was furthest from the hole, I had to go next.

We played out the rest of the sixth hole without much difficulty, and moved onto the seventh. By the time we got to the eighth hole, Diana and Josh had caught up and were waiting for us to finish so they could begin.

Declan leaned across the seat to me conspiratorially. "Mind if we let them play ahead? That way you won't feel any pressure to hurry, and I don't have to endure Diana's bitchy face at every hole."

I could feel the tickle of his breath against my ear and it sent shivers across my overheated skin. He was way too close for comfort. I shook my head, laughing nervously. "Good idea. I hate being the cause of that face."

He pulled back a few inches and gave me an incredulous look. "I don't think it's you causing that. I'm pretty sure she was probably born with it." Just before he got out to go over to them, I heard him mutter, "I don't know how Ryan ever stood that every day."

Ah, yes. Again it crossed my mind that I had no clue what the real history was between Declan and Diana. I wondered if I'd ever find out what the truth was.

As we sat in our cart under the shade of a big maple and watched them play the hole in front of us, I quietly confided, "Josh was *not* happy about having to be her partner. He said he felt like he was being punished for something."

Declan chuckled. "I bet."

"Why didn't you partner up with him?" I asked. "You two are friends, right?"

He glanced over at me. "Yes. But I already had the partner I wanted."

"What happened to them? They back out on you?"

"Nope," he replied, shifting his gaze back to Josh and Diana.

Oh. *Oh!* I felt heat rise to my cheeks again as I realized what he meant. Grabbing my water bottle and taking a swig, I noticed my fingers shaking a little.

My anxiety reduced a bit by the time we'd played a few more holes. At one point we were stopped by the edge of a small river, again waiting for our turn. I swiped sweat off my brow with my forearm and stared longingly at the water. "I'd love to go leap in there right now to cool down," I sighed, fanning myself with the scorecard.

"Me, too," Declan said. "Imagine the rumors that would fly if the two of us stripped down and jumped in the water?" He laughed.

I laughed with him, but I couldn't quite hide the tremor in it. What I was now imagining had nothing to do with any potential rumors, and a whole lot to do with the thought of us swimming naked together. Skinny-dipping with Declan? I needed to get that idea out of my head pronto. Damn him for even bringing that image to mind in the first place. Damn him and his piercing blue eyes. Damn his sexy lopsided smile. Damn his toned body that I'd love to see sans clothing. *Argh*! I really, *really* needed to think about something else.

Luckily, it was our turn to play. And later as we drove the course, we began talking about music again, and some of the concerts we'd been to, and it wasn't long before our easy rapport fell back into place.

When I told him I'd seen David Bowie play live, he exclaimed, "How old *are* you, anyway?"

"I'm twenty-nine. But I've been a Bowie fan since I was a kid. Why? How old are you?"

"Thirty-four."

"You don't look it."

He laughed. "I sure feel it some days. No, actually some days I feel seventy-four." He shook his head, as if to clear out something he'd rather not think about. "God, I'd love to see Bowie. If he plays Richmond again, we should go."

I froze, not sure how to respond. He wasn't really asking me to go to a concert with him, was he? His casual comment sounded a bit like he was implying…a date. Which he wasn't. Absolutely wasn't. We were both married. Going to a concert together, not to mention a concert in another city together, would not be a good idea. Even just as friends. I mean, of *course* it would be just as friends, but even still. I realized I had to say something though, or risk looking rude. Deciding to just keep it simple and honest, I replied in a low voice, "That would be awesome."

Even if it was never going to happen.

I was feeling rather pleased with myself when we got back to the clubhouse. On the final hole my ball had landed in the sand trap right beside the green. Declan had passed me a sand wedge, and with one sharp swing, I'd managed to pop it up right beside the hole. He'd whooped and high fived me, telling me what an awesome chip it was. He'd clearly been proud of me. And for a split second there, I'd thought he was even about to hug me.

After we returned the cart, he tallied up our scores. "We actually didn't do too bad," he assured me. "For your first time, you played great!"

"I had an excellent teacher," I said as we smiled at each other. "Are you heading inside?"

"I need to hand in our scorecard, and then I'm going to change. I'll see you in there."

It felt a bit like a dismissal, and I couldn't help being sort of disappointed, although I had no real reason to be. I took Morgan's clubs back to my car, and then went to the clubhouse restroom to freshen up before the socializing part of the tournament began.

Sam found me when I came into the dining area and dragged me over to a corner table to sit with Evan, Josh and herself. Before long, Ryan joined us as well. We'd all gotten two free drink tickets from the Social Director, and Evan got up to get us a tray of mojitos. When I saw Declan join him at the bar, I wished I'd gone over to get my own drink. Then, as I watched, a beautiful woman with flaming red hair approached them. Declan turned to her with a smile, slipped an arm around her waist and greeted her with a kiss. My stomach dropped as I realized I was looking at Laura Logan.

So much for spending any more time with him this evening, I thought. A crazy urge to skip dinner and just head home came over me. When Evan returned with our drinks, I downed mine in about four large gulps.

Sam turned to me in surprise. "Whoa! What's the rush, Amelia?"

I shrugged, flashing her a small grin.

"Hey, no explanation necessary. If I'd had to spend the last two hours in a golf cart with Declan, I'd need a drink, too." She laughed. I didn't.

I leaned closer. "Thought this was a spouse-free event? I didn't know I could've invited Scott."

Sam looked confused. "It is. Why do you ask?" I glanced toward the bar and her eyes followed the path of mine. "Oh. Well, it's *supposed* to be. Declan Kavanaugh, as per usual, clearly thinks rules don't apply to him." She rolled her eyes. I just snorted, feeling the alcohol start to hit my sun-fried brain. Maybe she was right about him after all.

Much as I still wanted to leave, I decided to hold off until after dinner. I slid my second drink ticket across the table top to Josh. He arched a brow at me. When I nodded that it was okay, he pocketed it without comment.

I had intended to hurry through my meal and then make some excuse to bail out early. The food was delicious, but I just wasn't hungry anymore. To be honest, I kind of felt sick to my stomach. I tried to convince myself it was because I'd been out so long in the heat, and then chugged down a mojito, but I knew there were other factors.

I deliberately didn't look around for Declan, instead trying my best to focus on the conversations around me. They were used to me doing more listening than chatting, so I didn't think my discomfort would be noticed.

At last I gave up the pretense of eating and pushed my plate away. Just when I thought I was going to succeed in escaping, I heard Josh say, "Declan! Laura! Great to see you again. So Declan, how did you guys finish up today?"

Crap. Now I was going to have to be involved in this conversation whether I wanted to or not. I pasted on a small smile and looked up at them. They were standing to my right, behind Josh. Declan had one hand braced on the back of Ryan's empty chair, and Laura's fingers were wrapped around his arm. Wrapped *possessively* around his arm, I thought.

Declan glanced at me. For some reason he didn't seem quite as cheerful as he'd been when we'd parted ways earlier. "We did decently well, coming in twelfth out of thirty-two teams."

"That's good," I said carefully. "Guess I didn't bring you down as bad as I thought I would." He had golfed an awesome game, single-handedly saving our score, I felt.

"Don't be so self-deprecating. You played great." He turned to Laura. "This is my golfing partner, Amelia York. I hear you two went to high school together."

Laura smiled, sticking out one perfectly manicured hand. I gave it a quick pump. "How are you these days, Laura?"

Making small talk with Declan's wife was pretty low on the list of things I wanted to be doing at the moment, but I managed the best I could. She claimed she didn't really recall me very well, but I couldn't tell if she was being truthful about that or not. We chatted about some mutual friends from Swann's Landing for a couple of awkward minutes. Then she spotted someone at another table she needed to speak with, and they hurried away.

I won't lie—she actually seemed pretty nice. She didn't appear to be the bitch that some small and very petty part of me had hoped she'd be.

At that point, I decided I'd had enough of this particular work function and I said my goodbyes to the others. As I headed for the doors that led out to the parking lot, I noticed Declan walking by himself back up to the bar. For a moment I contemplated going over, thanking him again, and letting him know I was leaving.

I thought about it. I knew it would be the polite thing to do. But in the end I didn't. I just walked out those thick doors and went to my car. Declan was not good for me in any way, shape or form, and I knew that continuing along the emotional road I was headed down would only lead to heartache. And that was the last thing I needed.

Chapter 8

Declan

The trajectory of my day went sort of like this: mediocre, fucking amazing, and then, as often seems to happen to me, it all went to complete shit.

It started off innocuously enough, with a client meeting in Appomattox with Marilyn Silver, which I rocked. I used my charm and knowledge to help her convince them, and from the sounds of it we'd have a signed contract in our office in the morning. She'd taken me out for lunch and a beer afterwards to thank me, since the client would be hers and therefore so would the anticipated commission. She was a widow, and she just loved to flirt with me, wedding band on my finger notwithstanding. Which made having lunch just the two of us, well…let's just say amusing. Fucking awkward would probably be a better description. I knew she intended I assume she was kidding around. Unless of course I ever decided to take her up on her alluded offers—then I've no doubt she'd become quite serious about the prospect of getting into my pants. Not to be immodest, but I was used to being flirted with, and I knew how to handle it. Marilyn was an attractive woman in her late forties, but it was neither her age nor her looks that held me back. First off, she was a colleague, but second, and more important, I was taken. If I'd wanted some pussy on the side, I could've had plenty, but ever since I realized Laura was the one I wanted to spend my life with, I hadn't looked at anyone else. So, as always, I politely ignored Marilyn's not-so-subtle come-ons, just as I did the countless others I got on a somewhat regular basis.

When we got to Falling River Country Club, I left her with her partner, found Amelia, and promptly forgot about everything annoying in my life. And though she was kind of nervous at first, she eventually got the hang of it, and we had a great time golfing together. For reasons I chose to not look too close at, I was able to relax around her. We chatted and laughed, and it was all really easy. It struck me that easy was something I hadn't felt around any adult but Josh in a very long time.

I had no idea Laura was going to show up for dinner. I'd assumed I'd grab a ride back to Lynchburg with Colleen, or Evan if he was sober, or maybe even Ryan. But my wife left work early for once and decided to meet me. Not that I was unhappy she came—she just took me by surprise. Any ideas I might have had about having a drink and more conversation with my pretty golf partner went out the window the moment Laura's fingers touched my arm. I knew I'd done nothing to feel guilty about, yet I felt a twinge of guilt anyway when I turned and saw her there. The truth was, for a brief moment I'd actually been hoping those fingers belonged to Amelia.

And—God help me—I was, just for a split second, disappointed to see Laura standing there. Hence the guilt. I loved my wife. I loved my family. The last thing in the world I wanted to do was jeopardize any of that. I needed to smarten right the fuck up and get a hold of myself.

So I put my arm around Laura and kissed her. And after dinner, I made a special point to take her over to Amelia's table so I could introduce them. I wanted to keep everything completely above board. No secrets, therefore nothing for me to feel guilty about, right? Then why was I so goddamn ill at ease for the entire two minutes the two of them chatted?

I needed to put a lid on those unwelcome feelings pronto and crazy-glue that motherfucker down. Amelia York meant nothing more to me than a new co-worker and, quite possibly, a new friend.

Sure, she was sexy as hell, but looking at her wasn't a crime. Talking to her wasn't inappropriate. Being her friend was not a betrayal of my wedding vows. So why did I feel so uncomfortable when Laura took my hand and led me away from her?

A few minutes later, I was on my way back up to the bar when I noticed the back of Amelia's head as she left the dining area. For some reason I changed direction and slipped out the double doors behind her. She was walking across the parking lot toward her car, and disappointment flooded me as I realized she was heading home. I don't know why her leaving without saying goodbye bothered me, but it did. Conflicting feelings ricocheted around inside my head. I mentally grabbed every last one of them and shoved them down, down, down as far as I could.

Leaning against the wall next to the door, I watched her get into her car and drive away as the setting sun painted the clouds pink and orange along the horizon. I'm sure she never even noticed me standing there.

The air was finally beginning to lose the suffocating grip of midsummer heat, and I stayed where I was for a few minutes, just breathing and trying my best not to even think. Then door beside me flew open and my brother's voice shattered my little moment of peace.

"What are *you* doing out here?"

Great. Just what I need right now. I sighed. "Nothing. Just getting some air."

"You followed Amelia out." Ryan posed it like an accusation, not a question. Leave it to my brother to assume the worst of me. He got that straight from our old man.

Clawing back my temper, I answered in as even a voice as I could muster. "I didn't follow her. I didn't even talk to her—just saw her taillights as she drove off. Stop trying to spot trouble where there isn't any. Haven't you got enough problems of your own to deal with?"

He angled his body to face mine, and straightened his back so he glared down at me. I guess it was supposed to make me feel intimidated or something. Sure didn't work, I know that.

"You wanna know what my problem is, brother?"

I closed my eyes for a second in frustration. I knew damn well what he was doing, and I couldn't let myself be baited. Not when my emotions were balanced on a tight rope as it was. "Nope. But I bet you're gonna tell me," I replied evenly.

"You. You're my fucking problem, Declan." His face was dead calm, a bad sign. I wondered if he'd reacquired any more of his little yellow friends. I made a mental note to ransack his car later. And his damned office, too. Fuck my life.

"Why's that? 'Cause I clean up your messes?" I probably shouldn't have goaded him, but he just made it so damn irresistible.

"My life would've been far better if you'd just stayed away. Why the hell did you have to come back here? Things were going great for me before you came back. I was happy. I was in love. But ever since you returned, my life has gone to shit. Why, Declan? Why can't you just leave me the fuck alone?"

Yeah, this definitely looked like it might get ugly. I used every ounce of restraint I had to hide my rising temper. "That's not true and you know it," I gritted. "Who's the one keeping you clean? Keeping your secrets for you?"

"Secrets! That's *rich* coming from you. You know *all* about secrets, don't you? Secrets like how you were fucking my wife?"

I clenched my fists against my sides, shaking my head incredulously. Not this again! I'd thought maybe we were finally past this same goddamn argument. I'm not proud of it, but yes, I slept with Diana. Once. Before they were ever married. It was a moment of very drunken weakness, and we both regretted it. At some point after she and my brother married, the idiot confessed our dalliance and all hell broke loose. Ryan never trusted either of us after that. He managed to convince his paranoid self that she'd continued to fuck me, and let his insecurities destroy his marriage.

I opened my mouth to deny his accusations yet again, but he wasn't finished. A shrewd look came over his face, and a knowing grin twisted his lips. "You've always preferred other men's women, haven't you, Dec? So they won't expect any commitments? Are you fucking Amelia York now? She does have sweet little tits. I'd love to get my hands on those."

At that, I just lost it. All my hard fought self-control went right out the damn window when he mentioned Amelia. My fist seemed to have a mind of its own, and it connected squarely with his face. Needless to say, he went down hard on his ass on the concrete. The complete and utter shock on his face was satisfying as hell.

My sense of satisfaction lasted only a second, however, because our father chose that exact moment to step outside.

Dad took one look at Ryan lying on the ground rubbing his jaw and turned to me accusingly. "Declan!" His voice was filled to the brim with disgust and disappointment. "You are at a work function! Whatever's going on between you two this time—keep it private. Or, better yet, maybe you should just keep it to yourself."

He reached a hand down to Ryan and helped him up. "You okay, son?"

My brother looked a little dazed, but otherwise was no worse for wear. He would have a bruised jaw by morning, but his ego didn't even get scratched. "Thanks, Dad. I'm fine." They both glared at me.

As he herded Ryan back inside, he turned back to me. "I think it's time you went home." He didn't ask what we were fighting about, and he really didn't care. As long as Ryan wasn't hurt and I didn't embarrass Patrick in public, that was all that mattered.

I slumped back against the wall again, sighing in frustration as I massaged my throbbing knuckles. I really should've been used to this shit from my brother by now. As for being blamed by my father, well that was old news, too. Yet every once in a while it still kind of got to me. Sometimes I still felt like that little boy who was never good enough, never smart enough, and could never make my dad proud, no matter how hard I tried.

Pulling my phone from my jacket, I texted Laura to meet me at her car. Amelia wasn't going to be the only one leaving this event without saying goodbye.

One morning about a week later, I was sitting in Josh's office. We'd just finished going over some numbers for a quote for a chain of Virginia-based coffee shops, and I was more than pleased with the results. If I won this business, it could mean a nice future cash injection for both the company and my bank account if they went national, which I had a very strong inkling they were on the verge of.

"So, how was golfing with the BFH?" I asked, leaning back in the chair. That was one of our little private jokes. Bitch From Hell equaled Diana.

He laughed dismissively. "Oh, you know. I am nothing if not a man of great patience. I'm friends with you, aren't I?"

"Your point being?" I said with a raised brow.

"Exactly. No, really though. It wasn't so bad. I let her beat me, of course."

"Of course," I agreed. We were both well aware Diana always had to feel like she was better at everything than everyone else. But personally I'd never have underplayed to feed her ego. She already had her superiority complex down to a fucking science. I'd have blown her ass right off the green and enjoyed every last second of it. Josh, however, was not me. And she was his boss. So I got it.

"And how did you and Amelia get along? She was pretty nervous before we left the office that day."

Hmm. She hadn't told him I'd given her a lesson the week prior? Interesting. I wondered if she'd told anyone at work. Somehow I doubted it. I smirked, imagining Blondie's reaction to that particular piece of news. "What would she have to be nervous about? The rest of them tell her I'd eat her alive or something?"

Josh snickered. "Probably." He looked me right in the eyes. "She seemed kind of uncomfortable in the clubhouse after. And she took off right after dinner. Did anything happen while you guys were golfing, Declan? Please tell me you weren't a dick to her."

I held his gaze and kept my face serious. "I wasn't a dick to her." He looked skeptical. Flashing a smile, I elaborated, "Really. I know it boggles the mind, but I wasn't. We actually get along great."

"Girl obviously isn't as smart as I thought," he deadpanned.

Laughing out loud, I said, "She's a fucking genius. Way brighter than all the rest of you assholes put together."

When Josh finished chuckling, he mused, "I wonder what was bothering her that night then. I just assumed it was something you'd said or done. Frankly I'm still not convinced it wasn't."

"I have no idea," I said, but I wondered as well. Josh thought she'd been acting weird over dinner, and straight after she'd zipped out of there like she couldn't wait to escape. Something had to have been up.

Simplest way to find out? I'd just have to ask her myself.

Amelia

I'd spent most of the last seven days telling myself it would be far better if Declan and I kept our relationship strictly business. Being friends just wasn't going to work out well for my emotional well-being if I couldn't shake this idiotic crush. And my reaction to seeing Laura at the clubhouse last week had only made that more clear. I shouldn't feel the need to run away every time I saw her. I shouldn't get those distracting waves of jealousy. I couldn't take any more chances that my growing attraction to Declan might make me act inappropriately. If I couldn't squash it so that we could be friends, then I'd just have to keep my distance from him as much as possible.

We hadn't had any communication since the golf tournament, and I was hoping that might last for a while longer. Frustratingly, there was also a not-small part of me that missed seeing his smile. Right now, I was not a big fan of that part.

Scott and I had taken my parents canoeing at Staunton River State Park over the weekend. We'd camped overnight one night, and the two days had flown by in a whirlwind of activity. I'd even gotten to spend some much-needed alone time fishing with my dad early Sunday morning, something we hadn't done in years. His health seemed much better and my worries about him were beginning to ease. The mist hovering over the water and the still morning air as we sat in the canoe were more inspiring to me than any church service ever could have been. The only sounds were the occasional splashes when a fish leapt from the water after a bug for breakfast, or the creak of the wooden canoe as we shifted our weight. We barely needed to talk; we just enjoyed the peace and each other's company.

I was tempted more than once to tell Dad about Declan, and maybe even the extent of the emotional turmoil I was feeling, but in the end I didn't. My father wouldn't have judged me, but I also didn't want him to worry. Which he very much would have.

I was worried about myself enough for the both of us.

When I returned to my desk after lunch and noticed I had an e-mail from Declan, I had mixed feelings. A strange combination of chagrin, anxiety and pleasure came over me the moment I saw his name. His message was brief and to the point.

Time to drop by? I'll be here until 1.

I glanced at the clock in the bottom corner of my screen. It was 12:33. His e-mail was time-stamped 12:19. Not much of a window left. He hadn't said what he wanted to see me about, either. There was no mention of a client.

Leaning back in my chair, I drummed my fingers against the edge of my desk. What to do, what to do. Did he just want to chat? Was that a good idea? Sure, I could drop everything and hurry over to his office, like he apparently expected me to. On the other hand, I could let the time run out, and if he asked later, tell him I hadn't seen his message soon enough to pop by.

The latter idea was probably the smartest choice. I knew it was. So I deleted it without replying and opened the next one to see what Sam needed. I even went back to the file room to retrieve the file and get started on her request.

However, not three minutes later I found myself with my heart lodged in my throat, nervously knocking on the edge of Declan's open office door. My lack of willpower when it came to this man was astounding.

When he saw it was me, he broke into a wide smile. "Hey," he greeted me. Crooking two fingers in a beckoning gesture, he said, "Come on in."

I dropped into one of his chairs and fought back the grin that craved to mirror his own. I didn't know what this was about, but I was determined to keep it short and professional.

God, he looked good. He wore yet another black button-up. No one should be allowed to look that delicious in a simple black shirt. It was frankly unfair to the rest of the men sharing the planet with him. *Time to stop drooling and pay attention,* I chastised myself. Imagining what his bare chest would look like as I undid the buttons of that shirt was not helping at all.

He narrowed his eyes as he looked me over. "You're tense again. Something wrong?"

I was confused. "Again? Why do you say again?"

"Last week at the tournament," he replied. "When we came up to your table after dinner, you seemed anxious. And then you left right after. I hope it wasn't anything I said." He smiled as he finished, as if to assure me he was kidding about the last bit. Unfortunately he was closer to the truth than he realized.

I was shocked he'd been able to pick up on my state of mind both now and last Thursday night. Was I really so obvious? I was also surprised he'd seen me leaving the clubhouse. I honestly hadn't believed he'd even notice. Clearly I'd been wrong.

I didn't want to lie. "I wasn't feeling very well, and just wanted to get home as soon as possible." My voice lowered a little. "Sorry I didn't say goodbye."

"That sucks," he said, waving off my apology. "Are you still sick?"

My cheeks grew hot once more. "No, I'm fine. Thanks." Well, okay, that was a little white lie. I was most definitely not *fine*. I decided this conversation needed to move right along and get to the point. "What was it you needed today? You didn't say in your message."

"Do I have to need something? What if I just wanted to talk to you? Would that be alright?" He was grinning at me again, waiting for my reaction.

I didn't know what to say. Being friends with Declan was a slippery slope. It would be far better for my emotional well-being, and my career at BWK, if we kept things strictly professional. And yet…yet I found I really wanted to be this man's friend. I got the distinct impression he didn't have many of them. And I genuinely enjoyed his company, even if he did make my stomach turn cartwheels.

With a tentative smile, I said, "Yes. That's fine." I was undoubtedly making a big mistake encouraging this, but I couldn't seem to stop myself.

"Good." He looked pleased. "So, tell me about your weekend. What goes on in Swann's Landing on a Saturday night, anyway? Everyone in town hang out at that one bar?"

"Something like that. But I wasn't in Swann's Landing this weekend." I told him about my camping trip, and fishing with my father. He mentioned he used to camp with Ryan when they were small, but he hadn't gone in about twenty years. The reflective expression on his face made me think it was an activity he missed.

"Maybe you could take Alexis some time?" I suggested. I honestly couldn't picture the put-together Laura Logan roughing it in a tent, but perhaps she had a hidden adventurous side.

"That's a great idea," he agreed. I didn't ask if Laura would go, too.

On impulse, I described a Fourth of July camping trip I'd taken in my late teens with a bunch of girlfriends, and how much fun we'd had partying at the State Park, nearly setting one of our tents on fire with our drunken antics.

"Are you still in contact with your old friends from high school?" he asked.

"Some of them, yes. Others only at Christmas when they're home visiting their families. But we all stay in touch over Facebook."

"Ah, Facebook. Yeah, I keep hearing it's a great way to stay connected with people," he mused.

"You're not on Facebook?" I thought everyone was these days.

"Nope," he admitted. "I'm behind the times with social media. Never saw the point, really. But there *are* some friends I'd like to touch base with again. Maybe I should try it. What do you think?"

"I think you should. Come join the twenty-first century, Declan," I teased. "If it's too confusing for you, I'd be happy to walk you through it. You can put the app on your phone so you don't have to wait until you're home in front of your computer."

He pulled his phone from his jacket pocket and tossed it to me. "Go ahead, Ms. Smarty-pants. Install Facebook on there and set me up."

I clutched his phone in my hand, staring at him. "Seriously?"

"Seriously. And don't forget to add yourself to my contacts."

My eyebrows shot up in surprise, but I downloaded the free Facebook app and set up his account for him. Before I handed it back, I friend requested myself as he'd asked. "Done. You'll need to change your password to one I don't know. I think there's a tutorial that'll walk you through it."

Declan laughed. "Don't worry, I'm a fast learner. And if I have questions, I know who to bug." He glanced down at his watch and frowned. "And on that note, I hate to cut this short, but I've got a meeting on the other side of town that I need get to."

I stood up. "No problem. I should get back to work anyway."

He shook his phone in my direction before re-pocketing it. "Thanks for this. Chat with you soon then." I didn't know if he meant on Facebook or in person, but either way, those crazy butterflies started winging around inside me again.

On my way back to my desk I realized I still had the CD I'd made for him in my purse where it had been all week. *Crap.* Oh well, I'd give it to him next time I saw him. And I was confident there would be a next time soon.

Chapter 9

Amelia

Before I went to my desk the next morning, I stopped by Declan's office to finally drop off the CD I'd made. The Sales department was always pretty deserted at that early hour, but I knew he sometimes took advantage of the quiet to get some work done without interruptions.

Today wasn't one of those days. Lazy dust motes twirled in the rays of sunshine slicing through the slats of his window blinds. Stepping inside to prop the disc against his keyboard, I happened to glance at the dual photo frame sitting beside his monitor and was suddenly overcome by the most surreal sense of déjà vu. Whipping my head around to face the door, I half expected him to be standing there watching me, like he'd been in my dream from weeks ago.

Of course, the doorframe was empty. I realized I'd unconsciously pressed my fingers against my lips. *God*, that had been *some* kiss. I leaned against the side of his desk for a second as I recalled it. I knew it was only a dream and could never really happen, but it had felt so real! Scott had never made me feel that way when he kissed me. No one had.

Before I could squash it, a maliciously honest little thought zipped across my mind: *I could go the rest of my life never knowing what it's like to be kissed like that.*

Later that night, I walked into Finnegan's to meet my friend Liv Webb. We'd known each other since we were kids, and she was one of the few friends who'd also remained in Swann's Landing. The rest had scattered themselves far and wide across the country after high school.

I scanned the dimly lit room until I located a petite woman in a black suede jacket with curly honey-colored hair sitting at the bar. She had her back to me. A mug of beer was clutched in her fingers, and a martini glass half full of blue liquid sat in front of the empty barstool beside her.

"Liv!" I hurried over and greeted her with a hug. "And you ordered my first drink for me? You're the best!"

She gave me a wide smile. "I can't believe I haven't seen you in over two months! I wanna hear all about your new job and everything else. How's your dad doing?"

Two months? That had to be some sort of record for us. It felt like with every year that passed we saw each other less and less. I didn't like it, and I resolved to make more time for my friends going forward. I couldn't let the people who were important to me slip through the cracks.

"He's much better, thanks." I took a sip from my glass. Yum. She'd ordered me a Blue Hawaii, like I often drank when we were in college. Scott used to tease me that they made my tongue look like a giraffe's. I smiled at the thought. Maybe tonight would end up being a blue-tongued night.

"Awesome," Liv said. "I have some news I'm dying to tell you, actually." She proceeded to describe a guy she'd met at work a month ago. His name was Ben, and she was clearly smitten. I swear she actually glowed when she talked about him. They'd already gone out twice, but hadn't slept together yet, and she was hoping tomorrow might be their big night.

Her last relationship had been a rocky one, with possibly more lows than there'd been highs, so I was happy she'd met someone new. I hoped this guy would turn out to be just what she needed. Her excitement was contagious as she talked about him.

Listening to Liv tell me how good a kisser Ben was made me wish, just for a fleeting second, that I was single and could re-live that magical moment of a first kiss again. Before a few months ago, the thought that I'd never kiss another man, never be with anyone but Scott, hadn't really crossed my mind. Now that little fact kept sneaking into my head no matter how hard I tried to ignore it. And I'd be lying if I said it didn't bother me.

I was nearly finished my second drink by the time the conversation turned back to me again.

"But enough about Ben. Sorry! What's up with you? How's your new job going?" I knew Liv was being polite and trying not to monopolize the conversation too much with talk about her new guy, but after two Blue Hawaiis while she went on about him, my tongue had started to loosen. I really needed to tell someone, and I'd always trusted her.

"It's great," I replied with a smile. "This is the first job I've ever had where I actually can't wait to get to work in the morning."

"Seriously? Wow. I'm glad it's working out for you. What're the people like?"

She'd given me the perfect opening. Should I tell her about Declan or not? There were plenty of arguments for 'not', but I was afraid I might burst if I didn't get this out of me soon.

I motioned to the bartender to bring me another drink, and then began to describe my co-workers. I started with the easy ones: Sam, Kaitlyn and Josh. It turned out Liv knew Josh's girlfriend, Holly, from the gym. I made a mental note to invite her and Ben when we made plans to meet up for drinks with them.

Noticing a booth had emptied, I picked up my glass and dragged Liv over to it. If I was going to confess this stuff, I wanted a bit more privacy.

As I sipped my third martini, I told her about Diana, and what I knew of her history with Ryan. Which of course led to me talking about Declan—pretty much where I figured our conversation would end up sooner or later.

I had a comfortable buzz going, and I couldn't help smiling as I described the CD he'd made me, how he'd taught me to golf, and our afternoon at the tournament. When I finished detailing yesterday's conversation about how he'd made me install Facebook on his phone and add myself as his first friend, Liv frowned, reaching out to squeeze my forearm.

"Amelia York! You're gushing! What the hell's going on? Are things not okay with Scott?"

My face got hot. "No, we're fine. And I'm not gushing", I protested. "*You* were gushing! Your excitement maybe just rubbed off on me a little, that's all." But she was totally right—I *had* been gushing.

Liv shot me a skeptical look I recognized all too well. She'd known me for a long time, and she knew how to read me. "Spill. Right now. You have a crush on this guy?"

Chewing my lower lip, I looked down at my fingernails. Then I got out my phone and opened Facebook. Declan had uploaded a profile photo, although so far he'd done little else. I pulled it up and turned the screen toward her.

She grabbed my phone from my hand and scrutinized the picture. "Wow. You work with *this* guy? He's drool-worthy, Ames. Declan Kavanaugh. It says he's married." She looked up at me with an arched brow.

"Yeah, he's married to Laura Logan. Remember her?"

"You're kidding? Of course I remember her—I watch her on the news most nights. Huh. I don't think I've talked to her since high school." Liv handed my phone back. "So let me get this straight: you, Mrs. Scott Templeton for the past four years, have a crush on Mr. Laura Logan, your sexy co-worker?"

Another rush of heat blossomed over me. Sweat trickled down my spine. Breaking eye contact, I examined my nails again. "It's not like that, Liv. We're just friends."

From the corner of my eye I saw her take a sip of her beer. She laughed, and I looked back up. "You were gushing and now you're blushing. I'm a frickin' poet." Then her expression turned serious. "Don't lie to me. You obviously have the hots for him. And who could blame you? He's gorgeous."

I smiled ruefully. Shrugging, I relented. "He really is. But don't worry," I assured her. "Nothing's going to happen."

"Oh, I know it won't. I know you—you'd never do that to Scott. You can look all you want, as long as you take your lust right back home to your hubbie. Hell, it might even be good for your sex life! God knows after twelve years together you could probably use all the help you can get!" She giggled and drained the last swallow from her mug.

I laughed along with her, but inside I wasn't so sure it was funny. Truthfully, I hadn't been all that interested in sex with Scott these days. And not just for the past few months, either. It was a fact I'd been avoiding admitting to myself for quite some time now. I loved him. I still thought he was attractive. But I didn't feel any real passion for him anymore. I still *wanted* to feel it, but it had definitely waned. When Scott kissed me, it no longer turned me on and made me want to take things further. The spark was gone. Acknowledging that to myself made me feel horrible. Scott deserved so much better. I was an awful wife.

Liv got up to get herself a refill, but as she passed me I stopped her with a touch to her elbow. "It's nothing, really. Forget I said anything, okay?"

She gave me a look of more understanding than you'd think a petite woman with three beers in her could manage. "Forget what? And by the way, your tongue is blue." She smiled and leaned over to kiss me on the forehead before heading to the bar. I rolled my eyes as I wiped off her sticky lip gloss with my napkin. *God*, I'd missed spending time with her.

When Liv returned, the subject changed to her brother and the financial crap he'd been putting their parents through, but I found I was no longer focusing very well. The alcohol had made me feel fuzzy all over, and the only track my mind could latch onto featured a pair of clear blue eyes.

Declan

Amelia sat in my office, idly twisting her necklace's pendant between her fingers as she talked. Somehow our conversation had turned over the past ten minutes from her telling me how much she enjoyed being able to help us help our clients to a story about visiting some of her friends in Richmond last winter and going out clubbing. As she described where they'd gone dancing, I couldn't help but picture this very put-together woman in front of me scantily clad in club clothes. The very thought of sweet little Amelia letting her hair down and showing off her wild side made my cock stir. *Down, boy. So* not the time.

"I remember those days," I said a bit wistfully. "It's been too long. Back when I was young and single, I used to love going out drinking and dancing." I tactfully stopped myself from adding *and picking up hot chicks and fucking their brains out.*

Amelia combed her fingers through her hair and exhaled a quick breath. "The last time I was single, I was *way* too young to go out clubbing."

"Really? How long has it been?" I asked, surprised.

"Twelve years. I've been with Scott since I was seventeen." She sounded like she was confessing to something shameful.

"Wow. That's a long time. I can't even imagine," I admitted.

"Why? How long have you been with Laura?"

"Five years. It's the longest relationship I've ever had."

"Did you have many other girlfriends before her?" she wondered.

I chuckled. "Yeah, there were a few. I used to travel a lot more for work, and I met women all over the place. Around ten years ago, I lived in Baltimore and had a girlfriend there for a while."

"Oh, yeah? Did you break up because you moved back here?"

"Nope. I broke up with her for the same reason I broke up with all of them—because she got too clingy. I was a bit of a player back then. Didn't have any interest in being tied down to just one woman for any length of time. Once they started in with all the neediness, the having to always know where I was, the jealousy, the needing to be reassured all the time, I ended it. Which more often than not was a messy process." I shook my head and smiled, lowering my eyes as they glazed with memories.

"Then the phone calls and messages would start." I pitched my voice higher to mimic a whiny girl. "Why are you ignoring me, Declan? I love you, Declan. You can't do this to me. I know you love me, too." I sneered a little on the word *love* to emphasize my point.

I looked up to study her reaction. She didn't seem like she was disappointed by my admission, she just looked attentive. Even Josh would have rolled his eyes at me after that little diatribe and told me what an asshole I was. And he'd have been right. But Amelia didn't appear to be judging.

I sighed. "Can I tell you something?"

She nodded, regarding me with interest.

"I never loved any of them," I confessed. "Not one. Sometimes I just said I loved them back 'cause I knew that's what they wanted to hear. I never really loved anyone 'til I met Laura. She was nothing like the other women. She didn't bullshit or play games. She was confident, she knew what she wanted in life, and she went after it. And something just clicked. I admired and respected her, and I realized I wanted her to respect me, too. So, I smartened the hell up. My life was pretty screwed up before I met her, but she gave me a reason to care. A reason to change."

Amelia's head tilted a bit as she absorbed all of this. Suddenly, a big smack of obvious hit me upside the head. This woman in front of me had most of the characteristics that had always attracted me to my wife. Not only physical beauty, but the intelligence, drive, and self-assurance that had made me fall for Laura in the first place. This realization was mind-fuckingly staggering. I understood in that split-second of awareness that if circumstances were different, if we were both single, Amelia was a woman I could seriously fall for. And that scared the living shit out of me.

"Wow," she said. "That's impressive. She must be your soul mate."

I chuckled a little at that. "I don't know. Maybe. I'm not sure I believe in stuff like soul mates. And relationships change over time, at least ours has. Not just because we became parents, either. We're both..." I paused, trying to come up with the right words. "We're very different people. Which is good, I know, but it's not always easy. We're not perfect. We argue. We disagree on lots of stuff. I know I drive her crazy sometimes. Hell, I often wonder how she puts up with me." Shrugging, I added, "But at the end of the day, we make it work."

"Huh. Scott and I never argue."

My eyebrows drew together skeptically. "Come on."

"No, really. We don't. He's pretty laid back. I get upset sometimes, but he just either listens to me vent or leaves me alone until I calm down. He never fights back. Not that I necessarily want him to. It's just…we have a really strange dynamic, I guess." She looked almost apologetic.

To me, no fighting meant no fire. No passion. I opened my mouth to say this, but then I thought better of it. I wasn't sure it was a good idea to continue discussing either of our marriages, and I got the distinct impression she was feeling the same way. Instead I said, "I guess your husband and I are very different. I seem to be able to butt heads with anyone, whether I want to or not. People around here go on the defensive with me real easily."

The corners of Amelia's lips twitched a few times. Then she grinned. "Can I give you some unsolicited advice, Declan?"

"Shoot."

"I can't speak to your in-person conflicts, as I've never witnessed one, but your e-mails are often pretty abrupt. Their tone can read as demanding. So, I get why your written communications might sometimes rub people the wrong way." She flushed, and I sensed she was worried I might not react well to her words.

"Thanks for being honest with me," I said as calmly as possible. "Can you give me any examples?"

"Well, you rarely say please or thank you, for one. Some people feel you come off like you think you're better than them."

"Do they? Okay, duly noted." I tried to keep my tone and demeanor relaxed so she wouldn't think I was getting annoyed. If anyone else had said that stuff to me, I might have dismissed them. But Amelia's opinions deserved my attention. I took what she had to say seriously.

"Don't you want people to react less defensively to you? They think you have no respect for them." Her voice carried the tiniest hint of reproach.

Straightening my back in my chair, I looked her right in those expressive big brown eyes. "I don't. People have to earn my respect. They all talk about me behind my back, and say the only reason I have this job is 'cause of my father. They've treated me like shit for years. Respect is a two-way street. They don't deserve it."

"So you don't respect anyone here?" She got very still.

"Josh. Colleen. And now you. That's it," I admitted.

"Why me?" she asked softly, holding my gaze with serious eyes.

I thought about that for a moment. "Because you're different."

"Different how?"

"I don't know—you just are," I lied. I did know how, or at least I was starting to get a pretty good picture.

Again, Amelia studied me so intensely it felt like she was trying to get inside my head. She nodded. "Good. Having your respect is important to me."

"Why's that?"

"Because we work together, and I need that in my working relationships. But, more importantly, I need it from my friends." And she flashed me the shyest little smile when she said the word *friends*. Man, she was so fucking beautiful. She really was the whole package. Just for a second I wondered what kissing those sweet lips would be like. Then I shoved that idea out of my head. I was treading on very thin ice with those kinds of indulgent thoughts, and I knew it.

Amelia stood to leave, but she turned back to me as she reached the door. "Just one more thing before I go, since we seem to be sharing this afternoon."

I smiled, making a twirly finger motion for her to continue.

"Accountants hate the phrase 'sharpen your pencil'. Using it is a sure-fire way to get our backs up. And you're less likely to get the results you want if you annoy us before we even consider your request."

"You're just full of advice today, aren't you?" I chuckled.

"Bye, Declan." She wiggled her fingers at me and walked out of my line of sight.

I'd just tucked Alexis into bed, and was sitting in my office responding to some e-mails. A snippet of lyrics from some song on the CD Amelia had given me played on repeat in my head, and my foot absently tapped out the beat against the chair leg. I made a mental note to check the track listing next time I was in my car for the title and artist so I could Google the guitar chords.

By some small miracle Laura was home tonight. At the moment she was waiting for me to come and watch television with her in bed. I hoped this time the show had lots of action and maybe a crime to solve, and wasn't one of those stupid hospital dramas which always seemed to be more about who's fucking who than saving some secondary character's life.

Before I closed my laptop to join her, I logged onto Facebook to see what was new with the few friends I'd connected with since Amelia'd signed me up. There might have also been a small desire to check out a photo or two of her on her profile. No big deal—just to see what she looked like when she was relaxing with her friends and not in work-mode. Maybe I'd even find one of her in a sexy going-out-clubbing outfit. But that wasn't the reason I'd logged on. Nope, not at all.

I noticed a little red square with a number one in it above my inbox icon. When I clicked on it, I saw I had a new message from someone named James Miller. My eyes narrowed at the screen. Who the fuck was James Miller? I couldn't remember having ever met anyone by that name.

Curious, I opened it.

> *Dear Declan,*
> *I hope I have found the right Declan Kavanaugh. Judging by the photo and location on your profile, I think you might be the person I seek. Your mother was Kathleen Ryan, correct? I know you don't know me, but I have been searching for you. I have something very important I need to tell you. I'll explain more when we speak.*
> *Please respond to me at jmillertime@gmail.com or call 555-991-0012.*
> *Thank you,*
> *James*

Chapter 10

Declan

It was a dark and stormy Monday morning five days after I'd received that strange Facebook message. I sat in a coffee shop not far from Lynchburg Regional Airport sipping a shitty cup of black sludge and waiting for James Miller to show up and explain what he'd sought me out for. Already I could feel the beginnings of a pressure headache twisting behind my eyeballs. The goddamn cigarette smoke drifting over from the old ladies gossiping nearby wasn't helping. Needless to say, I wasn't exactly in a chipper mood.

I glanced up when the bell over the door tinkled. A thin man of around fifty wearing a dripping gray trench-coat and fedora stepped inside. His face was narrow and lined, and he had a distinct air of apprehension about him. He looked around, and as soon as we locked gazes I knew this was the man I'd been waiting for. A wide smile lit up his entire demeanor when he saw me.

"Declan Kavanaugh?" he asked, approaching my booth. His eyes, which were a shade of blue eerily similar to my own, burned with emotion. When I nodded, he slid onto the bench seat opposite me, doffing his hat and unbuttoning his coat. His hair was dark and messy, also much like mine, although threaded with streaks of silver.

My stomach tightened with a queasy sensation as I studied his craggy, square-jawed face. Did I know this man after all?

Reaching a hand across the table, he said, "James Miller. It's great to finally meet you." His grip was firm.

I signaled to the waitress and she brought Mr. Miller a cup of coffee and freshened up my own. Once she walked away, I turned back to him. I had no interest in wasting time with pleasantries. "You knew my mother?" I asked bluntly.

"Very well," he replied, his expression growing solemn. "I was devastated when I heard of her death."

I nodded, accepting his years-belated condolences, and waited for him to get to the point. His handshake may have been confident, but the look in those strangely familiar blue eyes was anything but. "I don't know an easy way to tell you this, so I'm just going to say it. Declan, I'm your father."

My eyes shot wide, though somewhere inside I think I'd known from the moment he'd sat down. It wasn't like me at all to take a stranger's word at face value, yet I was sure he spoke the truth. For a few long seconds I was at a rare loss for words. Then I managed to get out just one. "How?"

He sighed with relief. "You believe me. Thank God. Because I'd be willing to take a blood test if you didn't." He took a tentative sip from his steaming mug, grimacing at the taste. Raising his eyes to mine again, he said, "I can see so much of her in you. She was so beautiful. And I loved her dearly. But we were really young, Declan. Young and stupid. Especially me."

I kept silent, waiting for him to continue. He seemed to be searching for the right words.

"I've got no good excuse for what I did. When Kath told me she was pregnant, I was terrified. We were just kids ourselves. I was only nineteen, in my first year at college—I wasn't ready to be anyone's dad. I was barely responsible enough to take care of myself, let alone a wife and child. I loved your mother more than anything in the world, but I wasn't strong enough to be there for her when she needed me most. For a while I tried, but the closer it got to her due date, the more I panicked. I was a coward, and I took the easy way out. I'm not proud to admit it, but I ran scared. I left her. I left you both. And I've been sorry as hell for it ever since." He breathed out the last sentence all at once, like a repressed sigh released at long last.

"I later heard she married Patrick Kavanaugh, and that he raised you as his own son. I figured it was probably for the best, so I never contacted her again, never asked to meet you. I thought you'd have a better life never knowing the truth. Even after I learned of Kath's...passing."

"What changed?" I asked, trying to maintain my cool and look skeptical, but pretty damn sure I was failing at both. I believed every word this man was saying, indubitably, which surprised the living shit out of me because blind trust was almost a foreign concept.

He took a deep breath. "I did. I've been trying to convince myself for a long time to just leave things alone, to not throw a wrench into your life all these years later. But I got some news a few months ago. I don't mean to cast a pallor of gloom over our little father-son reunion, but I don't want to lie to you. I found out I'm dying. I only have maybe six months left. And I knew I needed to meet you and tell you the truth while I still had a chance to try to make things right."

My brows shot up at his second stunning revelation. "I'm sorry to hear that," I murmured. I took another swig of my coffee, now lukewarm and stagnant. Maybe I should have said more, expressed more shock or dismay, but at the moment I just didn't have it in me.

I knew I should be feeling *something*: sadness at his terrible news, anger probably, because he walked out on my mother, joy at having this opportunity handed to me to get to know my real dad and more about my mom, even relief at finally sort of getting why Patrick had always been such a dick to me. But I felt none of those things.

"I know it's a lot to take in," James said. "I don't expect you to accept all this straight away. You need some time." He reached into his jacket pocket, pulled out a business card and placed it on the table in front of me. It was for a nation-wide insurance company, Buffalo office. He was a salesman, too. I shook my head in disbelief.

"I'll be in town for another couple days. Give me a call at that number if you feel like talking again."

"Got it," I forced out. An invisible python seemed to be wrapping its coils around my throat.

He got to his feet and shoved his fedora down to rest on his ears. Before he left, he turned back to me. "And Declan?" With some difficultly I lifted my gaze back to those blue eyes so like my own. "I won't be offended if I don't hear from you. In fact, I'd completely understand."

Then James Miller, my *father*, walked out the door. And I sat there for another full hour, drinking offensive coffee and staring at that little white rectangle in my fingers as the ceiling fan hummed overhead.

When Laura crawled into bed beside me that night, I didn't mention meeting James. I was still processing everything, and had no clue what I was going to do about any of it yet. I couldn't decide if I wanted to see him again, get to know him, grow to care about him, only to lose him like I had my mother. I didn't know if I wanted him to meet Alexis and Laura, have them come to accept and maybe love him, only to have him ripped away. But if I didn't contact him again, now that I knew the truth, how could I ever live with myself? No matter how I looked at it, it seemed like a double-edged sword. So I just tossed and turned and stewed.

The next day at work, I had a bitch of a time concentrating on anything for long. I kept pulling out James' business card and rubbing it between my fingers, staring at those little black digits.

Eventually I just couldn't stand it anymore. My brain felt like it might explode if I didn't talk to someone about it. Before I could change my mind, I picked up the phone and called Amelia.

"Good morning, Declan." The sound of her voice instantly soothed one or two of my frazzled nerves.

"You know my extension off by heart?" I asked, knowing the digits, but not my name, would have appeared on her call display screen. I couldn't help grinning. She'd memorized my number.

I heard a small laugh. "Yes. How was your weekend?"

"Revelatory. Do you have time to pop over at some point today? I'll, uh, explain in person." I couldn't fully cover my edginess.

She didn't ask any questions. She didn't make any excuses or put me off. She just said, "Be right there."

And about sixty seconds later she was standing in front of me looking at me with concern. "What's going on? You look stressed."

Amelia

As soon as I heard the strain in Declan's voice, I dropped everything and rushed over. His face was drawn and tense, and his hair was even messier than usual. He'd obviously been running his fingers through it over and over. I was willing to bet he hadn't slept last night.

"Could you close the door behind you, please?" he asked me. I noted he'd said *please*. Frowning, I did as he asked and took a seat. He pursed his lips, staring out the window, and I waited patiently for him to say something.

When he didn't, I prompted, "Declan?"

He sighed. "Something happened yesterday. And I really need to tell someone."

And he wanted that someone to be me? I was flattered he already trusted me enough to want to confide in me.

"You can tell me anything," I assured him. "It won't leave this office, I promise."

He explained, sometimes haltingly, about the strange Facebook message he'd gotten last week, and about meeting the man who claimed to be his real father yesterday. It was clear he believed this James Miller was telling the truth.

"Wow." I shook my head. "That's just…mind-blowing! How are you handling it?" That was a pretty major bombshell. I couldn't even imagine. Everything he'd always believed to be true his entire life, he'd just learned was a lie.

"I think I'm still in shock."

"Are you going to call him?"

"I haven't decided yet." He fiddled with the business card as he spoke. It flashed white between his fingers.

"I know it's none of my business, but why haven't you told Laura yet?" The question had been bugging me since he'd started to talk. This was *huge*. I would've thought his wife would be the very first person he'd want to share it with.

"There's more," he said matter-of-factly. Then he explained that James was dying. Declan wasn't sure he wanted to bring this man into his family's life just to have him ripped away again. After what he'd gone through when he was young, I understood why. I couldn't fathom what it would be like to finally meet my real father, and then be told I could only have a few months with him. No wonder he was so torn over what to do.

"Are you okay?" I asked softly.

His brows shot up and his eyes met mine. For a few seconds he just stared at me. "I don't know," he admitted.

I wanted to reach out and comfort him in the worst way, but I wasn't close enough for arms reach, and getting up and going to him would mean premeditated touching, which I thought might be crossing a line. So I made myself stay put, sitting on my hands to keep them still.

"What would *you* do? Do you think I should call?"

"You really want my advice?"

Declan nodded, his face serious.

I considered the situation for a moment. Then I took a deep breath. "I'd call him. Forgive him, if you can, and take advantage of these last few months. Let Alexis meet her grandfather. Don't let this opportunity slip away."

He was silent again. He held my gaze, but his expression was unreadable.

"Did I overstep my bounds?" I asked. "If I did, I'm sorry."

His eyes widened. "No! Not at all. I asked for your opinion, and you gave it to me. And you're right. You're totally right. I'm gonna call him. I'll tell Laura tonight."

"I think you're making the right choice," I said, rising to reach for the door. It wasn't smart for us to be alone in his office with the door closed for any longer than absolutely necessary. Neither of us needed any rumors to start.

Just as my fingers touched the doorknob, Declan stood and closed the distance between us. He put his hand on my shoulder, and I turned and looked up into his eyes, my heart suddenly pounding so loud I was sure he could hear it. Heck, Ryan could probably hear it from two offices down.

I held my breath as he stared at me. His face was less than a foot from my own. He was so close. Too close. I could see the black outline around the circumference of his baby blue eyes. I could count every dark lash that framed them.

Whatever this crazy connection was that we had between us, it was currently thrumming at full resonance. My throat was so dry I didn't think I could speak as I waited to see what he would do. My skin shot up several thousand degrees where he touched me.

Say something! Do something! Anything! Please don't just look at me like that, or I might lose my mind.

"Thank you, Amelia," he murmured, breaking our thrall as he dropped his hand back to his side. "I really appreciate you coming over this morning. I just needed to talk it out."

"You're welcome," I replied, my voice unsteady. "That's what friends are for." I opened the door wide, and turned back to him.

He was gazing at me again. He seemed to have developed a habit of that lately. It was very disconcerting, yet I loved the intensity of his focus when it was directed at me. He opened his mouth as if to say something, but closed it again. Then he smiled. "Have a great rest of your day."

"You, too."

When I got back to my desk, a stern-faced Diana was waiting for me. She leaned against the edge of my cubicle wall with a thick case-file in her hands.

"You've been gone a while," she observed with a pointed look.

"Sorry," I said. "I got caught up in a discussion. What can I do for you?" Diana was very observant. I suspected she'd be able to tell if I lied.

"A discussion with Declan?"

The temperature seemed to drop a degree or two. How had she known I'd just been with him? Someone must have seen me go into his office and shut the door. Frowning, I realized just how lightning-fast word could travel around here.

I flushed; I couldn't help it. "Yes. But I'm here now. What do you need from me, Diana?"

She straightened and took a step toward me . Her dark brown eyes drilled into mine. I could've sworn she was about to say more on the topic of me being in Declan's office, but she didn't. "I wanted to talk to you about this quote for Gonzalez Barristers you did yesterday. Ryan came to me with more info."

We went over the calculations together, and she showed me where we could reduce the price further. I was left with the distinct feeling I'd screwed up, although I knew for a fact I hadn't. The reduction she found came from something she learned after the fact, and my original quote was as accurate as it could have been with the details I'd had at the time. Her demeanor was dismissive as she gathered up the file and strode away. I wasn't sure I'd ever get used to being treated like just another peon by my manager. But I was still determined to impress her, even if it nearly killed me.

On my drive home, my mind was tumbling over my earlier conversation and close encounter with Declan, when my cell phone rang. As I was stopped at a red light, I pulled it out of my bag and answered.

"Hey," Scott greeted me.

"Hey. What's up?"

"Just letting you know I won't be home 'til about six. Put on something pretty and be ready to go out, okay?"

"What? Why?" I was momentarily confused. Dress up? Go out?

"Just because. It's been a while, and I feel like wining and dining you. We can go dancing after, if you want."

The light turned green, but I didn't notice. "Really?" I asked.

"Why not, right? See you later. Love ya." He hung up before I could respond. I stared blankly at the phone in my hand until the car behind me honked and startled me. Tossing it onto the passenger seat, I hit the gas.

Scott and I hadn't gone out to a nice dinner just the two of us since I'd found out I'd gotten the job at BWK and we'd had a reason to celebrate. We hadn't gone out dancing in a lot longer than that. He didn't even really like to dance—he'd only gone with me in the past when we were with a group, because he knew how much I enjoyed it.

Normally I was the one who planned date nights, but I'd let it slide the past few months. Not on purpose; I guess I'd just had other things on my mind. Now he wanted to take me out and spoil me, for no reason I could think of other than he loved me. And I'd spent the majority of the day thinking about another man.

Guilt and self-disgust overwhelmed me. I pulled over to the side of the road, leaned back against my headrest, and covered my eyes. What the heck was I doing? I was not this kind of person. I married Scott because he was an amazing guy, and I was lucky he'd fallen for me. No matter what attraction I might feel for Declan, I loved my husband.

My throat tightened, and I felt tears welling up. I gasped for air as they overflowed and began to stream down my face. I couldn't wipe them away fast enough. Low sobs erupted from my throat. This was not me. I couldn't lose sight of who I was. I couldn't let myself fall for someone else. I couldn't do that to Scott.

I hadn't had a good cry in a long time. I'd teared up with worry when my dad had his heart attack a few months back, but not a full-blown bawling session. I tended to not lose control unless I had a very good reason to. But now the guilt overwhelmed me. I wasn't wailing in agony, but I just couldn't stop my tears. For nearly ten full minutes I sat there, soaking through tissue after tissue and gasping as the radio played in the background.

Then I forced myself to pull myself together. I dried the last of the wetness off my abraded cheeks, and, sniffling a bit, drove the rest of the way home. I was ashamed for letting this happen, for having feelings for someone else. This just wasn't the woman I knew I was, or who I wanted to be. What Scott deserved was a wife who gave him all the love and attention he needed, and I decided I was going to be that for him again. I was going to go home, make myself pretty and go out and have a great time with my husband.

And I vowed I wouldn't allow Declan Kavanaugh to slip into my thoughts unbidden anymore.

Turned out it was just another vow I'd end up breaking.

Chapter 11

Declan

At five o'clock I powered down my computer, fished that annoyingly distracting little business card out of my jacket pocket for the hundredth time, and picked up my phone. My finger hesitated over the keypad. I set it back down again. Did I really want my family to meet James? Maybe I should just spend some time with him over the next few months and not tell them? Then they wouldn't get to know him, or grow to care about him, and would be spared the grief. It was too late for me, I understood that now, but I could still protect them from the pain of losing him right after he'd become a part of their lives.

Then I remembered Amelia's words from earlier: *Don't let this opportunity slip away.* I knew I'd regret it if Alexis and James never got the chance to meet. That wouldn't be fair to either of them. They deserved to know each other, and I wouldn't be the one who prevented it. Sighing, I picked the phone back up and called the number before I could change my mind again.

He answered on the first ring. "James Miller." His voice was calm, but had a little rough-around-the-edges timbre reminiscent of a former pack-a-day smoker.

"It's me."

"Declan." He sounded relieved. "So glad you decided to call."

I cleared my throat awkwardly. "Yeah. Not sure what I'm supposed to say."

"What do you want to say? If you want to tell me what a coward I was for not doing right by your mother and you, go ahead. I deserve it."

Sighing, I said, "Nope."

"Okay." He grew quiet, waiting for me explain the reason for my call. I wondered if he was fiddling with something, which was an annoying little habit I had when I was stressed.

"How much longer are you staying in town?"

"Do you want me to stay?"

I paused for a second or two. "Would you like to meet your granddaughter?"

"More than anything," he replied immediately, and I could hear the smile in his voice.

We arranged a time for him to come to the house a few evenings later for dinner, and I hung up. What the fuck had I just agreed to? On the one hand, I was curious as hell about this man who'd contributed half of my DNA. On the other, I was pretty damn sure I'd just set my family up for future heartbreak. Laura was in for a massive surprise when I told her all this. I hoped she'd understand why I hadn't said anything sooner.

As I stepped out my door, I glanced up the hallway toward my brother's office. It was dark inside. Most of the staff in our department had already left for the day. My mind flashed back to our little altercation after the golf tournament and I decided this might be a good opportunity to do some snooping.

Slipping into his office, I closed the door gently behind me and went straight to his desk. I began pulling out drawers, peering into the backs of them for hidden contraband. I wish I could say I didn't find anything, but I scored almost right away. Middle wide shallow drawer, all the way in the back inside an old film canister, I discovered a blister-pack of yellow tablets. Two of the six were already missing. I fucking *knew* it. Sighing in exasperation, I tucked them into the same inside jacket pocket as James' business card.

Just as I did, I heard the soft snick of the door opening behind me. *Shit!* I shook my head, grinding my teeth with frustration. My timing had been just the *worst* lately. Turning, I saw Ryan standing there, his eyes flashing with fury.

"What the ever-loving fuck are you doing?" he asked in that deceptively calm voice that meant he was about to lose his shit.

No point in lying—I'd been caught red-handed. "Snooping through your desk drawers. What does it look like?" I snarked. "Seems I hit the jackpot, too." I reached into my jacket and whipped out the blister-pack, waving it at him. "At work, Ry? Really? How can you be so goddamn stupid? Did I get *all* the brains in the family?"

He lunged at me, trying to grab the pills from my hand. Cramming them into my pants pocket, I leapt backward. Unfortunately the back of my knee caught on the edge of his chair and I fell flat on my ass. Fucking Fate. Vindictive little bugger.

Before I knew it, Ryan was on top of me, his face a seething portrait of rage. I tried to examine his eyes as they seared holes into me. Nope, no pin-point pupils this time. He wasn't stoned. Which was good, but also kind of bad. It meant he was in control, and probably ready and able to beat the shit out of me if I didn't get back onto my feet ASAP.

I struggled to free my wrists from beneath his knees. Just as I got one loose, he drew back a fist and sucker-punched me right in the gut. All my air blasted out in a rush. *Motherfuck!*

Ryan just grinned that stupid thin-lipped grin of his. What little strength I had left abandoned me, and I groaned in pain.

"Get the fuck off me," I gasped.

He was livid. "Stay." Punch. "Out." Punch. "Of. Punch. "My." Punch. "Life." Punch. None to the face. All to the stomach. Little shit knew just what he was doing. My midsection felt like it was in flames. Thank God I actually used my gym membership—my tight abdominal muscles provided some protection to my inner organs. I was no doctor, but I knew he could've done some damage with all those hits to the gut.

Ryan delved into my pants pocket and retrieved the pills, popping them inside his shirt pocket with no thought at all, as if someone noticing them sticking out meant nothing to him. "I don't need your interference. I don't need your fake concern. I don't need *you,* brother. Got it?" He straightened, towering over me. I just stared up at him, panting and trying to refocus my vision. My lungs weren't drawing enough oxygen to form words around the red haze of pain.

As he stepped backward toward the door, I managed to drag myself to a sitting position and somehow found my voice again. "You should be glad I help you, asshole," I panted. "Since we're not even really brothers." I sounded exactly like I'd just gotten the shit kicked out of me, but he heard every goddamn word.

His eyes shot wide. "What the fuck are you talking about, Declan? Not brothers? If only I could be so lucky."

"Consider yourself lucky then, dick. You and I are only half-brothers. I met my real dad yesterday."

All the anger and resentment fell away from his face. He gaped at me. Quite literally—his jaw damn near touched his chest. Then he frowned. "You're full of shit."

Hauling myself up, I fell heavily into his chair and clutched my midsection. It hurt like a motherfucker. I would be black and blue tomorrow. And I really did not owe this douchebag any sort of explanation. But I told him what had happened anyway.

He sat down on the corner of his desk, pills and punches forgotten for the moment. "Are you gonna tell Dad you know?"

Of course. Let's worry about Patrick's reaction. That's clearly the most important thing to focus on right now. I figured the man would dance a jig once he found out I knew the truth. No more having to pretend he sired me any longer. It'd likely be the happiest day he's had in years.

"I don't know. I don't know anything yet. Probably I'll tell him, yeah. Just not sure when. Hell, I haven't even told Laura yet."

"I'm the first one you've told?" he asked, shocked. Just for a second there I saw a flicker of the brother I used to know—the one who once idolized me, who was once my friend, hiding deep in his eyes.

I saw no benefit to telling him I'd already confessed all this to Amelia. "Don't make me sorry I did."

"I won't. And speaking of sorrys…" he trailed off, looking at me guiltily.

"Shut up," I said, attempting a small grin. "And give me those fucking pills. I shouldn't have to explain. You know damn well why."

The corner of his mouth twitched, and for a moment I thought he might refuse. Then he reached into his pocket and pulled them out. Tossing them onto his desk in front of me without a word, he turned and left.

It took me a while to feel well enough to walk without needing to clutch the walls for support, but then, moving slow and careful, I did the same.

Amelia

I lay in bed watching the clock, waiting for it to hit seven so I could get up for work. I'd turned the alarm off a while ago, knowing I wouldn't need it to wake and figuring I'd save Scott the annoyance. He snored softly beside me, oblivious to the sunshine sneaking around the sides of the curtains.

We'd had a nice, relaxing evening out Friday night. He'd taken me to Fratelli's, a new Italian place on the outskirts of town. We'd had a few glasses of wine, a fabulous meal, and shared some tiramisu for dessert. Our conversation covered everything from Liv and Ben, to my sister-in-law Morgan's new guy, to the plans Scott had for his students when school started back up. It was all very comfortable.

Though he'd been willing, after dinner I'd decided not to subject him to dancing. Instead we'd gone home, caught a movie on Netflix and snuggled in bed. And, yes, we made love. I tried hard to get into it, tried my best to block Declan's face from my mind and focus solely on Scott. I knew Scott; I knew just what he liked, and I was determined to be the woman he needed me to be.

But later, after he'd rolled over and fallen asleep, I'd stared at the ceiling. My stomach had ached. My mind had ached. I'd felt hollow, like there was something missing.

With a sigh I'd gone downstairs, turned on the television at low volume and wrapped myself in a blanket on the couch. Then I'd let my mind unclench. I'd given in and allowed myself think about Declan again. Fantasize about Declan, to be specific. I'd closed my eyes and imagined his voice whispering lurid suggestions into my ear, felt his fingers trail across my skin instead of my own.

I'd muffled my gasps in the blanket as I'd brought myself to release thinking about the wrong pair of blue eyes, the wrong set of lips, the wrong man. I'd finally fallen asleep, exhausted and ashamed.

I sighed and threw the covers back. Monday. Thank goodness. Like most people, I used to dread Mondays. But now I looked forward to them, because they brought the chance of seeing Declan.

Since Scott was still asleep, I quietly grabbed a navy dress from my closet and took it with me into the bathroom to shower and get ready. I examined at my face in the mirror, and my dark circles glared back. My eyes were red and itchy, probably from a combination of late summer allergies and nowhere near enough sleep. Contacts were not an option. It was going to be a rare glasses day.

The birds outside the kitchen window chirped cheerfully as I finished my toast and coffee. There was still no sign of my husband, but he was a teacher—he had every right to sleep late over the summer, and I tried not to begrudge it. Labor Day was fast approaching, and he'd be back to the grind soon enough. Summer was nearly over. A pang of melancholy hit me at the thought.

When I got into the office, my department was still dark and silent. I flicked on the overhead lights before going to my desk. It was rare for me to be the first one in. Kaitlyn usually beat me by ten or fifteen minutes, but her cubicle was empty.

As I was going through my messages a few minutes later, I heard footsteps behind me.

"Mornin', Amelia. You holding down the fort all by yourself?"

I smiled as I looked up. "Good morning, Josh. Yep, Kaitlyn must be running late."

He raised his eyebrows as he looked me over. "Glasses? That's a new look for you."

Flushing a bit, I shrugged. "Yeah. I haven't been sleeping very well lately. My eyes were too sore for contacts this morning, hence my old glasses."

"It works. You've got that hot librarian thing going for you." He gave me an over-exaggerated leer, and I wondered what Declan would think of my new look if we saw each other later.

"You think?" I laughed, flipping my hair over one shoulder as I batted my lashes at him.

"Very Amy Pond from *Doctor Who*." He chuckled. "Hmm. Don't tell Holly I said that."

I shook my head, smiling. "Our secret. I can't tell her anything if I never get to meet her, though. We still have to set up a date for drinks at Finnegan's."

Josh's grin grew wider. "Thanks for the reminder. I'll check with her tonight and get back to you. Deal?"

"Deal."

He disappeared into his office, and I went back to work, still amused by his reaction Maybe the glasses weren't so bad after all.

The morning flew by. There were lots of rush requests, and two accountants were on vacation, so we were short-staffed. Everyone was focused on their workload and not chatting much. The familiar sounds of keyboards clicking and pencils scratching surrounded me. Every now and then I'd get up from my cubicle to stretch my legs, making my own trips to the file room instead of asking Mandy to bring files to my desk.

Kaitlyn and I worked through lunch, and by the time three o'clock rolled around, the backlog had reduced to a more manageable level. My brain was feeling a little fried from so much focusing, and possibly also from wearing glasses all day when I wasn't used to them. I pushed them onto my forehead and rubbed my temples. Taking a big gulp from my water bottle, I contemplated how to make the next hour vanish so I could go home and relax.

I was saved by a phone call.

"You busy?" Declan asked.

"Yeah, but I'm ready for a break." I smiled, my mood instantly brighter.

"I've got a few minutes to spare. Come on over."

It was all the invitation I needed. "Be right there."

I popped into the washroom first, and frowned at my reflection. My hair was disheveled and frazzled looking. I combed it with my fingers, trying to flatten the loose strands back down. Then I reapplied my lip gloss, scrutinized myself again, and with a sigh decided it would have to do. Hot librarian, huh? I thought I looked hot more in the literal sense than the figurative.

I splashed water on my cheeks in an attempt to reduce my flush, took a deep breath and headed for the Sales department.

As I sat down across from him, I noticed Declan studying me more intently than usual. I shifted in my seat and began to fiddle with my pendant. Such focused attention from him made me feel like I was under a microscope.

"What?" I asked, smiling self-consciously.

"You're wearing glasses." He was still staring. His pupils were slightly dilated. If I didn't know any better, I'd swear there was a hint of lust swirling in those baby blues.

My face grew hot. "Yes. Itchy eyes this morning. Contacts weren't an option."

"I like it," he declared in low voice. That voice was pure sex. All the muscles in my lower belly tightened.

"Josh told me I was working the hot librarian look," I joked, trying to lighten the thickening atmosphere around us.

It worked. Declan laughed out loud. "He called you that?"

I nodded, grinning.

"I would have gone with sexy secretary, but okay. That works, too." There was definitely something about his expression. Was I just transferring my own attraction to him, wanting to read stuff that wasn't really there? He was kidding around with me, but his words made me burn from the inside out. I was overheating. Was the air conditioning not working this afternoon? Looking down at the unneeded file in my lap, I considered fanning myself with it. Time for a subject change.

"Did you call him?" I asked abruptly, referring of course to James.

"Yep," he said. "He's coming over tonight for dinner."

"Really? That's great! I bet he can't wait to meet Alexis. What was Laura's reaction when you told her?"

Declan's expression grew serious. "She was happy for me, and excited to meet him. Until I told her he was dying. Then she decided it'd be best if he didn't meet Alexis."

I frowned. "What did you say to that?"

"I told her the same thing you said to me: that it wasn't fair to let this opportunity slip away, for any of us. I told her I'd regret it if I didn't let Alexis know her grandfather, and she'd end up resenting me for it later. Laura said it'd be too hard on her to meet him only to lose him. I refused to budge on the matter. Tempers flared. I stood my ground. She finally gave in. Pretty sure everything'll be fine tonight." He sighed and looked away. "She can't protect our daughter from stuff like that. It's important that Alexis meet him. And it's not like Laura's the greatest judge of what's best for her anyway."

"Pardon?" He'd kind of muttered that last line and I wondered if I'd heard it right.

"Sorry. She just…" He stopped, sighing again. He seemed to be debating whether to answer me or not. I was just about to tell him it was cool if we dropped the subject when he continued. "It feels like she puts her job over her family. She works late a lot and doesn't spend enough time with Alexis. It just gets to me sometimes, that's all."

Whoa. This was some pretty personal stuff. I thought about what he'd just shared for a moment, unsure how to reply. Then I said, "That's why my mom doesn't think I should start a family yet. She says I need to put my career first right now, and that I'd never be able to do that once I have a child."

"Is that what you want? To wait?" he asked, studying my face once again.

"It's complicated. But I'm not ready to have kids yet." Of those two things I was very sure.

"What about your husband?"

"What about him?"

"Does he want to start a family now?"

I chewed my bottom lip. "Um. Yeah. Yeah, he's ready."

"And your career's really what's holding you back?"

"Yes. No. Sort of. I don't know." I sighed. This was not a conversation I was comfortable having with Declan. Someday perhaps, but not at the moment. I shifted in my seat again and declined to elaborate.

"Have I hit a nerve?" he wondered, narrowing his eyes. "Sorry. None of my business, I know."

I shrugged apologetically. "No, it's fine. Another time maybe."

He nodded in understanding and reverted to the previous topic. "No matter how much Laura claims she gets it that Alexis needs her around, she really doesn't. She still gets home after our daughter's asleep most nights. She keeps assuring me things will get better, but nothing ever changes. One of these days something's gonna give, and she might not like how it all shakes down when it does. I just think by twenty-nine she should be at a place in her life where she can understand the need for better career and family balance."

He paused and refocused on me. A smile reappeared where that deep frown had been. "But enough somber talk. Sorry I keep bitching to you about my family issues. I really shouldn't. James is coming over later, and I think it'll be a good night. I can't wait to see the look on his face when he sees Alexis. Patrick says she's the spitting image of my mom."

I smiled back, both grateful that he let me out of confessing my own issues, and stunned that he'd chosen to share such personal stuff with me again. "It's no problem. You can tell me anything. I don't mind." Standing up to make my exit, I continued, "You'll have to let me know how it goes tonight. Don't forget to take pictures."

"I will. I'll e-mail you some if you want."

"Cool." I paused and added, "Hey, for some reason I thought Laura was a year ahead of us in school. I didn't realize we were the exact same age."

He focused all of his attention on me again. Prolonged direct eye contact with this man did crazy things to my insides. Hypnotized, I couldn't look away.

"I obviously have a thing for younger women." He delivered that line with no hint of joking, and he did not break our connection.

Any skill I had for grace under pressure flew right out the window. I swear I nearly snorted snot right out my nose. One hand flew to my face to try to conceal my reaction. He did *not* just say that. My stomach twisted. My throat went dry. I thought my face might actually be on fire.

You can't say stuff like that to me! You can't. You just can't.

"I…um…I'd better get back to my desk," I faltered. I knew I couldn't stay there a single second longer and pretend to keep my cool. If I tried to carry on any more conversation, I'd surely end up embarrassing myself, or worse, both of us.

"Have a great night, Declan," I blurted as I dashed out the door. I thought I saw a confused expression flitter across his face before he flashed me a parting smile.

This man was going to be the death of me.

Chapter 12

Declan

Laura got home nearly on the dot of six, only thirty minutes later than she'd promised, and frankly sooner than I'd expected. James had already been at our house for nearly an hour. When she came in, he and Alexis were playing Barbies in the family room while I fixed dinner.

I'd introduced him to her as Grandpa James. She already had a Grandad, Patrick, and Laura's mom and dad liked to be called Nana and Papa, so I didn't think she'd be confused adding in a third grandfather. To my amused surprise, Alexis warmed up to him fast, and of course, he fell instantly in love with her. Watching the two of them get to know each other did strange things to my emotions. At one point I had to walk away from them to regain my composure. I tried to keep an ear on their activities from the kitchen. Her childish giggles never failed to make me smile, and I could just picture the matching one on James' face.

It all went off without a hitch. Alexis was too young to ask awkward questions about why she'd never met him before, and he was so good with her that it was easy to tell he'd had experience with young children. I realized I had no idea if I had any other half-siblings, or nieces and nephews. My entire concept of family was changing faster than I could wrap my head around it.

Later, once we'd finally gotten Alexis settled in bed, I poured some of the good whiskey, and the three of us sat down for some grown-up talk.

"You're from Buffalo, right?" Laura opened the conversation with something easy.

"Yes. I've lived there for the past twenty-two years."

"Upstate New York is beautiful. We spent a weekend on Lake Canandaigua when we were first dating, didn't we, Declan?" She flashed me a smile and I nodded.

"So, James, are you married?" she asked. I was thankful she had so much experience interviewing people. She was an expert at digging out information, and I was curious to find out as much as I could about him.

"I was. I'm not anymore," he replied.

"Kids? Grandkids?"

James glanced at me. "I have a daughter. Her name is Miriam, and she's twenty-six. She's single, no kids. Alexis will probably be the only grandchild I'll ever know." He smiled fondly when he said my daughter's name. "I need to thank you both for allowing me the opportunity to meet her."

Laura slid me a sideways look, but I ignored it. I knew she still wasn't at all thrilled about our daughter getting to know James and then having to lose him in a few months.

"You don't need to thank us. I'm glad we were able to do this." I gestured between us.

"Me too," he said.

"Does Miriam know about me?" The idea of having a sister out in the world somewhere whom I'd never even heard of before boggled my mind. I wondered if she looked like James. Or anything like me.

His forehead creased. "Yes, I told her when I first found out I was sick. I wanted her to know I was going to try to find you. I'm sure she'd love to meet you guys at some point."

Laura latched onto that opening to turn the conversation to his illness. "We're saddened to hear about your declining health, James. Do you mind me asking you to tell us more about it?" I leaned forward in my chair, anxious to hear his reply.

He gave her a thin smile. "I was planning on it. It's only fair you know the facts." With a small sigh, he continued, "I have a non-malignant brain tumor. It's slowly expanding and destroying the tissue around it as it grows. Unfortunately it's in a part of my brain where it's considered inoperable. My doctors say I might have six more months, nine on the outside."

"What are your symptoms?" I asked, forcing my tone to remain neutral.

"They're sporadic still, but as it grows, they'll get worse. Some short-term memory loss, although my long-term is still pretty good. On my bad days, I get dizzy spells. Nausea. Vomiting. A couple weeks ago, I lost my eyesight for a scary minute or so, but it returned. Once it starts to press more firmly against my optic nerve, my vision will dim and I'll eventually go blind. But hopefully that won't happen until close to the end." He spoke like he'd accepted his fate.

I was feeling some nausea of my own at the thought of what he'd have to go through. Logically, I was aware I didn't really know this man, but still, the idea of him dying made me feel sick and cold inside. Emotions were swirling around that I wasn't sure I'd ever felt before. I knew I should say something sympathetic, but I couldn't seem to come up with anything that felt appropriate. What's appropriate to say to a dying father you barely know? I dragged my fingers through my hair.

Laura saved me from having to respond. "We're so sorry. Is there anything at all we can do? Do you have medical insurance?"

His eyebrows lifted, and he exhaled a soft sigh of frustration. "I don't need money, if that's what you're asking. I just wanted to make amends with my son and meet his family—that's all."

Guilt enveloped me. Last night Laura had brought up the possibility that James was looking for us to pay his medical bills, and while I dismissed her concerns, I'll admit it had crossed my own mind.

"No, no," I protested. "We didn't think you only wanted to meet me to guilt me into a cash injection. Laura was just making sure you were covered. I want to—*we* want to help out however we can."

"I have insurance," James stated firmly. "I sell life and health insurance. I'm fully covered."

Right. I knew that. I'd forgotten to mention that fact to Laura, though. Stupid. I should have known better.

"Okay," she replied with a smile. "Glad to know your medical bills won't be a problem. Is there anything else we can do to help out during this difficult time? Have you seen any specialists? I have a contact at the U. of V. Cancer Center in Charlottesville. They do specialty work with brain tumors, as you might already be aware. Perhaps I could make a phone call on your behalf?"

Before James could even reply, I turned to her, wide-eyed. "Great idea! That'd be excellent."

James chuckled. "Shouldn't that be my line, Declan?" He directed his gaze back to my wife. "Thank you, but it's really not necessary. I've had three diagnoses already. They all agree it's inoperable."

"That may be true," I said, "but what does it hurt to get a fourth opinion? Or a fifth? Maybe there's some other avenue of treatment you haven't even heard of yet. It's worth a shot."

He sighed. "Of course. You're right. I'd put up with another round or two of poking and prodding if it could extend my time with my family. I'll take as much as I can get."

I noticed a flicker of a frown cross Laura's face before she whisked it away. She was thinking again about the potential effect on Alexis if—when—James passed away. Pasting on her brightest smile, she said, "I'll make a call tomorrow, and let you know if I can get you in. How long are you staying in Lynchburg?"

"Not long, but if you succeed in getting me an appointment, I'll plan my next visit around it. Maybe I can convince Miriam to come with me." He met my eyes, and I grinned with approval. Meeting my half-sister should happen as soon as possible, as far as I was concerned. We had a lot we needed to discuss.

Laura stifled a yawn I wasn't sure if she'd faked for our benefit or not. "I'm heading upstairs. I have some work I need to get done before bed." She stood and took James' hand. "It was wonderful to meet you, James. I look forward to seeing you again soon."

Before she could pull her fingers from his, he rose and planted a kiss on her cheek. "Likewise. You have a beautiful daughter and a lovely home. Thank you for having me over."

After she left, I topped up our glasses and sat back down. James had driven over in a rental, but I was prepared to pay for a cab back to his hotel if I couldn't convince him to spend the night in our guest bedroom.

"I take it you're still working?" I asked as I passed him his tumbler.

"I've been gradually reducing my client list, but I do have some I still need to visit, so I have to return to Buffalo soon."

"Understood. If Laura can get you into the U. of V. Center, you'll come back with Miriam then?"

"I'll be back, yes. I can't speak for Miriam, but I think she'll join me. I know she wants to meet you and your family."

I nodded. "I'd like that, too." Leaning back into the soft leather, I rested my feet on the coffee table. "So, tell me about my mother. Anything and everything you can remember."

James' face lit up with a wide smile. "I knew you'd ask me that, because it's exactly what I'd want to ask me, if I were you."

After a sip of whiskey and a deep breath, he began talking. He'd met Kathleen Ryan at the University of Richmond during their first week of classes. He said he'd taken one look at her and just known, without a shadow of a doubt, that she was the one for him. They'd become inseparable, connecting on a deeper level than he'd known was possible. James fell head over heels in love with her long before they'd ever even kissed.

She'd been dating another guy when they'd met, which was why their relationship started off as an ever-deepening friendship. He'd known he was falling hard for her, and he'd just hoped she'd someday start to see him the same way. James refused to give up on what they had between them, and she told him later she'd felt the same. He'd been shocked to find out she'd had a similar reaction when she'd met him—instantly smitten. She'd felt guilty about it, but in time hadn't been able to deny their connection any longer. A few months later, she'd left her boyfriend for James.

And they'd been perfect together—crazy for each other and happier than either had ever been before. Until she'd discovered she was pregnant.

James looked so goddamn sad and guilty when he got to that part that I stopped him. There was no need for him to rehash the same painful territory again. I knew he'd thought he was doing the best thing for both of us when he'd walked away. I also knew he'd regretted it every day since. That regret had been obvious from the moment he'd sat down opposite me in the coffee shop last week. I couldn't imagine living the rest of my life consumed by such remorse.

He shut his eyes for a moment and sighed, then downed the rest of his whiskey. "Do you think you can ever forgive me, Declan?"

I didn't reply at first, thinking how best to reassure him. Finally I just went with, "Already have."

He stood and I did the same, thinking he was ready for me to show him to the spare room or call a cab. To my surprise, he pulled me into a hug. I froze for a moment, shocked as hell. Then I clapping him on the back and stepping away. I couldn't remember the last time Patrick had hugged me. Pretty sure it had been well before my mom got sick.

At James' request, I called for a taxi, and promised I'd be in touch the next day. Once he was on his way to his hotel, I poured another generous two fingers into my glass and dropped back onto the couch. I had a lot of new information to process. I wasn't conflicted with how I felt about James, or the difficult journey we were about to undertake together, but his story about meeting my mother had me reeling.

Instead of it reminding me of when Laura and I first met, like you might assume it would, all I could think about when he'd been talking about my mom was how I'd been reacting to Amelia. Problem was, our situation was way more complicated than two teenagers making eyes at each other when one of them already had a boyfriend. With every fiber of my being I'd been resisting falling for Amelia York, but if I were being honest with myself, I knew damn well it had already happened. Weeks ago. Maybe the first day I met her—much like how James had described his response to my mother.

Fuck.

Amelia

I hadn't spoken to Declan in a few days, although he'd sent me a short Facebook message saying the evening James came over to meet his family had gone well. I was curious to ask him more about it, but so far we hadn't found time to connect.

I'd just finished typing up an e-mail to Sam, when the phone rang. My heart leapt as my eyes darted to the display hoping to see Declan's extension. Unfortunately it was Diana. She didn't waste any time on pleasantries, asking me to come to her office. The aforementioned heart didn't just return to its regular place in my chest; it sunk to my feet. Whatever she wanted, I knew it couldn't be good.

Straightening my spine and squaring my shoulders, I walked into Diana's office projecting as much confidence as possible. She looked up at me from whatever she was reading and gave me small smile. "Have a seat, Amelia."

I sat. And I forced my features to stay relaxed as I waited to see what this was about.

"You've been with us for…what? Two months now?"

"Yes," I agreed, although it was a bit longer. I wasn't going to nitpick.

"Are you happy here?"

Well that wasn't what I was expecting. "Very much so," I answered truthfully.

"Good. I'm glad to hear it." She leaned back in her chair and studied me. "You get along well with everyone?"

Where was she going with this? "Um, yes. I think so."

"Now that your training is complete, I've been going over some of the pricing you've done." I couldn't help but think her expression had gotten a little shark-like.

I forced a smile. "Great. Did you find any areas of concern?" I was confident my work was excellent, but I was not confident at all of Diana's opinion of me as her employee.

"You've been working on an awful lot of Declan's clients." Like a bird taking flight, one dark, perfectly tweezed brow rose on her forehead.

"Have I? I hadn't noticed. Is that a bad thing?" I tried to keep my tone light.

"I'd hate for any of my accountants to be accused of favoritism," she remarked, leaning forward again to rest her elbows on her desk.

"I could see why that would be a cause for concern," I said. "But I can assure you it's not the case with me. I treat every request I get equally, prioritizing their importance by level of rush, then in order in which they were received. Just like Josh trained me."

That eyebrow lifted again. "You and Declan have developed a friendship beyond merely co-workers, haven't you?"

Uh oh. My guard shot straight up, and I felt my heart rate accelerate along with it. "Yeeees, I guess you could say that," I answered slowly. "Is that a problem?"

"Actually, yes. It could be perceived as one. In your role here, becoming close with an Account Manager could be a serious conflict of interest if anyone were to question the work you did for him…or her." Now she smiled at me again, and I didn't like that smile one bit.

Heat flooded my cheeks. I wanted to tell her that who I was or wasn't friends with was none of her fricking business. I wanted to point out that Josh and Declan were good friends, had been for some time, and no one seemed to have a problem with that, but I didn't want to cause issues for Josh. For all I knew, maybe she *did* have concerns about their friendship. I needed to talk to him about this as soon as possible.

"I don't play favorites, Diana. Never have and never will. You can audit my work all you want—you won't find any preferential treatment. No quotes on Declan's groups that go above and beyond how we'd normally price. I evaluate each request on its own merit, and make my calculations accordingly." My temper was starting to boil, and I'm sure a hint of it probably came out in my little speech. I needed to get out of her office before I said something I'd regret.

"I can't tell you you're not allowed to be friends with someone, obviously," she said. I bit the edge of my lip and forced my mouth to remain shut. "However, I'm warning you right now—it's a bad idea in this workplace. People could interpret what they see in ways you might not like. And I'll be keeping an eye on your work, as you mentioned. Any sign of favoritism and you could lose your job. This discussion can be considered your warning."

My hands trembled with fury. I stood, nodded to her that I understood, and walked out. I didn't go to Josh's office—that would have to wait. I strode through the hallways to the farthest ladies' room from Accounting, and locked myself into a stall.

I was livid. She had no right to doubt my work ethic. And she certainly had no right to hint that I couldn't be friends with Declan and keep my job. I wanted to punch something. Or *someone*. Instead, I clenched my fists in my lap as hot tears filled my eyes. I wasn't a violent person, and I wasn't prone to fits of rage very often either, but Diana had managed to push every one of my buttons.

I sat there for a while, swiping away my tears with a scrunched up piece of toilet tissue, which also removed or smeared most of my eyeliner. Then I returned to my cubicle. I noticed it was nearly 3:30, which meant I could leave soon. And thank God for that. Only another half-hour until I could escape this stifling environment and breathe again.

There was an e-mail waiting for me from Declan.

How goes your day?

I sighed and typed: *Not so great.*

Not thirty seconds later he replied: *What's wrong?*

I'm about ready to punch a wall.

Why?

Thinking we should really just exchange phone numbers so we could send each other short, non-detailed texts, I responded, *I don't want to get into it right now.*

Come over here.

Again with the lack of a please. My irritation spiked, although rationally I knew he just wanted to see me in person to find out why I was upset.

I'm way too stressed out right now to have a civil conversation. I'll explain later.

The truth was I didn't want to see Declan in person for two reasons. One, I was still super agitated, and I didn't want to tell him about my talk with Diana until I'd calmed down. I'm a bit embarrassed to admit that the second reason was about vanity. I'd wiped away most of my makeup with my frustrated tears, and what little remained was smudged. My eyes were red and puffy. I looked like crap, and I didn't want him to see me like that. Call me vain, but it mattered to me. I wanted him to always see me at my best.

Another reply: *Please come see me before you leave.*

My lower lip quivered. *Damn him!* He'd remembered my advice; there was the missing please. I realized he just wanted to try to help me feel better the way I'd done for him the previous week. I loved that he wanted to be there for me when he thought I needed it. And I did need someone to talk to. But that someone would end up on the receiving end of a major rant, and I didn't want to put him through that. Our conversation would have to wait.

I glanced at the time again, and was relieved to see it was nearly four o'clock. I needed to go home. I just couldn't deal with seeing Declan right now.

I'm sorry, I have to go. I'll talk to you next week.
Then I left.

Later that night, I was propped up in bed with my laptop balanced across my thighs, trying to pay attention to some sitcom. Scott was down in the rec room watching baseball, which I had only a passing interest in, so I'd come upstairs for some alone time. I'd told him over dinner about my conversation with Diana, leaving out the identity of the Account Manager in question. He'd listened sympathetically, but I knew he didn't really get it. How could he? My career was very different from his, as was my relationship with my manager. I'd changed the topic to something else so he wouldn't have to pretend to be interested in my complaining.

Ever since I'd gotten into my car earlier, I'd been feeling guilty about blowing Declan off. I hoped he wasn't ticked off that I didn't go see him. I needed to explain and make things right.

On impulse, I pulled up Facebook and opened a new private message. I typed quickly, not wanting to lose my nerve.

Hey,
Sorry about earlier. Hope you weren't annoyed that I didn't come over.
Diana hauled me into her office and accused me of giving your requests preferential treatment. She told me it wasn't a good idea to be friends with you, and that she'd be keeping an eye on my work from now on. She even said if she ever found anything that suggested favoritism that I could lose my job. I told her I'd never done anything like that, and never would.
I thought it probably wasn't a great idea to be seen sitting in your office this afternoon. And frankly I was way too

angry to speak calmly about it. I won't let her or anyone
else dictate who I can be friends with. Sorry again about
this afternoon. Hope you understand.
Have you heard any more from James? Did you guys
make plans to spend more time together? I guess we'll
have lots to chat about next time we speak.
Hope you have a great weekend with lots of Alexis time.
Amelia

The next morning I woke up to the sound of the shower running down the hall. I stretched my arms out over my head and yawned. Since it was Saturday, I rolled over and pulled the sheets back up, thinking I'd fall back asleep for a while. Then I recalled my discussion with Diana yesterday. And right on the heels of that, I remembered the message I'd sent to Declan last night.

I sat up, grabbed my laptop off my bedside table and opened it. Sure enough, there was a reply waiting for me.

WTF? I wasn't annoyed before, but I am now. She's gone
WAY over the line. She actually had the balls to tell you
that you shouldn't be friends with me? That bitch has NO
right to say that to you. And questioning your
professionalism and work ethic? She'd be a damn fool to
lose you if you quit and I really want to tell her to go f
herself on your behalf right now. This makes me really
angry. But try not to let her ruin your long weekend. I
hope you're able to forget about it for a few days. I
should be in the office Tuesday afternoon. Maybe see you
then.
D.

I sent a quick '*Thank you*' and closed the lid. I was still annoyed about Diana, but I couldn't repress a smile at Declan's unflinching support.

Chapter 13

Amelia

Almost every second of that long Labor Day weekend seemed to drag. I felt like I was in a daze for most of it. My emotions whirled from anger to guilt to sadness and back again. I just wanted to hide from the world.

For a few hours I actually managed to. We'd been invited to Scott's mom's place for dinner Saturday night, but I begged off, claiming painful cramps—woman's issues were always an excellent excuse—so he wouldn't question me staying home.

All I wanted was to curl up in bed and try to sleep, try to shut off my cascading thoughts. I hadn't been sleeping well for quite a while now. I hadn't been very hungry lately, either. I'd noticed my waistbands were looser, and when I hopped on the scale I wasn't surprised to see my weight was down. I knew I needed to start getting more rest, but no matter how hard I tried, I always ended up lying awake until stupid late, then waking back up far too early.

Once Scott left, I poured myself a glass of wine and gulped it down, hardly tasting it. Then I refilled the glass. People joke that you know you have a problem if you drink alone, but at the moment I really didn't care. Alcohol often made me sleepy, and that was my goal. I just wanted to pass out and not dwell on my failings anymore.

With one glass of wine in my belly and another half-full one plus what remained in the bottle in my hands, I returned to the bedroom. The beginnings of a nice, comfortable buzz were already swirling through me. I propped myself up on the bed, turned on the television and took another sip.

A movie was just starting, one that had come out a while ago. It starred Kate Winslet, and was about two people, bored and unhappy in their marriages, who met at their children's playground and soon began an affair. I rolled my eyes, laughing a little at the weird symmetry to all my recent inappropriate yearnings, but I couldn't help it; morbid curiosity won me over. Before long, I found myself all caught up in the story. At the end, they didn't wind up together— both stayed with their families and their spouses never found out. I was surprised they didn't get caught and suffer negative consequences. Most stories about extramarital affairs wind up with the cheaters having their lives torn apart because of it. This one didn't have that kind of moral message, which was unusual and possibly food for thought, if I were capable of doing any heavy thinking tonight. But my brain was done in.

I switched off the television and downed the last of… my fourth glass? No wonder I felt so lethargic. I got up to dispose of the bottle so Scott wouldn't question its presence on my night table. After brushing my teeth, I crawled back under the covers. It wasn't late yet, but I was definitely drunk. Sleep was close at hand.

Declan's face swirled through my mind. I imagined him spooned up behind me with his arms wrapped around me in a comforting embrace. For a moment it was almost as if I could smell the light scent of his cologne and feel his fingers tracing patterns across my stomach.

For the first time in weeks I fell right asleep.

On Sunday evening, we met Josh and Holly at Finnegan's for drinks. Liv and Ben were running late, but they showed up later. I'd hoped being around the group of them would be a good distraction for me, but it didn't really work.

As I sat beside Scott, his arm draped across the back of the booth behind me, listening to the other couples tell us how they met and seeing how happy they were, treacherous thoughts played through my mind. To be honest, I felt envious. I'd known Liv since we were kids, and I saw the way she looked at Ben. I knew what it meant. She wasn't just smitten—she was in love. And though I hadn't known Josh for very long, I could see the same smile on his face, the same devotion in his eyes when he looked at Holly. When was the last time I'd looked at Scott that way? Everyone said relationships evolved over time, and marriage took hard work on both sides to keep it strong, but the way I was feeling lately—it didn't make sense. Was this normal? It sure didn't feel normal. It felt like something was very, very wrong.

Ben and Liv openly clasped hands on top of the table. Josh had one arm around Holly's waist as he sipped his beer and chatted. Scott and I sat with more than a foot of space between us, not touching. I don't know if he noticed or not, as it was pretty much our usual these days, but after observing the dynamic between the other couples, I certainly did.

As the guys talked about the Orioles chances of winning the pennant race this year, I tuned out, absentmindedly spinning my wedding band around my finger. Liv shot me a questioning look. She knew me well enough to detect my unease. With a smile, she invited me to join her in the ladies' room. Grateful, I got up and followed.

"You okay, Ames?" she asked as soon as we stepped inside. The cacophony of music and conversation out in the lounge dulled as the door slipped shut behind us. The washroom was thankfully deserted.

I thought about my reply. Liv had known Scott as long as I had, and considered him a friend. It wouldn't be fair for me to dump my issues on her. I knew if I did, it would just make her feel obligated to stand by me, and maybe uncomfortable around Scott. I didn't want to force her into that position.

"Yeah," I lied, turning toward the mirror and pulling out my lip-gloss. "I'm tired, that's all. Ben's a hottie, and he seems really nice. I think you lucked out this time, girl." I took a chance, hoping diverting the topic to her new relationship would distract her from asking about me. It did, but not for long.

Liv gushed about Ben for a bit, admitting what I'd surmised—that she was head over heels for him. I gave her a big hug and told her I was super happy for her.

"Are you really sure you're okay?" she wondered again as we were about to rejoin the others. "You seem kinda spacey tonight."

I shrugged. "I'm fine. Just not sleeping well lately. You know how it is." I hated not sharing my issues with her; it felt so wrong.

"It's nothing to do with that guy at work, is it? Sorry, but I had to ask after our earlier talk."

Breaking eye contact, I braced my palm flat against the door and pushed. "Not at all," I mumbled, walking out ahead of her. If she knew I was hiding something, she didn't question me more about it. Which made her a far better friend than I was.

Declan

James had gone back to Buffalo. Ryan was at Patrick's, hopefully keeping his trap shut about what I'd found out. We'd spent the previous day with Laura's mom, as her father had been working, which was probably a blessing in disguise. Labor Day Monday it was just my little family all on our own.

I sat cross-legged on the floor in Alexis' bedroom playing *Snakes and Ladders* with her. Well, it's actually called *Chutes and Ladders* these days, but in my mind those chutes would always be the long, scary snakes from my childhood. She kept trying to cheat—sneaky little thing—and I made a point to always insist she re-count her squares. It was a great way to get her to practice her counting, and kept her amused while learning. Unsurprisingly, Laura was off somewhere else in the house.

"Six!" Alexis squealed with delight after she spun. She went to move her cardboard piece that was shaped like a dark-haired little girl.

"Hold on, missy," I said, taking a hold of her small wrist. "The arrow is right on the line. Spin again."

She gave me the world's cutest pout. "Daddy, it's on six. See? Right there!" She pointed at the tiny fraction of an inch the plastic arrow leaned past the line toward the six.

I gave in, as she knew I would. "Fine, take your six. See where it gets you." I eyed the long blue chute that descended from the square six spaces away from the one on which her piece sat.

Alexis carefully counted out the squares as she hopped her girl across the board. "One, two, tree, four, five...awwww. No fair!"

"Should have listened to me and spun again," I laughed. "Tough luck, kiddo."

"You could give her a break once in a while," Laura said dryly. Looking up, I saw her leaning against the white doorframe.

I snorted. "She has to learn to play by the rules. We're nearly done. Wanna join the next round?"

"Mommy, play with us," Alexis begged, her blue eyes wide. I could never resist those eyes, so much like my own and, I now realized, James'. They sucked me in and made me putty in her tiny hands.

"I can't right now, sweetie," Laura told her. "I need to get some Mommy stuff done. Maybe later, okay?"

I frowned. "Maybe later" were two words we heard too damn much from her these days. "You can do your Mommy stuff later," I said firmly. "You're just scared a three year-old might kick your butt at *Snakes and Ladders*."

"It's Chutes, Daddy!" Alexis scolded me. "I keep telling you! Chutes!"

"Whatever," I chuckled. Looking up at Laura and holding her gaze, I said, "C'mon. We're not taking no for an answer this time."

My wife shot me an irritated look much too fast for Alexis to see, and resignedly lowered herself to the floor. She pasted on a smile and said, "Hurry up and beat Daddy, honey, so I can show you both how it's done."

Alexis giggled and passed the spinner to me. Her laughter was hands-down my favorite sound in the world. As I took my turn, I tried to remember the last time I'd heard Laura laugh genuinely and realized I couldn't. We used to laugh together all the time. When had that changed?

I pushed those thoughts away and tried to focus on some happy time with my family, since moments like this seemed few and far between these days.

I was watching yet another cooking challenge on the Food Channel, just about to turn it off and head up to bed, when Laura came downstairs. She was smiling.

Taking a seat beside me, she said, "There's something I need to talk to you about."

Uh oh. Call it a gut feeling, but, smile or no smile, I sensed this wasn't good.

I muted the television and turned to face her. "What's that?" I asked, keeping my expression neutral.

"I've just been speaking with Dan at the Manhattan studio. He told me confidentially that Greta Cormier is pregnant. They're going to be looking for her replacement shortly." She sounded ridiculously stoked and irritation surged through me. I already knew where this was headed.

"She does the Sports desk. You hate covering Sports."

"I know. But it's an in, Declan. In New York! This could be just the opportunity I've been waiting for."

"A temporary in," I corrected. "For a maternity leave. What would it be? A three month contract?"

She sighed, unwilling to relinquish her excitement. "Probably. It could be as long as six, but I doubt it. Greta won't want to be gone from the public eye for long. Not that I blame her."

Of course she didn't. Why would she think the woman might want more than a few months home with her newborn? Why would she assume anyone might prioritize their child over their fucking career? I tried to tamp down my rising annoyance.

"But it would be three months that could change the entire path of my career! If they like me, I might be brought in permanently when there's a spot open. And it would put my face in front of millions of viewers every night, which makes me way more valuable to other large-market stations. I'd be a fool not to take this opportunity. You see that, right?"

I didn't know who she was trying harder to convince, me or herself. Suddenly I realized how self-assured she sounded. My eyes narrowed. "He already offered you the contract, didn't he?" I asked flatly.

She flushed and looked away, which told me all I needed to know.

"Laura." Anger had seeped into my tone. "Answer the damn question!"

"Yes. Not officially yet, but he assured me it's mine if I want it." She still wasn't looking at me.

"Let me guess. You accepted?"

Her eyes shot to mine before darting away. "You know how important this could be for me!"

"You accepted a three to six month contract in New York, away from your family, without even talking to me about it first? Are you fucking kidding me?" My volume rose higher. I was seething. Clenching my fists at my sides, I stared at her, willing her to meet my eyes.

Finally she looked back at me, and I saw she was retaliating with some anger of her own. "You're not being fair. Opportunities like this don't come along that often for someone working in small town cable news like me! I had to commit when Dan asked me, or he would've just called the next person on his list. And it's not like I'll be gone for three months straight if this goes through—I'd come home every weekend."

I laughed. It sounded like dry leaves crackling. "You're right. Take the job. It's what you've always wanted. Don't worry about us. I'll take care of everything here while you're gone. Hell, it won't be much different from now anyway." I rolled my eyes as I grabbed the converter to flick the television volume back on.

"What's that supposed to mean?"

Glancing back at her, I arched a brow. "Just that your career comes first. Always has." She started to protest, but I cut her off. "Don't. Don't even try to deny it. We both know you'd be lying if you did. You make decisions that affect us without even talking to me. You're at work more than you're home. Jesus, Laura. If it wasn't for Alexis needing her mother so damn bad, I'd tell you not to bother coming back on weekends. Just stay in New York the whole time. At least then we'd know not to expect you."

"That's completely unfair. You're really going to pull a guilt trip on me about this? Hold me back from a chance you know full well I've been waiting ages for? I can't believe you!" She was as angry as I was, but for very different reasons.

I sighed. "It doesn't matter what I think anyway, does it? You'll do what you want. So go ahead. Take the job if they offer it officially—I won't try to stop you. Just don't be surprised when Alexis gets used to not having you around."

"I don't want to be away from her. Or you. You know that."

"Do I? I don't think I do. But your mind's made up and nothing I say is gonna change it, so I think this discussion is over." I pushed the volume button on the remote and fixed my gaze on the screen, although I was focusing so hard on controlling my temper I wasn't even seeing it.

She put a hand on my arm. "Please try to understand. It's only three months."

I shook her off. "Three months for now. And if you get offered more, then what? You'll expect us to drop everything and uproot our lives to New York, right?"

She didn't reply, but I felt her whole body stiffen.

"That's what I thought," I said after a few seconds.

"Goodnight, Declan," Laura sighed, rising. "There's no use talking to you when you're like this." As she got to the foot of the stairs, from the corner of my eye I saw her turn back. "Oh, and I finally got a chance to speak with Dr. Wong at the Cancer Center in Charlottesville today."

That got my attention. I looked up at her. "And?"

"You can tell James he has an appointment on September 16th at seven AM. It's the only time they could fit him in." She went up the steps without another word.

The words "fed up" didn't even begin to describe how angry I was with her, the appointment she secured for James notwithstanding. She just didn't fucking get it. I felt like she'd never grasp that her family should always come first, that marriage is a partnership, and that her child needed a mother far more than she needed any extra wealth Laura's goddamn career might provide.

And, selfishly, I was getting sick and tired of always having to be the responsible one, having to pick up the slack and take care of everyone else. Laura, Ryan, my clients—they all depended on me, whether they'd admit it or not. Not that I begrudged being the primary caregiver to Alexis. I didn't at all. I loved spending time with her more than anything. But what I was seriously lacking in my life was time for myself, when I could forget about all my responsibilities for a while. A time-out.

I needed a fucking time-out in the worst way.

Amelia

Wednesday afternoon was almost over and I hadn't still heard a peep from Declan since his Facebook message to me late Friday night. At exactly five minutes to quitting time his extension flashed up on my phone, and I smiled. He asked if I had time to pop by after I finished up and, since I was in no rush to get home as I knew Scott would be staying late for football tryouts, I agreed. I wanted to talk to Declan in person about last week's Diana Incident anyway. But mostly I just wanted to see him.

When I got to his office, I started right into explaining my discussion with Diana in greater detail, including how upset I'd been afterwards. I could see Declan's irritation growing as he listened to me recount it, and his abrupt tossing out of "bitch" after I told him she'd said it was a bad idea for us to be friends solidified it. I finished by apologizing again for not coming to see him before leaving.

"I saw you walk out to your car," he said.

"You did?"

"Yep. I was concerned after our e-mail exchange. You looked so upset I actually knocked on the glass to try to get your attention."

Really? Huh. I couldn't suppress a pleased smile. I mean, I knew it was true—I knew from his e-mail—but hearing him admit he'd been worried about me meant a lot.

"I didn't mean to worry you. I just…it just didn't seem like a good idea to come over right then." What was I supposed to say? That I didn't come because I'd been so upset I'd cried away my makeup in the washroom like an over-emotional teenager, and I didn't want him to see me looking like crap? Not likely.

"But you're fine with it now?"

I shrugged. "I've been doing a lot of thinking since Friday. I've realized that I work better…you and I work better together…when we talk things out. And as Diana said, she can't dictate who I can be friends with. So screw her." I grinned at him, but it slipped from my face when I realized what I'd just said. Oops. Maybe a bad choice of words, since, according to Sam, Declan actually had.

"Been there, done that," he chuckled.

My brows flew up. Did he really just say that? Was I finally going to learn the truth about Diana and the Kavanaugh brothers?

With a small snicker I said, "Yeah, I heard some rumors to that effect."

"Of course you did." He shook his head, smiling wryly. "They're all so sure they know what really happened. And they're all wrong."

"So what really happened? If you don't mind me asking?"

"I'd rather you know the truth." He picked up a pen and began twirling it in his fingers as he spoke. "I did sleep with Diana—once—a long time ago. About a year before she married Ryan. We were both pretty drunk at the time. Well, I was, anyway. I never touched her again. Years later, for some dumb-ass reason she told Ryan about our little indiscretion. Guess she still felt guilty and needed to purge. My brother freaked. He assumed we'd been fu…sorry…fooling around behind his back the whole time. He wouldn't believe either of us when we denied it was ever more than once. Still won't, actually."

He paused and looked at me. "His paranoia and mistrust destroyed his marriage. Can you believe that? Diana may be many things—arrogant bitch comes to mind—but as far as I know, adulterer isn't one of them."

A pang of guilt hit me at his last few words. How could I ever judge anyone else's actions when I was having such difficultly remembering my own wedding vows?

I realized with a start that Declan had told me more private details about his life over the past couple weeks than Scott had in the first few years I'd known him. Not that it was the same—Scott's family dramas were nothing compared to the things Declan had confessed. But, still. I was flattered he felt comfortable enough with me to share this stuff.

"That's messed up," I said. "But it explains some things. I accidentally overheard her and Ryan arguing a while back. Now I understand what they were talking about." I almost told him I was pretty sure Diana was still in love with his brother, that she'd been nearly in tears after he'd stormed off, but I stopped myself. No matter how angry I was with her, that was too private a moment for me to divulge. "And you're right. Everyone thinks you two were having an affair while they were married." I sighed. "I hate all the gossip. It can destroy people's careers, marriages, entire lives even."

"Yep," he said. "But at least now *you* know the truth. Sleeping with her was the worst decision I ever made. It would be easy to just blame the alcohol, but it was my own fault. I was well aware she was Ryan's girlfriend, and I never should've laid a finger on her. It ruined my relationship with my brother, and I've regretted it ever since.

"I'm so sorry. I really hope Ryan can forgive you someday." My heart clenched for him. This clearly still caused him pain.

He nodded. "I hope so, too." Then he broke into a grin. "Let's change the subject, shall we? How was your long weekend? Josh told me you guys all met for drinks Sunday night? If I lived in Swann's Landing, I would've come out and joined you."

"Oh, yeah?" I responded with a small smile. Inside I shuddered. Having Declan there, with or without Laura, would have made things a hundred times worse for me, anxiety-wise.

"Why not?" he asked. "Or wouldn't you have wanted me there?"

I pressed my lips together. "Spending an evening hanging out with you would be cool." Not to mention terrifying.

"We should make plans to go into Richmond one night. Meet up for drinks. Maybe see a band."

Whoa. My eyes widened. I think my heart stuttered. Did he really just invite me to go to Richmond with him? Did he have any idea what kind of effect saying stuff like that had on me?

"Are you serious?" I asked in a voice so low it was nearly a whisper. He was looking right into my eyes again. I realized I was sporting a goofy grin like some love-struck adolescent.

"Sure," he replied casually. "I think we could both use some downtime. I sure as hell know I could. You game?"

My throat felt drier than the Sahara, but my smile didn't falter in the slightest. What exactly was he inviting me to do? And was I game? Was I?

Before I could give any more thought to it, words just began to tumble out. "You're right, I really *could* use some downtime. My friend Indira lives in Richmond. I could stay at her place so I wouldn't have to worry about driving back home after." *Oh my God.* What had I just agreed to? It was like my mouth had a mind of its own.

"If we picked a Thursday night, I could arrange a meeting Friday morning so I'd have reason to book a hotel in the city overnight. I have several clients in Richmond. Shouldn't be a problem. That way most of my expenses would be a write-off. Win-win!"

He was grinning as he thought things through out loud. I was just stuck on the word *hotel*. Instead of commenting more, I nodded along with him. I had no idea if this was just casual talk about potential future plans that friends discuss but ultimately end up going nowhere, or if he was serious and this might really happen. I was stunned by his suggestion and not processing it all very well.

"...up with me?"

Crap. Missed some of that. Blushing, I said, "Pardon?"

"Would you tell your husband you were meeting up with me?"

I frowned. Another pertinent question. Though it seemed impossible, I swear my cheeks got even hotter. I chewed my lip for a moment before mumbling, "Um, no. No, I don't think so. I think that would just...complicate things."

Declan was staring into my eyes again. My stomach twisted, both from our current topic and his gaze. It was obvious he was thinking very seriously. Was he imagining Laura's reaction if he told her he was going out drinking in a different city with another woman? I wished I could read his mind.

"You're right," he replied, nodding. "It could definitely complicate things."

I promised I'd talk to Indira, or Dee, as I affectionately called her, about a visit, and get back to him with some potential dates. Then I said I needed to head home. My brain felt like mush. I had way too much to mull over, and I really needed the alone time of my drive to think.

My emotions were ricocheting between extremes as I got into my car. I was overflowing with excitement at the idea of a night out with Declan, not to mention the hotel room he'd so casually dropped into the conversation. I wouldn't even have to sleep at Dee's on that Thursday night if I didn't want to—I could just tell her I was coming in after work on Friday. I could spend the afternoon shopping after Declan left for his meeting, and then meet her Friday evening and make a second night of it. As far as Scott would know, I'd be spending both nights with Dee.

But then the other fifty percent of my reaction kicked in: the disbelief, the overwhelming fear and guilt. I broke into a cold sweat just contemplating it all. What kind of a person was I becoming? Could I ever respect myself again if Declan and I did cross the friendship line?

Cranking up both the air conditioning and the volume on the radio, I sang along as loudly as I could to try to drown out the conflicting voices in my head and in my heart.

Chapter 14

Amelia

That night sleep again refused to come. Scott had asked why I'd been so spaced-out earlier, and I'd told him I was just distracted by work-related issues. Which wasn't a lie. This time. But if I went to Richmond and hung out with Declan, I knew there would be other, far bigger lies in my future.

Around two AM, I decided I couldn't just lie there beside my snoring husband any longer. I got up and tip-toed downstairs to the rec room. Once more I turned on the television, lowered the volume, and wrapped myself in the soft blanket draped over the couch.

When I was nice and cozy, I leaned back, closed my eyes and allowed my mind to drift. I imagined what meeting up with Declan in Richmond might be like. I figured I'd probably head straight to the city after work, maybe leave my car at Dee's and walk downtown. Declan and I would've planned to meet up somewhere. But where? Someplace not too crowded, with low lighting. And soft music. And good food. And, of course, a bar. I realized I knew just the spot. I'd been there with Dee and some of her friends last spring. I couldn't recall its name, but it wouldn't be difficult to find out. It was a narrow hole-in-the-wall with couches all down one side and in the back, and a long bar along the other. If I remembered correctly, they had cheap martinis every Thursday night, too. It'd be perfect.

So I'd take him there. Maybe he already knew the place, but in my fantasy, I assumed he didn't. I'd lead him to the couches in the back where it was more private. Then I'd sit down across from him and we'd order a couple of martinis. We'd relax and chat. Maybe I'd say I couldn't hear him well enough and use the excuse to move over beside him, to lean in closer. As my liquid courage grew, I'd flirt a bit. And he'd flirt back.

I'd only have two drinks, though. The last thing I'd want would be to get stupid drunk and end up sick. Not only would that be crazy embarrassing, but I also wouldn't be able to remember much of our night. So, two drinks only. Three at most.

After a while, we'd leave and go for a walk. Maybe we'd stroll through Capitol Square. At some point we'd end up holding hands. Would it be Declan that initiated it? Or me? I imagined him casually reaching over and catching my fingers in his as we chatted and laughed and walked. His hand would be warm and a bit sweaty, his fingers rough and masculine. Before we got out of the park, we'd stop below a big tree and he'd press me up against it and kiss me. And my legs would nearly give out from finally having his lips on mine, so I'd wrap my arms around his neck and thread my fingers into his hair to keep myself upright. It would be amazing. And when we'd come up for air at last, we'd hurry back to his hotel room.

And then…then…

Then we'd make love. And it would be the most incredible, passionate and loving experience of my entire life. He would get lost in me and worship me and make me feel like I was the only woman in the world to him.

Gah.

That final thought was like a dash of ice water to my overheated senses. Because that was just it. No matter what might happen between us in Richmond, or anywhere else for that matter, I wouldn't be the only woman in Declan's world. I'd be the Other Woman.

My throat tightened, and I heaved a frustrated sigh. This was ridiculous. I needed to stop deluding myself. This was far more than just physical attraction; I had real feelings for him. Strong feelings. Feelings that dragged me along a path toward him whether I struggled to resist or not. I'd already fallen hard, and it was high time I admitted it.

I had no idea if Declan felt the same way about me. There'd definitely been some hints he might, such as his "I obviously have a thing for younger woman" comment. Not just that he'd said it to me, but the *way* he'd said it, while staring right into my eyes. I'd felt like he was trying to look inside me, trying to gauge my reaction. And now, this suggestion to go out drinking in Richmond together? What was I supposed to make of that? Was it completely innocent? Did he just want a night out with a friend where we didn't have to worry about loose lips spreading gossip? Or did he want more? He'd made a point to mention that he'd get a hotel room. Was he hoping us drinking together would lead to other, more intimate things? Things like what had happened with Diana years ago that he regretted so much? Surely the thought must have crossed his mind. Declan was far from stupid.

The very last thing I wanted was for us to have an amazing night together, and then have him regret it forever afterward. I'd lose him for good if that happened, and I couldn't even fathom the thought of him never being a part of my life again.

Argh! I was going to make myself crazy if I didn't stop over-analyzing this. I needed to make a decision. Was I going to take a leap for once and allow myself to be selfish and wild? To be reckless with my heart?

And Scott's and Laura's and maybe Alexis' as well, whispered that persistent little voice of reason in my head. Not that it was in any way wrong, but God, sometimes I hated that voice.

Or was I going to keep on being the responsible, practical, but unfulfilled Amelia I'd always been?

No matter what I did now, someone would get hurt. *I* would get hurt. Best case scenario? I'd eventually have to break my loving husband's heart and leave him, which would be beyond horrible. And that would be the *best* case. The worst case…well, I didn't even want to go over again the myriad ways this could—and probably would—blow up in my face. I'd already memorized every last one of them.

I didn't see any option that wouldn't lead to heartache.

Another night of barely sleeping. My morning coffee had become my crutch. I'd gone back upstairs in the wee hours, eventually managing to pass out sometime after four. And I'd woken up again around six, unable to fall back asleep for even another minute.

So I sat at my kitchen table, gripping my cup and squinting in the brightness. Irritatingly cheerful sunlight streamed through the window, reflecting off the blue floor tiles I'd picked out at Home Depot two summers ago. I'd carefully chosen those tiles, the curtain fabric, the countertops, and the appliances when we did the renovations. I loved my little kitchen. I loved my house, too. This was my home. How could I even consider doing something that could rip it all away?

This was the sort of day that should make me feel happy just for existing, yet here I was yawning and worrying and goofing around online.

You ever ask for a sign from the Universe to help you understand something or make a decision? The past few days I'd been begging for such a sign. And, strange as it may sound, as I scrolled down my Facebook home page, the Universe deigned to give me one.

A post of Liv's from the night before caught my eye. It was yet another inspirational image share, which seemed to dominate my friend feed these days. This one was a pink rectangle with a drawing of a smart looking woman on the right side. Words of wisdom were scrawled in black across the left: *It's never too late to change course. If this is not the life you want, love yourself enough to try another path.*

My breath caught in my throat, and I had to squeeze my eyes closed for a moment. With a sigh, I read it again. I swore Fate had put that out there just for me to see.

I took a deep breath and went still.

What if I did try another path?

What if I stopped fighting and just let the tide take me where it may? As my dad had told me, sometimes I was going to have to make hard choices, and sometimes I needed to do what was best for me, not for other people.

I closed my laptop, rinsed out my mug and got ready to head into the office. No matter how guilty I felt—and I definitely felt guilty—I knew what I wanted.

For me.

I got into work extra early again. Before organizing my day's workload, I took a minute to text Dee suggesting we needed to plan a girls' weekend, and asked which Friday might work. I didn't mention sleeping over at her place on Thursday, figuring I'd cross that wobbly bridge when I came to it.

An hour or so later, she replied: *Great idea! It's been way too long. This month's nuts for me. How about Sep 27 or Oct 11?*

I told her I'd confirm a date as soon as I could. First I needed to run the options by Declan to see what worked for him.

Having no idea if he was in the building or not, I sent him a quick e-mail saying I needed thirty seconds of his time. Hours passed with no reply. That seemed a bit odd, since even if he was on the road, he always checked his messages on his phone.

Right before I was about to head home, I received: *In an all-day meeting. Sorry, try to find you tomorrow.*

The next day he showed up at my desk. When I looked up from my monitor and saw him standing there, I sucked in a surprised breath. He was wearing a suit. It was charcoal gray with thin pinstripes, and it fit him impeccably. An azure blue tie brought out the color of his eyes. He looked good enough to eat.

"Hey," I managed, gawking.

"Hey. You needed me for something?"

Blankly I replied, "I did?"

"Your e-mail? From yesterday?" He shot me that disarming grin of his and my temperature spiked.

"Oh. Um." I paused. I couldn't exactly suggest potential meet-up dates with Kaitlyn right across the aisle, and Evan on the other side of my cubicle wall. Thinking fast, I grabbed a yellow Post-it notepad and scrawled *Sep 26 or Oct 10*. I handed it to him, hoping he'd understand what I meant.

"Right," I continued with a smile. "Sorry. Just wondered if you've heard back from Blair and Sons yet? Did we get the account?"

Declan's eyebrows shot up as he read the note and then looked back at me. His lips twitched with amusement. My tongue unconsciously darted out and licked my own lower lip in response. Realizing I was staring at his mouth, I raised my gaze.

The corners of his eyes crinkled as he replied, "Yep, just got the confirmation this morning. Thanks for all your help."

With any luck Kaitlyn had overheard him thank me. It'd become important to me that they realize Declan wasn't as bad as they thought. "No problem," I said. It felt like our eyes were having a different conversation than our mouths. On impulse, I swept my hand his way and added, "You're looking very dapper today."

"I just got back from a client meeting in Roanoke. Very high-end law firm, so I thought I'd better dress the part. What do you think of the suit?" he asked, still smiling away. It occurred to me that we almost always had massive grins on our faces when we were around each other.

I'd often seen Declan dressed in business casual, sometimes wearing a sport coat, and even in a tie a few times, but this was the first time I'd ever seen him wear something as professional as a suit. He looked like he'd just stepped out of an Armani ad. Drop dead gorgeous.

Chuckling softly, I scanned him up and down. Was that a blush I saw rising in his cheeks? "You look amazing," I murmured. *And lickable.* I wondered which of us was pinker.

I wouldn't have thought his smile could grow wider, yet at my words, it did. "Thanks. And I'll have an answer on your other question as soon as I can." He tucked the small yellow note into the breast pocket of his jacket. "Talk to you later." Then he winked at me and walked away.

I didn't end up speaking to Declan in person again until a week later. On Friday he let me know he was in his office, so I stopped by on my way out. I hated going an entire week without seeing him. It made me antsy.

As soon as our eyes connected, I felt myself relax. It was like my heart heaved a grateful sigh. He looked tired, but when he saw me his entire countenance brightened.

Instead of sitting down, I leaned against the credenza beside his desk. I couldn't stay long this time; I had to get home and start dinner. For some crazy reason Scott and I had invited both our families over. Since my mother and his mother rarely agreed on much, I was anticipating a stressful evening.

"So," I started, as he grinned that lopsided grin—the one that made those tiny butterflies in my belly whirl and dive. "Any luck booking that client meeting yet?"

His smile faltered, and he glanced down at something on his desk. "Not yet, no. So far the timing hasn't panned out. I'll keep trying, though."

I didn't know whether I felt more disappointment or relief. Delays meant I could still brush off the reality of what we were discussing.

After I asked about James, he told me his father had an appointment at the Cancer Center in Charlottesville on Monday, and was flying in this weekend with Declan's half-sister.

"You have a sister? Wow, another new family member. How've you been handling all this?" I was still shocked by it. I couldn't imagine how he must feel.

"It's a lot to take in," he admitted. "I'm still trying to process."

I shrugged. "I bet. So, what's he like?"

"James?"

"Yeah."

"He's..." Declan trailed off, thinking. Then he smiled. "He looks a lot like me, just older, greyer, and thinner. We seem to share a sense of humor, penchant for drink and, apparently, taste in women." He gave me another one of those piercing looks.

Before I could comment, he continued, "He's stubborn and stoic and proud. And he loves his family unconditionally. I hope you get to meet him one day."

My eyebrows shot up. I wasn't sure how *that* could ever happen. "I hope I do, too," I said honestly. "How old's your sister?"

"Twenty-six. Her name's Miriam. No husband or kids. That's all I know about her. But hopefully I'll get a chance to speak with her privately this weekend." His forehead furrowed. I knew he was thinking about his father's failing health.

"You're really going to have a lot of your plate over the next while," I said, my subtle way of offering him an out if he was having second thoughts about us meeting up.

"I know," he sighed. "But that's exactly why I need something to look forward to. A de-stressor." So he had understood the escape I'd just given him. And declined it.

"You'll need to book a room with a Jacuzzi!" I laughed.

Oh my God, what did I just say? Blushing hotly, I pretended to be interested in my purse strap. I'd meant to joke about him needing to relax, not to imply…well. Stuff.

"I've booked so often with certain hotel chains that I usually get upgraded, but I've never once seen a room in Richmond with a Jacuzzi. Not sure if such rooms even exist in that city. Maybe we should make plans in Roanoke or Norfolk instead—I bet I could find a Jacuzzi room there." He chuckled and wrote something down on a pad by his computer. A reminder to check with clients in other cities?

I made a non-committal reply about the different city idea, and then said I had to get home. He assured me he'd let me know as soon as he found a date that worked.

Forty-five minutes later, I was in my bedroom changing when something important struck me. The eyes staring back at me from my dresser mirror flared wide with shock. I dropped onto the bed, and covered my face with my hands. I had told Declan Richmond would work because I could stay with Dee. If he was seriously suggesting we go out drinking somewhere else, then I'd have nowhere to spend the night. I'd need a hotel room, too. So was he just musing out loud? Did he realize changing locations might mean I'd end up staying with him? Was that his intention all along? I blew out a loud puff of air and told myself not to be so fricking naïve. Declan was a smart guy. He knew. He must have.

Which meant…

I gulped. Which could only mean he wanted more than just friendship on our little night out. Which meant he felt this pull between us, too. And he wanted to act on it.

My entire body trembled. I couldn't seem to catch my breath for a few long moments. Suddenly every last aspect of our flirtation and all that had been hinted at became way too real.

Declan

It had been a long, stressful week, and it wasn't even over yet. Laura and I had been avoiding all meaningful conversation; we said what needed to be said, but very little else. She hadn't mentioned another word about going to New York if the contract was offered. Most of the time I hoped it'd all just blow over. But there were moments when it really got to me, when I actually wanted it to come up, wanted her to have to confront me with the fact that she'd chosen career over family yet again, wanted her to have to face telling Alexis that her mother was leaving her for three months. Dickish of me, I know. But I hated all this tiptoeing around each other. I was always on edge now, not knowing what she was thinking, or when the ball was going to drop. It seemed like my family was slowly being torn apart in painstaking little increments, and I despised every second of it. Something sure as shit needed to happen soon. But damned if I knew whether that *something* was to wait and let things heal on their own, or just rip off the proverbial Band-Aid and let 'er bleed.

The not knowing was driving me fucking bananas.

I'd spoken to James several days ago to tell him about the appointment Laura had arranged for him. He was very grateful, and called me back last night to say he'd be down tomorrow with Miriam. I insisted they both stay with us. Besides wanting them close, I also needed the distraction at home in the worst way.

My workweek had been crazy busy too, with never-ending meetings eating up almost all of my time. I hadn't had a chance to speak with Amelia since those fleeting few moments at her desk the week before. It was stunning to realize how much I missed her when I hadn't seen her in a while. When I finally found a moment to call, and she agreed to pop by on her way out, I felt lighter. And as she stepped into my office and flashed me that shy little smile of hers, everything became right again.

What that said about me and my growing desire for her, I was scared shitless to look too close at. I just knew I was happier with her around.

Recently we'd been discussing the possibility of meeting up for drinks in Richmond, and she'd even given me a couple of dates to work with. Though it had been my idea, and I had no doubt we'd have a great time, I was feeling conflicted as hell about it. It was true I needed a break, and I enjoyed spending time with her. She made me laugh and relax like no other adult could. But I was no longer able to deny the major connection between us. It wasn't just that she was hot—I was starting to develop real feelings for this woman, which made everything that much more complicated. It wasn't smart—in fact, it was stupid as hell—but I desperately wanted to spend time alone with her away from prying eyes. Problem was, if we did, especially if we went drinking, I wasn't sure I'd be strong enough to keep things strictly platonic. And if I slipped up and made a pass… Man, I could really fuck up everything. I'd probably ruin our friendship. And our working relationship. And if she told anyone, it could ruin more important stuff, too. I'd learned my lesson with Diana. I couldn't destroy either my family or this precious thing I had with Amelia. I wouldn't. I knew I needed to take this…this…this *attraction* and bury it. Deep.

So why did I let my mouth run off about hotel rooms and Jacuzzis when she was in my office a few minutes ago? Did I have no self-control around her? Because, shit, if that were true, then there was no way we should be spending time alone together. If I'd learned anything from my past mistakes, it was that I had a tendency to fuck up the good stuff in my life. I'd managed so well so far with Laura. I loved my daughter, and though she was driving me batshit crazy these days, I loved my wife, too.

No matter what I felt for Amelia, it would be a huge mistake to act on it. I didn't want to lose either her friendship or her respect, and I sure didn't want to risk imploding my family. I had to smarten the fuck up. But how could I turn off what I felt without losing Amelia from my life? That was the huge question I had no answer to.

My cell phone rang, startling me out of these maudlin thoughts.

"Declan?" an alarmed female voice shrieked. "Are you in your office? You need to get out to the parking lot right now!"

"Diana?" Panic flooded me at her tone. "Why? What's going on?" Jumping to my feet, I grabbed my jacket and keys.

"It's Ryan! I found him in his car. And I can't…I can't wake him up!"

Shit! I dashed out the door and down the hall, heading for the rear exit. "On my way! Is he breathing? Did you call 9-1-1?"

"Yes to both. I know he's been using again, Declan. What if he's OD'd?"

Chapter 15

Declan

I paced a worn out track in the linoleum of the waiting room at Lynchburg General Hospital, waiting to hear news about Ryan. Patrick sat nearby, alternating between flipping through scattered newspapers and watching the television mounted on the ceiling. Diana was slumped in a chair on the other side of the room, staring into space with her arms crossed over her chest. Every once in a while I heard her sigh. I was too restless to sit down, gripped tight with worry.

Ryan was off somewhere beyond those swinging doors having his stomach pumped. I felt like I'd assured every hospital employee I'd talked to, not to mention Patrick at least twenty times, that my brother was *not* suicidal. What happened had been an accident, a miscalculation, a major fuck-up. I figured they'd still insist he talk to a shrink after, but whatever fallout occurred from that would be entirely on him.

Patrick couldn't understand why Ryan still had painkillers to take too many of, even inadvertently. He'd asked me some very valid questions, and I was starting to get pretty sick and tired of covering up for my brother. I said the words, "I don't know. You'll have to ask

Ryan that," over and over. I told him I didn't think Ryan was depressed, and I was positive he hadn't been trying to take his own life. As expected, Dad was pretty rattled by all this. He'd thought he knew Ryan so well; it disturbed him to discover there were things—possibly dark things—his baby boy had hidden from him.

I knew the feeling.

Eventually an overworked-looking nurse stepped into the waiting room. "Mr. Kavanaugh?" she asked. Patrick and I immediately moved in front of the poor woman and stared at her anxiously. Diana perked right up to listen.

"Will my son be okay?" Patrick asked the nurse.

"Can we see him now?" I interjected before she could reply.

Her eyes shifted toward me briefly, then returned to Patrick. "You're Ryan Kavanaugh's father?"

He nodded.

"He'll live. He's asking for you." I detected a note of irritation.

Patrick and I exhaled simultaneous sighs of relief. The nurse turned to lead the way, and we both began to follow. Looking back at me, she shook her head. "I'm sorry, sir. The younger Mr. Kavanaugh was quite specific. Only his father."

I rolled my eyes. Patrick gave me a nod before proceeding down the long hallway after her. With a sigh, I dropped into an orange plastic chair across from Diana. Lovely way to spend a Friday night.

"Ungrateful little prick," I muttered.

Her eyes met mine. She looked as relieved as I felt. It was a far cry from earlier, when I'd found her frantic beside my brother's unresponsive body. I'd been shocked to see something I'd never seen in her eyes before: fear.

"He won't see either of us," she stated flatly. She sounded exhausted.

"Yeah, well, this time he's not gonna get what he wants. When Dad heads home, I'm going in." I flinched a little when I referred to Patrick as Dad, but Diana didn't know the truth, and frankly, old habits die hard.

She straightened up in her chair, steely determination on her face. "I'm going with you."

I just shrugged. I really didn't give a shit if she tagged along or not. She knew his little secret now.

Speaking of which. "You told me you knew he'd been using again. How'd you figure that out?"

She rolled her eyes, snorting. "I know him, Declan. Better than anyone."

I started to point out that she was living in Denial Land, to remind her that those days were long over, but then I stopped myself. What the fuck did I know? Maybe she was right. Maybe she did still know him better than anyone, even now.

"So you're telling me you just knew? Some sort of psychic connection between you and my dumbass baby brother, is that it?" I snarked.

Ignoring my jibe, she replied, "I started getting suspicious a couple months ago. He was obviously stoned when I phoned one night. Called him on it face to face the next day, and of course he denied everything. But I'm not an idiot; I've seen the signs before. I knew he was getting high again, but what could I do? He refused to let me help."

"Clearly you *are* an idiot, Diana. If you were so worried, why didn't you come to me about it?"

"Since when do you give a crap about my issues? Or his? You washed your hands of us both a long time ago."

Rolling my eyes again, I said, "You couldn't be more wrong." A nasty headache was pulsating beneath the pads of my fingers as I rubbed my forehead. This day could not end soon enough.

She arched an eyebrow, waiting for me to elaborate. I thought about Ryan's fuck-up, and how it could have easily cost him his life. I wondered how long he might have lain there if Diana hadn't come along and found him. But we *did* get him help in time, and apparently there was no lasting damage. My brother was still breathing and I owed that entirely to her. So I heaved a heavy, mock put-upon sigh and then quietly explained to her how I'd been helping him every time he'd fallen off the wagon since the day he moved out of their house and out of their marriage.

When I finished detailing our little showdown in his office a few weeks ago, leaving out the part about James of course, she was staring at me in shock.

"Did it ever once cross your tiny little mind that covering up for him all those times and not telling anyone was doing him a massive disservice? He needs help! And he was never going to get it if you kept making the problem go away. You want to know why he keeps falling off the wagon? Cause there's never been any consequences for it! No reason for him to want to try to stay clean! God, Declan! I can't believe you—you were basically enabling him for *years*!"

"Keep your voice down," I warned her, glancing around the otherwise empty waiting room nervously. You never knew when a nurse might pop in, and Patrick could return at any moment.

"I did what I thought was best for my brother," I gritted out through clenched teeth. "I didn't want Dad to find out, or any of his friends or co-workers. I made sure he didn't lose his job. It was what Ryan wanted. I protected him."

"Protected him from what?" she asked incredulously. "Himself?"

Pressing my lips together, I focused on a dirty smudge on the floor below my tightly clamped fingers. "Something like that," I muttered.

Diana wasn't quite done yet. "Then this is as much your fault as it is his. The both of you are fucking imbeciles, always trying to fix everything yourselves. I wish you would have just come to me and told me what was going on. I could have helped him."

I scrubbed my hands over my face and through my hair. Sighing, I responded, "I wish my brother would forgive me for sleeping with you. I wish our father didn't think I was a screw-up. I wish…" I paused and took a breath, shaking the image of Amelia's smile from my mind and re-gathering my thoughts. "I wish a lot of things. We just have to live with the hand we're dealt and the choices we make."

Patrick chose that moment to step back into the waiting room. Diana and I stood and walked over to him.

"How's he doing?" she asked.

"He'll be fine," he replied gruffly. "He can go home tomorrow, probably. They have to run some tests on his kidneys to make sure the drugs didn't damage them. And he has to talk to the in-house psychiatrist. If he gives the okay, then Ryan should be released before the end of the day."

"I'll pick him up," I offered.

"That's okay, I'll get him. He's coming home with me for the weekend. He shouldn't be left alone yet." Patrick sounded weary and every last one of his sixty-three years.

"He can stay with us. I'll keep an eye on him."

"No, Declan. He's coming with me, end of story. I'm heading home to get some rest. I suggest you both do the same." He darted a glance between us that made me wonder if he assumed I was still screwing Diana on the side, even now. It wouldn't surprise me. Now there was a depressing thought. He pulled on his coat and walked away.

The moment Patrick disappeared, I headed for the swinging doors leading to the patient recovery rooms with Diana hot on my heels. Neither of us had any clue which room Ryan was in, but we were bound and determined we'd find him.

A bleached blonde nurse of about retirement age stopped us before we got very far past the waiting lounge. "Can I help you?" she asked with suspicion.

I flashed her one of my patented panty-dropping smiles and turned up the charm. Glancing at the name badge pinned to her generous bosom, I replied, "Yes, actually, *Velma*. Can you please show us the room my brother is recovering in? Ryan Kavanaugh?"

"And you are?" She tried to sound strict and official, but she couldn't resist returning my grin.

I stared directly into her heavily lined blue eyes. "Declan Kavanaugh. And this lovely lady beside me is Ryan's wife, Diana."

The nurse glanced over to Diana, her smile faltering a little. "Oh, Mrs. Kavanaugh. Right this way. Your husband's in room eight." And just like that, she led us straight to him. Easy-peasy.

Ryan looked over groggily as we entered the room. It was sterile-smelling and cramped, with a bed, a side-table and a chair taking up most of the space. His face was pale, and there were dark hollows under both eyes. Oxygen tubes fed up his nose, and an intravenous tube was taped to the back of one hand. Charcoal smudges still stained his lips. He looked like he'd just survived a round trip to Hell, which I suppose he kind of had.

Diana sat down in the chair and reached over to clasp his hand. "Oh, Ryan," I heard her murmur. "What did you do to yourself? You scared the shit out of me." Her eyes glistened like she was holding back tears. With some surprise, I realized she was still very much in love with my baby bro. So she wasn't a bitter, empty shell after all. Huh.

I decided to make my visit quick, and leave the two of them alone. Perching myself on the edge of his bed, I smirked down at him. "You know, brother, if you wanted our attention, there was no need to be so dramatic. A simple phone call would've sufficed."

His eyelids fluttered a bit as he tried to focus on me. A small smile curved the corners of his lips. "Was...was an accident." His voice was creaky and rough. I figured his throat was abraded from the tube they'd rammed down it to pump his stomach out.

"Oh, I know. I know it was." I put a hand on his shoulder. "Believe it or not, I'm not gonna yell at you for nearly offing yourself. By the looks of you, I'm sure you already feel shitty enough. But I warned you this could happen, and I wouldn't be me if I didn't say I told you so."

"So...sorry," he whispered. He began to cough. Diana grabbed a tissue from the bedside table and brought it to his mouth, gently wiping off as much of the charcoal as she could. She glared at me as she stood to drop it into the wastebasket.

"I know you're sorry. But the cat's out of the bag now. You're gonna have some explaining to do to Dad." I glanced over at Diana before returning my gaze to him. "She saved your life today, you know. You owe her. And I told her all about your little problem, so maybe the two of you should talk?"

Standing up to leave, I patted him on the knee. "See you tomorrow."

As I turned to go, I heard him mumble my name, and I looked back at him, one brow arched in question.

"Thank you," he croaked.

Suddenly my throat was too tight. I'd almost lost my brother. This close call had been *way too* fucking close. Brushing him off, I muttered, "Thank her." Then I made tracks out of there as fast as I could.

When I got down to the parking garage and started my car, the memory of him slumped over his steering wheel popped into my head. And I just fucking lost it. I leaned back into the leather and squeezed my eyelids shut, but I couldn't manage to stem my tears. The little shit almost *died*. If Diana hadn't discovered him when she did... Fuck. I'd never been so terrified in my entire life.

Whether he hated me or not, whether he ever forgave me or not, whether we were full siblings or not—none of it made one goddamn speck of difference anymore. I just needed my little brother alive.

Amelia

Dinner with my parents and Scott's mom and sister on Friday night went as well as could be expected. Sandy only asked us when we were going to start a family once, which was minimal for her. My own mother jumped in to defend my ambiguous reply by assuring her I was making the right choice to concentrate on my career. I sipped my wine and silently watched with growing unease the two of them debate the appropriate timing of my future motherhood. Six months ago, I would have found this conversation slightly uncomfortable, yet amusing. But now listening to them argue over my choices like I wasn't even there made me feel like some sort of doll, existing just to fulfill their desires for me. Scott was trying to ignore them by chatting with Morgan as if the louder discussion wasn't happening. My dad reached over and patted my knee below the edge of the table. Giving me a sympathetic look, he asked if I needed help cleaning up and followed me into the kitchen.

"Just ignore them, Amy. They only want what they think is best for you," he murmured as I began to rinse off a dirty plate.

"I know, Daddy. I just feel like they've both got my future all figured out. But how can they, when I haven't?" Shutting off the tap, I braced my fingers against the countertop and stared out the window into the night.

He put a warm hand on my shoulder. "You will. You'll know what to do when it feels right. Just trust your gut."

"I guess. But what if I make the wrong choice?"

"There are no wrong choices. There are only different choices, which lead you down different paths. The choice you make is the one you're supposed to make at the time. The path you don't take is the one you were never meant to be on. You just have to believe in yourself, hon."

My dad was a wise man. "I know. But sometimes it's just so hard," I complained, pressing my lips together.

"Yes, it is. Being an adult is hard. You don't have your parents making decisions for you anymore—you have to do it yourself. But you know I believe in you."

I gave him a hug and thanked him. We washed up the dishes together and chatted about lighter things.

No other awkwardness went down after dinner, and by the time I started getting ready for bed, I was no longer dwelling on either my mother or mother-in-law's plans for my life. I half expected Scott to bring up the baby topic again, but he didn't.

He did mention that I'd been looking tired lately, but it was the only thing he said to imply he'd observed any changes in either my appearance or my mental state. I assumed he noticed more than he let on, though. He'd known me longer and better than nearly anyone, with the exception of my father. I assured Scott I was fine. To my relief he let it drop.

Before I drifted off to sleep, I thought about Declan. And I remembered my father's words.

I knew the path I wanted to take. I no longer doubted how I felt. But it still terrified me.

Declan

I didn't sleep much that night, and when I did, reoccurring nightmares plagued me. I must have had at least five or six different dreams of not getting to Ryan in time, of finding him in his car, or slumped over his desk, or sprawled across his kitchen floor, face gray and eyes empty. Eventually I gave up trying and retreated downstairs to numb my brain in front of the television until the rising sun woke Alexis, and I could step into Daddy-mode.

James and Miriam arrived on the 11:15 AM flight from Buffalo, and all three of us met them at the airport. My half-sister had blazing cherry-red hair, hazel eyes and a shitload of piercings. Her short hair framed a pretty heart-shaped face. She was a small girl, and her all-black outfit and heavy combat boots made her appear even smaller. My first impression was that she looked nothing like James, but when he introduced us, she smiled at me and the resemblance became clear.

"Nice to finally meet you, Declan," she said, as James went to retrieve their bags from the carousel. Even her perfect white teeth were small.

"You, too," I replied, accepting her outstretched hand. Her fingernails were painted neon green. I wondered if she really had a chip on her shoulder or if her aggressive appearance was all just for show.

Alexis held onto my fingers tightly, nervous to meet this strange woman who had arrived with Grandpa James. Miriam knelt in front of her and looked her in the eyes.

"You must be Alexis. I've heard so much about you," she smiled. "I'm your Auntie Miriam."

Alexis tucked herself against my side. "Say hello, hon," I urged her. At that moment, James returned with their baggage. I felt Alexis' body relax when she saw him.

"Grandpa!" she squealed, ignoring Miriam in favor of the man who'd played Barbies with her not long ago. She pulled away from us and promptly flung herself into his waiting arms.

I turned to my half-sister. "Don't mind her. She'll warm up to you soon. She's just shy at first." Seeing that James had already picked Alexis up and was twirling her around, I added, "Well, normally."

Laura was watching James and Alexis closely. I introduced her to Miriam, picked up my sister's suitcase, and then the five of us were on our way.

We took them to lunch, and afterward gave them a driving tour of Lynchburg and a walk through Riverside Park before heading back to the house.

Miriam immediately set about making herself at home. After tossing her bag into the smaller of our two spare rooms, she began to peruse our CD collection in the living room, making clicking noises with her tongue as she scanned the titles. At one point she informed me playfully that I needed a musical re-education, and she'd e-mail me some links to her favorite bands. I laughed, thinking of the mixed CD Amelia had given me sitting inside the glove compartment of my car. I decided I'd take Miriam for a drive in the Mustang sometime and see if she liked Amelia's choices any better. Laura's tastes ran more to new country, which I could put up with, but it would never be my first choice. From her reactions to what she'd seen, I doubted Miriam was a fan.

There was no chance to speak with her alone that night. After we got Alexis to bed, we opened a bottle of wine and chatted about our careers and back-stories for a few hours. I could tell James was fading fast, and since the two of them had been up since dawn, they both apologized before retiring. I told Laura I'd clean up and she, too, went upstairs. She and I were still ignoring the New York-shaped elephant in the room, which mostly meant avoiding any unnecessary conversation with each other. It was awkward as hell, but I didn't know what else to do about it.

I checked in with Patrick and learned Ryan had been released into his care around dinnertime. He had to go back in on Wednesday to discuss his psych eval. I told Patrick I'd take Ryan for that, and surprisingly he didn't argue with me. It crossed my mind that perhaps he was apprehensive to learn the results.

Since all the various people I had to worry about were safe and sound for the moment, I took a moment to sit back, sip my whiskey and just breathe. I had no idea what kind of shitstorm the next few days might bring, but at the moment I felt like I was up to dealing with it.

On Sunday morning, Laura got a phone call and then informed me she was heading to Swann's Landing to help out her mom for the afternoon. Instead of her going alone like she'd intended, I decided James and Miriam might enjoy seeing a bit more of Virginia, so I piled us all into my wife's car.

We dropped Laura off, and then I gave them a tour of the town at best as I could. James and Alexis played I Spy in the backseat and Miriam sat in the front beside me. My daughter and her new grandfather had been thick as thieves since he'd arrived. I doubted she'd even noticed Mommy wasn't in the car anymore.

Adopting my best Tour Guide persona, I showed them what I knew, which wasn't all that much: mostly the historic downtown with the Stormy River winding through it. Miriam seemed delighted, rolling her window down and snapping photos with her iPhone of whatever caught her eye.

I'd intended to keep going out to the wooded park just outside town where the waterfall was—it was picturesque as hell—but before we even passed the white Doric columns of Town Hall, Alexis loudly informed the entire car that she was starving.

Pulling into an empty space in front of Finnegan's, I asked, "You guys ready for a lunch break?" I was met with a chorus of agreement.

We grabbed a booth near the front and settled in, Alexis insisting she sit between James and me. Miriam watched her with amusement. I'm not sure she knew what to make of my little princess yet.

From where I sat I had a direct view of the bar. As we waited for someone to bring us menus, I noticed a couple back there. The man leaned against the polished wood, and the woman perched beside him on a barstool. She had long dark hair that obscured the side of her face as she chatted with the bartender. From behind she reminded me a lot of...

Across the restaurant I caught the musical notes of her laugh and I froze, momentarily mesmerized.

Amelia.

I jerked my eyes away as a cute blonde waitress arrived at our table. After she left to get our drinks, I couldn't resist stealing glances at the guy with his elbows braced on the bar. Amelia's husband was tall with dirty blond hair. He had broad shoulders and an athletic build, and he wore a plain gray t-shirt and jeans. What was it she'd said he did? Taught at the high school? Yeah, that was it. In the auto shop. So he was a blue-collar kind of man's man. Huh. I wondered if that was the type of guy she was attracted to. While I had enjoyed team sports years ago, these days I was more of a golfing in the summer, skiing weekends in the winter kind of guy. And my collars had sure as hell never been of the blue variety.

After the waitress returned balancing a tray laden with glasses, and we gave her our lunch orders, Alexis pulled on my sleeve. She drew my head down to hers and informed me in her strident child's whisper that she "needed to pee!" Miriam smiled and offered to take her to the washroom, but I declined, knowing my daughter still wasn't comfortable enough to go off alone with her brand new auntie.

When her needs were met and we exited the restroom, I heard a sharp intake of breath behind me. I turned around curiously to find Amelia standing in the hallway. She stared at me in shock.

"Declan?" Her eyes flicked down to Alexis, then back up to me. "What are you doing here?"

I smiled at her. "Amelia. Fancy meeting you here. I dropped Laura off at her mom's, and was giving my father and sister a tour while we killed time waiting for her." Shrugging, I added, "We got hungry."

Alexis tugged on my hand to get my attention. "Daddy? Who's that lady?"

Startled, I broke my gaze away from Amelia's and looked down at my little one's curious face. "Alexis, I want you to meet someone. This is my friend, Amelia."

"Amelia, this is the love of my life, my daughter, Alexis."

Amelia still had that deer-caught-in-the-headlights expression. She blinked, then seemed to come back to herself. Squatting to Alexis' height, she grinned at her. "I'm so pleased to meet you." Amelia held out her hand. Alexis was not used to people treating her like a big girl and wanting to shake her hand, but she cautiously extended her fingers to Amelia's.

When Alexis remained silent for a few moments, I offered quietly, "She's shy."

Amelia's smile grew wider. "Alexis, you are a very pretty girl. You have the most beautiful eyes I've ever seen. They're just like your Daddy's."

Her expression faltered and her small eyebrows drew together. "Everybody always says I have Daddy's eyes. But they're not! He's got his own!"

Any tension Amelia may have had seemed to melt away, and she broke out laughing. I chuckled along with her. Alexis looked between us, not understanding the joke.

Amelia glanced up at me, and then returned her attention to the confused child in front of her. "You're absolutely right. He's got his own. Your eyes are unique, just like you are. I'm sorry, I don't know what I was thinking."

"That's okay," Alexis said, back to happy.

Rising to her feet, Amelia flashed me a smile. "It was great bumping into you, but Scott and I are waiting for take-out, and it's probably ready by now. I should get back and pay."

"Understood," I said, nodding.

"It was wonderful meeting you, Alexis," Amelia told my daughter. "Your daddy is going to be in for a world of trouble when you get older. All the boys are going to fall in love with you."

Alexis stared up at her and screwed up her face. "No, they won't! Ew!"

"That's right," I chimed in. "Boys are icky, right, Lex?"

"Icky-sticky," she agreed solemnly.

"Except your Daddy," Amelia said. We stared into each other's eyes. She seemed a little troubled. Not for the first time, I wished I knew what was going on inside her head.

"See you next week," she told me, waggling her fingers at Alexis as she headed back to the bar and her waiting husband. Something clenched inside me when she walked away, like she was taking something vital with her, something I wanted desperately to hold on to.

As I took Alexis' hand and began walking back to our booth, she whispered, "Daddy, I like her. She's really pretty."

"Yes, she is, honey. And so do I," I whispered back.

Chapter 16

Amelia

Running into Declan and his daughter in the back hallway at Finnegan's had rattled me. When I returned to the bar, Scott was waiting with a large paper bag full of hot food, so I quickly paid our bill. On the way out, I shot a sideways glance at the booth Declan and his family occupied. I only caught a quick glimpse of his father, but I saw right away that Declan's description of James was spot-on. He looked a lot like his son. Declan's half-sister had short, bright red hair and wore a black leather jacket; that was all I had time to notice.

I was quiet on the drive home, lost in my thoughts. I didn't even sing along when one of my favorite songs came on the radio.

"Something wrong, hon?" Scott asked, glancing over.

Everything, I thought, staring unseeingly out the passenger window. *Everything is so wrong.*

"No, why?"

He shot me another look before returning his eyes to the road ahead. "You were in a good mood at Finnegan's. Now you're not. What changed?"

I mentally scrolled through a selection of possible answers, but I didn't like any of them. Telling him the truth was not an option.

"I…" I faltered, sighing. "I don't know, Scotty. Just tired I guess."

"You've been tired a lot lately," he observed.

I closed my eyes and pressed my lips together. "I know."

We pulled into our driveway, and he grabbed the bag of take-out and went inside. I ate a little, but my hunger had ebbed away along with my cheerful mood. When I got up to rinse off my plate, he commented, "You haven't been eating much lately, either. Are you sick?"

"No. I don't know. Maybe." I kept my back to him as I put the dirty dishes in the sink.

"Maybe?" I suddenly realized he was standing right behind me. Putting his hands on my shoulders, he turned me around so he could look right into my eyes. "What's going on? You haven't been yourself for weeks now. Tell me, so I can help you."

Before I could formulate a reply, his eyes grew wide and a huge smile spread across his face. "Are you…? Ames, are you pregnant?" He looked so happy at the thought.

I took in the excited expression on his face and promptly burst into tears. "No! No, no," I cried, wildly shaking my head. "I know you wish I was, but I'm not. Sorry to disappoint you."

Scott pulled me against him and wrapped his arms around me. "You're not disappointing me. It just crossed my mind that maybe…" He trailed off, sighing softly. "Anyway. *I'm* sorry for jumping to the wrong conclusion."

I extracted myself from him. "I know you want to be a dad, Scott. I know you do. I just…it's just not in the cards for me right now."

For a few moments he was silent. Then, quietly, he said, "Tell me something honestly. Have you changed your mind? Do you even want to have kids at all?"

I looked down at the floor. "I don't know," I whispered to the blue tiles.

"You don't know?" He put his hand under my chin and tilted it up, forcing me to look at him. Tears still rolled down my cheeks. "Are you sure about that?"

I felt like the worst wife in the entire world. I wanted so badly to lie to him, to say something that would make him happy. But I couldn't. This was Scott. My Scott. The handsome football player with the goofy sense of humor who'd won my heart when I was a seventeen-year-old cheerleader. My first love. My first lover. My husband. He deserved the truth.

"I can't…" My voice cracked as a sob roughly pushed its way through. I forced the rest of my words out in a gasp. "I can't…can't…can't even imagine having a child." I did not add "with you" onto the end of that sentence. I wouldn't be that cruel.

He hugged me to him again, smoothing his fingers down my hair as my tears dampened the shoulder of his t-shirt. "Shh, shh. It's okay. Don't cry," he soothed.

"It's not okay," I sobbed. "It's not. It's the exact opposite of okay. You should find a woman who wants to have babies with you, Scotty. You deserve that."

He pulled back and looked into my streaming eyes. "Don't say that. The only woman I want is you. Always you. I love you."

Oh God. He was being so understanding, and I didn't deserve any of it. I felt about an inch tall. I couldn't stand it anymore; I pulled away from him and fled up the stairs, weeping the entire way. I went straight to our bedroom and dove under the covers, hoping against hope that he would give me some space to cry myself out in peace.

He did. One thing I'd always been able to count on was him giving me time alone when I really needed it.

Once my sobbing at last died down to sticky eyes and hiccups, I got up and went to the bathroom to splash cold water on my face and brush my teeth. I found Scott lying on his side of the bed, television remote in hand, when I returned.

Slipping under the covers beside him, I whispered, "I'm sorry." My voice sounded raw, like it wasn't mine. Like a stranger's.

"Nothing to be sorry about. I know this has been bothering you for a long time. You need to remember that you're not your mom. Or mine. You're a grown woman and you get to make your own choices. You don't have to get pregnant just because someone else says you should, or because you think it's what I want. I'm not going anywhere—you're stuck with me for the long haul." He leaned over and kissed me on the forehead before flicking on the TV.

I wish I could say that his words made me feel better as he intended, but they only made it worse. A light wave of nausea swept over me, and I could feel a new batch of tears threatening, so I whispered goodnight to him and turned over.

I stared at the wall through two sitcoms and part of a late night talk show before Scott turned off the television at last. Then I listened to the sound of his snoring for another hour before I gave up and crept back downstairs.

Once I was curled up in the blanket facing the back of the couch, alone in the rec room with only the sound of occasional cars passing outside on our street, I finally fell into a fitful sleep.

I dreamed about Declan last night. And the night before that. And the night before that one, too. It was turning into a dangerous habit. Thank God I don't talk in my sleep. In the most recent one, he, Alexis and I were living together like a normal happy family. The version of me in that dream was totally comfortable being both Declan's wife and Alexis's stepmother. Since in my waking hours, I couldn't imagine being anyone's mom in any capacity, I was surprised at how natural it had felt.

I ended up spending the entire night downstairs, awakening only when the rising sun streamed through the window and across my face sometime before six. I was showered, dressed and had breakfast ready by the time Scott came down into the kitchen, which was unusual during the school year. He didn't question my early rising, or bring up our difficult conversation from the night before, for which I was grateful.

When I got to work, I pulled out my phone to text Dee that I still didn't know which date for a visit worked yet, but I'd try to get an answer this week. Before I could message her, I saw I'd received a text from Declan. My pulse jumped. It had no words, just two photos. One was a cute shot of Alexis sitting on James' lap, both sets of blue eyes focused on Declan behind the camera. The second was an image of him, Alexis and James together, all with matching smiles. Declan looked so happy. I couldn't help but grin when I saw it, but I was also pleased I now had a photo of him to pull up whenever I wanted to see his face.

I dove right into my to-do list. Concentrating on what I needed to accomplish enabled me to push all negative thoughts about my marriage, and positive thoughts about a certain Account Manager to the back of my mind.

Yawning deeply, I printed off the spreadsheet I'd just completed and tucked it into the file. I heard Kaitlyn call my name and I turned to her, startled. The morning had whipped by so fast I hadn't realized it was past noon, and we were late for lunch. We hurried to meet Sam, fully aware of how much she hated sitting at our table alone.

The room was swarming with people and the loud din of overlapping conversations. "Hey," Sam greeted us as we took seats across from her. I narrowed my eyes. She wore a somber expression, which was unusual for the normally cheerful blonde.

"What's up?" Kaitlyn asked.

"You guys haven't heard about Ryan?" Sam turned to me. "Declan didn't tell you?"

I shook my head. "I haven't spoken to him today. What's going on? What happened to Ryan?"

She leaned forward and whispered confidentially, "Apparently Declan and Diana found him unconscious in the parking lot Friday after work. They had to rush him to the hospital!"

"What? You're kidding!" Kaitlyn exclaimed, forgetting to lower her voice in her surprise. "Is he okay?"

Sam looked worried. "It sounds like he's gonna be fine. His dad took him back to his place when he was released on Saturday. I think he's still there. He probably won't be in the office for the rest of the week. I shouldn't even be taking lunch today, but I really needed to get away from my phone for a few minutes."

"Do you know what happened?" I whispered. I had a sinking feeling I already knew the answer.

"No clue," she replied. "No one seems to know, and Mr. Kavanaugh wouldn't say when he called me." Then she looked pointedly at me. "You're friendly with Declan, right? Maybe he'll tell you."

I frowned. If what I suspected was the reason for Ryan's collapse, I wasn't sure Declan would confide that kind of immensely private stuff. Maybe. He'd told me a lot of personal things already, so it was possible. But even if he did, I had no intention of babbling to Sam or anyone else. I knew Sam was just concerned about Ryan—anxiety was written all over her face—but if she learned the truth, it needed to come from Ryan, himself. Not me.

"I don't know. I don't think he'd share personal info like that with me. But next time I see him, I'll ask how Ryan's doing, okay?' The only reason I knew Ryan might have an addiction in the first place was because I'd heard Diana accuse him of being high that day in the file room. It wasn't because of anything Declan had told me. However, if Declan hadn't know about the drug use before, I was sure he did now. My heart ached for him. He had enough to deal with without adding this to his already crowded plate.

Sam was pretty stressed out, and our lunch was cut short because she needed to get back to her desk. I was worried about both Kavanaughs. Diana had kept her office door closed all morning—a clear sign she didn't want to be disturbed. I suspected she was concerned about Ryan, too. And God forbid she showed any sign of weakness to the rest of us.

The news about Ryan stayed on my mind all afternoon. I was restless. I kept getting up and moving around, switching between tasks. I called Declan's office multiple times, but it always went straight to voice-mail. I left no messages. After the fifth failed attempt, I remembered he'd told me he was taking James to Charlottesville early this morning to see a specialist. Maybe he wouldn't be in today at all.

I was anxious to find out what had really happened on Friday, and how Declan was dealing with it. On my way out, I decided to walk through the Sales department to the rear exit on the off chance I might catch him in his office at the end of the day.

Luck was on my side—he was behind his desk. I could hear him talking on the phone before I stepped into the doorframe, and, as always, warm pleasure spread over me when I heard his voice. He didn't sound too impressed with whomever he was speaking to, but as soon as he saw me standing there, a real smile surfaced. It gave me a little thrill deep inside that he always seemed as happy to see me as I was to see him.

When I quietly inquired about Ryan, Declan stood and closed his office door. I took my usual seat, and he began to explain what happened. He told me everything, starting with his brother's knee injury so long ago, all he had done over the years to try to keep Ryan off the painkillers he'd become addicted to, and ended by describing the accidental overdose on Friday. The words spilled from his mouth as if he'd been bottling all this up for far too long.

It was obvious how much of a toll recent events had taken on him. When he admitted how scared he'd been that his brother would die in the parking lot before the ambulance arrived, I stood and walked over to him, eliminating the desk barrier between us.

Placing my hand gently on top of his, I murmured, "You okay?"

He stared down at our fingers. Realizing what I'd done, I withdrew, embarrassed.

"I'm fine," he said a little gruffly. "I was less fine at the time, but now…now, I'm okay."

I chewed my lower lip, doubting the truth of his words. Awkwardness seemed to fill the room, and I didn't like it at all. I resumed my seat, but now he wouldn't meet my eyes.

It seemed like a good time to change the subject. "What about James? How did his appointment go today?"

He glanced up at me in surprise. "You remembered that?"

I nodded, lacing my fingers together to prevent them from fidgeting.

"They poked and prodded him, and ran a bunch of tests. Now we wait for results."

Declan definitely wasn't himself. I assumed worrying about Ryan and James all weekend had drained him of his usual spark. Deciding maybe my presence wasn't making things any easier, I grabbed my purse and stood to go.

"I hope they find a way to help him," I said sincerely. "And I hope Ryan gets the help he needs, too."

He nodded, getting to his feet to reach for the doorknob. Before he could open it, I did something I swear I wasn't planning to do. I pulled him into a hug. It was a quick one, the hug of a friend comforting another friend, but in those few seconds of pressing myself to him, every nerve ending in my body sang.

As I stepped back, I whispered, "Just don't forget to take care of yourself, too."

The rest of the week passed without incident. Or any more communication from Declan. I presumed the first date I'd given him,

September 26th, wouldn't work for us to go to Richmond, as it was less than a week away and I'd heard nothing. Which left October 10th. Maybe.

When the following week also went by without hearing from him, I began to assume the second date wasn't going to fly either. I knew Declan's life was crazy these days, so I wasn't really surprised, but I was disappointed he didn't at least let me know it was a no-go.

Finally I broke down and e-mailed, because not knowing for sure was driving me up the wall.

The meeting times I inquired about a few weeks ago? Can I assume they're both in conflict with other scheduling?

I didn't get a reply until the following day.

Yeah, sorry. That isn't looking feasible right now.

My stomach dropped. I don't know why—I can't say I wasn't expecting it. I can't even say there wasn't a part of me that was a bit relieved, as the layers of guilt had only grown deeper lately. But a much bigger part of me was disappointed.

Things hadn't felt right between us since I'd spontaneously hugged him. There had been no office visits, no cubicle drop-ins, no random phone calls or e-mails just to see how I was. I'd passed him once in the hallway, and he'd smiled and said hi, but he hadn't stopped to chat.

I suspected I was overanalyzing things, but I just couldn't help it. I didn't want to regret the hug—he'd looked like he needed one, and friends offer comfort to friends. I was worried I'd screwed up and crossed some imaginary line Declan had created for himself. Maybe all his talk of us going out drinking together was just that: talk. Maybe he'd never intended to really go through with it. Maybe he had no idea how much his flirting messed with my head.

My logical brain assured me he was probably just wrapped up in his personal life and his clients, and simply didn't have any time to spare. It was the most probable explanation.

But whether it was real or imagined, the recent distance between us really unsettled me.

Several more days crawled by. I still hadn't heard from Declan, and I worried that the closeness we used to share might be over. I wanted to make things right in the worst way, but had no idea what had gone wrong, or how to fix it.

I was sitting in Josh's office, just finished discussing one of Ryan's clients that he'd helped me work out some complicated pricing for. Columbus Day weekend was fast approaching, and he was telling me about his plans to whisk Holly away to some secluded bed and breakfast in the foothills of the Blue Ridge Mountains.

"Are you going to propose?" I wondered with a massive grin, only half-teasing.

Josh's eyes bugged out comically. "No! Well…not yet anyway. Things are going great though. It could happen." He smiled. "Who knows? Maybe by Christmas."

I laughed. It was good to see him so happy. Changing the subject, I asked, "Have you talked to Declan lately?"

His face grew serious. "Yes, actually. Why?"

I shrugged. "No real reason. I just haven't in a while." I tried to sound nonchalant.

"You two are pretty close these days, huh?"

"I guess. I haven't spoken to him much the last few weeks. But I know he's got a lot on his plate. How's he doing?"

Josh gave me a look. "You should probably ask him that yourself."

"I know," I sighed. "There just hasn't been an opportunity."

Josh stood and closed his office door. Turning to me, he asked, "What's going on? I know something is. He asks me about you. You ask me about him. You don't seem to be talking to each other right now for some unknown reason."

Frowning, I pushed a loose strand of hair behind one ear. Josh was a friend, and I trusted him, but he was also Declan's friend. I hadn't told anyone what was going on—either in my head or in reality—between us. It'd been eating away at me for months, and I was desperate for someone to confide in.

Exhaling a puff of air I said, "It's complicated."

"Amelia. Tell me. Before I jump to some conclusions of my own." His tone brooked no dissent.

Worrying my lower lip between my teeth, I considered what to say. There was no going back if I confessed this stuff to another person. I would be putting myself out there to be judged by someone I really respected.

I didn't begin at the beginning. How could I tell Josh about that moment when Declan and I had locked eyes across the room? How could I admit out loud that our connection had been formed the very instant we saw each other? I couldn't. So, with a deep breath, I started with the offer of golf lessons and went from there.

Without going into a lot of detail, I told Josh about our conversations in Declan's office, how I'd shown him how to set up Facebook, and how concerned he'd been after Diana had accused me of playing favorites. I admitted that we'd grown into the habit of confiding in each other more and more personal details about our lives. Josh knew about James, and I said I'd been the first person Declan had told when he'd found out.

Josh was studying me closely. "You have feelings for him," he observed. It wasn't a question.

Staring down at my twisting fingers, I nodded.

"Think it goes both ways?"

I looked up. "Josh, do you really want to know all this?"

"I think you need someone to talk to. That's what I think. I can be that person, if you want me to be." His small smile was kind, and I knew I could trust him.

"I do." I went on to tell him about Declan's 'I obviously have a thing for younger women' comment, which elicited an eye roll and an amused grin in reaction. When I hesitantly mentioned our discussion about meeting up in Richmond for drinks sometime, his humor fell away again.

"Hmm." One eyebrow cocked. "You know what you're doing?"

"Not even slightly," I replied with a nervous laugh. "But it doesn't matter. It's not going to happen now."

"That might be for the best. What changed?"

I explained our most recent interaction, saying that plans had just kind of slipped by the wayside. And I confessed how I'd spur-of-the-moment hugged Declan in his office nearly three weeks ago when he'd looked so shattered, and how distant things had been between us since.

Josh listened carefully and didn't judge. Finally he asked, "Does he know how you feel about him?"

My cheeks grew hotter. "No! Well…I don't think so."

164

He was quiet for a few moments. Then: "You wanna know what I think?"

"Yes," I said anxiously.

"I think you should tell him." He held my gaze, his face still solemn.

What? My eyebrows flew up. I definitely wasn't expecting that. "I don't know if I can," I said, shaking my head.

"Trust me. You need to tell him the truth." He sounded much surer about it than I was.

"How? How would I even begin to do that?" *I can't! I can't!* echoed through my brain.

"You know his birthday's coming up?" Josh picked up his pen, jotted something on a slip of paper, and handed it to me.

I looked down at the date and grinned. "No. I had no idea. Thanks for telling me. What do you suggest?"

"I suggest nothing. But now that you're armed with that info, I'm sure you can figure out something all by yourself." He tented his fingers, peering at me over the top.

"Maybe I could take him out for a birthday lunch? That would give us a chance to talk away from here," I mused.

Josh nodded. "Good plan. You two really need to do some sharing. Once it's out in the open, I think you'll find it easier to face."

My twisting gut screamed otherwise. "Thanks for listening to me this afternoon. I guess I needed someone to talk to." I flashed him a grateful smile as I got up to leave.

"I'm always here for you if you wanna talk. And nothing you say will ever leave these four walls. Understood?"

"You're the best. Thank you." Then I went back to my desk to try to figure out how exactly I was going to corner Declan and convince him he should let me take him out to lunch for his birthday…which he didn't know I even knew about.

Chapter 17

Declan

I'd just gotten into the office from a client meeting on the outskirts of Richmond. It had been a very early morning, and the foremost thing on my mind was getting a cup of black coffee into me and then processing the newly-signed paperwork in my briefcase.

Colleen greeted me as I passed her desk. Stepping into my office, I thought I overheard her say, "He's here."

I dropped off my jacket and headed for the cafeteria for that coffee. Cradling the hot cup in my hands, I alternated between blowing on the surface and taking small sips as I walked back. When I returned to my desk, I was surprised to find Amelia waiting for me.

We hadn't had one of our chats in my office in several weeks now, not since the Monday after I'd run into her with Alexis. The last time we'd talked, I'd confessed all Ryan's issues to her, and I guess she'd taken pity on my emotionally frazzled state or something, because she'd startled the hell out of me by giving me a hug on her way out.

The amount of sheer voltage that'd shot between us when she'd pressed herself against me for those few seconds—it'd felt like my fucking heart was being defibrillated. All thoughts had flown out of my head but one, which involved us being decidedly less clothed. I hadn't said a word to her after she'd pulled back. I think she'd told me to take care of myself. Then she'd walked away and we'd barely spoken to each other since.

It wasn't that I'd been avoiding her. Not really. I'd just had a lot to think about the past few weeks. Ryan had finally done something intelligent for once in his life and checked himself into what they call "partial rehab", which meant he could go to work, but evenings and weekends had to be spent at the facility for the first six weeks. After that, the intensity of the program was dialed down a bit if both parties agreed he was making acceptable progress. I made a point to visit him every evening I could squeeze it in, and on weekends I brought Alexis with me so we could play a board game or go for a walk with him.

The results of James' battery of tests at the cancer center had come back, and a new line of experimental treatment was being set up for him that would start at the end of next week. For the month of November, he'd be staying at the facility during the week, and returning to my place on weekends. Then they'd run more tests and reassess how best to continue. I was cautiously optimistic, although James appeared more pragmatic about the whole thing. It seemed to me he'd accepted his fate a long time ago. If his hope for recovery had improved, he didn't show it. He was neither particularly negative nor positive about his health; he just seemed to enjoy every day as it came, and accepted what life he had left to live. I admired the hell out of him for his attitude. I was pretty sure if I were in his place I wouldn't be able to be so damn Zen.

As for Laura, well, things between us were still uncertain. We were trying to act like everything was normal, talking about what needed to be discussed, going through all the usual motions, but my heart wasn't really in it. To be honest, I was so wrapped up in James' and Ryan's issues when not in the office, that I'd mostly been able to suppress my feelings about Laura's potential out of state job, and focus solely on the people who demanded my attention most: namely, Alexis, my father, my brother, and my clients. My wife's issues came in at the bottom of the list. If that made me an asshole, so be it.

And if I'd possibly used all these distractions as excuses for not making time to see Amelia lately, well, who could really blame me?

It just seemed like maybe me forcing some distance between us was what I needed to garner some better perspective on what I really felt, and what I really wanted to do about it.

What I hadn't considered was the effect my stepping back would have on her.

When my eyes connected with hers, I froze in my doorway. As always, I was more than a little pleased to see her, but I kept my face purposely unexpressive.

"Hey," I greeted her cautiously. Setting the steaming cup down on my desk, I took my seat and swiveled to face her. "What can I do for you today?"

Her eyes narrowed in a small frown for a second before she replaced it with her usual smile. Man, I'd missed that smile. I instantly gave up resisting; I couldn't help mirroring it.

"I know you're busy, but I promise I won't take up too much of your time. I have something I want to ask you. Actually, make that *tell* you, as I'm not taking no for an answer," she said firmly.

My eyebrows shot up. Intrigued, I replied, "Oh really? Well, by all means, do tell."

"A little birdie informed me you have a birthday coming up."

Shit. That was pretty much the last thing I'd been expecting her to say. My thirty-fifth birthday was next week, and I'd frankly been hoping to avoid it. I snorted and shook my head. "Marshall's gonna pay for that," I muttered under my breath, but I knew she heard me.

"And," she continued as if I hadn't spoken, "I'm taking you out for lunch to celebrate. It doesn't have to be on the day of, as I know you probably have more important things to do that day, but hopefully the same week. Okay?"

"You don't have to do that," I protested, hands lifting with my palms out toward her.

"Yes, I do. I really do. I'm not giving you a choice, Declan. Just tell me a date that works, and I'll plan it. We're going. We've barely talked to each other in weeks, and I miss you. I want to do this."

She missed me? At those words, tight tendrils snaked around my heart. *Not half as much as I've been missing you,* I thought ruefully. Sighing, I relented. "Fine, fine. Okay. Lunch it is. Can I get back to you?"

"Nope," she said with a smirk. I shook my head again and grinned at her. She sounded a lot like me just there.

"Stubborn much?" I teased.

"Very," she assured me. "Thought you knew that by now?"

"Kinda figured it out, yeah. Yet another thing we have in common." And then we both started to laugh. Amelia's laughter filled me with intense happiness. Any residual tension flew right out the window, and I relaxed completely.

She swiped under her eyes, still smiling so widely her teeth gleamed. "You think?" she managed to get out, before succumbing to snickers again. It wasn't even really all that funny, but neither of us could seem to stop.

Pressing my lips tightly together to hold back another round, I retrieved my phone from my pocket to pull up my calendar.

I knew without looking that I hadn't booked in anything on my birthday. I'd been intending to forget about it. In the past, Laura and I often went out for lunch on each other's birthdays, but this year I didn't think either of us was craving any extra one-on-one time. If she did ask, I'd just tell her I had a client meeting I couldn't get out of. But I was pretty sure she wouldn't.

Pretending to be examining my schedule, I frowned studiously at my phone. Then I looked back up at her. "How does October 30th work for you?"

Her face was glowing from laughter, and at my words her brows shot up. "You don't have plans that day already?"

"Not yet. Speak now, or forever hold your peace," I said with a grin. Then I realized I'd made a reference to something heard during a marriage ceremony, and my amusement fell away. Wedding memories were the last damn thing I wanted to be thinking about.

"Great," she replied, getting up to leave. "Book it. See you next Wednesday then."

"Next Wednesday," I agreed. "If not sooner. Oh, and Amelia?"

She glanced back at me curiously.

"Missed you, too," I told her softly. Her cheeks grew even pinker, and that sweet little smile reappeared before she turned and walked away. I swear that smile could melt the hardest heart. Was that what I had been attempting lately? Trying to harden my heart to her, trying to keep her out?

I realized I was fighting a battle already lost. She'd broken down those barriers some time ago. Amelia York was firmly ensconced in there.

The rehab center where Ryan spent his weekends was located a few miles outside the city. Alexis sat in the backseat singing along to one of the more repetitious songs on the CD Amelia had given me as I drove past tall fields of waving cornstalks. Halloween was fast approaching, and the local pumpkin patches and corn mazes were doing brisk business on this beautiful Saturday morning. An autumn chill permeated the air. You could feel the first signs that winter was on its way.

When we arrived, we found Ryan sitting on a bench under a maple tree on the sprawling front lawn. Diana sat beside him, one hand resting affectionately on his knee. When she saw us, she quickly withdrew her fingers. I raised a questioning brow her way, but she ignored me.

"Uncle Ryan!" Alexis called. She ran over and plopped down on my brother's right.

"Hope we're not interrupting," I greeted them facetiously as I approached. They both knew I gave no shits even if we were.

Diana got to her feet, brushing any clinging debris from the backs of her thighs. "It's time I head home." She tousled Alexis' hair, and my daughter looked up at her. "Great to see you, kiddo."

Alexis regarded her curiously but didn't reply. She had no memory of Diana once being her aunt.

Diana reached out and touched Ryan's shoulder gently. "See you tomorrow," she told him softly before heading in the direction of the parking lot.

"Tomorrow?" I questioned, taking her spot on the bench. Bracing my elbows on my knees, I turned to look sideways at him. "You two mending fences?"

Ryan glanced at Alexis, who had picked up some yellow and orange leaves from the ground and was making them dance through the air. Then he met my eyes. "Something like that, I guess."

"Does this mean…?" I didn't even want to ask, but I couldn't help myself.

170

He sighed. "I may have…overreacted somewhat in the past," he admitted.

I stared at him, eyebrows somewhere up in my hairline. "Overreacted? You don't say. Are you telling me you finally believe us?"

"I believe…I believe you both made a mistake. And I'm done punishing you for it." He dragged the fingers of one hand through his hair. "She saved my life. You both did. And I'm…grateful. Really."

"I know you are," I said quietly. "You forgive her, then? Giving her another shot?"

He exhaled a small laugh. "I don't know what we're doing. Enjoying each other's company for now, I think. But yes, I've forgiven her." He tilted his head and looked at me straight on. "You, too."

I had been about to wonder out loud how the hell anyone could possibly enjoy Diana's company, but his last comment shut me right up. I swallowed over a sudden lump in my throat and dragged my eyes from his to examine something off in the distance.

Luckily Alexis picked that moment to need to show us a large red maple leaf she'd just discovered behind our bench. Instead of going inside to play games, she dragged us on a walk around the large property with her, pointing out every rock, twig or leaf she found beautiful along the way.

I felt lighter than I had in years.

Amelia

It took me a long time to decide what to give Declan for his birthday. I'd had less than a week's notice, and as I'm sure is obvious, I was someone who usually had everything planned out well in advance. I scanned through the files of music on my laptop for at least twenty minutes before I chose one. In the end, I picked Pete Yorn's debut album, *musicforthemorningafter*, as I thought its simple 'guy and guitar' sound would appeal to Declan's tastes. It was also one of my personal favorites, and I hoped he might love it as much as I did.

But giving him another ripped CD wasn't good enough. I wanted my gift to be something more personal, something that would mean a lot to him for years to come. I wracked my brain trying to think of a great idea. I scrolled through the personal e-mails from him I'd kept looking for something to jump out at me, but his messages never offered much detail. Glancing down at my purse on the floor, I got a sudden inspiration. I retrieved my phone and pulled up the photos he'd sent me a few weeks ago, studying the one of Declan, Alexis and James together. Their matching blues eyes told a three generational story. It was perfect.

On the way home from work the next day, I stopped at the mall and had the photo printed out in 8"x10" matte finish. Then I asked them to mount and frame it in a simple, modern stainless-steel frame. Once it was padded and wrapped, I hid it in the trunk of my car.

The following day I did some research online and made a reservation at a small bistro on the south side of Lynchburg. It had great reviews, and the hostess assured me she could give us a table in the back where we'd have privacy.

Once everything was in place, I just had to wait, and hope like crazy Declan wouldn't find some way to back out on me.

And that I wouldn't lose my nerve.

The morning of Wednesday, October 30th, I arrived at work a good hour earlier than usual. I hadn't gotten much sleep, but I'd taken extra time applying my makeup, and had been generous with the dark-circle concealer. I'd also carefully selected my outfit: a dark red pencil skit paired with a black, white and red geometric-patterned blouse. It had a low scoop neck and ruffled peplum at the waist; I swear it was the girliest thing I owned. I had not been blessed with generous cleavage, but I knew the benefits of a good push-up bra, and I used it to full advantage with this outfit. I scrutinized myself in the bathroom mirror and smiled at my reflection, pleased with the results. I hoped Declan would like it, too.

I deliberately parked in the back parking lot and entered the building through the rear door so that I'd walk through Sales on my way to my desk. There was only one light on in one office, Marilyn Silver's. The rest of the department was dark and silent—just as I'd been hoping for.

Slipping into Declan's office, I left the bag with the CD, framed photo and a small card signed, *Hope this birthday is one you'll never forget, A,* on his chair where he couldn't miss it. Heart lodged firmly in throat, I went back to my desk to distract myself from my increasing anxiety with the day's workload.

I'd asked Diana for permission to take a half-day off, so I wouldn't have to return to the office after lunch. I figured no matter how our conversation went, I'd be way too keyed up to come back and try to work. A buffer of a few hours to either go home early or drive around and think about things seemed like a smart plan, and I had some time saved up from coming in early so many mornings.

Yesterday I texted Declan the name of the restaurant and what time to meet. He'd replied with two whole letters: *OK.* It still felt a bit strange to be texting each other, but at least this way if he ended up running late or needing to cancel, he'd be able to reach me. Much as I really didn't want him to back out, I knew I'd be relieved to delay this conversation.

It was yet another one of those mornings where the minutes crept forward at an agonizing pace. I was jittery and once again had difficulty focusing. I got up and did some filing in the file room for a while. When that was done, I sat in Josh's office with him. He was the only person who knew Declan and I were supposed to have lunch today.

As soon as Josh noticed how nervous I was, he began teasing me and making me laugh, succeeding in taking my tension down a notch or two. I was surprised when he mentioned the framed photo I'd left in Declan's office. Apparently he'd been over there earlier to drop off a bottle of birthday booze and Declan had shown it to him. Josh assured me it was a smart idea because Declan couldn't feel weird about me spending money on him, since my gifts were homemade.

When I got back to my cubicle, the little red light was flashing on my phone. I hadn't realized how long I'd been away from my desk. Surprised, I discovered the message was from Declan, thanking me for the gifts and telling me he'd see me soon. I was still anxious about our impending conversation, but hearing his voice and knowing I'd made him smile, knowing that he was looking forward to spending time with me, made me feel better.

I still had an hour to go until I could leave, and that final hour— well, let's just say I noted every single minute passing. When at last it was nearly over, I got up and went to the ladies' room to check my make-up, reapply my lip-gloss and freshen my antiperspirant. Nervous sweat was pretty low on the list of things I wanted to smell like. At that thought, I retrieved a small bottle of my favorite perfume from my purse and rubbed some on the inside of my wrists. Now that I was leaving the office, the scent couldn't offend anyone's delicate sensibilities.

Taking one last appraisal in the large mirror above the sinks, I decided I looked nervous. Cute, but nervous. Hopefully Declan wouldn't notice.

How was I ever going to get through saying what I wanted to say to him? There was no way to avoid the fear, but I didn't want to stammer and come across like some crushing fourteen-year-old girl. A glass of wine could help, so I decided to save discussing any sensitive topics until after I had some Merlot in me.

On my way back to my cubicle to power down for the day, I stopped in Josh's doorway to let him know I was leaving. His head tilted to one side as he scanned me up and down.

"You look great," he told me with a grin.

"Thank you. Wish me luck?"

"You don't need luck. Just tell him the truth. You'll be surprised how much easier things'll be between you once you're not keeping secrets anymore."

I sighed. "I hope so."

"You'll knock him dead, Amelia"

I laughed. "We'll see. Have a good afternoon. And if you need me…"

Josh's brows lifted.

"Don't call," I finished, grinning.

I shut off my computer, grabbed my jacket and headed straight to my car. I had no idea how many minutes it took to drive to the restaurant, but I'd allowed myself twenty.

With city traffic, it actually ended up taking closer to thirty. When I arrived at the address the website had given for *The Murano Bistro*, my mouth fell open in shock. It was on the main floor of the South Lynchburg Sheraton. A low knot snarled tight in my gut. I'd booked us lunch at a restaurant in a hotel. Where I intended to admit that I had more than just friendly feelings for him. *Crap*! What kind of a message was *that* going to send? That I planned to have him for

174

dessert? That was *so* not the impression I wanted to make, but there was little I could do about it now.

I spotted his unmistakable blue Mustang parked along one side, and I nudged my little car into an empty space nearby. As I got out and began to walk toward the front entrance my stomach dropped lower and lower as my nerves shot higher.

When I stepped into the lobby, I saw a small sign pointing the way to the bistro. Following it took me down a long hallway, and at the end I turned right and went along another. Then I took a left and wound around the indoor swimming pool. The scent of chlorine washed over me, and I saw a couple of kids splashing around. I went through a set of double doors, down another hallway and then took a right. If you're confused just reading this, imagine how perplexed I must have felt navigating it. The Sheraton couldn't have put their restaurant in front by the parking lot like every other hotel? I was starting to wonder if this place would be like finding the Minotaur at the center of the labyrinth. Smiling to myself, I imagined Declan as Theseus, slaying the dreaded horned beast to protect me.

At the end of the last corridor, I finally arrived at the entrance to *The Murano Bistro*. When I stepped inside, my eyes locked with Declan's as he approached me. He'd obviously been waiting.

"You made it," he smiled and pulled me into a hug right there in the foyer. I instantly lost my train of thought. His hands slipped around to the small of my back as naturally as if we touched each other every day. "I was afraid you might get lost trying to find it, like I nearly did," he said into my ear before stepping back and looking at me directly again.

He was wearing a light blue button-up that really made the color of his eyes pop. They just seemed to have an inner glow. I couldn't look away even if I wanted to.

"Happy Birthday," I managed to mumble.

"Thanks," he replied. "I listened to the CD on the way over. It's great!"

"I thought you might like it."

"I do. And the photo…I love it, Amelia. I already know exactly where it's going to hang." His eyes sparkled with happiness.

"Where?" I asked.

"On the wall in my office, so I can see it every day. It'll help to remind me what I put up with all the shit at work for. And of the thoughtful woman who gave it to me."

A hug and a genuine thank you from a cheerful Declan—what more could I ask for? Yet I was still completely freaked out. My palms were cold and damp with fear.

"Shall we find a table?" I asked shyly.

He turned to the hostess and told her we were ready to sit down. She led us to the back of the nearly empty restaurant. Apparently I hadn't needed to worry about privacy after all. We sat adjacent to each other at a square table, which put him much closer to me than I'd imagined the many times I'd played out this scene in my mind. Instead of looking at Declan, I picked up the menu and tried to study it. I wasn't hungry in the slightest, but I knew I should probably try to eat something. It was difficult to think about unimportant things like food.

We made small talk until the waiter took our orders and brought us each a glass of red wine. I took a sip, and as I swallowed, I realized the time had come for me to begin.

Here goes everything.

Chapter 18

Amelia

With a deep breath, I reached over and squeezed Declan's wrist. My fingers felt like ice.

"You're freezing," he observed with a small frown.

"Yeah. It's 'cause I'm super nervous." I pulled my hand back into my lap to clutch its partner.

"What've you got to be nervous about? Do I make you nervous?" And then he smiled that smile, the one that always made my heart race.

"Yes." I couldn't be more honest than that. "I need to tell you something, and it's…not an easy thing to spit out."

His eyebrows flew up. "I'm not sure I like the sounds of that."

"It's nothing bad," I assured him, understanding how much crappy news the poor guy had gotten over the past few months. "Honest."

"Then what is it? Don't keep me in suspense." His mouth curved into that half-smile as he looked at me expectantly.

My fingers, as they so often did, found the pendant of my necklace. With my other hand, I raised my wine glass and took a big drink. It was difficult maintaining eye contact with him for any length of time.

"You're freaked out," he observed in a low voice. "And you're making me freaked out just watching you. Amelia, please tell me what's going on."

All other sounds in the restaurant were drowned out by the cacophony of my throbbing heart. I tore my eyes from his again and pressed my lips together. How to even begin?

Swallowing thickly, I forced myself to speak. "You know how we were talking a while back about meeting up in Richmond? Going out for drinks together some night? And you were going to get a hotel room so you wouldn't have to drive after?"

I glanced at him and saw his brows draw together in confusion. "Yeah?" he replied cautiously.

I couldn't tell if he had any clue where I was headed with this, so I floundered on. "If we'd done that…gone out together like that…I might have…" I stopped and reached for my wine again, taking another gulp of the tart goodness. My fingers were clammy against the glass.

"You might've what?" He wasn't smiling anymore; his face was very serious. He was staring at me like he was trying to look right inside my head.

I had to look away. His expression was just too much. Sighing, I forced the words out in a rush. "Imighthavekissedyou," I whispered to my hands, once again clutched tight in my lap.

Declan was silent. I didn't peek up to see his reaction; I couldn't bear to. The silence stretched out until it felt taut as a rubber band. Once the tension became too much and it snapped back into place, I knew it would be me who'd get stung.

The waiter picked that moment to bring over our salads and give us a temporary reprieve. Relieved by the distraction, I drank some more wine and picked up my fork to dig in. It was something to focus on that wasn't Declan, or what I'd just admitted to. I still couldn't look at him.

As I chewed, I noticed that he hadn't touched his own food. I knew he was staring at me. I swear I could feel him willing me to look up at him, and I fought off the urge to give in.

Before I could take a second bite, he put his hand on my forearm to prevent me from stabbing more leaves. "Amelia…"

I darted a glance his way, quick as a blink, before I focused back on the bright green spinach in front of me. Was that worry I saw in his eyes? Pity? Understanding? I didn't know and was way too terrified to find out.

"I feel it, too," he said quietly, squeezing then releasing my arm.

My eyes shot back to his, and this time I forced myself to not tear them away. "You do?" I breathed.

"Yes. This connection we have between us? I'm not gonna tell you I don't feel it, because I do."

I just stared at him, waiting for the other shoe to drop.

He didn't make me wait long.

"The old me would have jumped at the chance to be with a woman like you. Hell, the current me wants to more than you know. But...I'm married. You're married. And I don't think I could live with myself if we did." His voice sounded off a little, like he was trying to force it to normalize and not quite succeeding.

"I know," I said, breaking eye contact again. "I feel guilty enough already just saying it out loud. But I had to tell you. I couldn't stand keeping it locked inside any longer."

"I'm sorry," he told me. And though I knew he meant it, I still felt sick hearing the words. "I mean, I could play the 'What If' game all afternoon, but it wouldn't change anything. I just...can't."

I laughed ruefully. "Go ahead. Ask me whatever you want."

He considered me for a long moment. Then: "What if...I had said, 'Let's go get a room right now'?"

I chewed my lip as I contemplated my answer. "Honestly? I would've considered it. But that's not why I asked you here today, not at all. I just wanted to talk."

"Really?" Declan smiled that sexy smile of his, and my heart began to gallop. I wondered if he was picturing what us getting a room here might entail. I know I was.

I waited for his next question.

"Okay. What if I'd said, 'Let's leave our spouses and run off together'?"

I sighed, looking down at my nearly untouched salad. Scott's face flashed into my mind, and the thought of breaking his heart. My throat tightened. "I don't want anyone to get hurt. I don't want to destroy your family, or mine. I just can't deny how I feel anymore." I

179

sucked in a frustrated breath. "God, I sound like a horrible person. You must think I'm the worst wife in the world."

Closing my eyes, my chin dropped to my chest. I became overcome by the need to escape this stifling room and the man staring at me. Where was the nearest washroom again? There'd been so many fricking *hallways*.

"Amelia, look at me. Please," he begged.

Raising my head, I forced my eyelids open and looked straight into those dangerous blue eyes. Why did that particular shade of blue have to pierce my soul so much?

"I don't think you're a horrible person. I don't. I've thought about you so much over the past few months I've lost count. Believe me, I'm not judging."

I frowned and started to rip my gaze away again, but before I could, he grabbed my wrist once more, insisting on my attention.

"I was single until I was twenty-nine. Where were you then?" he whispered, eyes locked on mine, and there was so much raw feeling in his words that my heart hurt.

Tears threatened. I closed my eyes and inhaled deeply, trying to force my overpowering emotions back into their cage where they so clearly belonged.

I'd thought getting all this off my chest would make things easier. I'd thought that, if for some crazy reason I discovered he felt the same way, it would lighten this weight that dragged me down, and make me happy.

But I was wrong on both counts. Learning he was attracted to me but refused to act on it because his guilt would be unbearable, after I'd just admitted I might give in, made me feel smaller than I'd ever felt before. Knowing we both felt this intense connection to each other, but our complicated circumstances would probably always keep us apart, was far more painful than I could have ever imagined.

I wanted to run away. I wanted to dig a hole in the floor and bury myself in it. I wanted to vanish into thin air and erase any memory of this conversation from his mind.

Instead I said, "So, what now?"

He looked pensive. "We're friends. That doesn't need to change. I don't want it to change."

I laughed, a short derisive snort. "I just admitted I wanted…more, and you shot me down. Which you were entirely right to do. Everything's already changed."

"Don't," he said firmly.

Glancing at him, I asked, "Don't what?"

"Don't do that. Don't close down on me like that. I want…I want the same thing you want. But we can't. You know we can't. Don't punish me for it. Don't stop being friends with me because of it." There was no doubting the crack in his voice that time.

His fingers were still on my wrist. I needed him to pull them away. I needed him to never let me go. I needed so many things from him I could never have.

I shook my head doubtfully. "How can ever I face you in the office after telling you this stuff?"

Declan narrowed his eyes and seemed to make a decision. Standing up, he tightened his grip on me, tugging me to my feet. "C'mon. Let's go talk somewhere more private." He threw some money on the table, and I followed him out of the restaurant. He didn't drop my arm.

Glancing into some of the public rooms as we walked past, he finally pulled me into a Games room. It had a pool table, an air hockey table, and some retro video games around the walls. More important, it was deserted.

He turned and stared at me with heat smoldering in his eyes. If I didn't know better, I would've sworn he was about to kiss me.

Letting go of my wrist at last, he sighed. "I know this sucks. Believe me, I know. This whole goddamn situation sucks. But I need you. You're the best thing that's ever happened to me in that office."

"What about Josh?" I asked, only half joking.

He smiled, but there wasn't much humor behind it. "Okay, yes, you and Josh. But Josh and I don't share this kind of intense connection I feel with you." His smile fell away, and he dragged one hand over his face and through his hair, giving it that just-fell-out-of-bed look. I had a crazy urge to smooth a few of the wilder pieces back down for him.

"Declan…" I started.

"No, I know. I know. We're both feeling pretty overwhelmed right now. Just promise me…promise me you won't make any rash decisions. Let's just take a bit of time to think things over."

"Okay," I agreed softly. "I can do that."

Suddenly he pulled me to him and wrapped his arms around me. My hands made their way seemingly of their own accord over his shoulders to rest on the nape of his neck, the ends of his hair tickling the backs of my wrists. As he bent his head and pressed his face against the side of my own neck, my fingers begged to thread through his thick hair and drag his mouth up to mine. Somehow, I resisted. Having his lips where they were was torture enough.

"I don't want to lose you from my life. I can't," he mumbled, his breath a furnace against my skin. And then he kissed my throat. At least I think he did; it all happened so fast, and my mind was frantically buzzing with everything we'd already said and done. Maybe he didn't plant a quick kiss to my neck. Maybe it was all in my head. But I swear he did.

Declan pulled away and looked down at me, cheeks flushed, eyes slightly hooded.

"You won't," I assured him. "Don't worry. I'm not going anywhere."

Yet another promise I wouldn't be able to keep.

Declan

When I got home after work, I gave my daughter a big hug and kiss before pouring myself two generous fingers of scotch from the bottle Josh had given me. I felt like my nerves had been put through the fucking wringer, yet my day was far from finished. James was at my place already, though I didn't have to take him up to Charlottesville until Sunday. He wanted to spend my birthday with me, and I knew he assumed this would be his one and only chance. Miriam had stayed behind in Buffalo to work, but she'd be down to visit in another week or so.

The four of us went out for dinner to celebrate—because it was expected of me, not because I particularly wanted to. I slipped into the father/son/husband role I had lately grown accustomed to, but what I really wanted more than anything else on the evening of my thirty-fifth birthday was some time alone to drink myself into a stupor and obsess over my afternoon with Amelia. It was doubtful any me-time would be in the cards tonight though.

After dinner and a rousing chorus of 'Happy Birthday' that had my family dissolved into giggles, we went back to the house, and I tucked Alexis into bed. James went in to say goodnight to her and I headed for the master bedroom where I found Laura changing.

She straightened and came over to me, slipping her arms around my neck. I couldn't help it; my entire body stiffened at her touch. She didn't seem to notice. Leaning into me, she whispered seductively, "Don't be too late gabbing with James tonight. I have a little birthday something for you later."

I swallowed and stepped back. Forcing a smile her way, I left without replying and headed for my office. I shut the door behind me and walked to the window, gripping the wooden sill in my fingers as I stared into the night. What the *fuck* was wrong with me?

Though the frequency had decreased due to our ongoing disagreements, it's not like I'd stopped having sex with my wife. We still did, although it had become a mostly wordless encounter, done in the dark, with far less affection than we used to share. She knew I was unhappy about her career choices, but she was also fully aware I had a high sex drive, and that she was a desirable woman. It had never taken her much to get me going. Passion's a funny thing sometimes—it isn't always about desire; anger or stress can trigger it, too.

But after such a revealing and emotional discussion with Amelia earlier, Laura's invitation for a birthday romp didn't appeal to me in the slightest. I only wanted to go downstairs and spend an hour or two shooting the shit with James, then find some place quiet where I could contemplate everything that'd gone down. I knew something had to have changed drastically if I had zero interest in sex with my hot wife. Again, I mentally chastised myself. Something was seriously fucking wrong with me.

No, scratch that. I knew *exactly* what was wrong with me, and she was a pretty co-worker with big brown eyes. Who was completely off-limits.

Sighing, I shook my perplexing issues off and went downstairs where I found James in the living room watching hockey. Pouring us each a drink, I joined him on the couch.

"How you feeling?" I asked, handing him his glass.

He glanced at me and shrugged. "Same old."

"Headache again?"

"Yeah."

We watched the game in silence for a while, although I wasn't really taking in much of it.

Taking a sip of his whiskey, James said, "You don't have to stay down here with me, you know. Go spend some quality time with your wife on your birthday."

At first I didn't reply. Then I just muttered, "I'm good."

James set his glass on the table and turned to face me. "Look, I realize we still don't know each other all that well. And I know I haven't been a father to you for very long, and probably have no right to stick my nose in. But I'm not blind yet, Declan—I know when two people aren't connecting. I lived through it with my ex, and needless to say it didn't end well. I know guys don't like to talk about personal stuff much, but I want you to know I'll listen without judgment if you ever feel like sharing."

I stared at him, my insides swirling the whiskey in my stomach until I felt a little queasy. He flashed a smile and turned back to the hockey, obviously giving me the option of ignoring his little speech. And for a while I tried to do just that. I resumed watching the game with him until the Sabres finally pulled their heads from their asses and scored a last minute tie-breaker to win.

"On that happy note," James announced, standing up and stretching, "I'm heading to bed. Hope you've had a good birthday."

"Wait," I stopped him. He lifted a quizzical eyebrow at me and dropped back to the couch.

"You're right," I admitted. "Things between Laura and me are...strained...these days."

"I'm listening."

Sighing, I began to tell him about my relationship with her: how we met, the unexpected pregnancy, our wedding, Alexis' arrival, and my wife's increasing focus on her career. I finished by explaining the offer to cover the maternity leave in New York City, and how she'd already unofficially accepted the contract before even talking to me about it.

James looked thoughtful. "I see. And now you're just waiting for her to announce she got the official offer and when she's leaving, right?"

"Yep," I said. "It's only a matter of time."

"Maybe she'll surprise you?"

"Not likely. This kind of opportunity at a big network is what she's been waiting for since before I met her. I'm sure she feels torn, and I know she loves us, but in the end, her career will take precedence. I know it will." My jaw clenched as I stared between my knees at my clasped fingers. From what I understood, it was basically a done deal already.

"Okay. Suppose you're right. Then what? Will you support her? Or will you hold it against her?"

I glanced up at him. "It's not a matter of me not supporting her. Sometimes I feel like all I ever *do* is support her. It's that she's hardly around for Alexis as it is, and accepting this job in New York will only increase that separation. She claims she'll be home every weekend, and she probably will be. For a while. Until it becomes every other weekend, because of some big event she has to cover. Things will come up that are more important than us, I guarantee it."

Swiping a hand over my face in frustration, I added, "Is it so wrong for me to want her to prioritize her daughter over her fucking job?"

James looked at me for a few seconds, brows drawn in tight. "I can't help noticing you keep talking about all this with regard to Alexis. Which is important, absolutely, but what about how it affects you?" Those eyes so much like my own seemed to see right through me.

I didn't reply right away. I didn't know how to answer that. Finally I said, "This is not about me, or my needs not being met. I'm not *that* selfish. My frustration is at how her actions affect our daughter. She's just a kid. She needs her mother around."

"I know, and I get that. But you're more than just a father, Declan. You're one half of a couple. And you're feeling like you're pulling far more than your share of the weight, not just in raising Alexis, but in your entire relationship. And I can tell you're backing off, distancing yourself so Laura going to New York will hurt less if it happens." His voice softened. "Am I wrong?"

I heaved another frustrated sigh. "No, you're not wrong. But there's so much more going on right now than just that stuff. This situation with her is only the goddamn icing on the cake. And I have no control over any of it. Laura. Ryan." I paused, then added quietly, "You." *And Amelia.* Underlying it all lay how I felt about Amelia, and the complex combination of guilt and pleasure it brought.

"Me," he said. "Yes, then there's me."

"You are not a problem, James. I'm glad to have you here. Really," I assured him.

"I'm glad to be here, too. It just pains me to see you under so much stress. If you were to ask me—which I realize you haven't—it seems re-connecting with Laura would be the easiest of those issues to remedy. Why don't you go upstairs and talk to her?"

I smiled, but it wasn't a happy one. "Hmm. Thanks for listening. I appreciate knowing your thoughts. I guess it's probably time we both turned in."

"Good plan. And I'm always available to listen. 'Night, Declan."

"Goodnight."

James made his way to the guest room and I trudged upstairs. From the hallway I noticed a lamp was still on in our bedroom. I stared at that glowing yellow strip under the door and debated whether or not I really wanted to go inside. Mentally bracing myself, I eased the door open a few inches until I could see the edge of our king-size bed. Laura was under the covers with her back to me. From the even sound of her breathing, it seemed she was already asleep.

Relief coursed through me. I wondered what kind of a man it made me that I felt so relieved I didn't have to talk to my wife tonight—or make love to her. Probably not a very good one.

I gently pulled the door closed again and went down the hall to my office. Instead of sitting at my desk, I flopped into the easy chair in the corner, tilted it backward and raised the footrest. Pressing my head into the soft leather, I thought about my very interesting thirty-fifth birthday.

I went over every word, every stare, every touch of my hour and a half with Amelia. I remembered the feel of the curves of her body pressed against mine. I recalled how hot the skin of her neck had been under my lips. It had felt right. It had felt natural.

She'd confessed to me that she had feelings for me. That she wanted to kiss me. That she wanted *more*. And though we'd both agreed we could never go there, I knew I wanted those things, too.

I wanted more.

And I couldn't have more. *We* couldn't have more.

And it was the worst feeling in the world. Because deep inside me was a voice screaming that what I felt for her wasn't wrong at all. It was right.

Really, really right.

Chapter 19

Amelia

The day after Halloween started like any other weekday. I got up. I went to work. I prayed that I wouldn't run into Declan. Well, okay, that part was different, but every other aspect of that Friday in the office was pretty typical. Forgettable, you'd assume.

I drove home and made dinner. As we ate, we had mundane conversation about Scott's students' projects, and the guy his sister was dating. I complained a bit about Diana's latest annoying assignment, and we both speculated on when Josh would propose to Holly.

Afterward, we sat down in the rec room to watch a movie together, me stretched out on the couch and Scott in the easy chair. Everything seemed normal. Everything felt like it always did. I had no idea my world was about to be turned completely upside down.

The phone rang.

Scott reached to answer it. I vaguely heard him say "Hello?" but I was focusing on the movie and hoped the interruption would be quick. He sucked in a sharp breath. As I glanced over at him curiously, he exclaimed, "Shit, no!" His eyes were wide and he stared at me in clear dismay.

A sharp bolt of dread stabbed me in the chest as I looked back at him. Something was wrong.

"Scott?" I asked, a quiver in the word.

He was listening to the other end of the line. In a stunned voice he said, "Let me put her on." After another dragging pause, he told them, "We'll be right there." Slowly, dazedly, he replaced the phone onto its base and turned to me. His eyes were glistening.

"What? Scott! What is it?" My tone was piercing and edgy and filled with terror.

"Ames, sit down," he said gently.

"I am sitting!" I yelled. Then I realized I'd leapt to my feet, so I dropped back to the couch. He came over and sat beside me, reaching to envelop both my hands in his large ones.

"I don't know how to tell you this," he began. The tears he'd been fighting escaped and began trailing down his cheeks. The only time I'd ever seen Scott cry had been on our wedding day, and those had been happy ones. My own eyes welled up in response.

"Your dad…" he whispered, and I instantly understood. My hand flew to my mouth in an attempt to stifle a wail. It was no use—it erupted from me loud and long, like a banshee's cry in the night.

Daddy!

"Nonononononononononononono!"

Everything after that was a blur. Scott pulled me into his arms and told me my father had collapsed after dinner, and my mom had found him unresponsive on the living room floor. The paramedics arrived fast, but this time they'd been too late to save him.

I was distraught, irrational. I scraped my nails through my hair. I cried, "Why didn't she want to talk to me? Why did she just hang up without talking to me?"

He had no answers.

We drove to my parents' house in stunned silence. By the time we arrived, I was nearly catatonic. The tears that had begun at the sight of Scott's just would not stop; they streamed down my face relentlessly. I barely spoke a word to my mother, or to Scott, or to the neighbors who stood in the living room I'd grown up in, consoling my mom with inane platitudes. I just stood there staring at the floor where my father had taken his last breath.

Suddenly I found I could barely take enough of my own. My lungs were so tight they had no room for silly things like oxygen. Gasping softly, I ran upstairs to my former bedroom. I fell onto the bench and pushed the window wide open, letting the cool November air rush over my sweat dampened skin. I sucked it back in huge, desperate huffs, but no matter how much I inhaled, it was never enough. There was a strange keening noise in the distance. It took me several long minutes to realize that sound was coming from me.

I heard the door open and Scott pad across the carpet toward me. The bedsprings creaked as he sat down. I ignored him.

"C'mon," he said. "I'll take you home. There's nothing more we can do here tonight."

Shaking my head wildly back and forth, I said, "No. No, I'm staying. You go." I had no idea whose voice that was, but it sure didn't sound anything like mine.

I expected him to protest, to come over and try to hug and comfort me like I knew he wanted to. But thankfully he understood that I didn't want sympathy or support from him right now. He just whispered, "If that's what you want." Reaching over to rub the top of my knee, he told me he was sorry, and that he loved me. And then he left me alone.

For a while I remained motionless on the window seat. I remembered sitting there as a child with my dad, snuggled up in his arms as he read to me. I could still hear him stumbling over the tongue-twisters in *Fox in Socks* and us both giggling hysterically. There'd been so many times we'd talked and played and laughed in this room.

I stood and went to my old bed, pulling back the quilt to curl up underneath. My tears dampened the pillow beneath my cheek. They refused to let up. I thought sleep would be impossible, but I was wrong. I drifted off in no time at all.

I wish I could say it was dreamless.

When I woke the next morning, at first I had no idea where I was. Cheerful sunlight streamed through my bedroom window and across the foot of my bed. Then it came flooding back and I gasped, feeling like I'd been sideswiped by the news all over again.

I pushed back the blankets and got up, shivering. I'd left the window open all night. Closing the sash, I pulled the curtains tight against the sun. It had no right to shine today. My sorrow begged for rain, dark and gloomy showers to prove God mourned right along with me.

There was a bag just inside the door with pajamas, toiletries, and clothing. I assumed Scott had dropped it off after I'd fallen asleep. Grateful for his thoughtfulness, instead of returning to my warm bed as I'd planned, I stripped off yesterday's clothes and headed into the adjacent bathroom for a shower.

Saturday passed in a blur of funeral arrangements and offered condolences from both friends and strangers. When it was just my mother and me, we barely spoke. I kept myself occupied by cleaning. Scrubbing out the bathrooms, vacuuming the rugs, dusting the knick-knacks that cluttered the living room—it made the hours when we weren't making funeral decisions or dealing with sad and well-meaning visitors pass faster.

Scott showed up just before lunch with take-out from Finnegan's, but I was already cutting sandwiches and telling Mom she needed to eat. He seemed surprised to see me up and functional, and at my mother's insistence sat down to eat with us.

He assured me he'd already called Josh and asked him to let Diana know what had happened, and that I'd be out of the office all of next week. Josh had asked Scott to let him know the service information once it was finalized. I replied that we'd already booked them. The visitations were tomorrow and the funeral would be held on Monday.

After lunch, Scott drove us over to Blair and Sons Funeral Home. *One of Declan's client's*, I thought idly as I stepped from the car. I wondered if he'd hear about this from Josh, and if he would show up at one of the services. Even through all my fog and grief, there was a tiny part of me deep inside that still perked up at that.

I knew this was going to be the really not fun bit. We needed to make detailed arrangements, sign documents, craft an obituary, choose flowers and a casket. My head hurt just thinking about it.

As it turned out, my mother made all the decisions, so I didn't have to contribute much. But when it came time to go downstairs and select a coffin, something in me balked. I got as far as the second to last step. Then I saw the rows of caskets: wooden ones in every shade, different colored ones, stainless steel ones, even child-size pink and blue ones in the back. Suddenly all I could envision was my dad lying inside one of them, eyes closed, white quilted satin pillow under his head. Being lowered into the cold, hard ground in one of those tight, narrow boxes. Locked shut and buried six feet under. Where I'd never ever see his face again.

I clapped a hand over my mouth to stifle my gasp. I managed to tell Scott I needed some air before rushing back upstairs and out the back door. Finding a secluded corner of the building to lean against, I squeezed my eyes shut and pressed the back of my head against the cold brick. I sucked in breath after breath, but I just couldn't seem to get enough. My heart jack-hammered. My chest felt tight to the point of pain. I fell to a squat against the wall. Was I having a panic attack?

After a minute or two, the invisible bands squeezing my ribcage eased up. As the sweat dried on my wind-chilled skin, I got to my feet, squared my shoulders, and made my way back inside.

Later that evening after dinner, when it was again just my mom and me, I finished clearing the dishes away and joined her in the living room. She was wrapped up in one of those angsty serial dramas on television.

I sat down beside her and watched it with her for a while. The melodramatic dialogue and overwrought characters made little sense to me, but my mind was too distracted to pay much attention to the plot.

During a commercial I asked, "So what are you going to do now?"

Mom seemed surprised. "Watch the rest of this, finish my wine, and go to bed."

"You know what I mean. Will you stay here?" I wondered if she'd sell the house, and a pang of sadness hit me at the thought. But I presumed it would be too much for her, both mentally and physically, to continue living here alone.

She glanced over at me. "Yes, I think so. For now, anyway."

I nodded. An issue for another day then. "Do you need anything else tonight?"

"No, thanks. I appreciate all your help today, Amelia. I know this is really tough on you." She patted my arm.

Tears welled up again. They were never very far away anymore. Twenty-four hours. It had only been twenty-four hours. Maybe this time last night he had still been alive.

"I just...I can't..."

"I know," she admitted. "Me, too."

Then I did something I hadn't done in very a long time. I hugged my mother tight and told her I loved her.

Declan

"What?" I exclaimed, my heart plummeting. "You're shitting me!" It was about nine on Monday and Josh sat in my office. He'd just told me the news about Amelia's father.

"I wouldn't shit you about something like this, Declan. The funeral is this afternoon, one o'clock at Blair and Sons in Swann's Landing. Come with me?" He didn't look like he would take no for an answer.

"I have a, uh, client meeting at noon, but I'll...um..." I swallowed thickly. "I'll meet you there."

After he left, I blew out a long exhalation. Poor Amelia. My heart went out to her. I knew how close she'd been with her dad, and I knew she'd be just devastated. Right now she needed the support of her friends, and I thought I probably still fit into that category. No matter what we'd said to each other last week, or how weird things may or may not be between us at the moment, I knew I should go. It was the right thing to do.

The problem was, I hadn't stepped foot into a funeral parlor since my mother's service when I was seven. Even driving past them made me shudder. Yes, I had one as a client, but Levi Blair and I always met in coffee shops when we did business. The very thought of going into one of those places, smelling all the flowers, seeing the dead person all painted up and on display in a wooden box for everyone to gawk at, hearing the mourners whisper and sob over the loss of their loved one—it made my panic buttons flare.

But I had to do this. I had to go support Amelia.

I buried myself in work, focusing all my attention on replying to e-mails, booking appointments, and dealing with client concerns. It only worked for so long. Before I knew it, it was time to leave for Swann's Landing.

As my Mustang closed the distance to my destination—at a far slower pace than I usually drove, I might add—I tried not to think about where I was headed. Singing along to the radio, fidgeting between stations, tapping my fingers restlessly against the steering wheel—I did anything and everything to distract myself. The urge to pull right the fuck over and make a giant U-turn tugged at me, but I fought it. I really wanted to be there for her.

My tires crunched in the gravel as I pulled into the crowded parking lot of Blair and Sons. As the service was about to start, the lot was nearly full. I saw the backs of a few black suits and dresses disappear inside the front doors.

I eased the nose of my car into the last spot in the far back. At first I couldn't even bring myself to get out. My heart was pounding. I took a few deep breaths and forced myself to open the door. My left foot lowered to the ground. Then, slowly, my right. Sighing, I stood up. I could do this. I could.

The strained notes of organ music from inside oozed out into the cool November air as I walked over the uneven gravel along the side of the building. My chest was tightening again, but I made myself keep going forward. Each step was more difficult than the last, like moving through water.

As I reached the corner of the front of the building, I caught a whiff of nauseatingly sweet flowers. And I pictured a coffin. A gleaming oak one, with large brass handles, the top third propped open and a woman's face clearly visible within. She had thick, black hair and deathly pale skin. And red lipstick—always the red lipstick. She'd reminded me of Snow White, awaiting her Prince Charming to come kiss her and awaken her. But real life wasn't anything like fairy tales. Even at my young age, I knew she wasn't going to wake up. She was gone. She wasn't ever coming back to me. And I needed her so bad.

A low gasp flew from my mouth and I clutched the brick wall for support. I wasn't a child anymore. I was a grown man. I could do this.

To my credit, I almost made it to the front door. Maybe if someone else had been outside and seen me, I would have been able to force myself to go inside. For appearance's sake, if nothing else.

But I was alone. Just as my foot hit the step to walk up to the porch and go through the front doors, I thought of James. And I realized this would be a prequel to what I'd have to go through myself in a few months. I imagined his face in that coffin instead of my mom's. And those desperate tendrils squeezing my chest snarled even tighter. My heart galloped out of control. I couldn't seem to get enough air. There was a rushing noise in my ears. Clutching desperately at the iron railing, I managed to steady myself. I felt like I was about to pass out.

And I'm not proud to admit it, but I fucking chickened out. As soon as I was able to get myself moving, I ran. You wouldn't think in that state I'd be able to run. You'd think, as I did, that I'd collapse into a fetal position on the pavement. But I didn't. I ran straight back to my car, jammed my key into the ignition, and sprayed loose gravel all over the parking lot in my haste to escape.

I never saw Amelia. I never saw Josh. And I felt like shit for being such a damn coward. I hated that I'd let them down, but I had to get the fuck away from that place as fast as humanly possible. I didn't care where I went—it just needed to be far from there. So I could breathe again.

Amelia

The days following my father's funeral seemed endless.

I stayed with my mother for a few more nights. Until she insisted she was fine, and that I go home and "take care of my neglected husband and get back to work." Her words. I rolled my eyes but did as she asked. Staying there kept me surrounded by memories of my dad, which was simultaneously comforting and excruciating. Mom was right—it was time to go home.

Scott had taken the Monday off work for the funeral, but he really couldn't take more time away from his students, so I found myself alone during the day. On Thursday there just weren't enough distractions to keep my mind occupied. Grasping a sudden wave of inspiration, I bundled up in a warm jacket and scarf, and drove out to the falls to go for a hike.

Dried leaves and twigs crunched under my shoes as I walked the narrow trail. My dad and I used to hike here was I was young, and I felt drawn to return on this sunny autumn day. I worked up a sweat as

I hiked, and the cool air felt heavenly on my overheated skin. Though there was no one with me, it didn't seem like I was really alone. I felt closer to him than ever.

The day of my father's funeral was little more than a hazy memory to me, a hazy, horrible, memory. The faces of the countless people who'd come up to offer condolences all blurred together. I'd shaken so many hands, accepted so many hugs. Very few of them had even really registered. I'd felt like an automaton, thanking them, telling them that my father would have appreciated it. I knew it was all a lie. What he'd have appreciated would've been still being alive, that's what he would have appreciated.

I paused under an ancient oak tree to take some deep, calming breaths. My eyes remained dry, amazingly. I wondered how long that would last.

Sam, Evan, and Kaitlyn had shown up, passing on the message that Diana'd had a meeting she couldn't miss. And Josh had come, of course. He'd whispered in my ear how strong he thought I was. There had been no sign of Declan. I'd been surreptitiously watching for him the entire time, hoping against hope he'd show up. I'd been searching for his face, for his presence to ground me, but he hadn't come. It was disappointing, but not really surprising.

We'd promised each other we wouldn't let our talk the previous week create awkwardness between us—*Oh God, was that only a week ago? It feels like so much longer*—but the truth was that it had, for me. Just two days in the office had passed since our lunch, but I'd studiously avoided going anywhere near the Sales department both days. I hadn't even left my desk at lunch, telling Kaitlyn I'd needed to finish something. I just couldn't bear the idea of facing Declan after confessing what I had.

Yet at my dad's funeral it had been his face I'd sought out. I don't even know why I'd hoped so much that he would come, but I had. And it hurt to discover he didn't think enough of me to be there.

I began walking again. Before long I was standing in the clearing near the base of the falls. A cold mist filled the air, dampening my clothing and skin. The roar of the water pounding against the rocks encompassed me. I swore I could feel the very earth trembling beneath my feet. If there was ever a place I could feel close to the spirit of my father, it was here.

On Friday morning I got up, got dressed and drove to Lynchburg. It had been a full week, or would be that evening, and I just couldn't stand to mope about home any longer. Work would provide a much-needed distraction, and when I returned Scott would be there, so I wouldn't have to spend much time alone. Which meant less time to think about things I wanted to avoid for a while.

My co-workers were surprised to see me in the office a day earlier than anticipated, and I accepted their condolences politely before throwing myself back into my workload. I wasn't really in the mood for chatting, and they seemed to understand. As expected, there was a backlog waiting for me. I embraced it wholeheartedly, if somberly. I still felt like I was drifting in an emotional fog, but concentrating on my calculations enabled me to cut through it and focus on the hard black and white of the numbers. And it worked, for almost the entire day.

When my phone rang toward the end of the afternoon, I was studying rows of figures searching for an error. I answered distractedly without glancing at the display.

"Accounting Department. Amelia York speaking."

"Amelia?" Declan sounded hesitant. "Surprised to hear you came in today."

I suppressed a sigh. Even now, even after everything I was dealing with, and everything we'd said to each other last week, just hearing his voice sent a wave of pleasure flooding through me. It was both annoying and wonderful.

"I needed to get out of the house."

"I'm so sorry," he said softly.

Yeah. But not sorry enough to find time in your busy schedule to reach out to me earlier, I thought sullenly. What I said was: "Thanks."

"Can you drop by before you leave? Please?"

A big part of me wanted to say no. The thought of seeing him in person after what had happened between us was daunting. So much had changed in just a week's time. But the pleading tone in his voice made me falter. Closing my eyes for a moment, I sighed, "I'll try. If I have time." Then I hung up. I knew it came out sounding kind of bitchy, but my emotions were in a stranglehold when it came to this man. And my father had just died. I had every right to be bitchy.

At 4:15 I powered down my computer, said my goodnights to my few lingering coworkers, and, with extreme trepidation, made my way to Declan's office. When I knocked on the edge of his door, he looked up and smiled, as he always did. Maybe it was just me, but his smile seemed a bit nervous.

He came to the door and glanced over my shoulder. Colleen had already left for the day, and I wasn't sure who he was looking for. Ushering me inside, he shut the door behind us. After everything, I was tempted to reach right back over and open it again. But I didn't.

In hindsight, perhaps I should have.

"I was heartbroken for you when I heard," he began. "I'm sorry I didn't make it to the service."

I lifted a hand, palm forward, in a 'stop' gesture. "It's okay," I said, my back stiff. "I was a bit busy. It's not like we would have had time to talk to each other anyway."

"No," he argued. "It's not okay. I should've been there. I tried. I got as far as the parking lot. And then I just…I kinda freaked out. My mom…and now, with James…"

Oh. *Oh*! I hadn't even thought of that. "Right. Of course. I get it, Declan. It's fine. It doesn't matter that you didn't come in."

"It does to me." Then he got up and tugged me out of the chair and into his arms. "I'm so, so sorry, Amelia. I know how much your dad meant to you. I know what it's like to lose a parent, and I wanted to be there for you, but when it came right down to it, I panicked. I failed you. And I feel awful about it. I don't want you to think I don't care, 'cause I do."

He held me tight. I could feel his breath in my hair. His aftershave was fresh and inviting like an ocean breeze. I retreated a bit to look him in the eyes, and his hands lingered on the small of my back. All my pain channeled into something else as I stared at him—something that took control of me. "I know you do," I murmured.

And I kissed him.

In my desperation, looking for something real and solid to tether my out of control emotions to, I kissed him.

And he kissed me back.

At first.

198

When I pressed my lips to his, he stiffened for a second. Only a second. Then he pulled my body against him, his fingers sweeping up my spine and into my hair. Angling his face, he opened his mouth to me, kissing me fully. He tasted a bit like coffee, but I didn't mind. I clung to him like he was the only lifeline in my darkness.

My hands crept to the sides of his neck and then up to cup his jaw. I got lost in him. My temperature skyrocketed. My heart raced. My nerves shot up flares. I couldn't stop myself; I moaned into his mouth.

Abruptly he pulled away. Turning his back to me, he clasped a hand over his face.

"No," he mumbled. "We can't. Not like this." He looked back at me, and his eyes said it all.

I crumpled inside.

Reading my reaction immediately, he grasped me by the upper arms and held me in place, preventing me from fleeing.

"Don't. Don't freak out. This? Us?" He gestured between us. "You're not thinking straight right now."

"Yes, I am. I know exactly what I want." I reached up and laid my palm against his cheek. "I want you," I whispered.

Declan stepped away from me once more, shaking his head in denial. "Your father just died, Amelia. When something as mindfucking as that happens, people don't make smart choices."

"This is the right choice. I know it is. And I know you feel it, too," I told him defiantly. My brain was going numb again, turning to ice.

A plethora of conflicting reactions played across his face in rapid succession. Then he sighed. "What I feel is not the point. Your emotions are all screwed up. They're not reliable. You shouldn't make any major life decisions when you're reeling from a loss. You'll only end up regretting it later."

As I stared at him, his words began to sink in. I thought about how much faith my dad always had in me to make the right choices, and I was ashamed. I frowned and took a step backward. Swallowing guiltily, I mumbled, "You're probably right."

"I know I am. Trust me."

"I'm so sorry," I said, reaching for the doorknob. "Not just for…this, but for everything I said last week, too."

"I won't accept any apologies. You have nothing to be sorry for," he assured me emphatically, but I knew different. "I'm glad we're close enough to be honest with each other, to trust each other. You mean a lot to me."

"My friendship, you mean?" I knew my cheeks were flaming.

He frowned, but replied, "Yes."

Pulling open his office door, I shouldered my purse. "Goodnight, Declan." I didn't look back as I walked away.

Chapter 20

Declan

Well, shit.

I sat in my office for a long while after Amelia left, staring at the portrait of James, Alexis and myself on the wall and thinking over what just happened.

She'd kissed me.

Fuck.

Amelia York had kissed me. And I'd kissed her back. Sure, I'd come to my senses and forced myself to put a stop to it, but *still*. I'd kissed her back.

And it had been *amazing*.

So now what was I supposed to do? Forget all about it? Not even remotely possible. I'd never forget *that* kiss for the rest of my life, no matter how long or short it may be.

There aren't even adequate words to describe what kissing Amelia had felt like. It felt like I wanted to do it again, that's what. And again. And again. I wanted to kiss her for so long and so deeply that hours would fall away and we wouldn't even notice. I wanted to kiss her until we passed out from exhaustion wrapped up in each other's arms. I wanted to kiss her and kiss her and kiss her some more, while doing other things to her, things that would elicit more noises like that soft little moan she'd made against my lips. Except louder.

God dammit! I wanted to punch something in the worst way.

I was so very, very fucked.

Instead of going straight home, I called the sitter and told her I'd be an hour late. Luckily, she didn't mind. I needed to go to the gym and work off some intense frustration.

Once I retrieved Alexis, we grabbed some take-out and went straight up to Charlottesville to pick up James after his first week of treatments. He looked a bit tired, but none too worse for wear.

By the time the three of us got back to the house, it was well into the evening. Alexis was yawning and begging Grandpa James to read her a bedtime story. Since I knew how much he missed her when he was away, I gave her a quick kiss and let him tuck her in.

Laura was working late again. When she got home, I was watching TV in bed, almost ready to pass out. I already had a pretty good idea of who'd be starring in my dreams.

She came into our room and perched on the edge of the bed, looking at me. "I'm going to New York next weekend."

Flicking off the television, I rolled to look at her. "Interview?" I asked dryly, arching a brow.

"Yeah." She went into the bathroom to brush her teeth. Once she was under the blankets, she turned to face me. "So are you going to be able to forgive me if I take this position? If I even get offered it, that is."

"Isn't this interview just a formality?"

"Probably. But I won't know for sure until I sign the contract. Answer the question, Declan."

"Will I forgive you?" I barked out a short, derisive laugh. "This has never been about me, Laura. It's about Alexis. And your unfailing ability to make career choices that keep you away from her." Rolling onto my back, I fixed my eyes on the ceiling.

"I wish you could try to see things from my point of view." She sounded frustrated. *Welcome to the club*, I thought.

"Oh, I do. I just don't happen to *agree* with your point of view." My voice was steely. Earlier, I'd felt guilty as hell for kissing Amelia back, but at the moment I didn't regret it one fucking bit.

Heaving a sigh, Laura muttered, "That's what I thought." Then she turned off the lamp and angled her body away from me.

I lay there staring up into the dark for a very long time before sleep finally drowned me in its blissful oblivion. Dirty dreams of forbidden kisses and illicit rendezvous were nowhere to be found.

Laura's weekend in New York came and went. She brought Alexis back a pink and black 'I Heart NY' t-shirt and claimed she'd had a fabulous time. I didn't ask any questions. No contracts seemed to have been offered or signed. Yet.

Thanksgiving came and went. We entertained the entire family at our house for dinner: Patrick, Ryan, Diana, even James and Miriam joined us. I'd told Patrick the prior weekend about meeting James, and he'd taken the news stoically, as I'd thought he might. When he'd gruffly told me he was glad for me, I didn't blow him off. I'd actually gotten the distinct impression he'd really meant it. Wonders never cease.

James had just completed his four weeks of treatment, and he and Miriam were heading back to Buffalo on Sunday morning. He was supposed to return to the Cancer Center in two weeks' time to go through another bout of tests, and then decide what the next step would be from there.

Ryan had one more week of rehab left, and then he'd be a free man again, although therapy sessions twice a week would continue for a few more months. Shocking to exactly no one at this point, he and Diana were seeing each other again. I wanted to be against it, but honestly I really couldn't. He seemed happy. I was happy for him.

As for things between Amelia and me, well…we weren't exactly avoiding each other, but—not going to lie—it'd been weird. I wished like hell we could somehow snap our fingers and go back to the comfort level we'd had with each other before, but in reality it just wasn't that easy. Neither of us went out of our way to spend time together anymore, not since the kiss. It saddened me, and I missed her, but I knew she needed time—time to grieve, time to think, time to work through everything. Christmas would be here before she knew it, and the holidays were undoubtedly going to suck ass this year. I'd decided to give her space until January, then once we were back to work again I'd make a point to instigate a chat. Some separation might help us both clear our heads.

It really fucking sucked, but I thought it was for the best. I filled the emptiness she left in my life with the usual things: clients, my daughter, my father, and my brother. Sometimes even my wife. But no matter what other distractions I had, they never completely worked. Even on the nights when I fell into bed too tired to think, dreams of Amelia would come. I could never let go of her at night, even when I managed to succeed for small periods of time during my waking hours.

It was a chilly December day. I'd had to scrape a thin layer of frost off the Mustang's windshield that morning, and I'd heard snow was in the forecast by the weekend. I sat in Josh's office spinning a pen in my fingers. I'd just finished telling him about James' next round of experimental treatment to further shrink his tumor that would start next month. Deciding to lighten the mood a bit, I switched to the topic of the approaching vacation.

"Are you taking Holly anywhere special for the holidays? Getting out of Swann's Landing for a break?"

"Yep," Josh replied, smiling. "The day after Christmas we're heading to the Bahamas for a week in the sun. I cannot wait. Sunshine on my skin, bottomless drink in my hand, and all the food I can eat. Sounds like heaven."

"It does," I agreed. "First vacation together—that's a big test of a relationship."

"Well, we already did a weekend away in October. That worked out so well I thought we'd try a whole week this time." His face grew serious. "She's the one, Declan. I'm gonna propose on Christmas morning. Already got the ring."

My eyebrows flew up. "Seriously? Wow, dude—major step there. Sure you're ready for 'til death do you part?'"

His grin stretched from ear to ear. "Yep, I'm sure. I'd even promise to obey if she asked me to."

"You'll be doing that either way," I smirked.

Laughing, he nodded. "Probably. So what are the holiday plans for the Kavanaugh household?"

"I'll be entertaining a house full of family most of the first week, and working from home and hanging out with Alexis the second. If work's as slow as I think it'll be, I might take her down to my cousin's place in Florida for a few days over New Year's."

"Just you and Alexis? Or Laura, too?"

I snorted. "Who the hell knows? She'll probably have to work, so I assume it'll just be the kiddo and me."

"Things still unresolved between you two?"

I flipped the pen into the air and caught it. "Her future career path is still not carved in stone. But she'll know any day now. Surprised it's taken this long."

"And then what?" Josh arched a eyebrow my way.

"Then my wife moves out for three months, that's what."

"You sure, man? You sure she won't turn them down?"

"It's her dream job. Why would she choose to stay in Nowheresburg with us when she could chase the bright lights and fame New York dangles? So she can co-anchor the evening news in Swann's Landing? Not fucking likely," I replied with an eye roll.

"She might surprise you, Declan. And even if not, you guys will still see her on weekends, right?"

I shrugged. "We'll see."

Josh's brows drew together as he studied at me. He opened his mouth as if he wanted to say something else, offer me some sort of platitude or advice I assumed, but then he shut it again.

"Okay," he said. "I hope things work out for you, buddy, I really do."

I did, too. The big question was what exactly 'working out for me' really meant anymore.

I got my answer to one of those questions that very evening.

I was in the kitchen tossing a salad to go along with the chicken roasting in the oven. Alexis sat on the couch in the living room watching *SpongeBob Squarepants,* and Laura wasn't due home for at least another half hour, maybe longer. So I was taken by surprise when I heard the front door open and my wife breeze in.

"Lex!" she called. "Want to go to Alessandro's for dinner? I'm taking us out!"

Alexis ran to greet her squealing, "Yes!" at the top of her little lungs.

My gut clenched at Laura's words. I knew right away why she wanted to go out, and I resented the hell out of her choice to tell us her big news together in a public place, instead of giving me the courtesy of a private head's up where I'd be able to react honestly.

With a frown, I turned off the oven and removed the half-cooked chicken. I was wrapping it up to put in the refrigerator when Alexis bounded into the kitchen shouting, "Daddy! We're goin' to 'Sandro's for pizza!"

"I heard," I replied with a forced grin.

Laura appeared in the doorway wearing a big toothy smile. "I thought we'd go out to dinner to celebrate."

"Celebrate what?" Alexis asked her.

"I'll tell you guys when we get there, sweetie. Go get your boots on."

As our daughter ran to the front closet, I glared at Laura. I opened my mouth to say something sarcastic, but before I could she'd spun on her heels to go help Alexis with her winter jacket.

Sighing, I put the meat in the fridge and joined them, determined to play the role of supportive—if taciturn—husband for the public part of our evening.

Alessandro's was a local favorite. Well known for their traditional Italian pizza and loud, family-friendly atmosphere, the place was packed. We waited more than twenty minutes before we were finally ushered through the noisy dining room to our table.

After the waiter took our order, Laura turned to Alexis. "Mommy has some amazing news, honey," she announced. I tensed all over. Alexis looked up at her mother with big eyes.

"Remember when I went to New York for the weekend last month?" Laura asked, digging in her bag and pulling out her iPad as she spoke.

Alexis nodded.

Laura turned it on and began to type. She angled the screen toward Alexis. "Remember this photo? That was the view from my hotel room. That's Central Park." She scrolled through some more shots. "And this is the Central Park Zoo. Would you like to go there?"

"Can we?" Her blue eyes shone with excitement.

"Definitely! And to a very huge, famous toy store called FAO Schwartz. And to see the Statue of Liberty." She pulled up photos of each to show Alexis.

"So cool! Can we go this weekend?"

I was getting more annoyed by the minute as I listened to my wife tempt our daughter with all the amazing things New York had to delight her with if she came to visit. These exciting ideas were being planted specifically to distract her from the fact that her mother would no longer be home during the week.

"Not this weekend, sweetie. But Mommy is going to be living there for a few months soon, and when you visit, we can do lots of fun things like this." She glanced up and met my eyes briefly before returning her gaze to Alexis.

"We're moving to New York? When?" She looked so thrilled, and it broke my heart.

"After New Year's." Laura took Alexis' small hands in hers. "You and Daddy are going to stay here, and I'll be going there during the week. But don't worry, we'll see each other every weekend, and we'll have so much fun when you guys come visit me. And it's not for forever. In three months I'll be back home again."

Alexis frowned. I could almost see the wheels turning inside her little head as she processed what her mother had just said. It was very tempting to toss my two cents in, but I knew it wouldn't be fair to affect my daughter's reaction to this big news. I forced my mouth shut and waited to see what she would say.

Finally a small smile broke over her face. "We can come visit you? And we can go to that toy store? And the zoo?"

Laura's grin widened in relief. "Of course!" She began to explain to Alexis how they would still be able to see each other every day using Skype to video chat, and how she could even read her bedtime stories over it. As expected, Alexis thought the idea of using Daddy's iPad to talk face to face with Mommy from bed every night was the coolest thing ever.

I sighed quietly. Laura was one smart cookie; there was no doubt about that. She'd known exactly what to say and do to win Alexis over to the idea of her leaving. She'd planned this all out, and it was working like a charm. But she wasn't going to be the one to have to comfort our not-even-four-year-old when she woke up from a nightmare at two in the morning and wanted her mother. She wasn't going to be the one to have to explain why Mommy couldn't make it home to visit this weekend because a news story broke that she needed to cover. Reading Alexis bedtime stories over Skype a few nights a week—because I knew damn well it wouldn't happen every night; hell, Laura barely found time for one story a week as it was—just wasn't going to cut it over the long haul.

The waiter, dressed like a gondolier in a black and white horizontal striped t-shirt and straw brimmed hat, arrived with our pizza. Laura tucked her iPad away and flashed me a smile as she began to dish up a slice for Alexis. I didn't smile back.

The entire drive home the two of them chatted excitedly about all the fun things they could do in the Big Apple when we came to visit. At one point Alexis exclaimed, "We can ride the subway! Won't that be awesome, Daddy?" and I agreed with her that yes, it would be pretty awesome. But mostly I kept my thoughts to myself.

Once we got back to the house, Laura made a special point of getting Alexis ready for bed and reading to her. When I went in to kiss her, she was already nearly out.

"Goodnight, pumpkin," I whispered, tucking the blankets up around her.

Her eyelids fluttered. "Are you sad, Daddy?" she asked sleepily.

I was momentarily taken aback. "No, baby girl, I'm fine," I assured her.

"Love you," she murmured, letting her eyes drift closed again.

"Love you, too." I kissed her forehead and tiptoed out of the room.

Now what was I supposed to do? Go into our bedroom and get into yet another argument with Laura? Head to my office to work or kill time on Facebook or watch television until so late she would be sure to be asleep when I came to bed? None of those felt right.

Instead I went downstairs, pulled my boots and coat back on and grabbed my keys. Slipping out the front door as quietly as I could, I hit the pavement. I walked around our neighborhood, and beyond, for hours. The night was cold and refreshing. Every breath I exhaled sent a puff of white into the air, and I crammed my hands deep into the pockets of my leather jacket. About a half hour from home, I realized I'd left my cell phone behind on my desk. But who the fuck would I call anyway? The only possible option was Josh, but what was I going to do? Bother him at home at this time of night to spew about my shitty evening? Not likely. Guys just didn't do stuff like that.

And to be completely honest, the voice I really wanted to hear more than any other, the only one who could possibly soothe my frazzled nerves and lighten my mood, wasn't even an option.

Amelia

So...yeah. I screwed up when I kissed Declan. I didn't want to regret it, because it was amazing—possibly the most amazing kiss I'd ever had in my life. He'd pulled me close, and kissed me back, and I knew he'd felt something. I wasn't sure about the extent of those feelings, whether they were mere physical attraction or if they went deeper, but they existed. And as I'd dreaded, things had been weird between us ever since.

We weren't as distant with each other as after I'd first hugged him. It wasn't like that. But we weren't friends the way we used to be, either. This time it was mostly my doing. The few times he'd invited me to come over and discuss a case, I'd asked him what he needed over the phone instead of dropping everything and heading to his office. He hadn't sat down with the group of us at lunch in nearly two months. The few e-mails we'd exchanged were work related, often with a polite 'how are you?' or 'hope life is good' tucked in there somewhere, but nothing more.

Things being awkward with Declan bothered me, but not as much as it had before. I'd been really struggling to deal with my father's death. Just when I thought I might be starting to get better, when I'd had a few days of near normalcy, it would hit me all over again, and I'd be down for the count crying my eyes out in the washroom.

It sucked. There was no other word for it. I missed my dad so much, and it sucked hard. I wasn't sure if I could ever truly feel happy again. Scott had suggested I speak to a grief counselor about it, and while I'd resisted the idea before, lately I was starting to think maybe he was right. Still, I hadn't picked up the phone to make an appointment.

Christmas was almost here. Normally I'd be full of holiday cheer and humming carols everywhere I went. This year I hadn't even put up our tree. Stockings were not hung by the chimney with care. Garlands didn't decorate the banister of the staircase. Mistletoe didn't dangle from the doorway to the kitchen. I'd told Scott I didn't want any presents. The only gift I'd purchased was a sweater for my mom. That's it.

I felt like Scrooge, but I couldn't seem to find it in me to care. Mostly, I just felt numb. If I'd had my way, I'd ignore Christmas completely and go hide somewhere alone to drink a toast or three to my dad.

But I'd recently found out Liv and Scott had been conspiring behind my back. A few days ago, they'd announced what I couldn't deny seemed like an awesome diversion. The four of us, Ben included, were heading off to Cancun on December 27th for a week of all-inclusive decadence. While I wasn't jumping up and down with excitement, I was relieved by the plan. Getting out of Swann's Landing over the holidays, and away from all the reminders of Christmases past, was just what I wanted.

So Josh was heading to the Bahamas, I was off to Mexico, and Declan was probably going to end up in Florida. All three of us would be spending New Year's Eve far away from home this year. And far away from each other.

When I got to my cubicle on the 24th, my last day in the office before vacation, I found a Starbucks gift card and a chocolate bar with a tiny silver Christmas bow stuck on top. There was no card, but I knew who they were from. A small ball of warmth started in my chest and expanded over me, as it always did when I knew he'd been thinking about me.

We may have been giving each other some necessary space lately, but Declan was still the brightest object in my orbit. And no matter what else I was dealing with, I didn't see that fact changing anytime soon.

Chapter 21

Amelia

The resort was beautiful. The days were sunny and hot. Both the ocean and pool were refreshing, and the ever-flowing fruity drinks kept my mind obliviously fogged most of the time. The food was delicious, and the people around me were cheerful. I, however, much as I tried to pretend otherwise, was not.

I was listless. I was distracted. Most of the time I was at least halfway drunk.

And no matter what I did to preoccupy myself, or how much I drank, I could not stop thinking about Declan.

I'd be perched on a stool at the bar with Scott, Liv and Ben, sipping a strawberry daiquiri and tuned right out of their conversation, because I was imagining I was with Declan instead. I'd be soaking up some sun on the beach with my eyes closed, pretending to sleep but actually fantasizing about Declan running across the hot sand after a dip in the ocean and dropping into the lounge chair beside me, laughing and shaking out his hair, deliberately splashing water onto my overheated skin.

I'd make excuses to go back to the room to change or grab something I'd forgotten, and I'd stretch out on the bed and pretend it was our room and he was lying beside me. I'd imagine we were spending the late afternoon making love and hiding from the rest of the world as the sun slowly extinguished itself into the sea.

My mind was lost in thoughts of him almost the entire trip. It was far better than thinking about home, and how once I returned I'd have to figure out how I was going to live the rest of my life without my dad.

New Year's Eve was spent at the resort's disco. The club was packed with mostly teens and twenty-somethings. Hot, sweaty, scantily-clad bodies closed in on us, gyrating to heavy beats. I chucked back a shot of ice-cold tequila and swayed to the music, the thumping bass reverberating in time with my heartbeat. Liv and I clutched each other drunkenly on the dance floor as we twisted and writhed, our skirts flaring out around us as we spun.

I was completely loaded. Time passed either in slow-mo or fast-forward, and midnight took me by surprise. A pair of strong arms wrapped around my waist from behind as the DJ lowered the volume and began the countdown. My eyelids slipped shut, I pressed my back into what I assumed was my husband's solid chest, and I pretended I was swaying with Declan. When the New Year arrived to deafening cheers, Scott spun me around and kissed me. I pulled him close, but didn't open my eyes.

In hindsight I'm not sure if it was good luck or bad, but right then a wave of nausea hit me, and I pulled away to rush to the washroom. After *that* unpleasant experience, which left me barely conscious and sobbing incoherently on the filthy tiles, Liv gathered me up and hauled me outside. Scott dutifully carried me back to our room and tucked me into bed before returning to celebrate with the others. I have no idea what time he got in.

For being in an exotic location with some of my favorite people, it ended up being one of the worst New Year's Eves of my life. Later on I realized that was because I couldn't be with either of the two people I most wanted to spend it with.

A few afternoons later, as we lay on our beach chairs sunbathing and reading while the boys played pool volleyball, Liv turned to me. "You okay? You've seemed kinda out of it this week."

I looked up from my magazine. "Not really," I mumbled truthfully. It's not like I didn't have a really good excuse for not being my usual self.

"You wanna talk about it?"

I considered it; I really did. The beginnings of a buzz from the margarita I was sipping had me on the verge of blurting out that I felt like I was on vacation with the wrong man. Somehow I managed to hold my tongue. Liv would only worry, and I really didn't want to make her more concerned than she already was.

Rolling over and sitting up, I dug into my beach bag for my sunscreen. As I squeezed out a large white dollop and began to rub it onto my shoulders, I said, "I know you're worried about me. And I appreciate that. I just…I just miss him so much." My heart ached at the admission. A surge of guilt hit me as I realized Liv assumed I meant my father, and though I did miss him terribly, it was Declan's face that had come to mind.

"I know you do, hon." She rubbed my shoulder. "Scott's worried about you, too. Have you given any more thought to seeing a counselor?"

Frowning, I lay back down and closed my eyes below my sunglasses. Just how much talking about me did Scott and Liv do when I wasn't around? And did I even care? I lifted my drink and took a long pull from the straw. Deciding I really didn't give a crap about much of anything right now, I said, "I don't know if I can talk to a stranger about this stuff. Maybe. I'll think it over more when we get home."

The sun blazed hot on my skin. Reading no longer interested me. I felt sweat-sticky and sunscreen-greasy. Instead of jumping into the pool to cool off, I decided it was time to go shower and steal a few moments for myself. Slurping down the rest of my drink, I began to pack up my things.

"Can you tell Scott I've gone to back to our room to lie down? I'll see you guys later for dinner."

Liv gave me a nod and small smile before focusing back on her book. She knew better than to push when I clearly wasn't ready, and I loved her for that. I trekked along the winding path to the low building where our rooms were located.

By the time I stepped out of the shower, the after-effects of the tequila had sunk in nicely. For some unfathomable reason I decided it'd be a good idea to freshen up my make-up before I laid down, so when it was time to meet the others I'd only have to throw on a dress and sandals and go.

I picked up my compact and brush and began to apply blush to my sun-kissed cheeks. As I stepped nearer to the large mirror behind the sink to get a closer look, my heel slid in a wet spot on the tile. Shooting forward, I lost my balance, instinctively grabbing the countertop to circumvent my fall. The compact wasn't so lucky; it escaped my grip and crashed to the hard floor.

Cursing in annoyance, I knelt to assess the damage. My pressed powder, blush and eye colors were all broken into a multi-hued mess. I gathered my still-rolling eyeliner and mascara and stowed them safely on the counter. Then I cautiously picked up the overturned compact and flipped it upright.

Though no sharp pieces had fallen out, the small mirror was broken. A spider web of cracked sections reflected my face back at me from ever-so-slightly different angles. Puzzle pieces that almost fit, but not quite. I stared at those shards, the brown eyes staring back huge and shocked and utterly foreign.

Gasping, I realized that's what my soul must look like. The Amelia I'd always imagined myself to be my entire life was now just like this mirror. Shattered. Unfixable. All the King's horses and all the King's men could never put me back together again. Not like I'd been before. That Amelia, the good girl who always did the right thing—she'd disappeared. I'd held onto her so tight and for so long, but she'd still slipped away from me. Maybe she'd never even existed at all. Maybe she'd always just been an illusion I'd clung to in order to define myself.

I didn't know, and it really didn't matter any longer. That girl was gone, just like my dad, and just like my dad, she was never coming back. That girl who'd fallen in love with Scott and promised to love him and only him forever until death do us part—she was gone, too.

I wasn't in love with Scott anymore. I cared about him deeply, but it was more like how you feel about a best friend or a brother, not a lover.

The compact slipped from my fingers and clattered to the floor again. I sat immobile on the cool ceramic staring into space. My mouth gaped in dismay as I realized something that had probably been true for a while.

I was in love with Declan.

Declan

I was only planning to take Alexis to Florida for three days, leaving on December 30th. But after Miriam and James packed their car with overstuffed bags and cartons of food and headed back to Buffalo on the 27th, I changed my mind. I needed to get the hell out of my life for a while, and since I was off for another week, it felt like as good a time as any to make an escape. I decided we'd forego flying and leave the next day to drive down to my cousin's place.

Laura wasn't too thrilled about us heading out a couple days early. She didn't like that I was taking Alexis away at all. I snarkily informed my wife that Alexis needed to get used to being apart from her for longer stretches of time, which earned me a dirty look. But it shut her up. I gave no fucks if she was pissed at me. For once I was going to do something just for my daughter and me. Time and space away right now was what I badly fucking needed.

The drive was long for a little one. I left before the crack of dawn so she could sleep in the backseat a few hours, and made sure to take plenty of stops along the way. Once we got to Naples, we had an awesome time with my cousin Nate, his wife, Lynn, and their twin five-year-olds, Griffin and Toby. Alexis had a blast playing with the boys, splashing in the pool and running circles around the backyard with their Great Dane, Loki. I spent most of my time goofing around with the kids or relaxing by the pool with a beer in hand, soaking up the sunshine. The second evening, I pulled out my guitar and strummed it by the campfire out back as the kids toasted marshmallows, their loud singing cheering the night.

Because I was far more relaxed there than I would have been at home with Laura, I pushed back returning to Lynchburg until January 2nd. I welcomed the New Year sitting in my cousin's hot tub holding a glass of wine and peering through the steam up at the stars. I was content. Almost. All that was missing was the right woman by my side.

The moment we returned home, the tension in the air re-solidified. Even Alexis seemed to feel it. She was cranky and miserable the entire weekend. On Sunday she wouldn't go near her mother, clinging to my side or playing alone in her room. I assumed she was upset Laura was leaving, which was understandable.

A half-hour before we had to head out, I went into her room.

"We have to take Mommy to the airport soon, honey," I told her.

Alexis was on the floor playing with her dolls. From the sounds of it, the dolls were not getting along well today.

"Don't want to," she mumbled.

I sat on the edge of her bed. "Lex?" She glanced at me. "Come up here," I said, patting the comforter next to me.

At first she ignored me and continued to play. After a second request, she got up reluctantly and sat beside me, her gaze downcast like she thought she was in trouble.

"I'm not mad at you," I assured her. "But I think maybe you're mad at Mommy right now. Are you?"

She looked up at me, eyes all big and serious, and nodded.

Draping my arm around her small shoulders, I tried to decide how best to handle this. "She's gonna be really sad if you don't come and say goodbye. She'll be alone and missing you all week, and she needs all the love and hugs you can give her to keep her going while she's away."

Alexis frowned. "I don't want her to go."

The sad note in her voice made my heart hurt, and I had to clench my teeth to restrain my rising anger. It always seemed to be just below the surface these days when it came to my wife and her choices. I sighed softly. "Me, neither. But it's what Mommy wants. And we have to be happy for her, because she's happy. I know it's not easy, but could you try? She really needs you to try."

I could tell Alexis was thinking hard about that. At last she gave me a small nod. "Okay."

Taking her hand, I led her downstairs. When she saw her mother, she went to her and gave her a hug. Laura flashed me a grateful look, her eyes shining with emotion. I was still as annoyed with my wife as I'd been before. Nothing about my feelings had changed. But I won't lie—seeing how much the two of them loved each other made my heart soften a bit.

Until Alexis ran back upstairs to get her dolls to take in the car with her, that is.

Once we were alone, Laura gave me a smile. "Thank you for whatever it was you said to her."

Shrugging, I said, "No problem. Didn't want you two to part angry."

Her smile vanished. "You mean like we are?" She arched a sardonic brow.

I sighed. "I don't know what you want me to say that hasn't already been said, Laura. Let's just get you to the airport."

"I know you're still angry with me. And frankly I'm not too thrilled with you, either. You've been a complete jackass about this whole situation from the start, and I'm sick of it. I think us being apart for three months might be just what we need right now to figure out if this marriage is still working for us." She opened the closet and dragged out her winter jacket.

I gaped at the back of her head as she flipped her hair out of the collar. "What the fuck does *that* mean?" I demanded. "I should consider this a separation while you're in New York? Is that what you want?"

Laura turned back to me. "Don't put this all on me. You've been distancing yourself from me for months—since the day I told you about this. Well, here's some time for you to decide if you want it to be permanent or not."

Was she fucking kidding me? I was seething. My face was hot. My fists clenched and unclenched at my sides. If I didn't know Alexis would reappear at any moment, I would've lost my shit.

When she came downstairs, I told them in as level a voice as I could that I'd meet them in the car. Laura picked up the smaller of the two suitcases, and they went outside. As soon as the door shut behind them, I ran upstairs and down the hall to our bedroom, grabbing my pillow off the bed and burying my face in it. With a primal roar, I bellowed out my impotent fury, hoping the cotton would muffle the sound.

That was it, for me—the last fucking straw that broke me down. My defining—although certainly not shining—moment. The moment when everything changed. Again.

Amelia

When I returned to work on January 6th, I was filled with an odd mixture of excitement and dread. I don't know how to explain it, but I simultaneously wanted to see Declan like crazy, and at the same time hoped to avoid him for a while longer. I heard nothing from him on Monday.

By the time Tuesday was half over, I thought I might make it through a second Declan-free day. It was almost time for lunch, and I was trying to finish up the spreadsheet I was working on before I took my break. An excited child's voice coming from the end of the hall on the other side of my cubicle broke my concentration. Narrowing my eyes, I wondered who'd brought their kid to the office. There was only one woman in my department with young children, and she was off with the flu.

Suddenly I caught the unmistakable timbre of Declan's voice. "Let's go say hi to uncle Josh first. We need to congratulate him."

Crap. Declan had Alexis with him, and they were headed to see Josh, who had gotten engaged over the holidays. That meant there was a pretty good chance they'd stop by to see me next. I have no valid explanation for why I panicked at the thought of that, but I did. All I knew was that I needed to get out of there pronto.

When I was pretty sure they'd gone into Josh's office, I looked across the aisle to Kaitlyn.

"Kaitlyn?" I called softly.

She didn't look up.

"Kaitlyn!" I repeated, louder and more insistent. With a start, she turned to me questioningly. "You ready to go?" I asked, dropping my voice to a near-whisper. It still came out sounding more strident than I'd intended.

Frowning, she glanced back at her monitor. "Sure. Just give me a minute."

"I'm going right now! See you in the caf." My tone was harsh, and I knew from the confused look on her face that I owed her an apology. But I was frantic. My blood pressure was soaring. I grabbed my purse, slammed the drawer it had been in, and nearly ran out of the department. I saw from the corner of my eye that Josh's office door was open, and I prayed Declan wouldn't pick that moment to glance out and notice me fleeing.

218

When I got halfway to the cafeteria, I realized there was a good chance they would make that their next stop and I nearly screeched to a halt. Spinning around, I made straight for the nearest exit. Change of plans—I was taking myself out to lunch.

I slid into my car and dashed off a quick text to Sam letting her know something had come up and I wouldn't be joining them. Gripping the steering wheel tightly in my fists, I began to take deep breaths. Was this another panic attack? If so, what had triggered it? Why did I freak out at the idea of seeing Declan and Alexis? I missed him so much; it had already been way too long since we'd last seen each other. And yet here I was, desperate to avoid him. What was wrong with me?

My appetite was gone, but I drove to a nearby park and sat in my car listening to my iPod for a while. When I got back to my desk, I was relieved to find no sign of Declan. I apologized to Kaitlyn for my strange behavior, and then tried my best to forget about it.

The following day, however, I was forced to confront the situation early on. Shortly after nine, an e-mail from him arrived: *Please come see me at your earliest convenience and bring the client file we discussed last.*

I had to chuckle. The client file we discussed last? Which would have been nearly a month ago, sometime in mid-December. I had no idea which company it was, and I was willing to bet he didn't either. It was obviously Declan-speak for 'bring a file with you so it looks like we're talking business.'

Sighing, I realized I couldn't put off seeing him any longer, nor did I honestly want to. I grabbed the nearest file folder off my desk, made a pit-stop in the washroom to check my appearance, then headed to the Sales department, nerves alight.

I stopped in his doorway, my heart pounding against the file clutched to my chest. "Hey," I said.

Declan glanced up in surprise. "That was fast." He'd gotten his hair cut since I'd seen him last. It was shorter at the back and sides, but still as messy-looking as ever on top. He looked downright lickable. No surprise there.

"Saw no point in postponing the inevitable," I mumbled, dropping into a chair.

"What's that supposed to mean?"

"Nothing," I sighed. "How are you? How were your holidays? Did you make it to Florida?"

He smirked. "If you'd stuck around yesterday, you'd already know the answers to those questions."

Crap. Did he see me hightail out of there after all? I hoped not. I debated playing dumb for a moment, before realizing he'd know I probably would've heard Alexis' shrill voice. "Sorry. I was running late."

He frowned for a second. "O…kay. If you say so."

I shrugged. This was awkward. I hated awkward. I just wanted things to go back to the way they were before—before I'd opened my big, stupid mouth. Suddenly I really didn't want to be sitting in his office any longer.

Before I could come up with some reason why I couldn't stay, he began to tell me about his Christmas break. James and Miriam had visited for a few days. He'd had an entire house full of people on Christmas. On the 28th, he'd driven down to Florida with Alexis and they hadn't returned home until January 2nd.

Then he shocked me with the news that Laura had accepted a three-month maternity leave contract in New York and had left this past Sunday.

My mouth fell open. "She's going to be gone for three whole months?"

He nodded. "During the week, anyway. Probably some weekends as well."

"Are you okay with that?"

Shrugging, he replied, "Not especially, no. But my opinion didn't matter much in her decision."

I was floored. "How can she want to be away from you guys for so long? I don't get it." As much as I loved my job, I couldn't fathom leaving my family for months to further it. And I didn't even have a child.

"I don't get it either. But am I surprised? Nope, not at all. It is what it is."

My eyes narrowed as I studied his face. "You're furious." I observed softly.

"I'm not exactly thrilled. My daughter will be without her mother for three months—the occasional weekend notwithstanding. But I'll be there for her, and she'll be fine. We'll be fine. We always are." His lips were set in a tight line.

"I'm sorry to hear that, Declan," I said, and I meant it. He had enough to deal with without this.

"Don't be. Like I said, it is what it is. I expected it. But enough about unpleasant things. I've been thinking about you. How've you been?"

I smiled, and he smiled back at me, a genuine one this time. I skimmed over my somber Christmas with my mom, and then begin to tell him about our trip to Mexico. He laughed along with me at my description of New Year's Eve at the disco and how I'd had too much to drink and ended up crashing out early.

Suddenly I realized this was probably the first time I'd laughed since before my dad had died, and the grin fell away from my face.

Apparently Declan was thinking something similar. "I've missed your laugh. I've missed you. It's been too long."

"Me, too," I admitted. He had no idea just how much I'd missed him, how I'd thought of him nearly every moment I'd been on vacation. Just being in close proximity to him had already boosted my spirits immeasurably.

"We should hang out more. You're good for my state of mind. Let's have lunch again. Next week?" His expression was so hopeful.

I went still, remembering our emotionally fraught lunch a couple of months ago. "You think that's a smart idea?"

Declan took a deep breath. "Doesn't seem like being smart has made either one of us very happy." His eyes locked with mine.

I couldn't argue. It was completely true. And I badly wanted to spend time with him, no matter what the context. So with a small shrug, I agreed. "Sure. Just tell me when and where."

He grinned happily, and I felt myself mirror it. My heart rate was nearly normal. I was relaxed and almost…could that be happiness? I hadn't been sure I'd ever be able to be happy again. In that moment, things between us finally felt back as they should be.

He told me he'd let me know once he figured out details, and I returned to my cubicle with a lightness in my step that hadn't been there for what seemed like a very long time.

Right at exactly four o'clock, my desk phone rang. When the extension flashed up on the little screen, I was surprised to see it was Declan's.

"How does Friday sound?" he said as soon as I answered.

I glanced at my day planner. "The 17th? Looks good."

"No, two days from now. I can't wait that long."

My breath hitched. "Okay, this Friday it is. Where and when?"

"We didn't really eat last time. How about the same place?"

Confused as to why he'd pick *there* again, I said, "Um, sure."

"Any chance you could take the afternoon off?" He sounded a bit tentative.

I paused for a few seconds, startled. "I guess I could probably come up with a reason to ask for it." Twisting the phone cord around my fingers nervously, I asked, "Why? What did you have in mind?"

"Remember what we talked about last time we were there?"

"Yes," I replied slowly. "How could I ever forget?"

"Do you recall our little 'What If' game?"

"Uh huh." My throat constricted. Where was he going with this?

I heard him take a deep breath. "What if I said lunch wasn't all I wanted?"

Oh my God. Squeezing my eyes shut, I braced my forehead on my palm. Just what exactly was he suggesting? I didn't know if I could deal with another rejection at this point.

"I…we…" I sighed. "I thought you made your stance pretty clear."

"I know, but…you don't understand. I can't stop thinking about you. Everything's changed since I met you." He lowered his voice an octave. "Every damn thing is different."

"Different how?" I breathed, nearly unable to speak.

His words were scarcely more than a whisper, but I heard them as clear as if he were right beside me.

"I want more."

Chapter 22

Amelia

I don't recall my drive home from work. I know I made it to my house safely, but I had no memory of any stoplights, turns, or other cars on the highway. I couldn't tell you a single song I heard on the radio. I couldn't even tell you if the radio was *on*. I don't know how many minutes it took, if I was speeding, or crawling along like my grandma. In hindsight, it's amazing I made it in one piece; I'd been running on autopilot.

Three words played on an endless loop in my head.

"I want more."

When I pulled into the driveway and shut off my engine, I just sat there, staring through my windshield at the garage door. Unclenching my fingers from their death-grip on the steering wheel, I saw they were trembling.

"I want more."

I didn't know if I wanted to laugh and run in excited circles, or burst into tears, curl up into a ball, and rock back and forth.

He wanted more. And, God help me, so did I.

Thankfully Scott's truck wasn't there, which meant I had the house to myself. I forced my mind to focus on simple tasks like getting out of my car, going inside, climbing the stairs to the bedroom, changing, then returning to the kitchen and pouring a glass of wine.

As I leaned against the counter sipping the merlot and obsessing over Declan's words for the seventeen-thousandth time, my phone buzzed. It was Scott.

Heading home. Want me to stop at the Palace?

My stomach rebelled at the thought of food. My mind rebelled at the thought of trying to act normal around my husband. Scott knew me so well. I was sure he'd see right through me.

Thinking quickly, I texted back: *Going to mom's in a few. Get yourself pizza. Might not be home til late.*

Next I called my mother and told her I was coming over. Time spent just the two of us would never be my favorite thing, but at the moment it sounded infinitely preferable to staying here. I ended up sleeping in my old bedroom again, but this time it wasn't my dad I dreamt of.

That was how I avoided facing Scott on Wednesday. Thursday night I had no choice. I had dinner ready when he got home, but I was nursing a nasty stress headache. My brain throbbed relentlessly. I swore tiny demons were using pickaxes on the inside of my skull.

As soon as I saw him, guilt began to claw at me, and I hadn't even done anything yet. How would I ever be able to face him once I had? Would he take one look at my face and see my deceit written across it in glowing letters? Would a big scarlet A appear on my chest, visible only to him?

I'd already had more than twenty-four hours to think things over. You'd probably assume I'd been fluctuating back and forth about whether I really wanted to go through with it, whether I really intended to betray my marriage vows. It would be logical to presume that. But you'd be wrong. I'd been over and over all those thoughts so many times since the summer, and I was no longer confused about how I felt. I was in love with Declan. Our timing was horrible, and I was scared out of my mind about taking the next step, but I knew we were meant to be together.

Scott told me about his day over dinner, and I listened, a little. Mostly I pushed food around on my plate and took increasingly larger sips from my wine glass, all the while wondering if it was possible for my head to actually implode from pain.

"-move to Canada."

"Who's moving to Canada?" I asked, only vaguely interested in the answer.

Scott laughed. "You haven't heard a word I've said, have you?"

I met his all-too-familiar deep blue eyes, and, yawning, covered my mouth. "I'm sorry. Just tired. You were saying something about John Tate? He's moving to Canada?"

He sighed. "No, I said, *we're* moving to Canada." My eyes widened in shock and he chuckled again. "Don't worry. We're not going anywhere. I was just checking to see if you were paying attention."

"I said I was sorry," I muttered.

For a few moments he just stared at me. I flinched under his intense scrutiny. "Have you given any more thought to seeing a grief counselor?" he finally asked.

Something sparked in me at that. I heaved a sigh and stood, taking my plate and dumping it into the sink with a crash. I couldn't hold back my annoyance. "This again? What? Do you and Liv tag team each other or something? You both think I'm losing my mind—is that it?"

"You know we're just worried about you. I don't get why you're so dead-set against it."

"I don't need a shrink! I just need you guys to give me some space!" I shouted. "You're smothering me! I need to deal with my grief in my own way. And it will take time! Maybe lots of time. Maybe I'll never get over it. I don't know! But what I do know is that I don't want to talk to some stranger about it!" My voice grew louder as irrational anger consumed me.

"So far I've been giving you nothing *but* space to deal with this your own way. And it's not working. More than two months have passed. It's time to start pulling yourself back together." His hand landed on my shoulder. I flinched and moved away, heading for the stairs.

"See, and there's another thing," he said with obvious frustration. I turned to look back at him. "You've shut down on me. It's my job to be here for you, and you won't let me be anywhere near you. You sleep on the couch, or at your mom's. When you're with me, you

225

barely seem to know I'm in the same room. Something is really wrong, Amelia, and maybe it was wrong even before your dad-"

"Don't say it," I warned, choking on the words as my throat closed up. "Just don't."

His tone softened. "He's not coming back. I'm so sorry, and I miss him, too, but he's gone. And you need to accept that or you're never gonna be able to move past it."

Tears overflowed and ran rivulets down my burning cheeks. "I can't," I whimpered.

He pulled me into him, squeezing me tight against his chest and stroking my hair. And for a moment I let him comfort me. For a fleeting moment I remembered what being in love with Scott had once felt like: protected, adored, secure.

Just for a moment.

Then reality crashed back down, and I tore myself away again. "I'm sorry, Scotty. You're probably right. I'll…I'll call my doctor tomorrow for a referral." I wasn't sure I really meant it, but I knew it was what he needed to hear.

"Good. I think it'll help you." He smiled at me, but I didn't smile back.

Swiping the tears from my cheeks, I turned to go upstairs, but he stopped me again.

"Ames?"

My eyes locked with his.

"You still my girl?" His face was wide open and honest, his grin the same one I'd known since the day we'd met so long ago, when we were both young and innocent.

I was mortified. No, no I wasn't. I was *so* not his girl anymore. I just didn't have any clue how to tell him that.

I kept my face blank and held Scott's gaze for a few seconds longer than was probably necessary. At last I nodded and continued up the steps.

Friday, January 10th—another day that changed the path of my life forever—dawned clear and bright and cold. Surprisingly, I actually slept the night before. Not much, but I did. Scott had left early for a staff meeting, which was propitious. I spent a long time in the shower, shampooing and shaving and scrubbing myself near-raw. Meticulous primping was not normally my style if I didn't have a formal event to attend, but this morning I took the extra effort. Straightening, then curling my hair, dusting on powder, applying a coat of waterproof mascara, choosing just the right shade of lip gloss—it felt like I was performing an important ritual.

None of the clothes in my closet seemed right for…whatever this was. Finally I pulled on a black skirt and light blue sweater. Slipping into my black heels, I decided it would have to do.

As I reached to grab a pair of earrings, I saw my wedding rings on my dresser. My insides tightened as I looked at them. My engagement ring had a small diamond solitaire, and my wedding band was plain gold. We hadn't had much money at the time Scott bought them, and I didn't have expensive tastes or any desire for flashy jewelry. But they'd meant so much to me. They still did, although now it was more for sentimental reasons.

I picked them up and slid them home. They would probably end up in my purse later, but at the moment they needed to be in their customary place.

Before I left the bedroom, I took a final glance in the mirror. I knew it could be the last time I'd be able to look myself in the eye and still see some remnants of the person I used to be. There wasn't much left of her, and after this afternoon, she would undoubtedly be gone.

I straightened my shoulders and glared at the woman reflected back at me. I was done with her. It was time for her to disappear, and I didn't think I'd even miss her. I was ready to become the new Amelia. I couldn't wait.

I pulled into a parking spot behind the South Lynchburg Sheraton, my heart lodged firmly in my throat. The word *nervous* didn't even begin to encompass how I felt. For a few long moments I just sat there, trying and failing to calm my racing pulse.

Taking a deep breath, I forced myself to leave the car and go inside. The lobby of the hotel was tastefully decorated, with clean, modern black and white everywhere. Potted plants of tall green ficus added splashes of color to the room.

I approached the front desk nervously. A pretty blonde with pale blue eyes greeted me with a wide smile. I briefly wondered if Declan had checked in with her, and if they'd flirted. Then I mentally chastised myself. Even if he did flirt with her, or anyone else for that matter, it was none of my business. I knew he was here for one reason and one reason only: me.

With a gulp, I told her the same thing Declan had explained over the phone earlier: that a key should be waiting for me under the name Amelia Miller.

"Welcome to the Sheraton, Mrs. Miller," the blonde said cheerfully. "You're in room 414." I accepted the key card she handed me and turned toward the elevators. Noticing the ladies' powder room on the right, I made a sudden detour.

Once inside, I removed my wedding bands and pantyhose and tucked them into my bag. They would only be an unsexy nuisance. Then I reapplied antiperspirant, touched up my mascara, and wiped off what remained of my lip-gloss, applying a clear balm instead. No point in getting lip color in places where it shouldn't be. And yes, I had very much thought about all this. A lot. Most of the past few days.

With one last glance into the big mirror above the sink, I made a kissy face at myself and said goodbye to that girl forever.

Then, with a pull in my heart I couldn't resist, I headed for the elevator.

I stood in front of the pale green door to room 414 for a long time, debating whether to knock, knock then use my key card, or just use the card and walk straight in. Turning around and going home was not an option.

Gathering my courage, I slipped the card into the reader and knocked gently before pushing open the door.

As I shut it, I looked up to find Declan standing a few steps away, eyes wide. He wore charcoal gray trousers and a royal blue dress shirt with the top few buttons undone. His hair was disheveled. His feet were bare. When my eyes lifted to his again, I flushed under his intense gaze.

"You look beautiful," he said in a low, somewhat rough voice. I wondered if he'd gotten as little sleep as I had last night.

I gave him a shy smile. I wanted to tell him he looked so good he literally made me weak in the knees, but the words refused to come.

He retreated so I could enter the room. My eyes were drawn to a bright green golf fairway on a large television on the wall. Across from it was a queen-sized bed, the coverlet rumpled where Declan had been lounging as he waited for me. Past it, near the window, were two white leather loveseats facing each other, and between them was a black wooden coffee table. Upon it sat a vase of roses, a bottle of wine and two glasses. Heavy white drapes were pulled wide, flooding the entire room with cheerful sunshine. Was it strange that my first instinct was to shut those curtains and hide us from the rest of the world?

Declan cleared his throat, going over to pick up the wine. "It's a shiraz," he observed. "Shall I open it?"

I shook my head. Wine might relax me, but I wanted to remember every last moment of this afternoon. It might be all we'd ever have, and I didn't want to obscure any of those future memories.

"Okay." He set it down, looking back to where I still stood against the wall. With a slight tilt of his head he asked, "You alright?"

A small laugh escaped. "I'm…just…"

"Scared shitless?" he supplied with a wry grin.

Nodding in relief, I confessed, "Yes. Completely."

"Me, too," he admitted, coming back over.

"Really?"

He closed the remaining distance between us, leaning forward until his forehead rested against mine, his hands braced on the wall on either side of me. His face was so close. I could count every dark fleck in his irises, trace every laugh-line creasing his skin. God, he was so, so close.

"Terrified," he murmured.

I looked into those mesmerizing blue eyes, now mere inches from my own, and I saw all the love I felt for this man reflected back at me. And it was exhilarating and frightening and everything I'd ever wanted all rolled up into one.

"You can still walk away," he said softly. His voice held a slight pleading note. I wasn't sure if he was pleading with me to go or stay.

I bit my lip. I wished he'd just kiss me already. "I don't want to walk away," I whispered. "Do you?"

"Uh uh." He was still staring at me. Neither of us moved. I don't think either of us was even breathing. Seconds, possibly millennia, raced past as we drowned in each other's eyes.

Finally he broke the trance. "Amelia?" One of his hands moved to cup my jaw, thumb stroking my cheek.

"Uh huh?"

"I'm gonna kiss you now."

And before I could utter another syllable, he did.

My eyelids slipped shut as his mouth met mine. His lips were soft and gentle, tentative even—like he was waiting for me to change my mind and pull away. But I had no intention of pulling away. When he kissed me, I forgot who I really was, who we really were. We became simply two people who needed each other more than our common sense insisted we shouldn't.

Winding my arms around his waist, I pulled him against me, pressing my chest into his. I wondered if he could feel my heart racing. All his caution seemed to drain away and he cradled my face with both hands, angling my head to deepen the kiss. At first I let him control things, but then desire spread out from that spot in my lower belly. I didn't just want him; I *needed* him: body, mind and soul.

My temperature was spiking. So hot. Too hot. I slipped my hands under Declan's shirt and ran them over his bare skin, the muscles of his back flexing beneath my fingers. He was burning up, too. We were both about to spontaneously combust right here in this rented room.

Our tongues danced as we explored every inch of each other's eager mouths. I was so wrapped up in kissing him I only vaguely registered him trailing his fingers along the sides of my neck, over my shoulders and down, coming to a rest at the small of my back. He moaned into my mouth and slid his hands up each side of my spine, lifting the hem of my sweater along with them. When he got to my shoulder blades, I pushed away from the wall, allowing cool air to rush against my overheated skin. But nothing could reduce that heat. I whimpered in protest as he tore his mouth away and tugged my sweater up over my head, tossing it onto a chair.

I'd worn a matching blue bra and panties set. It was the prettiest lingerie I owned. Actually, it was probably the only matching set I owned. Judging from the expression on Declan's face as he ogled my satin and lace-clad breasts, he very much approved.

Exhaling a rush of air, his eyes met mine again and his questing fingers found the zipper at the back of my skirt. I bit my lip in concentration as I pushed the top button of his shirt through its hole before moving to the next one. It was more difficult than expected as my fingers were trembling. At last his shirt fell from his shoulders to the floor. I stepped out of my skirt and heels.

My God, the look of hunger in his eyes as they raked over me. Had anyone ever looked at me that way before? I couldn't help it; I grew self-conscious under his intense stare and had a crazy urge to cover myself back up.

"You are so gorgeous," he said, clearly in awe. With a groan, he pulled me back to him and kissed me again. As I ran a hand up his smooth chest, he lifted me and carried me to the bed.

My head hit the pillow, and then he was above me, our mouths still joined. His kisses grew more intense. I quivered under his touch as he began to explore my newly exposed skin.

"You cold?" he whispered against my lips, lifting his head and tugging at the edge of the comforter.

"I'm...no, I'm fine," I said as I pulled him back to me. I wasn't cold; I just wanted more. More kissing. More touching. More *Declan*. His fingers feathered their way up my side, coming to rest over the lace covering my right breast and squeezing gently. When one fingernail began to trace circles around the hardening tip, I gasped in pleasure.

He chuckled low in his throat at my response, and that crazy-sexy sound—not to mention what his hands were currently up to—did dangerous things to my libido. His mouth left mine and trailed a path down the side of my jaw and along my neck, grazing my skin lightly with his teeth as he went. I threaded my fingers into his hair as he traveled lower, along my collarbone, over my shoulder. He slid my bra strap down my arm to make way for his kisses. Another involuntary shiver shook me when his lips reached their destination, latching on to a silk-clad nipple.

"Oh God…" I whimpered, arching my back to press myself more firmly against his mouth.

He stopped and looked up at me. "Tell me what you want, Mel."

"I want…" I sighed, my eyelids slipping shut.

"Tell me," he repeated, soft yet insistent, trademark smirk firmly in place.

"More…I want…more," I confessed, pushing myself a few inches off the bed to reach around and unhook my bra. I dropped back to the mattress and Declan tugged it down my arms and tossed it over his shoulder. Heat flooded my face as he stared at my naked chest, his longing and lust clear. He traced gentle lines across the swell of my breasts, down along their sides, and over my abdomen. Slowly, deliberately, he lowered his lips to capture one hard, pebbled peak.

Declan was a man who knew exactly how to please a woman's body. I'd only ever had one lover before, and I worried my inexperience with anything more than basic vanilla would be noticeable. I mean, I'd seen parts of a few dirty movies, read some racy novels, but I'd never actually *done* anything particularly adventurous in the bedroom. But I highly suspected he had, and I had no idea what he might expect from me.

He began to pinch and twist my unattended nipple in a delirious combination of light pain and intense pleasure as his mouth and teeth claimed ownership of my flesh. My body wasn't used to being tormented and tantalized like this, and frankly it loved every second of it. I could feel myself growing slicker and more desperate to feel his touch elsewhere.

He switched to my neglected breast, cupping it firmly before starting to lavish it, too, with attention. It felt scandalous and wonderful and I never wanted him to stop. The fingers of his other hand wandered over my ribcage, glided across my stomach, then gently traced along the elastic of my panties.

My control began to slip as he suckled me. The slightly abrasive wool of his dress pants rubbed against my knee as he hooked one leg over me, holding me in place. I squeezed my thighs together, trying unsuccessfully to relieve the tension building between them. I grew desperate. I needed to be touched. I needed Declan to touch me.

As if sensing my turmoil, he finally slipped his hand beneath the fabric. My breath caught with anticipation, and I unclenched my legs, allowing him where I wanted him most. He took his time caressing and exploring, getting to know every inch of me. When at last he eased a careful finger into me, I bucked upward and gasped.

His eyes lifted to mine with an arched brow. "You okay?"

I exhaled in a rush and nodded. All I could think about was the sinfully delectable way he was making me feel. I spread myself wider, giving him better access.

With a dangerous smile, he replied, "Good," and began to move his finger inside me, curling it upward and hitting just the right place. Groaning in approval, I raked a hand through his hair, tugging gently. At my response, he added a second finger, pumping them a bit faster. I inhaled sharply and held my breath as I focused on the sensations he was creating.

He resumed his ministrations to my breasts, now slippery from his tongue, while stroking me down below, rubbing his thumb over my most sensitive spot, alternating between oh-so-gentle and intense. I didn't have to tell him what I needed—he just knew. I felt like he already knew my body better than anyone ever had. My breath flew out in a rush and I squirmed below him, internal pressure building, building.

I moaned as my climax overtook me. All my muscles went stiff, and my entire body trembled and convulsed against him. Sweat beaded my forehead. Gooseflesh erupted over my chest. As my mind floated away, I ever so vaguely heard his distant voice commanding me to keep breathing, just keep breathing.

As I slowly descended to terra firma again, I realized he was watching me intently. Smiling, he pressed his lips to mine. "You are so incredibly sexy when you just let go like that," he whispered.

I took a few more deep calming breaths, self-conscious of how closely he studied me.

With some surprise I realized he still had his pants on. I stroked the side of his face with my fingers. "You look…" I trailed those same fingers down his muscular torso to his belt buckle. He arched a brow at me. "Entirely overdressed," I finished with a smile, hooking one finger into the leather strap and tugging it free.

"Couldn't agree more," he laughed, pulling back to stand and undo his belt. I glanced away, another wave of shyness coming over me. It was broad daylight. Sunshine flooded the room. And the man I was truly, madly, deeply in love with, but had never seen naked before, was stripping his pants off right beside me. I blushed at the thought.

I focused on pulling back the coverlet. The sheets were starched white cotton, softer to the touch than I'd expected. Slipping below them, I covered up and attempted to distract myself with the golf tournament on the television.

Declan climbed in next to me. Hearing a soft chuckle, I glanced at him questioningly.

"Isn't it a little late now to be shy?" he asked, reaching for the remote to turn off the TV.

Flushing deeper, I mumbled, "I know."

He wrapped a strong arm around my waist and pulled me to him. "One of us still has an item of clothing on," he teased, sliding a hand under the elastic of my panties to squeeze my bum.

"How can you be so relaxed about all this?"

Grinning that easy grin he seemed to save just for me, he replied, "Simple. I'm naked. You're damn near naked. We've both just jumped off this cliff together. What's there to be nervous about at this point?" He kissed me sweetly, continuing to caressing my curves.

"You're right. I know," I agreed when he pulled back for air.

"Say that again," he insisted, eyes widening devilishly.

"Say what?"

"That I'm right." That sexy smirk reappeared.

"Shut up," I laughed, pulling him in for another kiss, and as we did, he deftly tugged my panties down my legs.

Kissing Declan was definitely my favorite thing. I felt like I could kiss this man all day long. But he had some other ideas in mind for how to spend our afternoon together. Rolling on top of me, he pressed me into the pillow-top mattress. As our kisses became more fervent, I shifted my legs so he rested between them, the hard evidence of his desire pressed insistently against my thigh. My hands traced the outline of his shoulder blades, glided down the ridges of his spine, roamed over his body the way his had done mine. When my exploring fingers drifted below his lower back and grasped his amazing butt, he groaned against my mouth.

"Mel?"

Mel? He'd called me that earlier, too, hadn't he? No one had ever used that nickname before, and I realized I kind of liked it.

"Uh huh?"

Rising up on one elbow, he looked me straight in the eyes, his expression serious. "Any second thoughts?" he asked softly.

My throat tightened as I shook my head. "I want this," I murmured. "You?"

He stared at me, his formerly baby blue irises darkened with lust, his lips swollen from our passionate kisses, and I knew his answer before he even said it. "Not a chance."

Clarity refocused his face for a moment. "Condom," he muttered, rolling to the side. I grabbed his arm to stop him, and he arched a questioning brow my way.

"I'm on the Pill," I told him. "And there's never been anyone else."

"Really? You've only ever been with…" Declan's eyes widened as he got the message. I smiled shyly and nodded, stroking the side of his face.

"I've got a clean bill of health," he assured me.

I stared into those entrancing eyes. At the moment they were deep as the ocean and twice as likely to drown me. This was it. This was our time. And I loved him. Even though I knew the Universe could easily break me into a thousand pieces in punishment for it, I loved him.

"Okay," I whispered, shifting my knees apart as he settled back into place.

His mouth opened as if he wanted to say something more, but instead he pressed it closed. He planted soft kisses on my nose, my lips, my chin. Sliding one hand down between us, he ran himself through my wetness. Then carefully, ever so carefully, he pushed inside.

Oh God, oh God, oh God…

My lips fell open in a loud gasp. It felt so different from what I'd imagined, so much *more*. Having Declan within me was far more intense, both mentally and physically, than I could ever have anticipated. A sentimental lump wedged itself tightly in my throat. I'd waiting so long for this…this *joining*. It was overwhelming.

Instantly he stopped. "Am I hurting you?"

I shook my head and took a deep breath, pulling him against me and tucking my face into his shoulder so he couldn't see the emotion in my eyes. "You're perfect," I assured him, and he began to move.

His lips found mine again—he couldn't seem to stay away from them for long. We clutched each other as if we would never get enough, my fingers stroking his back as he pumped his hips against me. It was possibly the most…tremendous…sensation I'd ever experienced.

One of my hands tangled in his hair while the other slid down his lower back, pressing him ever closer. I loved the feel of his muscles flexing beneath my fingers. I was starting to realize I loved most things about Declan, except for the one tiny little fact that he wasn't really mine. If I was only going to be able to have him for these few hours, I was determined to make our time together count.

Tearing my mouth from his, I gasped, "On top," and he obligingly rolled us over. The covers fell away and a beam of sunlight landed across his chest. With a smile, I bent forward and licked a trail through it from his nipple, which elicited a delectable little moan, up to his throat, finishing back at his lips again.

Swiveling my hips down onto him, I braced my hands on his shoulders to steady myself. His fingers groped my breasts, squeezing and teasing me. The exhilarating pleasure-pain he created, the way my heart seemed to sing every time our eyes connected—it was entirely unique, entirely us. I could feel my control begin to slip again as I ground against him, my breathing accelerating along with my speed.

Declan sensed this, and he flipped me beneath him again, taking charge once more as our mouths rejoined. For the most part I was a strong, confident woman out there in the real world, but right here, right now? His self-assured dominance seriously turned me on. If he'd wanted to tie my wrists to the bedposts, I would've spread them wide and begged him to do with me as he wished.

As his previously unhurried thrusts picked up intensity, I lifted my knees higher, pushing my heels into the back of his thighs. This change of angle allowed for shorter, deeper strokes and part of him was now creating this amazing friction against me. Without warning, my orgasm ripped through me. My entire body clenched beneath

236

him. The noise I made was more growl than moan. It was low and guttural and raw, and I could hardly believe it had come from me.

He pressed his face into the curve of my neck, driving into me harder as I rode out the quivery aftershocks of my high. My fingers feathered up and down his sides as he panted for air, his own release fast approaching. With a shudder and a gasp, he bucked against me a final time before collapsing in a heap on top of me, utterly spent.

I held him close, one hand in the back of his hair, the other around his waist, and I kissed his damp temples, his chin, his closed eyelids, as he fought to catch his breath. Again, my emotions surged and delirious unshed tears itched at the corners of my eyes. As I looked at him, I was overcome by how much I loved him.

Rolling his weight to the side, his eyelids fluttered open, a happy, satiated smile gracing his face.

"My God, Declan," I breathed. "Do you have any idea how I feel about you?"

He gazed into my eyes, all serious, searching for something. At last, it seemed he found it. Pressing a finger to my lips, he leaned his forehead against mine, still staring at me like he couldn't get enough.

I was just about to speak again when he stunned me to silence by whispering, "I might, yeah. And Mel?"

"Yes?"

"Me, too."

Chapter 23

Declan

We fell asleep in each other's arms, Amelia right away and myself
much more gradually. I lay there watching her face as it relaxed into
oblivion, lightly stroking her sweat-dampened arm, her soft, tangled
hair. Long dark lashes fluttered against flushed skin as she started to
dream. Every slight edge softened; in sleep she seemed so young, so
innocent. Looking at her, I felt something shift inside me. I had an
uncontrollable urge to hold her close and protect her, to shield her
from anything that could ever cause her pain.

Which was ironic I guess, considering the most likely offender was
probably me.

I hadn't told her about Laura's insistence that I consider her three-
month absence a trial separation. I'd debated it, but ultimately
decided it would put more pressure on whatever this was between us
than we needed.

My feelings for Amelia were…intense. And growing with each
passing moment. I could love her. Maybe I did love her. But it
wouldn't be fair to give her hope or imply promises I might not be
able to keep. If Laura and I split, and she had reason to feel vindictive
about it, she could take Alexis from me. Mothers always got

preferential treatment from the courts if they wanted full custody, unless negligence was proven. Because of that, I wouldn't ask her for a divorce. If it happened, it had to be Laura's idea. And it couldn't be because she'd found out I'd been unfaithful. I was taking a massive risk right now with Amelia—there was no way in hell I was going to be the one to initiate ending my marriage. I refused to take the chance of losing my daughter.

This made things really fucking complicated and any potential for a future with the woman in my arms sadly unlikely. It wasn't that I didn't want to be with her on a permanent basis. I did. So much. It felt right—incredibly right—but the stakes were just too high. I wasn't willing to take a gamble I could easily lose. Not with Alexis. Not even for Amelia.

Sighing, I pushed those negative thoughts aside for now and closed my eyes, focusing on the comfort of her nearness and the soft sound of her breathing until I drifted off, too.

When I woke, it was 3:15, and Amelia was still out. I assumed she needed to head home around four as usual, and I also assumed she'd want to shower first. Reluctantly I realized I'd better wake her.

At some point she'd rolled over, and in my sleep I hadn't let her go. I was spooned against her back, one arm draped around the curve of her waist, palm flat on her stomach, and my nose nestled into her hair.

I could think of several ways to wake her up, and every last one of them made me harder than the last. Slowly I began tracing light patterns on her abdomen. She responded with a low humming sound in her sleep, which encouraged me to continue. The soft skin of her shoulder beckoned my lips, and as I dropped a gentle kiss there, she made that little moan again, shifting her body a bit closer to mine.

Smiling to myself, I let my fingers wander higher, cupping her breast, noting the weight of it in my palm. She was beautiful, perky and perfect, not too big and not too small, just exactly the right size for my hand.

As my fingertips circled a hardening nipple, she exhaled and unfurled toward me, giving me access to lower my mouth to it for a more personal greeting. As my tongue flicked over the puckered tip, her eyes flew open.

"Hey!" she gasped, laughing softly. My gaze lifted to hers, and her mouth curved into a sleepy smile.

Then she glanced over at the clock on the nightstand, and her face fell. "Oh my God! It's nearly 3:30!" She smacked my arm lightly. "How could you have let me sleep for so long?" she accused, her voice choking up on the last couple words.

I raised my face up to hers, concerned by the distress in her tone. I pushed a loose strand of hair off her forehead as she pressed her lips together, her eyes welling up.

"What's wrong?" I asked, stroking her cheek with my thumb.

"I slept away our afternoon together. We only had today and I wasted it." She sighed. "I wanted more time with you." A single tear escaped and slid down her temple.

"It's not wasted time. We were together." I leaned over and kissed her as I wiped that errant tear away. "I loved waking up with you. I loved that you were the first thing I saw when I opened my eyes. And hey," I glanced at the clock again, raising my brows seductively, "we still have thirty minutes or so."

That brought a small smile back. She ran her fingers into my hair, pulling my face to hers. After giving me a long, lingering kiss, she whispered, "I guess we both need a shower?"

That was all the invitation I needed. I threw back the sheets, picked her up, and carried her to the bathroom. After setting her on the countertop, I turned to start the hot water. When I looked back, she had twisted around, examining her reflection as she stretched the hotel-provided shower cap over her hair.

She must have seen the surprised look on my face as she met my eyes in the mirror. Shrugging, she said, "I can't very well go home with wet hair." I couldn't argue with that. And frankly, she looked cute as hell with that plastic polka-dotted cap on her head, a few strands of hair escaping here and there as she resolutely tried to cram them back underneath.

Her gaze dropped lower. I watched with amusement as her cheeks flushed and her mouth fell slightly open, the tip of her tongue darting out to run over her lower lip. I couldn't help but smirk as she stared at me. Earlier she'd averted her eyes, which I'd thought was kind of adorable. I'd figured as we got more comfortable around each other her shyness would ease up. It seemed I was right.

I took her hand and guided her into the shower. Grabbing the soap and unwrapping it, I begin to lather my hands. "You first," I told her. Before she could ask what I meant, I spun her around and started running the soap slowly along her spine, cresting it across her shoulder blades and up over the roundness of her shoulders. As I brought it down her ribcage, over her lower back and around the curves of her shapely ass, I heard her inhale deeply. Grinning, I continued slowly down the back of one leg, then the other.

"Now turn around," I whispered, straightening up.

She willingly obliged. And let me just say, I had no intention of kissing her then. The plan was to continue washing and exploring every inch of her body. But I looked into her eyes, and the emotion I saw staring back at me...I had no choice; I simply couldn't *not* kiss her.

Winding her arms around my neck, she pulled me against her. Her tongue slipped into my mouth, and the next thing I knew I had her back pressed into the wet tiles. Jesus Christ, the things this woman could do to my self-control. It all went out the fucking window when we touched.

But right now, I knew I had to stop. I was working toward a goal and I intended to see it through. Gathering all my fragile willpower, I dragged my mouth from hers and stepped back. She moaned in disapproval and reached for me, but I held her slightly away. "Uh uh," I teased. "Be patient. I'm not done yet."

I resumed my ministrations to the front of her body, sliding the soap across her chest and down both arms, then over her tight belly. Lathering my hands up well, I returned the soap to its shelf and ran the flat of my palms lightly over her nipples. She inhaled sharply, and I smiled at her reaction. Gently, I massaged each breast, before angling the spray to rinse them off. I leaned down and took one taut peak in my mouth, suckling until I heard a soft mewling sound from above. Then I switched to the other one, licking and nibbling as she squirmed.

The sounds that flew from her as my lips ravished her chest and my hands ran over her legs, finally finding their way up to her wet center, sent a burning tightness from my belly straight down. I didn't think it was possible to be more turned on.

It was time to take Amelia's pleasure to the next level. I guided her backward and positioned her against the ledge at the rear of the shower, then dropped to a kneeling position before her. She regarded me curiously, but I just smiled and nudged her knees apart, lifting them to rest on my shoulders.

When my mouth touched her, she gulped. As I tasted and explored her, the sounds she made grew louder, although more spaced out. She seemed to be holding her breath as long as she could between inhalations. Slipping a finger inside, I began to stroke her as my tongue swirled and pressed and flicked. It wasn't long before her breathy gasps turned into one long moan as her thighs clenched around my ears.

Extracting myself from the vice-grip of her legs, I stood to take her in my arms. Her breathing was heavy and she clung to me for support, pressing her face into the curve of my throat as she gripped my shoulders.

I gave her some time to recover, but then I couldn't wait any longer—I needed to kiss her again. Our kisses were soft and languid, filled with promises of lazy afternoons and gentle embraces. I loved how she kissed me. I think I got to know her—the real her—better and better each time. She was strong and confident one minute, seemingly shy and timid the next. Sometimes she took control; more often, she seemed to prefer when I did. I was good either way.

The more I kissed Amelia York, the harder I fell for her. We were already treading on incredibly dangerous ground as it was, yet with every gasp, every fumbled touch, every exhalation of breath into each other's mouths, I knew I was further lost. We were in too deep already and neither one of us was the least bit interested in trying to swim for the surface.

I pulled away and pressed my forehead to hers, staring into those intoxicating brown eyes. Against the damp, flushed skin of her cheek, I whispered, "Me, too," and she breathed the words right back to me. We were mirrors. We were echoes.

"Me, too."

"Me, too."

"Me, too."

Amelia

As I walked out of the hotel and got into my car, I was smiling. I mean, I was sad our time together was over, but there was no repressing the grin that stretched across my face from ear to ear. It's funny how the mind works. It felt strange to feel so crazy happy in the face of all the awfulness I'd been through recently, and knowing full well the guilt and pain that would come later. But right at the moment? I was blissful. I was ecstatic. I was *in love*.

And I was pretty sure he loved me, too.

He didn't say the words. Neither of us did. But we might as well have. I knew just what he'd meant when he'd looked into my eyes, read the truth in my heart and said, "Me, too."

The intense joy of reciprocated feelings, even if our situation was infinitely messed up and probably hopeless, filled me right to the brim. I wanted to sing at the top of my lungs. I wanted to shout from the rooftops. I wanted to tell everyone, even complete strangers, that I'd found exactly whom I didn't even know I'd been looking for.

His name was Declan. And I loved him.

I couldn't stop thinking about our afternoon. After another mind-blowing lovemaking session in the shower, we'd toweled off and slowly proceeded to get dressed in near complete silence.

He'd walked me to the door and told me he'd wait a while after I left before checking out. Then he'd pulled me to him one last time. I'd wrapped my arms tightly around his waist and pressed my cheek into the side of his neck, and we'd just held one another for several long, long minutes, just breathing each other in, trying to memorize every last thing about the other.

We'd kissed sweetly, full of tender emotion, and then I'd slipped out the door. There were no words that needed saying. We'd both understood all too well.

You know how when you're all wrapped up emotionally in a certain situation, songs, television shows, movies, everything around you seems to reflect your inner turmoil? Well sure enough, the first song that came on shuffle in my car as I drove home was that old Squeeze song, "Tempted". I stopped for gas and when I went in to pay, the radio in the small shop was playing Rihanna's "Unfaithful". As I gave the sullen teenager behind the counter my credit card, it morphed into the sappy "My Secret Love" by some awful boy band I didn't even recall the name of. Ugh. But that one's lyrics hit home even more than the others.

> *"My secret love, I can't say no.*
> *Secret love, can't let you go.*
> *Hate runnin' around, hidin' all the time.*
> *Have to be so careful to leave no sign.*
> *We both know it's wrong, but our love is just too strong.*
> *Can't stay away for long."*

It's a terrible song—one that always made me cringe. But it kind of summed up my life at the moment. I cursed its existence as I walked back to my car, already sure it would be stuck in my head the rest of the day.

I didn't know what to do with myself once I got home. At one point I realized I was just staring into the fridge, my original intent to look for something to make for dinner forgotten. Closing the door, I trotted up the stairs instead and pulled out my laptop to look at photos of Declan on Facebook. My lips still remembered the pressure of his; my body still remembered how it responded to his touch. If I concentrated, I imagined I could still feel him inside me.

The sound of the front door opening and closing threw an instant damper on my amorous reminiscing. I sighed in frustration. Crap, now what was I supposed to do? Quickly closing the computer and putting it aside, I went into the bathroom and shut the door.

Bracing my hands on both sides of the sink, I stared at myself in the mirror. Did I look any different? I sure felt different. I examined my mouth, my cheeks, my throat, my chest—everywhere exposed that Declan's lips had touched, and there was very little skin he'd missed. It all looked normal. Then I looked into my own eyes, and that's where I found the difference. They were no longer blank and empty, twin pools of silent misery. They were sparkling, bright, and happy. My eyes were alive again. That's where my change lay—not just in my heart, but pouring out of my very being. At last I had begun to heal. I know it sounds cheesy, but I felt like the love I'd found was a balm to heal my damaged soul.

Convinced Scott would notice the transformation if he looked too closely at me, I scrubbed at my face, a burning need to wash away my happiness before I faced him. My frantic mind kept insisting that if I could re-find my misery, the profound change I'd just experienced would become invisible.

I dropped to the floor and leaned my back against the door, squeezing my eyes closed and blocking out all thoughts of Declan. Instead, I focused on my dad. I thought about a specific moment: the day we'd cleaned out the attic together and the box of my old baby stuff that I'd found. I recalled how he'd understood that I didn't really want to have children with Scott, and had told me to stop trying to live up to the person everyone else expected me to be, to just be myself. And he'd assured me he'd support me no matter what choices I made.

Then I imagined telling Scott I was leaving him.

That was all it took. In my mind's eye, I could already see the destroyed expression on his face. A horrified lump promptly blocked my throat, my eyes welled up, and the tears came. Swiping them away, I pushed myself upright to go greet him. A quick glance in the mirror confirmed I no longer appeared happy, and therefore different from usual.

It turned out my generated sadness was unnecessary. Scott didn't seem to suspect a thing. Apparently my guilt was *not* actually written all over my face in glowing red letters. Still, when he asked me how my day was and I had to lie, my stomach cramped up. How was I supposed to fake normalcy—whatever that even was anymore— around this man who'd known me for over half my life? I didn't know how long I'd be able to keep up the pretense. I also knew sooner or later I'd need to sit down with him and have a serious talk about our future. My vote at the moment was for later. I wanted to delay that conversation, even if procrastinating made me an even worse wife than I already was—if that was even possible.

Instead, I pulled my usual brand of avoidance and called Liv to ask if we could hang out tonight. In a surprised voice, she said she'd been just about to call me to suggest the same.

We met at Finnegan's less than an hour later. As I slid into the booth across from her, I noticed she looked stressed.

"Are you okay?" I asked.

She smiled, shaking her head a little. "Isn't that what I'm supposed to be asking you?"

I waved my hand in dismissal. "My issues are all we ever talk about anymore. Tonight is about you. Tell me why you have that sour look. Something happen with Ben?" Her entire face seemed to droop when I mentioned his name, and I realized I'd hit the jackpot.

The server picked that moment to interrupt with our drinks. As she walked away, Liv concentrated on the label of her beer instead of meeting my gaze, picking at the edge of the foil with a fingernail.

"What is it? C'mon, you know you can tell me." I wanted to focus on someone else's concerns so I wouldn't think about my own. Not that I was pleased my friend had problems, but there was a small part of me that welcomed the distraction.

She bit her lip and lifted her eyes to mine. "I think…" She stopped and sighed. "'Ames, I think Ben might be cheating on me!" Her eyes shone with unshed tears.

My mouth fell open in surprise. I reached across the table and took her hand. "You're kidding! Crap, Liv. Why?"

"He's been acting really weird lately: staying at work late all the time, not spending nights at my place as often, barely having real conversations with me anymore. And there's this new girl in his department he's become friends with. I swear she gives me the stink-eye every time I walk by her desk." She rolled her eyes, and I gathered the dislike was mutual.

I could feel my face heating up as some of her story hit a little too close to home. "So he's been working late and has a new friend. That doesn't mean anything," I reassured her, although I wasn't sure how much I believed my own words. "Ben would never cheat on you."

"He talks about her all the time. I don't even think he realizes how much he does it. Carrie did this or Carrie said that, constantly. And he smiles like crazy whenever he says her name. I've had my suspicions for a little while, but now…now he hardly seems to touch me anymore. He hasn't told me he loves me in two weeks! Something is really wrong, I know it is." I could see her welling up further as she spoke.

A pang of guilt shot through me at the similarity to my own situation. Squeezing her fingers, I asked, "Have you talked to him about any of this?"

She shook her head wildly, a few droplets flying from the corners of her eyes.

"Why not?" I pressed.

Staring down at our joined hands, her tears tracked sticky, mascara-darkened paths on her cheeks. For a long time she didn't reply. Finally she darted a glance up to meet my eyes. "I'm scared I'll find out I'm right," she whispered.

I got up and went around the table, nudging her aside so I could slip onto the seat beside her. Then I wrapped my arms around her and gave her a sideways hug, laying my head against her shoulder. "No matter what, whatever ends up happening, I'm here for you," I promised.

She embraced me back before swiping at her face with a cocktail napkin. By unspoken agreement, we changed the topic to Josh and Holly's engagement, speculating about what their big day would be like. I swooned over the mental image of a dashing Declan in a black tux as the best man. Hopefully, things would be easier for us by then. Hopefully, by the time the wedding rolled around, we'd be in a position to be together publically.

Liv and I chitchatted about easy things. She was either distracted enough or understanding enough to not ask about my issues. And for the next hour or so it felt like things were almost normal in my world again, which was just what I needed.

Saturday, I spent most of the day at my mother's. The less I was alone with Scott, the more relaxed I was. Sunday, we went out to brunch with his mom and sister. Sunday evening I couldn't avoid it being just us, but between making dinner, watching television and playing around online, the hours thankfully passed without any meaningful conversation.

I forced myself to make eye contact with Scott and smile at him like usual, though my stomach twisted with guilt each time I did. All weekend I felt like a sham wife, a robot Amelia, programmed to say the right things on cue. I had to make myself eat, as my appetite was minimal. At night when I slid into bed beside my husband, I felt dirty, like I was betraying the man I loved. Which I was. I was betraying both loves, past and present, just by sleeping beside Scott like everything was still the same, like I was still the same person I'd been before.

The entire weekend I'd been waiting for him to challenge me on something: my peculiar not-as-depressed-as-usual mood, my spending as much time as possible away from him, my lack of an appointment to see the psychologist yet, anything. But he didn't. He seemed subdued a bit himself. He spent his time watching football or working on his lesson plans for the second half of the school year. To me, it really seemed like we were living nearly separate lives—more like roommates than spouses.

I wasn't oblivious enough to think this could go on indefinitely, though. This fragile and carefully enforced distance we were maintaining would have to be addressed at some point. It couldn't last, and it wouldn't be fair to either of us if it did. As much as I shrank from the thought, I knew I had to break his heart to set him free.

But not yet. No matter how guilty I felt, I just wasn't ready. I was far too scared still, too emotionally fragile, to put either of us through that right now.

Monday morning at work, I didn't know how to feel. I couldn't wait to see Declan, but I was worried things would revert back to awkward between us—or worse, that he'd treat me like just another co-worker. Logically I understood that we had to appear as no more than casual friends in public, but I knew it would be hard to take if he acted aloof with me.

I was also scared that he might be consumed with guilt and remorse. If he regretted being with me, I didn't know if I could handle it. And I hated feeling so vulnerable. Vulnerable was yet another aspect of the new Amelia that felt foreign. I couldn't remember ever feeling that way before about a guy. But things were different now. Somehow, and fully against my better judgment, I'd given Declan the power to utterly break me.

I didn't hear from him on Monday, so my fears weren't tested. The next day I chatted with Josh in his office for a while. He told me he and Holly were planning a long engagement, and that they'd decided to go the cheesy route and get married on Valentine's Day next year. After teasing him about the giant pink heart-shaped pillow I was going to make for them for a gift, I detailed some of my own wedding organizing stories, ending by recounting the untimely screw-ups that led to us having to make our own last-minute table centerpieces. This had entailed collecting mismatched flower pots and whatever random wilted blooms were still available from the closest discount florist, and Scott, Liv, and our families rushing to assemble twenty of them. Poorly. But those pathetic centerpieces became the subject of hilarious conversation the entire night, and we'd never forgotten.

Josh chuckled along with me. "You seem happier today. Lighter, somehow, than I've seen you in a long time."

I smiled. "Thanks. Didn't realize it was so noticeable."

"You're trying to hide your good mood?" His eyes narrowed in confusion.

"No, not exactly."

"Can I ask what's made you so cheerful? Or who?" One of his eyebrows arched knowingly.

Flushing, I sighed. "Is it that obvious?" I trusted Jos, but I wasn't sure I should admit anything. No matter how much he liked me, he was still Declan's best friend. Unless? Was it possible Declan could have told him?

"Only to me, because I know you both pretty well. I talked to him earlier today. He didn't spell anything out, but he couldn't stop smiling, either."

Josh was far too smart for his own good sometimes, but I wasn't able to contain my grin at his words. "Really?" I asked.

His voice dropped. "I'm not gonna pretend I think whatever's going on between you two right now is a good idea. It's not. You both know it's not. And I don't wanna see either of you get hurt. But I care about you, and seeing you both so damn happy warms the cockles of my cold little heart." He winked.

I laughed nervously. "What do you know?" I whispered.

"Only what I can see with my own two eyes. And it worries me. You both really need to deal with your own situations before you explore this stuff. You know that, right?"

Frowning, I muttered, "I know. I...we..." I sighed again. "You're right."

"Don't get me wrong; I want you to be happy. You deserve every happiness. Just please be careful. This could so easily blow up in your face. You could lose everything. And I don't want that for either of you." His face was the picture of seriousness now.

I stood to go. "Thanks, Josh. I mean it. And I'll be really careful, I promise."

"See that you do. And if you need me for anything, any time of day, you know how to reach me."

I walked back to my desk with the emotional load I was carrying a bit lighter just knowing my secret was shared with another, who wanted only the best for us and wasn't judging.

Later, I called the number on the card Dr. Fleming had given me for the grief counselor. I'd come to the conclusion getting stuff off my chest to a professional psychologist might be a good idea after all, especially considering the emotional path I was currently headed down. I booked an appointment for after work on Friday.

About 3:50, my desk phone rang, and Declan's cell number popped up on the screen. My lips twitched in a secret smile as I answered.

"Hey," I greeted him, my voice a little nervous.

"Hey. How was your weekend?"

Mindful of the ears around me, I cautiously replied, "Fine. Nothing worth noting. You? She come back?"

I heard him exhale. "Yeah. It was okay. No major conflicts."

"Glad to hear it."

"I was just...in a really good mood. Made it easier, I think."

"I know what you mean. I was...I'm happy, too. Josh even commented on it."

"Did he?" He chuckled. "Figures."

Declan paused for a second, then in a lower, more serious tone said, "You're happy. That's good. I wasn't sure how it would be...after...for you. Everything's okay, then?"

I suddenly realized why he'd called, and any remaining anxiety slipped away. He'd needed to know I had no regrets. "Much better now."

"Me, too."

"Me, too," I murmured.

Just saying those words to each other again sent a rush of pleasure through me. I became giddy. I'd never done drugs before, but I thought this must be what it felt like to get high, and why people became addicted to the euphoria. All I wanted was him. All other priorities and responsibilities faded away. If he'd asked me to run off with him and leave my life completely behind, I would've agreed in a heartbeat.

But it seemed a few shards of logic still remained somewhere deep inside. Even through my Declan-induced bliss, I recognized how dangerous to my well-being this entire situation was.

Chapter 24

Amelia

Friday morning I woke with a start, confused and upset after the strangest dream. In it, I'd gone to Finnegan's to meet Josh and Holly, and as I walked inside I noticed the place was nearly deserted. There was no sign of my friends. Then I spotted Scott at the bar with his back to me. A petite redhead perched on the barstool beside him. She leaned over and rubbed his knee in a very affectionate manner. I began walking over to make my presence known, but suddenly, to my extreme shock, he turned to her and kissed her. I mean, *really* kissed her—not some friendly peck on the cheek, but full-on tongue action. Neither of them had noticed me. Freezing in horror, I watched them make out. Fury boiled up inside me. I've never been a violent person, but right then I wanted to knock that girl right off her barstool. I was just about to march up and demand they tell me what the hell was going on when I woke up.

My heart was pounding. Pressing my head into my pillow, I glared up at the dusty ceiling and gripped the sheets. I took a few deep breaths to try to tamper down my riotous emotions. I knew my reaction made me a gigantic hypocrite, but I couldn't help it; I still thought of Scott as mine. He'd been mine for nearly as long as I could remember. He'd married me. He loved me. And messed up as it was, I still felt possessive toward him. I couldn't even fathom the idea of him with someone else. I knew it would upset me if I ever found out Scott felt about another woman the way I felt about Declan. And yes, I understood how selfish this made me. Scott deserved to be happy, and falling in love with someone else would inevitably be a big part of his finding true happiness. But we'd been vital to each other's lives for so long. My feelings for him couldn't just be switched off.

Sighing, I dragged myself out of bed. My first appointment with the grief counselor was after work, and I was already anxious about it. I didn't need any additional stress from dreaming about things that weren't even real. Yet.

Other than one brief work-related e-mail, I didn't have any communication with Declan all day. We hadn't seen each other in nearly a week, and it was killing me. I wasn't certain what our current relationship status was, if you could even call it that, but I hoped he was missing me as much as I missed him.

The psychologist's office was across the street and down a bit from Blair & Sons. As had become my habit since my dad passed away, I averted my eyes as I drove past the low red brick building and took a right into the parking lot of the medical center. Even still, I felt the pressure of those memories aching to push forth. I shoved them away resolutely, determined that I would not cry. Not right now. Not if I could help it.

Debbie Westwood was in her mid-to-late forties, with graying ash-blonde hair, dark eyes, and a warm smile. She met me just inside the door to her waiting room and ushered me into her office. Noticing there was no couch to lie down on as I'd pictured, I took a seat in one of the two blue armchairs opposite her desk.

Since it was our first meeting, I chose to limit what I discussed to my father, and how acutely I still felt his loss. I wasn't ready to admit the other major reason I was so stressed yet, not until I felt comfortable enough with her to consider divulging my deepest, most shameful secret.

As I talked, I tried to tamper down thoughts of Declan, but it wasn't easy. A week ago, I'd been happy in his arms. Now I sat in this overstuffed chair reminiscing about my dad and trying to ignore all the other messy feelings swirling around inside me.

My first impression was that Debbie seemed kind and sympathetic. She was a soft-spoken woman who asked me simple, direct questions about my relationship with both my parents. When she brought up my marriage, I became less forthcoming. I'm sure she noticed my increased reticence, but for now she chose not to press the subject.

After we talked about my panic attacks, she told me she wanted to recommend my doctor give me a prescription for anti-depressants. I wasn't too sure how I felt about that, but I promised I'd make an appointment to discuss it with Dr. Fleming.

When I returned to my car, I felt a bit better. I had another appointment scheduled for the following Friday, which gave me another week to decide if I was ready to talk about my marriage or my situation with Declan. Her suggestion that I consider medication made me hesitant, but maybe she was right. If it could help with these intense mood swings and bouts of panic, it might be worth it. I'd have to do some research.

Scott's truck was already home when I pulled into the driveway. The light shining from the kitchen window pierced the twilight and reflected brightly off the snow on our small lawn. Inside, I could see him pacing in front of the counter with his phone pressed to his ear. When I came in the door and shrugged off my coat, he stepped into the hallway and greeted me with a smile.

"How did it go?"

My guard instantly went up. "Fine," I replied as nonchalantly as I could. "I'm seeing her again next week."

"Great. I'm glad." He came over and to kiss me hello. I tried not to flinch or tense up, but I'm pretty sure I failed.

Scott pulled back and frowned, brows drawn in tight as he studied my face. Then his grin reappeared. "I made reservations at that Mexican place you like out on the highway. We need to leave in about ten minutes. That okay?"

Surprised, I said, "Um, sure." I glanced down at my outfit and decided I didn't need to change. Casa Marisol was certainly fancier than your average Taco Bell, but my work clothes would do. I went upstairs to splash some water on my face and touch up my makeup, wondering vaguely why Scott wanted to go someplace nicer than

Finnegan's for dinner. Did he want to discuss something serious? I shuddered. That thought made me nervous.

As we drove to the restaurant, Scott kept glancing over at me as he babbled on about his day. Finally noticing my sparse, lackluster replies, he grew silent.

When we arrived, we were ushered to a table in a secluded corner. It had a vase of roses in the middle. Flickering candles on either side sent undulating shadows up the white stucco wall. Scott pulled out my chair for me, then took his place opposite and stared into my eyes.

"Tonight's a big night. I wanted to make sure we did something special," he said with a small smile.

I narrowed my eyes for a split second before forcing my face to become passive. What was he talking about? A big night for what? I glanced around us. The restaurant was about half-full, but none of the other diners sat nearby. Their tables were also candlelit, but none had floral centerpieces. I looked back at the roses in front of me. They were peach, which had been my favorite color rose when I was younger. To be specific, there were five peach roses.

Five.

Just like the ones I'd clutched in my bouquet on our wedding day…which had been five years ago. My eyes flew wide. *Crap! Crap! Crap!* If there was some kind of award for the worst wife on the planet, I deserved it.

Face hot with shame, I pasted on what I hoped was a sweet smile. "Yes, it is," I replied. "And the roses are beautiful, Scott. Thank you."

"You're welcome."

I signaled the waiter and ordered a bottle of wine. Once he filled our glasses, I raised one to Scott in a toast.

"Happy Anniversary," I said, hoping I sounded sincere.

"To five fabulous years with the love of my life," he replied, clinking his glass against mine. "And to at least fifty more." This was not a man who had any doubts about me, or our relationship. He was confident we'd be together for the rest of our lives. My gut clenched. I knew there wouldn't be fifty more. There probably wouldn't even be one more.

How was I going to get through this? How was I going to believably play the happy wife celebrating a major milestone with her husband? I didn't even think I could even eat dinner, let alone act cheerful all night. And then later, once we got home…

At that thought, my belly lurched again. There was no way I could have sex with Scott. Not anymore. I wouldn't sleep with both of them. It was bad enough doing what I was doing, but to add that into the equation? No. Now that I understood how I felt about Declan, I couldn't cheat on him with my own husband. The very idea made me nauseated. It just wasn't going to happen.

I'm not proud to admit it, but I lied a whole lot more. I drank a few glasses of wine, ordered something spicy, and by the time we got back to the house I was complaining of stomach pains. That part wasn't untrue—I did have cramps, had had them for hours by that point, but they were from guilt and shame, not the food. I bolted upstairs to the bathroom and crammed a finger down my throat, forcing everything I'd consumed back out. Ten minutes later, pasty and drenched in sweat, I weakly told Scott my insides hadn't agreed with the meal. Needless to say, he didn't even try to kiss me goodnight.

I felt like utter crap, both mentally and physically, as I wrapped the blankets around myself in the bed we'd shared for the past eight years. I was an awful person. I'd lied to Scott so much recently it had become almost second nature. I'd been unfaithful to him in every way. And now I'd completely forgotten our important five-year anniversary. I knew we needed to talk about some very serious issues, but it just wasn't a conversation I was ready for yet. *Soon*, I promised myself as I laid there beside him; I'd break things to him very soon.

As I fell into an uneasy sleep, I wondered if my timing for anything important in my life would ever be right.

Declan

Laura came home the first weekend, as promised. After her parting comments to me the previous Sunday, I made a deliberate choice to leave her and Alexis alone as much as I could, spending my time in my office, or with James, who was visiting again as he had more appointments scheduled for the upcoming week. While she was back,

I moved some of my stuff into the upstairs spare bedroom and slept there. We tiptoed around each other, only speaking politely and succinctly when necessary.

When she'd walked in the door and caught my eye over Alexis' shoulder as they'd happily embraced, guilt stabbed through me. Looking right into the face of the woman I'd once promised to love for the rest of my life in front of God and all our loved ones—I couldn't help it; I'd felt a surge of shame and regret for my recent choices. At first, she seemed cautiously pleased to see me. A small smile curved the corners of her lips, and she raised a tentative brow my way. I don't know what it was that she saw on my face, but her eyes narrowed and went cold. She returned her attention to Alexis and began to tell her about her week in New York, and my heart hardened again. There was no mistaking the detachment that rolled down her face like a bulletproof blind. I decided then and there that keeping my distance as much as possible for the next three months was exactly how this was going to play out. If she didn't like it, it was her own fucking fault.

After five years of marriage, sleeping in different rooms and barely speaking to each other felt awkward as hell. I'm sure she'd say I was the one making things more difficult than they needed to be—and shit, maybe I was—but this was the simplest way I could deal with it. Or not deal with it, as the case may be. James had to have noticed things between us were tenser than ever, but he didn't try to offer any unsolicited advice, for which I was grateful.

I wasn't in the office much the following week, and when I was, my time was filled with meetings and deadlines. Other than a quick phone call on Tuesday, when I needed to make sure Amelia wasn't harboring any regrets, and that her guilt hadn't overwhelmed her too much over the weekend (but most of all because I couldn't stand not hearing her voice for another second longer) I hadn't been in contact with her.

The second weekend, wonder of wonders, Laura came home again. I mumbled "two for two" as she walked past me into the kitchen, but she didn't deign to reply. James had returned to Buffalo, so there was no one to provide a buffer between us but Alexis. Again, I mostly left them alone to have quality mommy-daughter time. I had some client appointments on Saturday, worked upstairs Saturday evening, and went over to Ryan's Sunday afternoon, returning only when I knew Laura needed to leave to catch her flight. As with the previous weekend, she didn't mention my aloof attitude once, but contrary to that weekend, I felt no pangs of guilt about Amelia.

It wasn't that I hated my wife—I definitely didn't. There was even a part of me that still loved her. I just didn't think that we were repairable anymore. And since I wasn't willing to take the risk of losing my daughter by initiating ending our marriage, it was better for me to just stay out of her way.

When Laura was gone I was the best possible dad to Alexis I could be, and when she was around, I felt the right choice was to leave the two of them to hang out together. Whenever I had a free moment, my thoughts were consumed by all the negativity in my life. Sometimes I just shoved all that crap aside and let myself get lost in the positive memories I had recently created with someone who allowed me an escape from my stress, someone who appreciated me, someone who just made me happy.

It'd been another insane day in the office, and the hours seemed to whip by at break-neck speed. One fire to extinguish after another had my head spinning and my temper short. Before I knew it, it was almost four. I hadn't had a chance to contact Amelia in days, let alone have any face time. Not seeing her left an ache inside me. I missed her smile. I missed her everything.

As I was looking into an inquiry about the pricing on a quote she'd worked on, I decided instead of e-mailing or calling, I'd stretch my legs with a stroll over to Accounting.

I knocked on the metal edge of Amelia's cubicle. Startled, she looked up and the moment those beautiful brown eyes locked with mine a massive smile lit up her face. Like a mirror, I reflected it back to her.

"Hey," she greeted me softly, clearly pleased. My gaze dropped to her lips, which were full and soft-looking, and I had a nearly uncontrollable urge to just bend down and kiss her right there. Parts of me previously relaxed shot to full attention at the thought.

"Hey," I returned, blinking in an attempt to shake off the rush of lust. Inhaling deeply, I continued in as business-like a tone as I could.

"I wanted to ask if you could confirm the parameters you used on your quote for McMillan Dairy. They think we might've omitted some considerations."

She frowned. "I don't have that file on my desk anymore. I'll have to go pull it from the back."

Sweeping an arm in front of me, I directed, "Lead the way."

Amelia arched a brow at me as I started to follow her. I just grinned, hoping like hell the file room would be deserted.

As we walked past Diana's office, she glanced over, but her attention was diverted by her ringing phone. *Saved by the bell*, I thought wryly. A few steps further, a small brunette girl who looked like she could still be in high school told Amelia goodnight as she passed us in the short hallway that led to the rear of the department.

"Goodnight, Mandy," Amelia replied.

There was a desk back there where their administrative assistant worked, which I assumed belonged to the young woman I'd just seen. Behind it, large windows brightened the area with late afternoon sun, and to the left was a plain white wall with an unmarked door. Amelia pulled open the top drawer and retrieved a key on a red lanyard. As she unlocked the door, she explained that after Mandy left each day the file room was supposed to be kept locked. I followed her inside, closing it firmly behind us.

She went behind of a wall of files, squatting to search a lower row of M's for McMillan Dairy. Her hair was pinned up in a messy bun on the back of her head, exposing the slender nape of her neck. A few strands had escaped and curled down, dancing over her shoulders. I couldn't help it; my fingers moved as if they had a mind of their own, lightly grazing her lower back, then tracing a gentle path up the soft fabric covering her spine to the skin on the curve of her neck.

The second I touched her she gasped, which only made me want to touch her more, elicit more of those sexy little sounds from her. When my hand brushed bare skin, she stood abruptly, turning toward me. Her eyes were shining. Her cheeks were flushed. She had just enough time to whisper my name before I pulled her to me and covered her lips with my own.

Unfortunately, she only kissed me back for a few delicious moments before bracing her palms against my chest and firmly pushing me away.

"We can't. Not here," she whispered, looking nervous. And sexy. God, she looked sexy as hell. The fact that we hadn't seen each other since she left the hotel room, and how turned on we both clearly were already, did not escape either of our notice. Her gaze slid down my body before reconnecting with mine.

"Door's locked and you've got the key," I reminded her, waggling my eyebrows suggestively. "No one can interrupt."

Sucking in a sharp breath, Amelia considered our situation. Her eyes flicked between the door and my mouth, forehead creased with indecision. Finally she whispered. "Diana's still in her office, and it's not that far away. If we got caught…"

I sighed. She was right, of course. With a regretful groan I took a step back from her. "I know." Squeezing her fingers, I told her, "You go back to your desk. I'll come out a few minutes later and head straight for my office. You can just e-mail me the information I need."

She nodded. Standing on tiptoes, she pressed her lips to mine again. "Sorry," she murmured sadly. "I want to be with you, too. I've missed you."

As she started for the door with the file clutched to her chest, I reached for her arm. "Mel, I need…need to see you, to touch you. Soon." Her eyes softened as she stared at me.

Then the smile I loved so much reappeared, eradicating all the worry. "You could meet me in a parking lot on the south side of town in about twenty minutes? We wouldn't have much time, but I think I could spare a few minutes before I'd have to hit the highway."

Now there was my girl, using her head to come up with a solution. "Perfect. I'll call you when I'm leaving to tell you where."

With a nod, she disappeared. I leaned back against the shelf of files behind me, trying to reassemble my jumbled thoughts. Being around Amelia tended to eradicate all my logical thinking. And kissing her…well, kissing her seemed to shut my brain right off. I got lost in her every single time.

I took a few deep breaths and tried to focus on recalling what I absolutely needed to finish before I could get out of here. Then I thought about meeting Amelia shortly thereafter and, with a devilish grin, pushed off the wall and got a move on.

Amelia

As I made my way back to my desk, I couldn't stop smiling. My formerly blah mood had soared the second I saw Declan's face. And when he touched me…well let's just say that old adage about sparks flying described my reaction well.

My heart pounded with excitement, knowing I'd soon have some alone time with him, however short. I quickly scanned through the McMillan Dairy file, double-checking all my calculations to make sure I hadn't overlooked anything vital. Finding no errors, I sent Declan an e-mail confirming my quote's accuracy.

Then I powered down my computer, said goodnight to Josh, and headed out. The temperature had dropped, and the wind swirled gusts of snow and debris between the rows of vehicles. Pulling the collar of my coat tightly around my neck, I hurried across the pavement to my car.

As I climbed inside and pulled the door shut against the cold, I heard my phone chirp inside my bag.

"Hey," I answered, knowing who it was without checking the display.

"Meet me beside the Food Lion on Ward's Road?"

"I'm leaving right now."

"See you in a few." Declan paused for a moment, and at first I thought he'd disconnected. Then I heard him mutter, "Not soon enough."

I smiled to myself. "Never is."

The Food Lion was a large supermarket I passed every day on my route to work, located along Highway 29, also known as Ward's Road. I'd even stopped there a few times when I'd needed to pick up last-minute groceries. The surrounding parking lot was huge and, fortunately for us, nearly empty. A few scattered cars were parked along the left, and several more were clustered near the main entrance, waiting for their shivering, bag-laden owners to return.

It was a frigid late January afternoon, dim and dull, soon to graduate to full-fledged dark. The wind rose and fell in gusts, driving whirling snow devils across the cracked asphalt. The steely sky overhead ushered dark clouds looming low on the horizon. As I scanned them, I wondered if they heralded an approaching snow storm, and if so, would I have time to make it home before it hit?

I pulled into a space along the right of the building. There was only one other vehicle nearby: a lone car shrouded with a thick layer of snow. It obviously hadn't been moved in days, possibly weeks. I doubted its driver would show up during the short time I planned to be there.

Hoping Declan would arrive soon, I turned my engine off, but left the radio on. I didn't want to have to sit alone in a rapidly cooling car for long. Inspired, I slipped the Jim Coltrane CD he'd made me last summer into the player while I waited.

The opening notes of "My Secret" filled the car.

> *"You are my secret, baby*
> *And I am yours*
> *We hide behind closed doors*
> *And nobody knows*
> *Nobody knows."*

My heart clenched. He was my secret all right, and nobody knew—not what we really were to each other. Only he and I carried that weight between us. That knowledge was at the same time both lighter than anything I'd ever felt before, yet heavier than either of us could hope to carry alone.

I began to softly sing along.

> *"Hate lying to everyone else*
> *Always havin' to keep you to myself*
> *I just wanna tell the whole world you're mine*
> *Lord, can'tcha give me a sign?*
> *Cause this secret's breakin' me, breakin' me down."*

A light tap on the passenger window made me jump. With relief, I saw Declan's face peering in at me. Somehow I'd gotten so wrapped up in the music that I hadn't seen him pull up alongside my car. He laughed as he opened the door and climbed inside.

"Did I scare you?" he teased, tugging off his black leather gloves. The corners of his eyes creased as he grinned at me, his cheeks red from the cold.

I smiled sheepishly. "I guess I really got into the song," I admitted.

"It's a good one." He paused as he thought more about it, then added, "Appropriate, too." He slid a hand around the back of my neck and tugged me to him with a soft, "C'mere." I snuggled closer and our lips met in a rush.

It didn't take long for my chilled body to heat up with Declan's hands and mouth burning my skin each place he touched me. His palms first cupped my cheeks, then my neck, then one hand found its way inside my jacket and around the bare skin of my waist under my shirt. I kissed him fervently, wishing we were alone in a warm, private room instead of partially exposed in my chilly Honda.

When I pulled away for much-needed air, his lips nibbled their way up my jaw to my ear. Sucking in a sharp gasp, I shivered as his hot breath tickled the sensitive skin right below my earlobe.

"I can't believe we're making out in a car!" I exclaimed with a laugh as he began to kiss his way down my neck, pulling aside the collar of my jacket for better access. "I feel like a teen trying not to get caught by my dad with a boy."

Declan shifted his face level with mine. "Did that happen often?" he asked, his eyes twinkling. "Getting caught making out with boys in cars?"

I giggled. "Not often!"

"But sometimes?" he pressed, studying me with amusement. "Were you a bad girl when you were a teen, Mel?"

"No! I was a good girl. I'm *still* a good girl!"

One dark eyebrow quirked skeptically. "Oh, really?" He smirked. "You sure about that?"

And just like that, all the lightness and mirth drained out of me. I sighed heavily and pulled away, staring down at my hands. "No. I'm not. I'm a liar and a cheat. I've been so caught up in my own issues, I even forgot my wedding anniversary last week. I had to fake it and lie through my teeth, which has become such a regular thing lately it barely fazes me. The lies just spill from my mouth one after the other." My voice quavered. "And I know what I have to do, but I haven't found the guts to do it yet."

"What's that?" Declan asked, his tone full of understanding and compassion. His large hands found mine and squeezed my icy fingers.

"Tell him that we're over. Break his heart into a million pieces. I loathe the idea of hurting him, but I can't continue this charade much longer. It's not fair to either of us—to *any* of us. Yet I keep putting that conversation off because I know how much it's going to suck." I paused and drew a deep breath. "God, I've turned into such a terrible person. My dad wouldn't even recognize who I've become since he died." Tears welled up in my eyes.

He gripped my shoulders with both hands and forced me to look at him. "Yes, he would. You told me once he promised he'd always stand by you and support your decisions, right?"

I nodded, wiping a few errant tears away.

"So don't be so hard on yourself. I know nothing about this is easy. It's not easy for me, either. And if you wanna call it quits, all you've gotta do is say so. The last thing I want is to make your life more difficult than it already is."

"I know. And you don't. I'm *happy* when I'm with you. I swear it might be the only time I *am* happy anymore. I don't want to lose you." I attempted a small smile, but I knew it was a wobbly one.

"Good," Declan said firmly, and pulled me against his chest, wrapping his arms around me and holding me close. He pressed his cheek to mine and spoke low into my ear. "I know how crazy all this is, but you're..." Taking a deep breath, he searched for the right words, his fingers stroking down my hair. "My life is full to the brim with worry and stress and responsibility. You're my calm, my easy..." He paused to look me in the eyes. "You're my escape. I need you."

"I need you, too," I whispered, and he squeezed me tighter.

Tiny snow pellets began to pepper the windshield. We both knew we needed to get back to our regularly scheduled lives. Our small time-out had to come to an end.

He kissed me again, slow and deliberate and full of all the emotions we still hadn't voiced to each other.

When he pulled back to go, he held my gaze once more. "When things get too much, when you're feeling lost and alone, just remember," he told me, partially quoting one of the songs on the CD I'd made for him so many months ago. I smiled as he tugged the door handle and pushed open the door, letting the icy air swirl inside.

"Remember what?" I asked, but I knew.

Declan stroked a finger down my cheek and along my jaw before stepping out of the car. "Me, too."

A sense of tranquility spread over me as I shifted into reverse and made my way back out to the highway. The hard snow assaulted the glass, and my wipers whipped it away nearly as fast as it made contact. The roads weren't too slick yet, but it wouldn't be long.

The last of the fading daylight ebbed away as I sped down the road toward home, or at least what used to be my home. I was about ten minutes into my drive when I realized I was still smiling.

Chapter 25

Amelia

We began meeting once or twice a week after that, in random spots not far off our regular paths. Usually right after work, but occasionally, when there were no other options, we'd get together over lunch. He'd climb into my car or I'd go to his, and we'd talk and touch and kiss. We never had sex; I assumed we both felt it would demean what we were to each other to make love in our cars. Ours was no sneaky high school romance—it was so much more than we could ever put a name to. I cherished those stolen moments each week when we could talk openly with each other, touch each other, and just be with each other.

It seemed like we were always touching from the moment the car door shut behind us. Even while we chatted about our day, our hands would be connected, or he'd be stroking my arm, or my fingers would be resting lightly on his neck. Skin against skin. Always. When he kissed me, his hands inevitably found their way underneath my top, tracing blazing trails across my back and down my sides, and sometimes in moments of passion, over my chest as well. We wanted each other far more than the fifteen minutes we allowed gave us time for, but somehow we resisted. Hotel rooms were mentioned in needy and regretful murmurs, but neither of us acted on booking one again. I think we realized the massive risk we had taken that first time, and didn't feel comfortable returning things to that level again. At least not right now.

Yet we just couldn't stay away from each other completely. So we met up, and during the short time we were together, we hung on like we never wanted to let go.

Monday, February 3rd was one of those bright, yet bitterly cold winter days. I remember it clearly because it was the first day of my Week From Hell.

It all began with an e-mail from Colleen requesting a quote for SleepAway Motels for an add-on we did not break out pricing for on its own, only in conjunction with other services. In my reply, I politely explained that I couldn't quote it independently, but would be happy to price it as part of a package if that's what the client wanted.

About an hour later I got another message about it, this time from Declan. He asked me rather bluntly to cost the service independently. Again, I clarified as professionally as possible why we simply couldn't do it. He responded within a few minutes saying that he'd had this service priced by itself in the past, and he needed it for this client. Not a *please* to be found. I insisted it was not an exception I was able to make.

When he came back yet again, this time with glaring annoyance seething from every word, my own anger sparked. A sick feeling spread through my gut as I realized this might end up being a bigger issue than I'd first anticipated. With chagrin, I recalled the stories Kaitlyn had told me about how Declan reacted when he didn't get his own way. He was well known to be pushy, demand things be done how he wanted, and then go over people's heads if he still got resistance.

I was confident I was giving Colleen and Declan the right information, but I still printed off the e-mail chain and, as Josh wasn't in his office, went in to speak with Diana. I explained the situation to her, what the client was asking for, what my response had been, and the messages I'd since received from Declan insisting I had to break it out for him. She looked over the request and agreed that my answer was correct. When I returned to my desk, I wrote a firmly worded e-mail back to him, with Diana copied in, explaining for a third time exactly why we couldn't price it as asked. I deliberately referred to it as the client's request and not Declan's so it wouldn't come off like a personal denial.

The whole situation left a bad taste in my mouth. Not only had the tone of his messages implied that I didn't know what I was talking about, but they also hinted that he thought I was being difficult deliberately. After all we'd been through together over the past seven months, and especially recently, it was the latter that hurt the most.

When Josh returned to the office, I went to ask his opinion on the matter. Like Diana, he agreed that my response had been right, but he also admitted that an exception or two had been made for one of Declan's clients in the past. At that, I closed my eyes and sighed in frustration. I suddenly understood just how this would play out. As usual around here, Declan was going to get his own way, and I'd end up looking like a fool for denying him.

I wasn't wrong.

Diana showed up at my cubicle about thirty minutes later with the SleepAway Motels case file in her hands. She dropped it on my desk, informed me irritably that she'd been on the phone with a pissed off Declan for the past twenty minutes, and that I was to price out the service as the client had originally requested. If I had any questions about how to do it, I should go ask Josh. Then she strode off in annoyance, as if somehow this headache was all my fault.

Within less than a minute of her leaving, yet another e-mail from Declan arrived, telling me essentially the same. It was curt and short, with no pleasantries or thank yous. Clearly, he was no more impressed with the situation than I was, although for very different reasons.

Rolling my eyes in frustration I did as I was told, calculating the price and sending it to him with both Colleen and Diana copied in. Although I was fuming, I assumed that would be the end of it.

And it was, for that day. I wondered if I'd still get a personal call or text from Declan to arrange a clandestine meet-up this week. To my disappointment, but no real surprise, I did not.

The following day, he e-mailed me first thing in the morning and requested I come over to discuss the SleepAway quote. I wrote back asking what he still needed, but he just replied, "Bring the file with you."

I got a sinking feeling in the pit of my stomach. I knew this conversation was going to be far different from how we usually interacted. But we needed to deal with this and get it out of the way. I'd already spent too much time reading and re-reading the e-mails he'd sent the previous day. Each review only made me more annoyed.

So when I walked into his office and dropped into one of his guest chairs to face him, I wore a stony expression. He flashed me a tight grin, but it wasn't his usual 'happy to see me' look either.

"I thought we should talk about what happened yesterday," he began, attempting eye contact. I didn't hold his gaze for long, instead looking down at the print-out of my quote.

"Was there a problem with my pricing?" I asked, trying to keep my tone businesslike.

His brows narrowed. "No."

"Then why am I here?" I closed the file and started to rise.

Declan frowned. "Why are you upset?" His eyes shifted to the open office door, and I knew he was thinking about closing it. This time, that was the last thing I wanted.

With a sigh, I sat back down. "I had very good reason for denying your request. And your e-mails made it sound like you assumed I was just deliberately being difficult, and didn't want to help you or the client. That's why I'm upset."

He scrutinized me, his expression unreadable. Finally he asked, "Weren't you?"

Anger erupted inside me at his confirmation of my suspicions. "No!" I shot back. "I'd never do that! And I would hope after all this time you'd know me well enough to know I wouldn't react like that. I always—*always*—make every attempt to get the pricing our clients are waiting for back to you guys as soon as humanly possible. When I have *ever* given you push back on a request for no reason? *Ever?*" I stopped to take a breath, realizing how much my voice had risen.

"You haven't before," he admitted, glancing at the door again.

"But you thought this time I was just being a bitch, didn't you? Look, I'm fully aware you've had problems with other accountants in the past. But I'm not them, Declan. I'm me. And you *know* me!"

He just stared at me, absentmindedly tapped his pen against the edge of his desk. When he didn't reply after a while, I said in a much lower tone, "I'm angry and hurt you would even *think* I'd treat you that way."

He sighed. "Hmm. Maybe we'd better just put this one to rest." Pasting on a smile and a more relaxed expression, he casually asked, "So how was your weekend?"

My mouth fell open in shock. *How was my weekend?* Was he freaking kidding me?

"Um…it was fine."

We regarded each other silently. In my effort to tamper down my fury, a thick lump now hurt my throat, promising imminent tears if I didn't get a better control over myself.

"I can't do this right now," I muttered, rising to my feet. "I've gotta get back to my desk."

His eyes narrowed again, but he just replied, "O…kay." He did not add "talk to you later" or anything else to imply we might interact again anytime soon.

I stalked back to my cubicle fuming, hoping no one else would dare say anything to upset me further. If they did, I was pretty sure I'd end up saying something I'd regret.

Sleep was a long time coming that night. I stared at the wall, unable to stop my mind from going over and over the e-mails and words we'd exchanged.

On Wednesday, I collected the new quote requests assigned to me and worked my way through them, as I always did every morning. Less than five minutes after finishing up and sending out a quote for one of Declan's potential new clients, I got an e-mail from Colleen asking us to delete that request because Declan had decided to decline it. I was a bit irritated, since I had just spent thirty minutes of my time working on something he should have reviewed prior to sending to Accounting.

While speaking with Diana later, I mentioned in passing that I thought it would be a great idea if the Account Managers would review their quote requests before their assistants sent them to us, as I was in the habit of doing mine first thing in the morning, and it was frustrating to find out I'd wasted my time, since this had happened more than once. As I might have expected, she was annoyed to discover that her accountants were sometimes not making good use of their valuable time. When she asked which quote was declined today so she could speak to Sales about changing the process, I didn't hesitate to tell her. I figured improving our time management was a good thing for everyone involved, so I went back to work and promptly forgot all about it.

I had an e-mail from Declan waiting when I returned to my desk after lunch. It said that if I had a problem with how something was handled between myself and his team, he would've appreciated it if I'd come right to him, as Josh apparently always did, instead of complaining to Diana and getting her involved.

The anger sitting dormant since Monday resurged through me. I forced myself to close his message without replying, aware of how stressed I was that he was obviously still unhappy with me. I'd been hoping this was over, and we could move past it, but unfortunately it seemed like I was wrong. I worked on other stuff for a couple of hours until I felt I could respond in a calm and professional manner. Then I explained to him that I hadn't gone to Diana about it, we'd just been talking, and it had come up. I said I'd received Colleen's message to decline after I'd already finished the quote, and that I wasn't thrilled about the waste of my time. After debating for a few moments, I added that I thought he was still upset with me about Monday's issues.

He replied a few minutes later, assuring me that there was no problem from his end, that he and Colleen had been nothing but professional, and that if there was any 'upset', it had come from my department. His tone felt accusatory and dismissive, and my hackles rose even more. My fingers were trembling with rage as they hovered over my keyboard, about to type a scathing comeback. Flailing about for the fleeting strands of what remained of my restraint, I minimized my inbox. An angry reply would only make things even worse.

When I left for the day I was still seething. I could focus on little else but our stupid conflict.

That night I again tossed and turned, far too wound up to sleep. I'd been withdrawn and sullen all evening, and Scott had noticed. He'd asked when my appointment was with my doctor to discuss the anti-depressant recommendation. I was still wary about taking drugs that would mess with my emotions, but I'd told him I was seeing Dr. Fleming next week. He'd seemed relieved. I couldn't help but wonder what exactly he hoped the medication would change about me.

The next day, I discussed the Declan debacle with Josh, who was sympathetic but had no answers for me. He assumed other outside issues were probably stressing Declan, and advised me to give him some time before trying to talk things out.

I buried myself in work in an attempt to distract myself from how unhappy I felt, but it wasn't easy. Things not being right with Declan completely threw off my ability to focus. Around three o'clock, I again re-read all the messages we'd sent to each other over the previous three days. I recalled our discussion in his office on Tuesday. I thought about the fact that I hadn't received a single personal text, phone call, or kind word from him the entire week. And I worried we might be in the midst of imploding in a permanent way. That thought terrified me. No matter how annoyed I was with him right now, I still loved him.

On impulse, I opened a new e-mail and typed: *Do you have any idea how much damage this week's issues have done to our friendship?*

It was almost time to go home, so I finished what I was working on and began to shut things down for the day. Just before I closed my inbox, a reply from him arrived.

Please come over to discuss.

I sighed. He wanted to see me. He'd even said please. I contemplated going, but I fast realized I was still too upset to have a rational conversation with him. If I spoke to him face to face right now, I was afraid we'd both say things we'd regret, making this divide between us even wider. So I decided to put it off. I told myself I'd reply in the morning, and possibly speak with him in person then.

I went home.

Friday, the final day of the Week From Hell, was dim and snowy, and I got into work late. Strong winds gusted white sheets horizontally across the slick highway, and my car ended up trapped in a long, slow caravan of white-knuckled drivers. By the time I finally arrived at my desk, there was a pressure headache stewing behind my eyes, and I had to spend my first hour calculating out two rush requests that had been awaiting my attention.

Just after ten a message came in from Declan: *Thought I would have heard from you by now to talk things over. Guess I was wrong.*

My eyes widened in surprise. Now he was disappointed in me again? Because I hadn't jumped and immediately come running to him when he beckoned? That all-too-familiar anger erupted once more and my heart began to pound as the accompanying adrenaline kicked in. Over the next few hours a succession of increasingly more inflammatory e-mails flew between us. Each time a new reply from him showed up, my blood pressure spiked before I even read the content.

Somewhere around 2:30 in the afternoon, I just stopped responding, which was what I really should've done hours earlier. I knew we were using company e-mail that was traceable if HR ever wanted to, and our thinly veiled business phrasing had become more and more antagonistic with each subsequent communication.

I decided that I was going to head straight out at four again and let Declan simmer. To be completely honest, what I really hoped was that he'd reach out to me on a personal level. I wanted him to call, or text, or show up at my desk and apologize. I wished he'd admit that he wouldn't be able to go home and relax this weekend until we were right again.

Then I realized something. I had no idea what was really driving his mood this week, or why things between us had escalated so fast. I was holding on to my temper and pride, wanting him to man up and come to me, but I was just being stubborn. I was the one who wouldn't be able to relax, or probably even sleep, if I didn't fix this before I left for the weekend.

So, when I shut down and got ready to go home, instead of heading straight to the parking lot, I made a detour through Sales. My nerves buzzed like high-tension wires; I had no idea what kind of a reaction I'd receive when I saw Declan. I didn't even know if he was still in his office until I approached and heard his voice as he spoke on the phone.

I hesitated outside his doorway, not wanting to interrupt. When I caught a few words, I understood this was not a business call. He was clearly irritated. As I listened, his volume rose in annoyance. "Fine! Have it your way, like you always do! I'll just deal with the fall-out for you, like *I* always do." Then I heard the unmistakable sound of the phone being slammed into its cradle.

Just as I was about to turn and walk away to give him a few minutes to cool down before I approached, bringing with me presumably more stress, he swiveled in his chair and caught me watching him. His eyes bulged in near comical surprise. I thought I detected the beginnings of a smile before he wiped it away.

"Amelia," he greeted me in level voice.

"Declan," I returned, equally cool.

I waited to see if he'd invite me in to sit down. Staring resolutely at me, he said nothing. After a moment, I stepped inside and closed the door behind me.

I sat down, and at first we just regarded each other in silence. His eyes were bloodshot and tired-looking, and his hair was even messier than usual. I could picture him raking his fingers through it over and over with every new e-mail from me he'd read. His black dress shirt was untucked, and empty paper coffee cups littered his normally neat desk. Declan was definitely not himself.

With a soft sigh, he broke our stalemate. "So what can I do for you?"

"I didn't want to go home for the weekend with things so messed up between us." I confessed.

He frowned. "I didn't want to go home last night without talking to you, either, but you apparently had no problem with that."

"I was angry."

"So was I."

"Why?" I wanted to know the real reason, whether it was truly all because of me, or if there were outside issues, and he'd been redirecting his frustrations.

"The first time or the second? Monday, it was because you wouldn't help me until I had to go over your head and force you to. The Amelia I knew always did everything in her power to help a client, and you flat out refused!"

"I already explained over and over exactly why I-"

274

"Then on Wednesday I'm blindsided by a bitchy e-mail from Diana demanding we review all our requests for pricing in advance, as we're wasting her accountants' precious time. She stated your complaint to her as proof. Which you *should* have come straight to me with if you had a problem. I thought that's how we worked—that we trusted each other enough to always go to one another to fix things first, before dragging Diana or anyone else into it!"

"And I told you I never meant to-"

"I thought we had each other's backs, but apparently I was wrong." He leaned back in his chair and fixed me with a challenging glare. It seemed like he was daring me to defend myself.

"Are you done?" I asked. "Or is there anything else you'd like to tell me off for?"

"No, I'm not done. You know what pissed me off the most? What disappointed me more than anything else?" His eyes flashed with hurt and anger.

I shook my head.

"That you refused to even come talk things out with me! That you just…just *left*! Like it didn't even matter to you!" He stood and turned toward the window, hands braced on the edge of his desk, refusing to look at me.

I started to understand. Darting a glance at the closed door, I got up and went to him. I touched his forearm tentatively as I assured him in a low voice, "It mattered to me. It mattered a lot. I hated that we were fighting. But every single e-mail you sent just made my blood pressure shoot up higher."

Declan swiveled to meet my eyes and the corner of his lips twitched. "I had the same reaction to yours."

"I know myself well enough to know if I'd come talk to you earlier, we probably would've ended up saying things we couldn't come back from. I needed some cooling off time, and I suspect you did, too." I squeezed his wrist. "Seems we're both pretty stubborn, huh?"

A small smile surfaced at last. He lifted a hand and gently ran the tops of his knuckles down my cheek. "Yet another thing we have in common."

Without thinking, I pulled him into a hug. His arms slid around my waist and pressed my body to his.

Remembering where we were, I pulled away with reluctance and returned to my chair. Though I was immensely relieved, I wasn't done with this conversation quite yet. "So what else is going on? There's obviously more crap happening with you this week than just our stuff."

Declan sighed as he sat back down. Then he told me he'd found out Monday morning that two of his more lucrative clients were taking their business to another advertising agency as soon as their contracts were up. He felt guilty that he'd been so distracted lately by all the issues in his personal life, and confessed that he hadn't been able to focus on work as much as he should have been.

"Was it your fault they decided to leave?" I asked bluntly.

He considered my question. "Not directly, no, but I should've-"

"Stop. It sucks, I know, but you can't take responsibility for that. Clients come and go. It happens in every agency. And if it wasn't because of something you did, then you can't blame yourself." He nodded, and it encouraged me. "What else?"

His brows shot up.

"I know there's more. What is it? Something with James? Ryan? Or did Laura tell you guys she wasn't coming home this weekend, and Alexis is upset?"

Eye widening in surprise, he admitted, "The last one. Just got off the phone with her confirming it's definite. Lex doesn't even know yet."

Sighing, I told him, "That sucks, too. It really does. No matter how much it doesn't surprise you, I know you were hoping for your daughter's sake this wouldn't happen."

"Exactly. But it's probably best she get used to it. It won't be the last time Laura will blow us off."

I paused as I realized something. "You felt abandoned—by her, which you're kind of used to, and then by me, which you're not. That's why you got so defensive."

He just stared at me, lips pressed into a hard line.

"Declan, I didn't abandon you. I had to work through my anger before I came to see you, but I still…you've still got me. I'm not going anywhere." As I reassured him, I gave him the first genuine smile I'd probably had all week.

He visibly relaxed at my words. "Perhaps we could continue this conversation elsewhere?" he asked quietly, a real grin of his own finally surfacing. Parts of me I hadn't even realized were tense eased at the sight of it. And, just like that, our Week From Hell was over.

Glancing down at my watch, I told him I could spare a few more minutes. "Food Lion, Wooley's Auto Body, or Feed 'N Fuel?" I asked teasingly.

And that was how, at 4:45 on a Friday, I ended up in the front seat of his Mustang parked behind the former Feed 'N Fuel on Ward's Road, snugly encased in Declan's warm arms.

Declan

Sometimes I do stupid things. Getting my fucking panties all in a knot over Amelia's e-mails this week was one of them. The quantities of shit that had gone down around me the last few days had left me feeling like all my life-lines had been cut, and I'd been set adrift. My whole life, it had been difficult for me to really trust others, and the few times I had, they'd invariably let me down. This week, it felt like I'd been fooled into deluding myself about Amelia, too—like now I'd let her in, I'd discovered she was just like all the others. Somewhere deep down a part of me knew I wasn't being fair in passing judgment on her so quickly, but then another message would arrive from her and I'd get pissed off all over again.

After our talk in my office at the end of the day Friday, we met for a few minutes behind a derelict gas station before she headed home. All my stress from being at odds with her all week fell away. We collided in a tangle of lips and limbs.

The release of all those pent-up emotions overwhelmed me as I kissed her. My hands had minds of their own; they roamed frantically over her soft skin, under her sweater, down the back of her dress pants, caressing every curve, but never stopping for long in any one place. It was like I needed to touch every inch of her to make sure she was real, and that she was still with me. I was hard as hell, and all I could think about was getting closer, being inside her. If I'd had my way, we would have had makeup sex right there in that gloomy, deserted parking lot.

Unfortunately Amelia knocked some sense into me, for which I was both frustrated and grateful. She couldn't stay, and I knew I had to pick up Alexis from the sitter in a few minutes.

Before she opened the door, she asked, "We're okay now, right?"

My eyebrows shot up. Hadn't we just been lip-locked seconds ago? How could she still be uncertain? "Completely. You even need to ask?"

"I just wanted to make sure. This week had me really freaked out. I hate when things aren't right between us."

"I hate it, too. And I'm sorry for overreacting. I got…" I stopped, unsure if I wanted to elaborate or not.

"You got what?"

With a soft sigh, I admitted, "I got scared."

She reached over and squeezed my large fingers in her small ones. "Scared of what? Me changing my mind? Deciding everyone else is right about you?"

I blew out a small breath. "That. And…how you make me feel. That scares the shit outta me."

She snuggled up to me again, threading her hands beneath my leather jacket to pull me close. "I know just what you mean. But you don't have to worry. I won't change my mind. Even when we're fighting, being with you makes me…thrive."

"Me, too," I admitted, and kissed her again.

As I watched Amelia get back into her own car, wave at me through her window, and drive away, it hit me. When we'd finally talked everything out earlier, she'd analyzed the situation and been able to see straight through my bullshit to what the real issue was. Even when we were butting heads with each other, she managed to figure out the truth—truth I hadn't even realized until she said it out loud. In that moment, I realized how completely head over fucking heels in love with this woman I was. There was no longer any point in even trying to deny it.

My heart started to race, and I let my head fall back against the headrest. I gasped as I fought to get enough air into my suddenly too-tight lungs. Squeezing my eyes shut, I tried to focus on evening out my labored breathing. *Breathe in. Breathe out. So you don't fucking pass out,* I chanted internally. I'd had intermittent panic attacks off and on since my mother died, and I knew how to deal with them. In a few more minutes this one eased up, too.

I'd been lying to myself when I'd thought I had some semblance of control over my emotions for her. There was no goddamn control. I was lost. And because of my situation, chances were I was also completely fucked.

Chapter 26

Amelia

The night was clear, frigid, and bright, with a massive bone-white moon hanging low over the horizon. It seemed to stare at me accusingly as Scott and I drove home from dinner at his mom's. Sandy, for maybe the first time ever, conspicuously did *not* ask us when we were going to give her grandkids. It made me suspect Scott might have told her about me not wanting to be a mom, which, in turn, had me wondering if she thought I was a failure as a wife to her son. I was already well aware I was a complete failure in that, without a doubt, but the thought that anyone else might see me that way disturbed me.

I'd had another appointment with Debbie Westwood the previous day. This time I'd opened up to her about my marriage, telling her I didn't see myself having kids with Scott. She'd gotten me to admit I loved him more like a friend than a lover these days. She'd then asked if I'd considered leaving him. I'd squirmed in my chair before acknowledging that the thought had crossed my mind. When she wondered what was stopping me, I'd confessed that not only did I hate the idea of hurting him, but I also wasn't ready to deal with the intense pain I knew taking that step would yield, as I was still getting over my father's death. I wasn't sure if she bought it or not, but at least she didn't ask me if there was someone else, though I was on pins and needles just waiting for that particular question. I hadn't mentioned Declan yet, but I was starting to trust her. I decided I'd give serious thought to revealing my most guarded secret soon.

Gazing at that huge round moon, I wondered if Declan might be staring up at it, too, wherever he was tonight.

Scott's voice dragged me from my thoughts. "So, how've you been feeling lately? Has talking to that woman been helping at all?" He shot a glance my way as he drove.

"Yes…at least I think so. It's probably too soon to say."

"I'm glad." He was quiet for a while. Then, abruptly, "Does she do marriage counseling?"

I sucked in a sharp breath. She did, actually. But I didn't know if that was something I'd even consider. If I told her the truth about Declan, I didn't think I'd be able to sit through marriage counseling with her. I did think Scott could use someone of his own to talk to, though—besides Liv, presuming he'd been discussing things with her when I wasn't around. Neither of them had said anything to me about it lately, but I just had a gut feeling. I wondered if she'd told him she thought Ben was cheating on her. Then I couldn't help but question if Scott suspected I might be doing the same. Suddenly the thought of Liv and Scott confiding in each other made me nervous.

"Amelia?" Scott's voice interrupted my musings, and I realized I hadn't yet replied. "You tuned out again."

"Sorry. Right. Um, yes, I think so. Why?"

He sighed in exasperation. "*Really*? You have no clue why I'd ask that?"

Okay, I was getting seriously uncomfortable with the direction this conversation was going. Contemplating an appropriate response, I stared out the window watching the dark houses slip past. We were nearly at our street.

"So you're not even gonna answer me?" His voice had risen along with his agitation. He was obviously frustrated, but not only did I not want to talk about this, I also had no idea what to say.

"I'm *sorry!*" I burst out. "I *know* I've been a sucky wife to you since my dad died! I know it. And I *know* you're not happy with me.

But I already told you I needed more time. What else do you want me to say?"

Scott twisted the wheel sharply and we careened around the corner, my shoulder slamming against the inside of the door. I cried out in surprise.

He didn't say a word until he'd lurched his truck to a sudden stop in the driveway. "*What I want* is some sign from you that you actually wanna fix our marriage!" he bellowed, swiveling his body to face mine.

I rubbed my sore arm as Scott glared at me. "You think it's broken?" I whispered, guilt and fear churning my guts to mush.

His tone softened. "I sure as hell know *something's* not right. And so do you. Hell, even Liv can tell that much. You're depressed, I know, but there's more to it than that. Things have been off since before your dad passed away. Please don't try to deny it."

I fixated on my fingers twisting in my lap and said nothing.

"Amelia?" Another sigh. "We always used to tell each other everything. Why won't you tell me what's really going on?" His voice had taken on a pleading note.

The tears I'd been fighting back began to slip down my cheeks, each one chasing the trail of the last. Pressing my fist to my lips, I leaned my forehead against the cold window.

"Your silence says it all." He leapt from the truck and slammed his door shut, jolting the entire vehicle and me within it. He stood there on the driveway with his back to me, head down, shoulders heaving, for several long seconds. Instead of going inside, he then strode down the sidewalk, disappearing into the dark.

I cried harder. My nose ran. I gasped shallow breaths into my too-tight lungs. My throat was so sore I could barely swallow. And still the tears gushed. I brought my knees up and wrapped my arms around them, curling myself into a ball.

I don't know how long I sat there rocking gently back and forth, the ticking of the cooling engine the only sound beyond my labored inhalations. When at long last it seemed that there was nothing left in me, I stumbled out into the cold and retreated inside my dark, empty house.

Sometime later I heard the truck's engine start up as Scott returned to drive off to who knew where. He didn't come home that night. I wrapped myself up in the blanket on the couch downstairs and, shockingly, did manage some sleep, but not much. Nightmares about our next confrontation kept waking me, causing my overactive mind to play out every possible scenario, each one more awful than the last.

Did he have his own suspicions about my faithfulness? I had to find out, so I could prepare myself. I needed to talk to Liv to try to discern what Scott really thought. And if he was only worried about my pulling away from him, then I had to decide if I'd consider joint marriage counseling. But that would mean lying not only to Scott, but to Debbie Westwood as well. No, I didn't think I could do it. I'd suggest he schedule his own sessions to talk about his feelings privately, and then if he wanted to discuss stuff with me afterward, he could. I truly didn't want Scott to be so unhappy. He didn't deserve any of this.

Of course, my other option was telling him flat-out that our marriage was over and facing the fallout.

I really missed my dad and the guidance he always offered. Yes, he'd be disappointed in me. No, he wouldn't approve of my recent choices. But he'd love and support me no matter what, even though I'd be letting him down. He'd know the right thing to say to get me moving again, to get me back on the track I needed to be on.

No matter how much I tried to tell myself the advice I suspected he'd give me if he could, I remained paralyzed. Whatever choice I made, someone would get hurt. I never meant for any of this to happen, and I loathed the thought of wounding Scott, or anyone else.

I felt like a massive failure.

Monday after work I went straight to the nearest pharmacy and filled the prescription Dr. Fleming had given me. It had been folded up in my purse for nearly two weeks while I'd debated if I really wanted it or not.

The accompanying list of side effects made me nervous, but I had decided I should at least give it a try. I'd been feeling extra volatile lately. Last week, I'd fought with Declan, last night, with Scott—it seemed clear I needed help dealing with this funk I was in. Maybe the antidepressants would take the edge off.

Around eight, I nervously swallowed my first small orange tablet. By nine, I felt drowsy and somewhat out of it. Scott knew I'd started the medication, and he seemed pleased I was finally making an effort to improve my situation. I went to bed early, and fell into a dreamless uninterrupted sleep.

Tuesday, I woke with a dry mouth, but otherwise felt better first thing in the morning than I had in who knew how long. If this was what taking these drugs was going to be like, with solid, restful sleep, I was all for it.

The rest of the week passed without a hitch. I fell asleep early every night, and slept like a woman without a care in the world, rarely even getting up to pee—which in itself was a small miracle. Every morning, I awakened thirsty, and sometimes between taking my little oval pill and going to bed, I felt kind of spaced out, but otherwise the side effects were minimal.

Scott and I seemed to be back on a fairly even keel, and he'd apologized for letting his temper get the best of him last weekend. I knew he hoped the drug would help me, and therefore help mend things between us.

Friday was Valentine's Day. I honestly had no idea what that even meant to me anymore. Did I celebrate the day people traditionally spend with their lover with the husband I was planning to leave in the near future, or with the boyfriend who was married to someone else? Frankly, I was tempted to call in sick and just hide under the covers to avoid the whole day.

But I didn't. I got up at my usual time, and when I came downstairs I found bacon and eggs plated and waiting for me. A vase of peach roses brightened our kitchen table, and I gave Scott a grateful peck on the cheek before digging in. The old familiar guilt poked at me, as it always did. Scott was too good to me. I didn't deserve any of this. All I'd gotten for him was a card.

When I got to the office, I couldn't help but wonder whether Declan would acknowledge Valentine's Day to me or not. I swore to myself I wouldn't get upset if he didn't. After all, he had no obligation to me whatsoever on this day, nor I to him.

There was nothing waiting on my desk, and though I got tiny stab of disappointment, I brushed it off and dug into my first quote. A while later, I pulled open my top drawer to retrieve a highlighter and found a box of candy hearts tucked inside. Like at Christmas, there was no card or note, but I knew exactly who'd left me this sweet surprise.

Opening the package, I tapped out a little pale pink heart into my palm. In magenta letters across the front was the message: LOVE YOU.

With a secret smile, I popped it into my mouth, hoping it was true.

On Saturday, I met Liv for drinks and tried to suss out what she and Scott had discussed about me. I didn't get very far, but it didn't seem like either of them suspected me of cheating, just of retreating into my depression. Before she could disclose much more, she broke down in tears, and I spent the rest of the evening comforting her. It turned out she and Ben had had a big talk just before she'd left to meet me, and they'd decided their relationship had run its course. Liv was, of course, devastated. I felt like a crappy friend for not noticing her distress earlier.

After two beers, a whole pack of tissues, and more hugs than I could count, she calmed down a bit. By the time we were pulling on our coats, she admitted she knew it was for the best. She laughed ruefully, saying she'd probably end up meeting Mr. Right packing groceries at Food Lion. I told her you just never knew when or where you might stumble upon your soulmate.

I felt bad for her, but I was also impressed that she was being so mature about things. They hadn't been together very long but I knew she loved him and that wasn't something you could just switch off.

During my drive home, I wondered how Scott would react when I finally told him we were over, and if he'd have someone's shoulder to cry on like Liv'd had mine. As I pulled into our driveway, I realized that shoulder would probably end up being hers, and I wasn't sure how I felt about that.

You know when you get blindsided by a seemingly inconsequential tidbit of info? Something that means very little to anyone else but you? I got such a bomb dropped on me the next week.

I was eating with the girls in the cafeteria. It was just the three of us, so Sam felt comfortable gossiping more freely. As I nibbled my sandwich, she glanced over at me and lowered her voice. "So you guys know how Declan's wife's working in New York until spring, right?"

Kaitlyn and I both nodded. I tensed, wondering where this was going. She didn't leave me hanging for long.

"Ryan told me this morning they're actually separated. Apparently she told Declan before she left to consider it a trial separation until she came back." Sam shook her head, rolling her eyes. "No wonder he's been more of a dick than usual lately."

My mouth fell open in shock.

Kaitlyn frowned. "That explains a few things," she mused. "Still, must suck for him."

Sam looked hard at me. "You look surprised. He didn't tell you?"

I blinked. "I had no idea."

"Well maybe he doesn't want anyone to know. Still, I thought he might've said something to you."

"We haven't had much time to chat lately." I wanted to add, *and if he had told me, I wouldn't have blabbed it to anyone anyway*, but I didn't. Shrugging, I tried to look sympathetic yet nonchalant.

Inside I was reeling. This wasn't just more office gossip or sad news about a co-worker's personal life—this was a big deal. Why hadn't he told me? I would've thought I'd be the first person he'd want to share that with. But apparently not. Instead, he'd confided in Ryan, who'd disclosed it to Sam, who'd told…well, probably everyone—which kind of sucked for Declan if he'd meant to keep it private. If he'd known he was separated before our afternoon at the Sheraton, you'd think he would have wanted to tell me that important piece of news. So the big question was: why hadn't he?

Shoving my chair back, I mumbled some weak excuse for leaving. When I got to the hallway outside the cafeteria, I stopped. Turning right would take me toward the Sales department, and possibly Declan if he was in his office, and I could ask him about it myself.

Turning left was the most direct route back to my desk. What did I want to do? He'd kept it from me for a reason. I didn't know what that reason was, but I knew there had to be one.

With a sigh I headed back to Accounting. I needed some time to think this over before I talked to him.

By the end of the day, I decided I wasn't going to tell Declan what I'd heard, although I did think he deserved to be made aware that everyone else knew. He'd just have to find that out from someone who was not me. If he'd wanted me to know he was separated, he would have told me—simple as that. Still, I hoped to see him, as we hadn't found time to meet up for over a week. I wanted to tell him about my fight with Scott, about the anti-depressants, and honestly, I just really needed to see him.

I texted him a single word: *soon?*

He called me back in less than a minute. "Great mind thinks alike," he chuckled. "Can you spare a few minutes after work today?"

After assuring him I could, we arranged to meet in the Food Lion parking lot.

Twenty minutes later, I was sitting on Declan's lap in my car, his arms wrapped around me, telling him all about Scott's big blow up and how I'd reacted. He listened sympathetically, lightly rubbing my back as I talked. I couldn't help but think how his situation differed from my own. When I once again said I knew I had to end things with Scott, that I wasn't being fair to him by keeping him in the dark, I gave Declan the perfect opening to tell me the truth about the state of his own marriage. He didn't take it.

Realizing he wasn't going to, I pressed ahead. When I admitted I'd started taking anti-depressants, he seemed surprised. He told me when he was a teen he'd been on them for a while, but he'd hated feeling like his emotions were dampened, and after a few months he'd quit. I wondered if he worried my feelings for him would be lessened by the medication. So far they hadn't been, not even a little. I made a mental note to prove it to him.

"I'm sorry you had such a shitty week, and I wasn't around to ease your stress," he said, his fingers still running over my skin.

My heart clenched., "I missed you," I whispered.

He kissed me softly, assuring me without words how much he'd missed me, too. When he pulled back for air, he leaned his forehead against mine, our eyes mere inches apart. I was sure I saw love in those eyes, but if that were true, why hadn't he told me about Laura's request for a trial separation? He knew I intended to end my marriage. Did he not see a future with me? Doubts I'd been trying to suppress all day flooded back in.

Before I could pull away, his eyes lit up, and he broke into a wide grin. "What would you say to escaping with me for a weekend?"

My eyebrows flew up. "You're kidding?"

"I'm dead serious. Remember when we talked about going to Richmond together months ago, but it didn't work out?"

I nodded curiously.

"Let's pick a weekend, and you can say you're going to visit your friend, and we'll go. Overnight on a Friday. Home by Saturday dinner. I'll make sure Laura's actually coming back. She's used to me not being around much on her weekends home—she won't question a thing. I'll take you out for a night on the town. I know an awesome little restaurant downtown. We'll have a blast! You game?" With every sentence he grew more and more excited.

His enthusiasm was contagious. Mirroring his grin, I said. "That could actually work. And I could really use the break."

"I know you could. We both could. And I think we need some time just us. To recharge." Declan's smile lit up my whole car.

"You just want me all to yourself in a hotel room!" I teased, running my fingers up his chest and over his shoulder to tangle in his thick hair.

"Damn right," he murmured, re-capturing my lips and showing me just how much he wanted exactly that, and for a while I forgot all about the secret he still hadn't shared with me.

Declan

Friday, February 21st was my daughter's fourth birthday. I'd texted Laura earlier in the week to make sure she'd be home, and once she confirmed, I made reservations at Alessandro's for Saturday night. Laura's parents, Patrick, Ryan, and Diana would be joining us. Since they were unable to make it down, James and Miriam had sent a package full of gifts. I knew James would be here the weekend after, and he'd make it up to Alexis for missing her birthday, but I still wished he was going to be around for moral support as I played Dad at a Happy Family Event.

When I walked into my office on Friday, I found two brightly-wrapped presents. The one dominating the middle of my desk was labeled, "To Alexis, Love Auntie Colleen." A second small flat one sat on my chair. The sticky note on the top simply read, "Happy Birthday Alexis." No signature, but I recognized Amelia's handwriting. From the feel of it, she'd been thoughtful enough to get my daughter a book. I wasn't sure whom I'd tell Alexis it was from, but I figured I'd just let her assume it was from me for now. If, by some miracle, Amelia actually became an open part of my life someday, we could tell her who really gave it to her then.

I had a two o'clock meeting I couldn't get out of, but as soon as it was over, I left the office to get Alexis from the sitter's early. On the way there, I stopped to pick up a bunch of Disney Princess balloons. My daughter heard my voice at the door and came running, skidding to a halt the moment she saw them.

"Happy Birthday, Princess," I told her, kneeling and pulling her into a hug. She spared me not even a glance, her huge blues eyes focused solely on the multicolored bouquet I held.

Scooping her up, I carried her back to the house. She immediately ran into the living room, took a look around, then instructed me just where she wanted her birthday balloons displayed. After we both arranged them to her satisfaction, I pulled one of the gifts off the kitchen counter and handed it to her.

Colleen had picked out a frilly blue dress and matching sequined ballet slippers, which Alexis, ever the mini-fashionista like her mother, instantly adored. Right away, she stripped off her sweater and jeans to try them on. I pulled out my phone and snapped some shots of her twirling and posing for me. I started to e-mail them to Colleen, copying in Laura as I knew she'd get a smile out of her daughter's fashion model stances. After a moment's hesitation, I blind copied Amelia in as well.

Alexis stopped dancing and looked up at the counter. "Is that one for me, too?" she asked, nearly bursting with curiosity.

I handed her the package from Amelia, and she tore off the wrapping without hesitation. As I expected, inside were two books: one about an impetuous little pig called *Olivia Forms a Band* and the other the Dr. Seuss classic *Oh, The Places You'll Go!* Alexis paged through them, looking at the brightly colored pictures. I promised her I'd read them to her before bed.

Then I took her hand and with a wide smile, led her into our attached garage. There in the middle of the concrete floor with a huge pink ribbon tied around it stood her very own big-girl bicycle. She squealed with delight the moment she laid eyes on it.

"As soon as the snow melts I'll teach you how to ride it," I promised.

"Really? Without training wheels?" she asked doubtfully, eyeing the extra wheels bolted onto the back tire.

"Eventually, yep. But you can keep them on until you get the hang of it."

She climbed onto the bike in her brand new blue dress and proceeded to peddle it in circles around the garage. It was a bit too big for her, but she managed pretty well. I could tell already it wouldn't be long before those training wheels would be collecting spider webs in the corner.

Alexis helped me make her favorite: homemade mac and cheese with mushrooms, peas, and extra cheese. After dinner, I brought out two red velvet cupcakes with pink icing and put two candles in each so she had four to blow out. This was the first birthday she'd ever spent without her mother, and I wanted to make it extra special. Unfortunately it didn't end up being the last.

I let her pick out her favorite movie, and we curled up together in the big bed in the master bedroom to watch it. She fell fast asleep curled up against my side before it was even half over. Instead of carrying her down the hall to her own room, I let her sleep with me.

Laura would be home before lunch tomorrow, but as far as I was concerned, right now Alexis and I were doing just fine without her.

My estranged wife breezed through the front door laden with gift bags at ten minutes to noon on Saturday. As expected, the minute she arrived the entire dynamic of our household changed.

While she showered Alexis with expensive toys from FAO Schwarz, and even a small silver charm bracelet from Tiffany's, I snuck upstairs to my office to respond to e-mails and make some calls. After a few hours of work, I changed into a button-up and came back down, putting on my best cheerful Dad expression. I found them icing cookies in the kitchen, my daughter's face a Pollock-esque mess of every color frosting imaginable. She was laughing like I hadn't heard her laugh in a long time, and it made me feel both happy and melancholy. Laura wouldn't have any clue that joyful sound had been mostly missing around our house lately, but I sure as hell did. Deep inside, I resented the fuck out of that fact.

I calmly suggested Alexis go get washed up and put on her new blue dress to get ready for her birthday dinner. Once she left the room, Laura turned her back to me and began cleaning up the mess they'd made.

I cleared my throat. "Sounds like you guys had a fun afternoon."

She glanced my way. "Yep."

"So…" I hesitated. "How goes it in the Big Apple?"

I heard her sigh as she wiped the center island clean of crumbs and smears. "It's great. I love it. Is that what you want to hear?"

Frowning, I said, "I don't 'want to hear' anything. I was just…just wondering how you were."

"I'm fabulous. Wonderful. Couldn't be better. Hope that helps you sleep at night."

The temperature in the kitchen seemed to drop a few degrees. "I sleep fine," I lied. "Can you say the same?"

"Like a goddamn baby," she muttered, showing me her back again as she rinsed out the dishcloth.

I snorted and started to leave the room to head upstairs and make sure Alexis succeeded in washing all the icing off.

"Declan?" Stopping in my tracks, I turned to face Laura. "At this point it doesn't look like my contract will be extended past the first week of April. That means I'll be coming home in six weeks as originally planned. We're going to have to talk about stuff once I'm back. You know that, right?"

"I know," I agreed, holding her gaze. "What I don't know is how that conversation is going to go."

"Me, neither," she admitted. "Will you do me a favor in the meantime?"

"What's that?"

"Will you give some serious thought to how you really *want* it to go?" Her expressive green eyes widened as she searched mine. I have no clue if she found what she was looking for.

"I think about little else," I said, turning and heading for the stairs.

Dinner with Ryan, Diana, and the grandparents wasn't as awkward as I'd thought it might be. Socializing with family and making sure my daughter was happy provided excellent distractions, and no one seemed to notice I didn't interact with Laura much.

Alexis was the center of attention, which she thrived on, and she got spoiled rotten by her adoring family. Seeing her eyes light up and hearing her giggle was all the balm I needed to sooth away my aggravation for a while.

When I finally tucked her into bed, read her one of her new books, and got her to sleep, I headed for the back bedroom as was my new habit when my wife was home.

I lay there on the spare bed for a long time without sleeping. The bright moonlight shined through the not-quite-closed curtains and bathed the room in an otherworldly glow. I thought about my slowly splintering family, and about Amelia, and about the vast gulf between the two. I loved them both, yet saw no easy way to bring them together. Unless Laura asked me for a divorce in April, my heart would remain divided.

And that division, those two separate parts of my life—they were slowly tearing me apart.

Chapter 27

Amelia

Two weeks later I was speeding down Highway 460 pushing my little Honda's engine as hard as I could, heading for a carpool lot about halfway between Lynchburg and Richmond. I was a few minutes behind schedule, and I didn't want to keep Declan waiting.

My new regime of an anti-depressant a day, while not exactly keeping the doctor away, was at least starting to take the edge off things. It didn't feel like my emotions were ricocheting as much as they'd been before. I'd developed some weird twitches that sometimes startled me during those strange otherworldly moments between wakefulness and sleep, but otherwise, the side effects had so far been minimal.

Scott seemed happier, which also relieved a small amount of the burden from my shoulders. As far as he knew, I was going to stay the night at Dee's after a girls' night out. Since my demeanor had improved lately, he thought me spending time with some girlfriends was a great plan. And yes, I felt guilty. I mean, how could I not when he'd seen me off with a smile and told me to have a fabulous time? Once again, I'd lied to his face. But as much as I was ashamed of it, I was also really excited to go on this little adventure.

I had something really special planned for Declan tonight. I'd found out earlier in the week that Jim Coltrane was playing a live show at The Oasis on West Broad Street, and I intended to surprise him with it later. A couple of days ago, I'd called ahead to ensure tickets would be waiting for us at the door. I absolutely could not wait to see the look on his face when Jim took the stage.

The daytime temperature had risen over the past couple of weeks, and nearly all the snow had melted. Evenings, however, were still pretty chilly, and it made choosing what to wear difficult. I decided to pack light. Nothing fancy, but I really didn't think I'd need it. Other than grabbing a bite out somewhere tonight and going to the show, I assumed we'd spend most of our time in the room.

My intention had been to head for Richmond as soon as four hit, but to my intense chagrin, Diana had stopped me to discuss one of Ryan's clients before I could escape. I'd extricated myself as soon as I could, but it'd still put me about ten minutes behind.

As I pulled into the carpool lot, I spotted Declan's blue Mustang parked off to the right. An insuppressible smile surfaced, and I slipped into the empty spot beside him. Grabbing my overnight bag from the backseat, I got out of my car and climbed into his.

He wasted no time, pulling me to him and greeting me with a passionate kiss. There was nothing remotely friendly about it; it was full of lustful promises.

When I broke apart for air, he trailed his lips up the side of my jaw. "Just you wait 'til I get you alone in that room," he whispered, his voice a low rumble in my ear. I shivered all over at the implications.

"What did you have in mind?" I asked softly. I'd meant my tone to be teasing, but it came out more like a needy whimper.

Declan pulled back a few inches and arched a brow. "Dirty, nasty, filthy things. Things that'll make you turn seventeen shades of red as you scream my name."

Gulping, my temperature shot up several degrees as images of our naked bodies tangled together flashed through my mind.

"You'll find out soon enough," he smirked. Then he dropped a quick kiss on the end of my nose. "Buckle up. I intend to get us there as soon as possible."

True to his word, his Mustang seemed to fly over the asphalt. I clutched the door handle surreptitiously, hoping he wouldn't notice my anxiety at the speed.

Far sooner than I expected, we pulled into an underground parking garage below the Lamplighter Guest House. After killing the engine, Declan ran a hand up the inside of my thigh, leaning into me until his breath tickled the shell of my ear.

"Almost there," he murmured.

I closed my eyes for a moment, holding my breath. He already had me so turned on I had to restrain myself from pulling him down on top of me right there in the car.

He grabbed both our bags from the backseat before coming around to open my door for me. Taking my satchel from him, I slung it over my shoulder, and he reached for my hand as we headed for the stairwell.

I smiled, looking down at our entwined fingers. We were holding hands. In a public place. Well, in a deserted parking garage, but still. Declan was holding my hand. It felt so natural and right, and I hoped he wouldn't let go anytime soon.

He didn't. Just before we left the stairwell to go into the main lobby, he turned to me with a smile and leaned over to kiss me. Then he pushed open the glass door and we went up to the desk to check in, just like any other average American couple spending the night at this hotel, just like it was a normal thing for us to do. He released my hand only to fill out the form the clerk pushed over the counter to him. As soon as he dropped the pen, his fingers promptly found mine again.

I loved it.

I loved *him*.

The anti-depressants had not dampened my feelings for Declan one bit. Nor had they reduced my sex drive, which was on the list of possible side-effects. I'd been a little worried about that one, but from how I currently felt, I knew it wasn't going to be an issue.

Our room was at the end of a long, red-carpeted hallway. As we approached the door, my entire body seemed to thrum in anticipation. He glanced at me with a small smirk, squeezed my fingers once, then dropped them. Swiping the key card, he pushed open the door, holding it with one arm outstretched so I could enter ahead of him.

I walked in and tossed my bag and coat on a nearby chair, turning to face him as I heard the soft click of the door closing. In one smooth motion he reached for my arm and twirled me in a half circle, and I abruptly found myself pressed against the wood by his body. His eyes, mere inches from my own, blazed.

"Did I ever tell you," he asked, his voice soft and dangerous and dripping with desire, "about the fantasy I had after we first met?"

Mutely, I shook my head, my gaze locked on his.

"It involved me having you up against the door in my office. Now let me see if I can remember how it went…"

My eyes widened and I gulped, suddenly overheated.

His hands slid down the outsides of my thighs, stopping at the hem of my skirt to toy with the edge.

"I know your skirt was up…*here*." He dragged the fabric up until it bunched around my waist.

"Declan!" I gasped, but he shushed me with a fingertip against my lips.

"No interrupting. Now where was I? Oh yeah. My mouth was…*here*." His lips dropped to the side of my neck, and at his touch my skin pebbled with goose bumps. I shuddered as his tongue trailed up the underside of my jaw.

"One long, sexy leg was…*here*." His voice became rougher as his hand slid down my ass to the back of my left thigh, lifting my leg and hooking it over his hip. I could feel how ready he was for me through the fabric of his pants.

"And I'm pretty sure those pantyhose were nowhere in sight." He thrust himself against me as his other hand squeezed my breast.

"You-" I broke off with a groan as he tilted his hips roughly into me again. "You had such dirty thoughts about me right from the beginning?"

"Oh, you have *no* idea, Ms. York," he whispered by my earlobe. My entire body quivered.

"Declan, I…we…can't."

He stilled and met my eyes, one brow raised in question. "Oh no?"

"I mean, we *can*, definitely we can, but not against the door to the room! Anyone walking by would hear. I don't really want a bellhop interrupting us—do you?"

With a devilish grin, he said, "All part of the thrill."

My pulse raced and my throat went dry, but I didn't refuse. I didn't say a word. I just nodded my assent.

"That's my girl." He resumed kissing me, and I wrapped my hands behind his neck, slipping them up into his hair and pulling him closer.

His fingers dipped below the waistband of my tights and began sliding them down my hips. Inch by inch he lowered them, his slightly coarse palms brushing over the skin of my thighs as he knelt. When his fingertips reached the sensitive backs of my knees, I closed my eyes for a moment and shuddered, exhaling a low moan of pleasure. I heard a chuckle from below as he kept going, slowly caressing my calves and ankles. He looked up and shot me a devilish grin as one foot at a time he freed me from their confines and tossed the offending garment aside. As he straightened, he paused along the way to kiss the front of one thigh, running his tongue in damp circles, making silent promises.

I fisted my fingers in Declan's hair and dragged him back up to my lips, but he only kissed me for a few moments. Then he pulled away again, his eyelids heavy with lust, and began to open the buttons on my blouse. My breath caught in my throat as I watched him slowly expose my skin, one small green button at a time. When the bottom one was released, he pushed the two halves of fabric aside.

"Beautiful," he murmured, gazing at my black bra in admiration before crashing his lips into mine.

I knew this wasn't going to be all slow and tender like our first time. We both had too much pent up desire for slow and tender right now. Sweet lovemaking could come later tonight. Or in the morning. Or after lunch. I wondered fleetingly if we'd even leave the hotel room tomorrow. Maybe not. I had no problem with that.

Our kisses grew deeper. His fingers, which had been busy drawing low moans from me as they teased my nipples through the lace, soon found their way to the top of my panties and roughly pushed them down. When they hit the floor and I stepped out of them, I heard the unmistakable sound of Declan's zipper.

Grabbing the back of my thigh and lifting, he curled my leg over his hip again, opening me wide. I felt him rub up against my wetness, and I whimpered, more than ready for him. He looked me in the eye, lifting his brows as if to ask permission. I nodded, biting my lower lip in anticipation.

He positioned himself and with a soft sigh of pleasure, pushed inside me. The feel of him at this angle and in this position was beyond intense. I sucked in a sharp breath as I adjusted to the sensation.

Shooting me a wicked smile, he began to move. He started off careful and deliberate, not exactly gentle, but not rough either. Lacing my fingers behind his neck, I dragged his mouth back to mine, kissing him with everything I had as I tilted my hips to meet his controlled strokes.

We were both really turned on. I mean, *really*. As amazing as it felt, I knew neither of us was going to last very long. His pace began to increase, and I did my best to keep up with the rhythm he set. My hands dropped to his bum and squeezed as he thrust into me, the rough cotton of his pants brushing against my bare skin, making everything feel all the more forbidden.

When Declan pushed aside the stretchy lace covering one breast to pinch and twist the pebbled peak, I couldn't help moaning. He silenced me with another deep kiss, and I could feel my internal pressure building. I was so very, very close.

Please...just...

Another sharp drive of his hips and I trembled all over, convulsing around him. Ripping my mouth from his, I cried out. Not a scream, not his name, just a rush of release and satisfaction. He pulled back and stared into my eyes as I struggled to catch my breath. His irises, though darkened and glazed with lust, were filled with adoration.

I wanted so badly to tell him I loved him, but I forced the urge back down. Instead I moaned, "God, Declan..."

With a cocky smirk, he whispered, "Brace yourself, baby." His hand dropped to the back of my thigh and pulled my other leg up around his waist so I was suspended by his strength alone.

My fingers gripped his shoulders as he pounded into me, the door behind my back shaking with each hard thrust. His breathing grew ragged. Sweat beaded on his brow. His eyes lost focus. His motions became rough and erratic, all sense of rhythm gone in his eagerness to finish. Driving inside me a final time, he shuddered and gasped and fell against me, his arms wrapping around my waist and tugging me close as my feet returned to the floor. I held him tight, tucking my face into the damp skin of his neck and planting a soft kiss there.

"That was…" I stopped and dragged in another deep breath.

Declan pulled away a few inches and leaned his sweaty forehead against mine. "Fucking incredible?"

"That about covers it, yeah," I said, smiling.

He stepped back, allowing me to move away from the door, and I slipped into the bathroom to clean up. When I came out, I retrieved my discarded clothing from the floor and went to get changed for the evening. We still had so much to do tonight, the most important of which he had no clue about. I couldn't wait to see the look on his face when he found out.

"What do you wanna do for dinner?" he asked, lounging across the massive bed with his head propped up on the pillows. With a lecherous wink he added, "We could just order room service."

"You're up for round two already?" I asked incredulously.

He patted the comforter beside him. "Why don't you come over here and find out."

"Tempting, very tempting, Declan, but I'd really like to go out tonight. We could actually go on a real date for once."

That earned me a grin. "You mean you want me for more than just my skills in the bedroom?"

I dropped onto the bed and leaned over to kiss him. "Well…you definitely have some talent in that department, I must admit."

His fingers slipped around the back of my neck and up into my hair, pulling me closer. "Just some?" he whispered, moving his lips against my earlobe. A shiver ran over me, and just like that I wanted him again.

Reminding myself how important tonight was, with some regret I pulled away and unzipped my bag, yanking out my jeans.

"Maybe you can demonstrate the extent of your skills later. C'mon. Let's get dressed and go find food."

Declan groaned and sat up, his hair sticking out in all directions. He looked exactly like a man who'd just gotten laid. With a sigh, he grabbed his duffel and disappeared into the bathroom. I heard the shower start a minute later and was tempted to sneak in and join him, but I knew if I did we'd never get out of here in time to make the show.

When he emerged ten minutes later, he looked sexy enough for me to seriously consider blowing dinner off and dragging him to bed. He'd changed into jeans that fit him like they were made just for him, frayed around the ankle cuffs, with no socks. The little fish tattoo undulated on the side of his foot as he walked. His chest was still bare, and it glistened with a few elusive droplets of water the towel had missed. Coming over, he bent his head close, running his fingers up my arms, enveloping me in his clean, fresh scent as he kissed me softly.

"Better?"

"There was nothing wrong with you before," I replied with a smile. "But yes, you smell amazing. If I wasn't so hungry…" I trailed off, glancing over to the bed.

"I can satisfy all your appetites," he promised, cocking an eyebrow at me.

"Oh I don't doubt that. But later, okay? Put a shirt on—I really want to go out tonight."

He shrugged as if to say "your loss" before pulling a black t-shirt over his head. Maybe I was a bit biased, but clothed or bare, the man looked delicious.

I knew where West Broad Street was in relation to our hotel, so I steered us that way. Strolling with our fingers entwined, in no particular hurry, pausing often for secret smiles and quick kisses, we made our way downtown. Eventually we found a little hole-in-the-wall pizza place and grabbed a booth in the back.

Instead of sitting across from each other, Declan squished in beside me, wrapping an arm around my waist and pulling me against his side. He teased me about my rabid hatred of olives when I insisted they not come within a foot of our order. Neither of us could stop beaming at each other, touching each other. We must have looked like teenagers in the throes of first love.

I don't think I even thought about Scott once. Not on purpose—we were just lost in our own little bubble, and any thoughts that brought negative feelings were immediately shoved away.

We polished off some beer with our pizza—it turned out Declan was hungry after all. Later we walked hand in hand down the street again, headed in the direction of The Oasis, although he didn't know it yet.

When I stopped in front of the bar, he looked at me questioningly. Scattered groups of smokers loitered around the entrance, blocking our view of the poster announcing the night's entertainment. I tugged his arm to bring him closer until we could read it clearly. In thick black letters it said: *Tonight Only - Jim Coltrane.*

Declan's eyes flared, his mouth falling open in shock. "Did you know about this?" he asked, turning to stare at me.

Grinning widely, I nodded. "Tickets are waiting for us inside. C'mon." I grabbed the thick brass door handle and led him into the darkened hallway.

The tall bald guy manning the entrance told us we needed to show tickets to get inside tonight, so I informed him I'd called earlier in the week and put two on hold. He pointed me in the direction of the bar.

Once I got the bartender's attention, I asked him to please look for a pair of tickets being held for me under the name Amelia Miller. After a few minutes of rising panic when he couldn't locate them, he called over the manager who remembered they were still sitting on the desk in the back office.

The Oasis was a fairly cozy venue, and the place was filling up fast. As all the tables were already occupied, we procured drinks and found a place to stand along the side of the room. We had a clear line of sight to the small stage, which was illuminated by a single spotlight. Caught in the beam was a microphone on an angled stand and a chair with an acoustic guitar leaning against it.

Declan put his beer on the ledge behind us and wrapped his arms around my waist, pulling my back against his chest.

"Thank you," he whispered into my ear. "You're amazing."

I twisted my head to look up at him with a grin. "I know."

"I'll thank you properly when we get back to the room."

"Yep, you will," I agreed.

Jim ambled into the spotlight about fifteen minutes later. By then, Declan had replaced his beer, although mine wasn't even half empty. I had a small buzz, but was trying not to distort my senses too much.

I examined the man onstage. He was of medium height, slim, around thirty, with shaggy reddish-brown hair and a full scraggily beard. A gray tweed newsboy cap sat low over his forehead, casting a deep shadow over his eyes due to the angle of the glare. His stage attire consisted of jeans and a plain white t-shirt with a loose-fitting brown corduroy jacket over it. Jim Coltrane was clearly a man of simple tastes. Sitting down, he picked up the shiny guitar and began to strum, looking down at his hands as they danced over the strings. After playing few chords, he lifted two fingers to signal the sound guy at the back before launching straight into "Heaven In You".

Declan gave me a squeeze and began to sing along softly to himself.

In another forty-five minutes, he had his fourth beer of the evening in hand, and I still nursed my second. Jim had disappeared into the crowd during intermission, and Declan was snuggling against me again. He put his chin on my shoulder and kissed me on that sensitive spot below my ear.

"He's such an amazing songwriter! I still can't believe you brought me here."

I just smiled, basking in the glow of his excitement.

A few minutes later Jim came back onstage and picked up his guitar. As he began to sing, Declan squeezed my fingers and exclaimed in a happy whisper, "God, I love you for this!"

All thoughts in my head evaporated, and I froze in his arms. It was loud in here, and I wasn't sure if my ears had tricked me. Did he really just say he loved me? I risked at peek at his face. He was staring at Jim, mouthing the words to "Georgia Girl" and looking completely enraptured, not to mention a bit intoxicated. Maybe he hadn't meant it the way it sounded? It didn't seem like he even realized what he'd just said.

I glanced up again. He took a swig of his beer and tightened the grip of his other arm around my waist. Seeing me looking at him, he smiled and dropped his lips to mine, his kiss tasting of hops.

No, I was sure he had no idea he'd told me he loved me. So, I tried to brush it off and focus on the show.

We swayed together to the music as Jim started in on a mournful ballad of lost love. Declan slipped his fingers under my t-shirt and stroked my stomach lightly, his pelvis pressed against my lower back.

Before long, Jim was thanking the audience and saying goodnight. Declan clapped and whistled possibly louder than anyone else in the entire room. He was grinning from ear to ear, and I couldn't help feeling proud that I was the one who'd made this happen.

We didn't linger, making our way through the crowd to the street outside. The temperature had dropped, as you might expect on a Virginian March evening, and I pulled the collar of my jacket around my neck and crammed my hands into my pockets as we started to walk back to the hotel.

Declan whistled one of Jim's songs, draping his arm over my shoulders as we moved somewhat awkwardly along the sidewalk. I knew he had a good buzz going, and it felt like I was kind of supporting him. When I stumbled on an uneven edge of pavement, he caught me with his other hand.

"Careful, baby," he cautioned.

"I'm okay," I assured him. Before he could put his arm around me again, I grabbed his hand, lacing my fingers through his.

"Your hands are freezing." He stuffed our entwined hands into his coat pocket for warmth. It made walking the rest of the way back much easier.

At last we made it into the warm seclusion of our room. Declan immediately kicked off his shoes, dropped his jacket on the chair, and fell on his stomach across the bed. I looked at him and smiled, shaking my head in amusement. He looked so cute lying there with his eyelids drifting shut and a crooked, sleepy grin on his face—just like a little boy who'd had a very long, exciting day.

I didn't say a word, grabbing my nightgown from my bag and heading into the bathroom to brush my teeth. When I returned, he was under the blankets and, I assumed, already out. Though slightly disappointed we wouldn't be enjoying a round two before sleep, I was more than pleased we'd already had such an amazing evening together. And he'd even said he loved me. Possibly. At least I was pretty sure I'd heard those words.

Pulling back the covers, I slid underneath and leaned over to brush his hair from his forehead and kiss him. "Night, Declan," I whispered. Then I switched off the lamp, intending to sleep.

After a few minutes, he groaned and flung back the sheets. He stumbled out, staggering around the end of the bed in the dark and swearing softly when he bumped into something on the way. The bathroom light flicked on, then vanished as he closed the door.

When he came out, I turned the bedside light back on, knowing he'd be even more blinded after the brightness. Once he fell safely back into bed beside me, out it went again. I figured he'd also be out in a few seconds right along with it.

Instead I felt an arm slide around my waist as he snuggled up to me. He began to kiss my shoulder and I rolled toward him, our lips finding each other. Now he tasted minty fresh, and I realized he was neither as drunk nor as sleepy as I'd presumed. His kisses grew more aggressive, claiming my mouth as passionately as he'd done after we'd first checked in.

Soon he tugged my nightgown up over my head and tossed it aside. He rolled onto me, his bare chest pressing against mine, and I realized he'd stripped off his clothes in the bathroom. The fingers of one hand stroked along my sides, while the other cupped the side of my jaw as we locked lips again. He settled his weight between my thighs, caressing my skin, handling me lightly, reverently, his kisses now gentle and sweet. The way Declan touched me—it spoke of nothing less than love. There was no other way to interpret it.

His lips broke free from mine and began to trail down the column of my throat, and I shivered. A man clearly on a mission, he traced a burning path over my chest, kissing each of my breasts in turn, pausing for a few moments to give them attention. My fingers threaded into his hair and I sucked in a sharp breath, flattening my abdomen as I felt the pointed wetness of his tongue travel across it, swirling around my navel, tickling its way down my lower belly. A thoughtful silence came over me as, shifting his body, he arrived at his destination.

Before he could begin, like an idiot I ruined the moment.

"Did you mean it?"

I didn't intend to say the words; they just slipped out of my mouth. I immediately wished I could suck them right back in, certain he'd have no clue what I was referring to.

Instead of replying, I heard him fumbling around on the nightstand. Light flooded the room again and he blinked at me in confusion, his face back at my level. "Mean what?"

"Forget it," I mumbled. "It's nothing." I was hesitant to elaborate, worried I'd sound too needy.

As my eyes adjusted, I saw him frown. "Mel, don't do that. What do you want to know if I meant?"

With a sigh I looked away. "What you said in the bar earlier…"

304

He was quiet for a few moments. I could feel the weight of his gaze studying me. Then, in a sudden whisper, "That I love you?"

I bit my lip and nodded, risking a glance back at him, every part of me but my heart utterly still as I waited for his response.

He stroked my cheek with absolute tenderness. His eyes were soft as he assured me with one simple word: "Yes."

Tears welled up. Taking his cheeks in my palms, I pulled his face to mine and kissed him. When we broke apart again, I finally, finally allowed myself to say it out loud. "I love you, too," I confessed, and he smiled.

We made love slowly. Neither of us reached to turn out the light; I think we both needed to be able to see each other's face. Declan and I, we were…we were happy, finally—our deepest, truest selves no longer hidden from the other. We were soft sighs of pleasure, skin sliding against skin, murmurs of devotion for what felt like mere minutes, but was were actually long hours heralding in the dawn.

Once I'd told him I loved him, I couldn't stop saying it. I told him again and again. I whispered the words like some long buried secret, like a condemned woman's final confession. I breathed my love for him against every inch of his body throughout that incredible night.

Every gasp, every movement, every word, I committed to memory. He brought me—no, we brought each other—to heights I'd never even imagined. Declan introduced me to pleasures I hadn't dreamed of, to things a man and woman could do together that I never thought I'd consider. Yet I did, with him.

I trusted him more than I'd ever trusted anyone in my entire life. With my heart and my body, yes, but also with the fractured, messy parts of me, the parts of me I believed to be unlovable—I gave my all to him and he accepted it and loved me anyway, in spite of all the broken bits with their sharp, pointy edges.

And I discovered that, contrary to what I had believed, some of those pieces still fit back together again after all.

Chapter 28

Amelia

The sensation of Declan's warmth leaving my body startled me into a sudden hazy awareness as he slipped out of bed and padded to the bathroom. Pulling the blankets up around my neck, I snuggled into them. I was nowhere near ready to wake up yet.

As I shifted my weight, I realized I ached in places I'd never ached before. Wrenching open one heavy eyelid, I checked the clock on the nightstand and my gaze landed on the dented tube lying beside it. My eyes slammed shut and I turned my face into the pillow. Vivid flashes of the night before flooded over me, making me blush hotly as I ran a palm along the curve of my backside. He'd unleashed something wild in me last night. A secret smile curved my lips.

When Declan returned, he climbed in beside me and spooned his body around mine again. His skin was cool from being out of bed, and I shivered when he pressed himself against me. In response, he cuddled me closer.

I couldn't help it—I yawned loudly, and I heard him chuckle low in his throat. That sound made something stir inside me, but I resolutely tried to ignore it. Going back to sleep was still my top priority.

"Good morning," he whispered, dropping a kiss to my bare shoulder. My skin tingled where his lips had touched.

"Morning," I muttered, pushing my head deeper into the pillow.

"Did I keep you up too late?"

"Mm hmm," I groaned.

"Wasn't it worth it?' Another kiss landed on my upper arm as his fingers gently stroked on my abdomen. Heat bloomed in my lower belly.

"Mm hmm," I mumbled a second time, already knowing I wasn't going back to sleep anytime in the near future.

Declan laughed, but instead of asking another question, he re-settled his body against mine so I could feel just exactly how awake he was. His hand drifted up to cup my breast, and I sighed softly, pressing my shoulder back against him to allow him better access. My nipple hardened at his touch, and he began to roll it between his fingers. I sucked in a breath, my arousal spiking higher as he teased me, my thighs squeezing together in a vain attempt to alleviate some of the building tension.

I twisted my head so I could see his face. His smiling blue eyes met mine as he leaned over to kiss me, his hand abandoning my breast to slip down under my side. Rolling me to face him, he pulled me snug to his chest. I could feel his heart beating against my skin as we kissed, slowly at first, but the intensity soon grew. His nimble fingers traced down the ridge of my spine, stroking my lower back, caressing the curve of my hip, and then along my thigh as he hitched my leg over his.

"Your skin is so soft," he whispered, pulling away for a breath. "So smooth. I could touch you all damn day."

"Please do," I said, grinning.

He was more than happy to oblige. His fingers returned to my breast, and he dropped his lips to it, laving circles with his tongue before taking it into his mouth. I moaned in pleasure as he lavished attention on first one nipple, then the other until I was writhing beneath him.

I wound my fingers into his messy locks and squirmed as he suckled me harder. The word *sleepy* was no longer part of my vocabulary. I was overheated, I was yearning for more, and I knew only Declan could give me the release I needed. In understanding, his hand abandoned my chest and trailed its way down to my wetness, slipping one finger inside me, curling it until it hit just the right spot. I gasped, tugging his hair to encourage him to continue. Even the slight discomfort left over from the night before wasn't enough for me to want him to stop—not even close.

He stroked me, kissed, licked, and nibbled me until I could hardly breathe, teasing me, bringing me right to the precipice before slowing so I couldn't quite fall over it. So many sensations—my brain was turning to mush. Finally, I couldn't take it any longer.

"Please?" I begged, any remaining pride now gone.

Lifting his face to stare into my eyes, he smirked and rolled on top of me, settling his weight between my thighs. I drew my knees up and held my breath in anticipation, but he didn't make me wait—he positioned himself and pushed inside.

I had to suppress a wince as he filled me and started to move. We'd made love most of the night, in every possible manner, in every possible position I could imagine and then some, and my overused muscles were protesting.

Arching an eyebrow at me, he stilled. "You okay?"

"Yeah. I'm just…just a bit…sore…is all."

He frowned and cupped my jaw, rubbing his thumb lightly over my cheek.

"Sorry, baby. Want me to stop?"

"No, no. Please don't. I'm fine. A bit tender, but fine."

He studied my face with concern for a few moments longer, then carefully reassumed his motions, noticeably slower than before. It turned out the slight sensations of pain only added to my pleasure and before long I was pushing back against his thrusts, our bodies moving together in unison.

We kissed sweetly; we touched reverently; we locked eyes and held on to both our physical and mental connection as we made love. We were in complete harmony with one another, as close, as intimate as two people could be.

He was as gentle with me as possible. I got to the point where I just needed more, and I coaxed him to move faster. I couldn't believe the plea "harder" flew from my lips. Who was this wanton woman I turned into when I was in bed with Declan? She seemed so much more in control of her desires than the Amelia I knew ever was.

When I finished, with a groan so loud I'm sure neighboring rooms heard, he followed almost right behind. He held me in his arms, bending his head to drop kisses to every available inch of skin he could reach.

I wrapped a hand behind his neck, pulling his face to mine again. We kissed tenderly, happily, and when we broke apart, I looked into his eyes and murmured, "I love you."

Smiling, he whispered, "Love you, too."

I wrapped a big soft hotel towel around me and stepped out of the shower into the steam. Noting my phone sitting on the countertop, I frowned, realizing I'd better check in with Scott. My fingers shook as I called home. Thankfully it wasn't a long conversation; I just told him I was having a great time and had been up really late the night before, which was completely true, that we had some plans this afternoon, but I'd be home around dinnertime, and I'd text him when I was on my way. He was busy marking assignments, and we agreed it was probably for the best I wasn't there. I pushed down the guilt that rose—I'd have plenty of time for guilt later. Right now I wanted this time away to be only about Declan and me.

When I opened the bathroom door, I heard his voice and I froze.

"Sounds like you guys had fun."

Pause.

"Yep, I promise I'll be home in time to eat with you."

Pause.

"I miss you, too, but I'll see you soon."

Short pause.

"Love you, too. Bye."

Then I detected the sound of movement on the bed and a clack as his phone hit the table.

Something inside me fell away and I silently closed the bathroom door, retreating to sit on the toilet lid. Tears rose to my eyes. Stupid tears. Jealous tears. I knew I had no right to react this way, but hearing him say those words to her—it stung. He'd said he loved me not half an hour earlier, and several times last night. And now he'd just said those same words to Laura. From whom he was currently separated. Or was he? I had no idea what the truth really was, because he hadn't told me. I had no idea if he still loved her or not. Maybe he did. Probably he did. Did that make his love for me any less? She was his wife, for God's sake. Who was I?

Just his dirty little secret, that's who.

My tears overflowed. I dabbed at them with wadded up squares of toilet paper as they trickled down the sides of my nose. I felt ashamed and demoralized. My chest ached—a deep throbbing pain much more intense than any of the real aches our vigorous lovemaking had created.

He'd said he loved me. He'd said he loved her. And whether I had any right to feel like this or not, the idea of sharing his heart killed me.

I didn't make a sound. I just sat there with my face pressed into the tops of my knees. I kept telling myself I was being ridiculous, but I couldn't help it. At last my silly waterworks dried up and I went to the mirror, splashing my face with cold water to lessen the redness that had blossomed around my eyes.

When I finally emerged from the bathroom, I found Declan propped up against the pillows, one arm tucked behind his head, watching the news on the big flat-screen television. The white sheets were rumpled up around his waist in stark contrast to his tanned abdomen. No matter how upset I was, a part of me couldn't help admiring the view.

"What took you so long?" he wondered, patting the mattress beside him. "I was just about to make sure you hadn't drowned. Hungry? I'm gonna order up some food."

"Not really," I mumbled.

He looked at me fully, examining my face with a small frown. "What's wrong?"

I sat on the edge of the bed and turned to him. Taking a deep breath, I asked, "Was that Laura you were talking to?"

Declan's forehead furrowed. "At first, yeah. Then Alexis. Why?"

Relief spread through me. *Of course* it'd been Alexis. I was just being an oversensitive fool by jumping to conclusions. But then I remembered what Sam had told me, and frustration boiled up again.

Deciding to be blunt, I asked him straight out, "Are you and Laura separated?"

His eyes went wide, his face flushed, and I knew even before he replied that it was true.

"I'm sorry. I was gonna tell you—I was."

"Then why didn't you?" I interjected, feeling that familiar itch start around my tear ducts again. I willed it away. I needed to be strong right now.

He frowned. "I wanted to. I seriously considered it. But I didn't...I didn't wanna give you false hope." Staring into my eyes, he took my hand in his. I pulled it away.

"False hope?" I wondered, my voice cracking a little. Anger rose, and with it, my volume. "You didn't want to give me *false hope*? You didn't want me to hope that if your marriage was over and I ended things with Scott, we could be together for real, out in the open? You don't want that with me? Then why did you tell me you loved me, Declan? *Why?*"

"Amelia, please. It's not like that. I *do* want that with you—more than you could possibly know. But it's just not that easy. I can't ask Laura for a divorce. She could take Alexis from me, and I won't risk it. She'd have to be the one to end it. Then, hopefully I could get joint custody and maybe try to make a life of my own." He sighed. "But as of right now, the ball is firmly in her court and there's not a damn thing I can do about it.

"Please try to understand. I can't take the chance of losing my daughter. It has to be this way, for now." He reached out and touched my cheek, turning my face to his so he could look right at me. His eyes silently begged me to see his side. "I'm so sorry I didn't tell you. I should have. You shouldn't have had to hear about it through office gossip."

"No," I agreed, "I shouldn't have. But I didn't think about that other stuff. I guess it's a lot more complicated than I assumed. I just wish you'd confided in me." Pulling away from his hand, I added, "It hurt that you didn't."

He looked beseechingly at me, chagrin creasing his forehead. "I'm sorry," he said again. "I *do* love you. You know that, right? You believe me?'

Pressing my lips into a tight line, I stared back at him. I blew out a puff of air. "I believe you. This just...sucks. That's all." Then I reached for him and pulled him into my arms. I felt a relieved exhale flutter my hair before he kissed the top of my head.

"It really does. Well, *this* doesn't suck." He ran a hand along the curve of my side up to my breast to emphasize his point. "*This* is amazing. If I had my way I'd have you in my bed every night and wake up beside you every morning."

Smiling, I pressed my lips to his stubbly throat and asked, "So are you still hungry?"

I heard a chuckle and his fingers reversed their path to slide back down and cup my backside.

"Starving," he whispered.

Declan

Having Amelia all to myself in Richmond was more amazing than I'd ever dreamed. The sex—no, the *lovemaking*—was better than I'd experienced in years. Maybe ever. Because being with her the way we were this weekend felt completely different. It wasn't just our intense physical attraction, although we could barely keep our hands off each other. It was how natural it felt to be together. I did something I rarely do: I bared my soul to her.

And she'd told me she loved me.

To say I was shocked when she took me to the Jim Coltrane gig would be a massive understatement. I was beyond shocked—I was completely fucking floored. No one I'd been with in the past had ever done anything like that for me. Something so simple as surprising me with tickets to see my favorite singer—you'd think it'd be a no-brainer, right? But nope. Never. Amelia was so different from any woman I'd ever been with.

At the show I'd had a few beers and…the words had just fallen out of my mouth. I'd said I loved her. When she later asked if I'd meant it, I told her the truth, and by some miracle she felt the same way. And yeah, I was well aware that chances of us finding a happily-ever-after together were pretty slim, but I swear hearing those three magic words from her was nearly the happiest fucking moment of my life. Damn close, anyway.

We'd made love until the wee hours, and fallen asleep completely sated and exhausted in each other's arms just as the sun was starting to poke its head over the horizon.

Later she'd blindsided me by asking about my marital status. Turned out she'd known I was separated for weeks already, thanks to my blabber-mouth brother and his gossipy assistant. I didn't realize how much my deliberate omission had hurt her, but once I'd explained my reasoning she'd said she understood. Then she'd held me tight, and before long one thing led to another. Again.

We ordered room service and ate lunch sprawled naked across the bed—certainly my new favorite way to consume food. Especially the dribbles of chocolate she let me lick off her stomach. And thighs. Which led to more…well, you know. Can you tell I was a happy man?

While lying wrapped around her, stroking her soft skin, I got a burst of inspiration. Leaning across her still-heaving chest to grab the phone, I called downstairs and booked us massages in the hotel's spa. She was nothing short of giddy about that, confessing she'd never been to a spa before, which made me all the more determined to spoil her. We rushed to wash and dress, and made our way downstairs.

Amelia and I changed into thick robes before being led inside a dimly-lit room with dark wood-paneling. Lavender scented the air. After disrobing, we lay on our stomachs under white sheets on side-by-side tables. Two attractive young ladies in pink smocks came in to greet us. The blonde massage therapist flashed me an appreciative smile before heading for Amelia. The redhead went straight to me. I saw Amelia raise her head and give the masseuse a skeptical once-over as she folded the sheet off my back and began to apply lotion. Smirking to myself, I realized Mel didn't love the idea of this woman touching me.

Turning my head face down into the head-rest, I felt small fingers dig into my shoulder blades, working the tight muscles there. I detected a small sigh from Amelia's direction and wondered if she was still watching. Frowning, I questioned whether these dual massages had really been such a great idea after all. Then I mentally shrugged. She needed it, and I wasn't about to cancel now. Plus, I was both flattered and amused as hell to note Amelia's jealousy. If we'd had male masseurs, I doubt I would've been thrilled to see some strange guy's hands on her either. That thought brought to mind the image of her husband touching her, which I quickly shoved away. Being possessive in our precarious position right now would only make things even more complicated. And yet there was no denying I wished I was the only man in her life.

I heard the blonde masseuse ask Amelia if she had any problem areas that needed extra attention, and lifted my head in time to catch her shoot me an accusing look. Clearly she considered her achy spots my fault. I just grinned, wondering how she'd reply.

She mumbled, "Not really," cheeks flaming beautifully, and I had to turn my face away. She looked so damn sexy I got a crazy urge to ask the gals to leave us for a while.

I was right though—the massage was just what Amelia needed. It relaxed her so much she actually dozed off a few times, which was also my fault for preventing her from getting enough sleep last night. It was difficult to feel too guilty.

As we dressed, we agreed we felt more stress-free than we had in months. For me, it wasn't just the massage, it was all of it: the concert, the sex, the love confessions. Being with Amelia for an extended period without having to worry or be Mr. Responsible made me feel lighter, younger somehow.

When we returned to the room, she declared she felt like a million bucks. I asked her cheekily if it was because of the massage or me. Wrapping her arms around my waist, she kissed me instead of replying, and we fell onto the unmade bed and made love one final time.

It was a bit softer, a bit sadder, knowing we soon had to leave that bed, that room, that city where we had just shared so many important moments, and return to our regularly scheduled lives. Neither of us wanted to let go of the other. We dressed and packed up in near-silence, all the laughter, all the passion, all the ease we'd felt forever etched into our memories.

I drove Amelia back to her car with the music turned up as she sang softly beside me, her fingers tapping out the beat against my thigh. The temptation to just keep on driving past the carpool lot, past Lynchburg, past our old lives, and whisk her away to start over somewhere away from everyone who would tear us apart nearly overwhelmed me. But then Alexis' smiling face popped into my mind and I pushed all those crazy ideas away, suddenly missing her little arms around my neck and wanting to get back home after all.

I pulled off the highway and into the parking lot, slipping the Mustang into the empty space beside Amelia's lonely little Honda. Then I turned to her, and for a few moments we stared at each other without speaking. I knew what she was thinking, probably because I was thinking it, too.

We simultaneously reached for each other and I pulled her against me, holding her tight to my chest. She snuggled her face into the curve of my throat and inhaled deeply.

"You smell so good," she whispered. "When I catch the scent of your cologne, I think of you and immediately feel happier."

"Oh that was my evil plan all along. It's Pavlovian," I teased. "Now whenever you smell it you'll have an irresistible urge to have sex."

"What if I smell it in a department store? Will I want to jump the sales guy?" She giggled. "I sense a flaw in your evil plan."

"No, silly. You'll only want to have sex with me." I smirked down at her smiling, upturned face. She was ridiculously cute when she looked at me like that. To be honest, I was only half joking. The thought of Amelia with another man made a sick feeling coil in my gut.

"Hmm. In that case, your plan is working perfectly."

"Yes. Yes, it is," I laughed, and then kissed her.

When we finally broke apart, she thanked me for everything, told me again that she loved me, and slipped out the door without looking back.

I watched her reverse out of her parking space and head down the on-ramp to the highway until her taillights vanished in the distance. A lump formed in my throat when I could no longer see her, although I couldn't say why.

Amelia

It was nearly six when I pulled into my driveway. My body still ached. I'd taken a couple of Tylenol before we left the hotel and they'd helped a bit, but I was still worried I might walk funny. If Scott noticed, I'd just tell him I drank too much and took a tumble on the dance-floor at the club—though it would be kind of weird to hurt myself falling down in the places I was sore.

315

I sat in my car for a moment staring out the windshield at the garage door. Dealing with my real life was pretty low on the list of things I wanted to be doing. What I really wanted was to reverse back onto the street and just drive. I didn't know where I'd go, maybe to Mom's, or Liv's, but I knew I didn't want to go inside and face my husband after spending the past twenty-four hours living in my happy little love-bubble with Declan.

Facing Scott made me feel guilty, but I felt guilty all the time these days anyway, so that was no different from usual. The problem was that now I understood just what I was missing out on. Real life seemed so much less bearable now that I knew what being with Declan could actually be like. Falling back into my old role felt dull and gray and tired.

The house was unlit but for a single lamp in the living room. I found my husband on the couch hunched over the coffee table, piles of papers spread out across it and on either side of him.

I needed to talk to Scott about the state of our marriage, but after learning what the real situation was with Declan's, I'd decided to wait and see what happened when Laura returned next month. I knew I was dragging things out even longer, and it wasn't fair to leave him hanging, but I had convinced myself on the drive back that waiting made the most sense right now. And Scott had seemed less…frustrated with me lately. Maybe his sessions with Debbie Westwood were helping him work through some things himself.

As I stepped into the doorway, he looked up at me. "Hey. How was your visit with Dee?"

I paused, wondering if there was any chance he could've found out I hadn't been with her. Choosing my words carefully, I pasted on a smile. "It was great! I drank too much though—I'm all bruised in weird places today from falling last night."

Lifting his eyebrows in concern, he asked, "You okay? You want me to rub your back later?"

The massage I'd had earlier flashed into my mind, as well as Declan's own hands on me. No, I definitely didn't want Scott to give me a back-rub. "Thanks, but I think I'll just have a hot bath. You hungry? Want me to whip up some sandwiches?"

"Sounds good. Before you do that though, come in here for a moment. I wanna discuss something with you."

My stomach dropped. What on earth did he want to talk to me about? With extreme trepidation I went into the living room and leaned against the chair closest to him.

"What is it, Scotty?"

He jotted a grade on the upper corner of the paper in front of him, put it on a pile on the couch, and looked up at me. "We need to discuss what you really want to do."

Crap. I didn't like the sound of that. Biting my lip, I asked, "About what?"

"Do you want a big party with all your friends? I wasn't sure if you'd be up for that. Or should we just have dinner with our families? Your thirtieth birthday is a big deal, Ames. I know you haven't been feeling all that social lately, but I don't think we should just ignore it."

Oh! My birthday. It's not that I'd forgotten. I knew it was coming up. I'd just had far more important things on my mind. And turning thirty wasn't exactly something I was excited about.

I went over my options and realized the answer was obvious. A night with just family would make me feel self-conscious. I didn't want to have to pretend to be happy, and I didn't want to deal with the topic of grandchildren if it came up again, which it probably would. However, a party with all my friends would give me plenty of distractions and a perfect excuse to have a few drinks.

"Okay," I said. "Let's do the party thing. I had fun Friday night, and I think I'm up for celebrating with our friends."

"Should we host it here, or have everyone meet up at Finnegan's?"

I thought for a moment. "Let's do it at Finnegan's. Then we don't have to clean, and we can always walk home after if we drink too much. Maybe they'll even have live music that night."

His attention returned to the paper in front of him. Without looking back up, he said, "Okay. I'll invite everyone. Can you let Dee know? And Josh and Holly? Anyone else from work you want to invite?"

Now *there* was a loaded question. "Um, yeah, I'll tell Sam and Kaitlyn." No matter how much I might wish otherwise, I knew there was no possible way I'd have the person I most wanted beside me at my birthday party.

I left Scott to his grading and went into the kitchen to make him something to eat. Not feeling very hungry myself, I headed upstairs to start running hot water into the tub. I hastily unpacked and stripped, tossing every piece of clothing I'd taken with me into the hamper. A sense of melancholy enveloped me as I clipped my hair up and returned to the bathroom. All I wanted was to sink down amongst the bubbles and steam, close my eyes, and reminisce about my time with Declan. The guilt I always carried these days couldn't be washed away with soap, but I found it could be temporarily alleviated by losing myself in those memories.

Chapter 29

Amelia

I woke up itchy: itchy legs, itchy arms, itchy back. I dragged my fingernails up the back of each calf and along my forearms, but my relief was short lived. Tossing back the blankets, I stripped off my pajamas and headed for the bathroom to examine myself in the big mirror.

Little red dots! With increasing chagrin I realized I was covered with them. It was driving me crazy. Sighing, I pulled on a loose-fitting dress for work so it wouldn't rub against my skin too much. I'd have to call Dr. Fleming as soon as his office was open and see if I could get in today.

My mind raced back over potential causes. Could it be from something I ate? The detergent the hotel used to wash their sheets? Maybe the soap or lotion from the bathroom or spa?

Two months ago I'd convinced myself I'd be somehow marked with scarlet A on my forehead, declaring my unfaithfulness to the world. Instead I'd been cursed with angry spots over my entire body, tormenting me with their constant demand to be scratched. I figured it was my deserved humiliation, my overdue adulterous branding.

When nine o'clock finally rolled around, I called my doctor's office and convinced his receptionist to squeeze me in for the last appointment of the afternoon. As expected, it was a very long, very uncomfortable workday.

Dr. Fleming took one look at my inflamed skin and, to my surprise, announced I was having an allergic reaction to my pills. When I protested that I'd been taking the medication for over three weeks already, he just shrugged and told me sometimes people had delayed reactions to anti-depressants. He told me to toss out the remainder of my tablets, wrote me a prescription for a different one, and said that the rash should clear up on its own.

I was just relieved it wasn't caused by something from my weekend with Declan. An allergy to my medication was easy enough to explain. Why I'd been at a hotel instead of at Dee's was not.

My thirtieth birthday dawned dull and rainy. I was so groggy Scott had to remind me three times to get up and get ready for work. I'd been taking the new tablets for a week and a half now, and unfortunately they didn't help me sleep anywhere near as well as the previous prescription had. And those annoying sleep twitches had gotten worse—they startled me awake multiple times a night. I was not in a good mood.

At last I dragged my butt out of bed and into the shower, and I made it to the office only ten minutes later than normal. Considering I usually arrived fifteen or twenty minutes early, it wasn't any big deal. As I turned on my computer, my phone rang.

A small smile pushed through my bleariness when I saw who it was. Before I could even get out a greeting, Declan began to sing *Happy Birthday*. The remainder of my bad mood melted away, and my little smile stretched into a massive grin.

"Happy Birthdaaaaay tooooo yoooooou!" His voice cracked on the last word and we both dissolved into laughter.

"Thanks," I said once my giggles died away. He knew exactly what I needed. As usual.

"You're welcome. How does it feel to finally hit the big 3-0? Feeling more mature? Responsible?"

I snickered. "Less, actually."

"Glad to hear it. Who needs mature, right?"

"Not me. At least not today."

There was a brief pause. "Can you come see me for a few minutes?"

"Sure," I agreed. "I'll be right over."

"Actually, I'm not in the office today. Could you meet me for, say, ten minutes at the park on Fillmore Street?"

"Oh. Um, I'll see what I can do. I'll text you yay or nay shortly."

"I won't keep you long, I promise." Then he disconnected.

After letting Diana know I had to run to the drug store on a quick errand and I'd make up the time, I texted him: *10 min.*

He replied right away. *See you soon bday girl.*

Reason number 342 why I loved him: he could always put a smile on my face.

Rain pelted down as I made my way to the park. Waves splashed up and away from each side of my tires. The small lot beside the park was empty, so I killed the engine and leaned back against my seat to wait.

Droplets beaded on my windshield and wound wobbly paths down the glass. The inside of the car was dim and cool, and I wished I'd thrown on a sweater this morning. Shivering, I turned up the stereo to drown out the shower.

I hated gloomy days like this; they made me melancholy. I ached for my father not being around to celebrate this momentous birthday with me. I ached for the holes I couldn't seem to fill in my life since he'd passed. Everything I wanted felt just that much more out of reach.

Suddenly headlights illuminated my face as a familiar blue Mustang pulled in beside me. Anticipation flooded me, obliterating my pointless gloom. I swear my demeanor lit up right along with the interior of my car.

By the time Declan slid onto my passenger seat, he was nearly drenched. He gave me an apologetic half-smile before leaning in to kiss me.

"Happy Birthday, baby. I wish I had more than a few minutes to spare for you today."

"It's okay," I assured him. "I'm just glad I get to see you at all. Honestly, I was surprised you even knew it was my birthday."

"Oh, I know plenty of things about you." Shifting his lips close to my ear, he whispered, "Like the sound you make when I touch you...*here*." His wandering hand under my jacket made his point for him—I whimpered at his caress.

Pulling away a few inches, he smiled and ran a still-damp finger down my cheek. "Sadly no time to recreate all those delicious noises today. Wish we could."

I sighed. "Me, too."

Leaning back against the seat, he reached inside his jacket and withdrew a little blue box. My eyes grew wide at the sight of it.

"Declan, no," I whispered.

He took one of my hands in his and placed the box on my palm, closing my fingers over it. "Open it," he said firmly.

My hand trembled with a mix of excitement and trepidation as I tugged the lid up. When I lifted the white cotton protective square, I gasped. A silver necklace with a ring strung on it lay below. The ring was a band of silver maybe an eighth of an inch wide, and in one spot along the circumference it had a twist.

For a long moment, I just stared down at it. Then I raised my gaze to meet his. "Th...thank you," I managed to mumble.

He chuckled, taking the box from my hands and pulling out the necklace. Instructing me to lift my hair and turn around, he fastened the chain around my neck. The cool metal of the pendant falling against my chest sent a quiver through my entire body.

I sighed. "You didn't have to get me anything," I admonished. "Especially not something expensive."

Declan ignored me, instead reaching over my shoulder and pulling down the driver's side visor to reveal the mirror behind. I examined my reflection closely. The ring was delicate and simple: no stones or engravings, just that cute little spiral.

"You like it?" he asked, meeting my eyes in the mirror. The raindrops snaking their way down the window made wiggly shadows on my cheeks, like the ghosts of ancient tears.

I bit my lip and swiveled to look right at him. "It's beautiful."

"You're beautiful." He kissed me again, sliding the palm of his hand along the outside of my thigh. When he pulled back, he glanced at the clock on the dash and sighed. "I'm really sorry, Mel—I have to run. But I wanted to see you today and give you your present."

"Thank you so much again." My hand rose to the ring, turning it around in my fingers, getting a feel for its weight, its smoothness, and that intriguing twist.

"You're more than welcome. Have an amazing birthday." He kissed me a final time and then jumped out into the downpour.

I drove one-handed through the wet streets back to the office, my left hand still curled around the pendant, my third finger threaded through the ring.

It was a perfect fit.

The band had just started their first set. Sam and Kaitlyn flanked me at the bar as we watched them warm up the small crowd. I sipped my second drink of the evening, determined to try to have fun tonight.

At the other end of the bar Scott was chatting with his sister and her boyfriend. I still hadn't talked to him about us separating. Not only because of my birthday, not only because I hated having to break his heart, but also because the very idea overwhelmed me. Selfish as it was, I was so scared to take that leap. The thought of packing up all my things and moving out of the house we'd bought together, spent the past six years in together, made a comfortable life in together—it made me feel nauseous even contemplating it. The other day I'd opened my laptop in the kitchen after work and began a tentative search for apartment rentals. Scrolling through places I thought I could afford, I'd glanced up and my gaze had landed on the blue plaid curtains over the sink that I'd sewn and hung myself. I'd wondered idly if I'd leave them behind or take them with me. Then I'd questioned whether Scott would stay here without me or if we'd put the house up for sale. A mental image popped up of a happy young couple sipping coffee over breakfast together in this kitchen, *our* kitchen. And I'd gotten a visual of those same once-cheerful curtains covered in dust, hanging over a window in some dingy little apartment. I'd slammed my computer shut in a panic.

But tonight I refused to let negative thoughts get to me. I was going to have a good time with my friends, and forget about my problems, at least for a few hours. Raising my straw to my lips, I surreptitiously scanned the room, searching in vain for the one face I knew I wasn't going to see.

I spotted Liv over near the restrooms chatting with some friends we'd known for years. Dee hadn't been able to make it due to a prior commitment, but she'd sent her love, along with a bouquet of balloons and a bottle of vodka which FedEx had delivered to my door just as I'd gotten home from work the night before. The birthday balloons with their weighted base now decorated a booth to my right where Josh and Holly were sitting. Colorful bags and boxes cluttered the back of the table.

I fiddled absentmindedly with my new necklace as I attempted to listen to both the band and Sam as she gushed about her most recent date with Evan. Yes, I was wearing it. I hadn't taken it off since Declan put it around my neck Friday morning. When I'd returned to the office, Kaitlyn noticed it right away and said it was pretty. I'd told her I'd noticed it in a shop window downtown and bought it as a birthday gift for myself. Scott had glanced at it politely, said it was nice and, as far as I could tell, hadn't given it a single thought since. Every time I stroked my fingertip over the smooth metal ring, I thought of Declan and smiled.

I'd broken down and sent him a text yesterday inviting him to come to my party. I'd convinced myself he was buddies with Josh, and Scott knew he was a work friend, so why not? His reply had been non-committal, something like 'I'll try.' Of course I didn't really expect him to show up. I knew him being here would likely be uncomfortable for both of us. So why did I keep flicking my gaze to the door, hoping against hope to see him walk in and search the room until his eyes connected with mine?

The answer was simple: because it was my party, my big night, and I wasn't sharing it with the person I most wanted to be with. It was yet another thing about our whole situation that sucked. We could never spend special occasions together. We could never meet each other's friends or families, or ride the Ferris wheel at the Fall Fair, or go for a walk hand in hand along the trail by the river I'd grown up near. We could never—or at least incredibly rarely—wake up beside each other.

And even once I left Scott, I *still* wouldn't be able to do any of those things with Declan. Not unless Laura asked him for a divorce, which I had no control over whatsoever.

As I was heading back to the bar to get a refill, a hand gripped my arm. I turned to look up into Josh's face.

Bending his head close to my ear to be heard over the music, he said, "He's not coming." He must have noticed my furtive glances at the door.

"Who?" I asked, feigning innocence, but of course I knew who he meant.

"You know who. I know you invited him, and I see you watching the entrance. But he's not coming. Can you really blame him?"

I sighed. "No. I guess I knew he wouldn't. I just kind of…hoped." I shrugged.

Josh's gaze dropped to the ring against my chest. He reached out and lifted it up, studying it as he ran his thumb around the outer edge of the metal. "This a birthday present?"

For a moment I debated saying I'd bought it for myself like I'd told everyone else. Then I nodded.

"From him?" He raised his eyes to lock with mine.

I frowned and nodded again. "Why?"

He looked back down at the ring. "You know what this is?"

"It's a silver ring," I replied, laughing. My head was dizzy from both the sudden movements and the alcohol in my system.

"This bit, this twist—this isn't just any ole' ring. It's a möebius strip."

My eyebrows shot up. "A what? A Moby's trip? What are you talking about?"

"Not Moby's—a *möebius* strip. Take it off and I'll show you."

We slid into the empty booth beside us, and I undid the clasp and handed it over, immediately feeling anxious when it no longer rested against my skin.

"Here, run your finger around the edge of the ring. Don't let it lose contact with the surface of the metal."

I did as he instructed, focusing through my buzz and sliding the pad of my index finger along the outer edge. When I got to the twist, I went around it and began tracing the inner surface instead. Once I returned to that little spiral, my finger again ran around the outside of the ring.

"Weird," I commented, looking back up at him and exhaling a perplexed laugh.

"It's an optical illusion. It seems like it has two sides, but really there's only one infinite one. It's a mathematical object. You didn't learn about these in school?" His tone was light and teasing on the surface, all seriousness underneath.

"I don't think so, but math class was a long time ago." I continued sliding my finger over the metal. "What does it mean?" I wondered. "Does it mean something?"

Just then, Holly came over, wine glass in hand, and pushed in beside Josh. "What're you guys looking at?"

"I'm just showing Amelia how the ring on her necklace is actually a möebius strip." He took it from me and explained it to Holly. She'd never heard of it either.

Turning to me, she said, "That's very cool. It obviously symbolizes eternity. Was it a birthday gift from Scott?"

I giggled and took an absentminded pull on my straw. Since my glass contained little more than melting ice, it just made a loud slurping sound, reminding me I'd been on my way to get another.

"No, I bought it for myself. I think it's cool, though." I retrieved my necklace from Josh's hands and refastened it around my neck. The moment the pendant fell back against my skin I felt better.

"Thanks for the lesson, Teach. I'm headed to the bar." Josh gave me a look I couldn't quite decipher as I rose and made my way to where Liv and Scott stood chatting with the bartender. Already I'd forgotten the name Josh had called the shape of my ring. A few minutes after that, I got distracted by Liv recounting her abysmal date from the night before, and most of what he'd told me about it, and what Holly had offhandedly interpreted it meant, slipped away.

I still glanced toward the door every now and then, but I knew it was pointless. I wasn't going to see him.

No amount of distraction could fully remove Declan from my mind. I drank and danced with my friends. I hugged everyone who wished me happy birthday, and laughed in all the right places at the comments they made. And at the end of the night I went home on the arm of the person I was expected to: my husband.

But inside I felt hollow. If this was what my thirties were going to be like—this perpetual emptiness that could only be filled once in a while by a man who wasn't even mine, then I wasn't too thrilled to be turning a year older.

I was vaguely aware of co-workers talking outside the partly open window while I sorted file folders in the file room annex. As I worked, the chatter began to die down as people finished their lunches and went back inside. For a few minutes, I heard nothing but the peaceful sounds of distant traffic and birds chirping, but then two very familiar voices interrupted the birdsong. I instinctively stilled and listened.

First I heard Josh, low and irritated. "The Bitch From Hell tore a strip off my ass again this morning. One of these days when she least expects it, I'm seriously going to lose my shit on her."

"What now?" Declan asked.

"Oh, the usual bullshit. I solved a pricing issue for one of Ryan's clients my way, the logical way, instead of her way, the kiss-ass way, that would have lost us money in the long run. The client was happy, but I guess her boyfriend's commission check might take a small hit because of it—like I give a shit as long as we keep the business! I'm just getting really fucking sick and tired of her superiority complex. I'm a senior accountant for a reason. One of these days she's gotta learn to trust me."

"Typical Diana. She won't ever change, dude. If you don't get off on verbal abuse on the regular you'd better hand in your resignation."

Josh sighed. "Man, what did you ever *see* in her? I mean, I know she's hot and all, but I hope she was at least a killer fuck for all the shit you've dealt with since."

I heard Declan snort. "Not gonna lie. She's more than just amazing tits—she's a fucking demon in the sack. It's no wonder my brother lets his dick overrule his common sense most of the time."

My stomach clenched at his crude words. I knew I shouldn't be eavesdropping on their conversation, but I couldn't seem to make myself step away from the window.

There was a loud laugh from Josh. "Demon in the sack, huh? She wasn't barking commands like a drill sergeant?"

Declan's voice dropped lower. "Let's just say I kept her mouth occupied as much as possible."

I got a sudden vivid flash of my boss on her knees in front of the man I loved. I felt sick. Yet I still didn't move.

Both guys snorted. Then Josh teased, "I bet she likes to be on top. Whips, chains, the whole nine yards. Hell, she probably wears a strap-on. Huh, Declan? Who fucked who exactly? Did Diana make you her little bitch?" They laughed. I did not.

This time I didn't wait to hear Declan's response. Grabbing a bunch of folders, I held them against me like a shield as I backed away from the open window. I ran into the file room, ducked behind a wall of shelves, and fell heavily to the floor, dropping the files to the carpet beside me.

At first, I actually tried to do some filing, directing my focus on locating the right space to put each one so I wouldn't think too hard about what I'd just overheard. Before long I realized I couldn't do it. I stared wide-eyed and unseeing at the shelves as my mind played back their conversation on repeat.

It wasn't that I was offended, exactly. I was fully aware guys often used those kinds of vulgarities when they talked to their buddies, often spoke of their sexual conquests in degrading terms. It didn't make it okay, but I knew it wasn't unusual. It wasn't that; it was just...the man out there with Josh was not the Declan I knew. It hit me that not only did I not know the side of him he showed to his friends, but I also didn't know what he was like around his family. I had no clue what kind of father he was to Alexis, what kind of son to James or Patrick, what kind of brother to Ryan. I didn't even know what kind of businessman he was with his clients. All I knew was what he chose to show me here at work or when we were alone, and I realized all he truly knew of me was the same. Neither of us actually knew each other as well as we'd convinced ourselves we did.

We really didn't know one another very well at all.

And as long as we needed to keep our relationship a secret, a private thing that had to be hidden away from the world, we never would.

Declan

I didn't go to Amelia's thirtieth birthday bash. Laura hadn't come home, and since it was my last weekend of just Alexis and me, I spent all my time with her. Even if I'd dropped her off at my in-laws to sleep over, I knew it wouldn't be right for me to show up at Amelia's party. It would've only made things weird for her, and she didn't need weird on her big night. And frankly I would have felt awkward as hell seeing Mel and her husband celebrating as a couple right in front of me. Neither of us needed the inevitable anxiety my presence would've brought. So I'd skipped it.

The following week I only saw her once at work and it was brief, but I noticed she was wearing the necklace I'd given her. It looked good against the light skin of her throat, and I was happy she seemed to like it. We didn't get a chance to meet up privately, but I wasn't too bothered. I was confident we'd have plenty of time for that.

At the moment, life was pretty good. Amelia and I were in a great place. James was in remission. He'd gone back to work and was feeling better than he had in years, although we knew there was always the risk that goddamn tumor might start to grow again. Ryan seemed to have his life back on track, and I no longer felt like I needed to keep an eagle-eye on him, perpetually waiting for him to fall off the wagon. I even had a conference in Vegas coming up in a few weeks to look forward to. Overall, I was happy. Nearly.

Laura was due back on Saturday, and I had no idea what to expect when she returned. I knew she wanted to talk about our future, both as a couple and as a family. I suspected there was a good chance she'd tell me she wanted to move to New York permanently to pursue her career. And I figured the word *divorce* would enter the conversation before it was through.

Was it wrong of me that I hoped that was what she decided, even though it would undoubtedly devastate Alexis? Sure it was. But our daughter was young. She'd get over it. She'd visited Laura in the Big Apple only once over the past three months, when my mother-in-law had taken for her a weekend in mid-February, and it sounded like they'd all had a blast. I was sure my soon-to-be-ex-wife would make it seem like a dream come true that Alexis would be able to come visit her there on a regular basis from here on out. One of Laura's greatest talents had always been gilding the fucking lily. I thought

Alexis would deal with our split fairly well, once the initial shock wore off. After all, she was used to spending the majority of her time with me already, so her life wouldn't really be all that different.

Every night that week I lay awake in the king-size bed that we'd shared for the past five years and thought about how our discussion would go, how I'd react to Laura telling me we were done. I'd be sad, sure, but I'd tell her I agreed that it was probably the right choice for us now, and that she deserved to follow her dreams if that was what was going to make her happy. I'd tell her we'd be fine, that we'd always be friends and co-parents, and that I wished her only the best.

I had it all worked out.

But Fate just loves to fuck with me, doesn't she?

Chapter 30

Declan

On Saturday, April 5th, Laura walked back into our lives with a suitcase in each hand.

When she breezed into the sunny foyer with a smile and a hug for Alexis, I mentally braced myself. The fallout of this little trial separation of ours was imminent. Soon we would have to sit down and talk like rational adults about where we saw our future heading, and if that future would include each other as a couple, or just as co-parents.

We tried to behave like a normal family all day. My smiles were even genuine some of the time, as Alexis hadn't seen her mother in two weeks and was happy as hell to have her home again. The two of them were clearly delighted to be reunited, and their joy rubbed off on me a little. We walked to the park to play with some of the neighbor kids, then jumped into the car and headed for Swann's Landing to have dinner with Laura's parents. By the time we returned home, Alexis was yawning, and Laura took her upstairs to read her a bedtime story. I waited down the hall until she left the room before going in to kiss my daughter goodnight.

"You're glad Mommy's back, huh sweetie?" I asked, tucking her blankets up around her chin.

"Is she really gonna stay this time?" She sounded so hopeful, but I could hear the doubt beneath the hope, and it hurt my heart.

I paused. I didn't know the answer to that myself yet. "Maybe you should ask her?"

"She says yes. I hope so."

I didn't know what to say. Instead, I smoothed Alexis' dark curls off her forehead and placed a gentle kiss there. "Goodnight, Lex."

"Night, Daddy." She punctuated her words with a big yawn as I slipped out of her room.

I glanced down the hallway and saw the light was on in the master bedroom. For about half a second I debated going in. Then I sighed and went downstairs. Plopping myself onto the couch, I switched on the Sabres game. I knew James would be watching it, and I figured I'd give him a call during the next intermission.

Laura came down the steps soon after and disappeared into the kitchen. A few minutes later, she returned with two tumblers of whiskey on the rocks and handed one to me. I glanced down into the glass before lifting my eyes back to hers and thanking her. I took my whiskey neat. We'd been together for over six years—she should've known that. But apparently she didn't. Or she forgot. Either way, I decided now was not the time to mention it; I just took a polite sip and suppressed my grimace.

She sat down beside me and took a deep drink before setting her glass on the coffee table. Without a coaster. The ice would make condensation form on the outside of the glass and leave a ring on the polished wood. For about two seconds, I debated the merits of ignoring that, too. Then I grabbed a leather coaster from a drawer and slid it under her glass. She frowned, but didn't comment.

For a while we watched the hockey game in silence. Finally, Laura sighed. Lowering the volume, she turned to face me.

"So…how've you been, Declan?"

I arched an eyebrow. "Fine."

When I didn't add anything further, she plowed on. "Have you given any thought yet to what you want?"

Fuck, yeah. I want a future that includes both Alexis and Amelia. But of course I couldn't exactly say that.

"What *I* want?" I asked. "Just get to the point, Laura. You've had three months in New York away from us, working your so-called dream job. You tell me—what is it *you* really want?"

"I won't lie; I loved working at the Manhattan station, even if I was just covering the sports desk. The people are amazing, and it was everything I'd hoped it would be. But no matter how much I enjoyed it, I was never fully happy."

She looked straight into my eyes. "You want to know why? Because I didn't have my family to go home to every night. I missed you guys. You might not believe me, but it's true."

I sighed. "I believe you. It's been obvious how much you missed Alexis. And she's missed you like crazy. She needs her mother around."

"I need her, too. I know one thing for sure: I don't ever want to be apart from her for so long again. I won't let us be separated like that anymore, I swear." She paused, putting her hand on top of mine on the couch. "I missed you, too. Things used to be so good between us, Declan. I know we're in a bad place right now, but...do you think they ever could be again?"

Swallowing, I glanced down at our hands. "I don't know," I replied slowly. "You were never satisfied covering small town news. Now that you've had a taste of the big leagues, how are you ever gonna be happy here, working at Swann's Landing cable TV? I honestly don't think you would be. And I have no interest in moving to New York. So I suspect the same issues are still gonna rear their ugly heads at some point."

She frowned. "I already spoke with Max. He's offered me my old anchor spot back, and I've accepted. I'm not going back to New York."

Narrowing my eyes, I pulled my hand away to reach for my drink. "Really?" I asked before taking a mouthful. Ugh, cold whiskey. I swallowed it down so it couldn't linger long on my tongue. "Why should I believe you won't still be unsatisfied here?"

"I want to be with my family. Whatever it takes. If you're here, then I'm here, too." She paused. "If you want me to be."

My brows flew into my hairline. "You say that now, but I know exactly how this is gonna play out. In six months, you'll start feeling trapped again. And you'll end up resenting the fuck outta me for holding you back. And next thing we know, we're right back where we were last fall."

"I won't, I promise you. If you're willing to try to repair this, then so am I. I've been thinking about it non-stop for weeks now, and I've made up my mind. I'll do my part; I will." Laura looked so serious, so hopeful, that I actually started to believe her.

I stared at her. A lot of complex emotions were swirling inside me at her promises, disbelief and shock being the primary ones. I tried to keep my face impassive, but I'm not sure I succeeded.

"Declan?"

Realizing I'd been unresponsive too long, I blew out a long sigh. "I'm sorry, but you can't blame me for being skeptical."

"I don't blame you. Things between us have been so strained for so long that it's natural you'd be skeptical. Why don't you sleep on it? Think about whether you want to try to work things out and see where they go. We can talk more about it tomorrow night maybe." She downed the rest of her whiskey and stood to take her glass to the kitchen before heading back upstairs.

I stayed on the couch and watched the rest of the game, but I couldn't tell you who won. I didn't call James. Sometime around one in the morning, I went up to the spare room and lay down on the bed, but I didn't sleep. I felt many things, but tired wasn't one of them.

When I finally did pass out, I had very fucked-up dreams. In the one I remember most clearly, Laura was yanking on my left arm while Amelia tugged on my right, Ryan had one foot, James the other, and I'm pretty sure Colleen was pulling my hair. They were all demanding parts of me, loudly talking over one another until I couldn't understand a single word any of them said. Before I knew it, they'd ripped my arms and legs from my body and run off with them, leaving me lying on the ground. I looked up and saw Alexis standing a few feet away staring at me with wide eyes. Her lower lip quivered and tears started to run down her chubby little cheeks. She cried, "Fix it, Daddy! Please, just fix it! Fix it!"

I woke up drenched in sweat, all limbs thankfully still attached.

Sunday passed in a blur. I mean, I did stuff, but my mind was distracted. Laura had thrown me for a major headfuck, and I was having trouble processing it. She was looking forward to returning to her old job anchoring small town cable news? She wanted to fix things between us and return to how we used to be? What the fuck? It was a pretty huge stretch to expect me to buy all that.

But…she'd seemed so earnest last night. A part of me did actually believe she wanted to try to repair our marriage. For real. And I had no goddamn clue what to say to her. I wracked my brain all day trying to figure it out, but couldn't come up with any painless options.

Finally, after watching my daughter's happy face from her bedroom doorway as Laura tucked her in, I made a decision. It was the best idea I could come up with that would have the least collateral damage.

After kissing Alexis goodnight, I headed for the master bedroom where I found Laura sprawled diagonally across the bed, typing away on her laptop. I shut the door behind me and sat on the edge of the mattress, waiting for her to finish. At last she looked up, one expectant eyebrow arched.

"Can we talk?" I asked.

Closing the computer, she shifted into a cross-legged seated position. "So talk."

Taking a deep breath, I tried to choose my words carefully. "You really want to try to fix us?"

"I do." Her face was still and serious.

"What if we're not fixable? A lot of shit has gone down, Laura. What if it's too late?"

She sighed. "Don't we owe it to ourselves…to Alexis…to at least try?"

I was quiet. She'd voiced exactly what I'd been thinking only minutes before. Much as I'd been hoping, and frankly expecting, that she would straight-out ask me for a divorce when she returned, I had to admit that maybe we needed to make one last attempt to see if our family could be put back together again. Our daughter's well-being came first. She would always come first.

"I think I can be open to giving it one more try," I conceded. "For her sake."

Laura exhaled her relief.

"Here's what I propose: you know I'm going to Vegas next weekend for the conference, right?"

She nodded, her expression curious.

"Come with me."

Her eyes shot wide. "Really?"

"Really. See if Alexis can stay with your parents for a few days. We'll go see a show, throw some cash at the slot machines, have a few drinks—it'll be fun. Maybe it'll remind us of old times. Maybe it won't. At least we can say we gave it a shot."

Truthfully, I didn't think any attempt to mend our fractured marriage would work. I believed we were doomed to fail, so what did it really hurt to give it another go? That way Laura would realize all on her own that we were beyond repair, and neither of us would be able to say we didn't make an effort to fix things.

"Well…as I'm going back to work tomorrow I could only go Friday to Sunday anyway. But yeah, I'll call my mom. I think I can swing it." She gave me a tentative smile. Much of her usual confidence had been missing since she'd returned. I knew she didn't want to tear our family apart any more than I did. But soon enough she would come to the conclusion I'd already reached. I figured that maybe I could speed things along faster if we had a few days away together.

"Great. I'll rebook the flight and hotel dates." With that, I left her to her thoughts. I had no idea if she expected me to start sleeping back in our bedroom with her, but I had no intention of it. Chances were we'd end up having to share a bed in Vegas, but I planned to use it for sleeping only. If worse came to worse and things between us got extra strained, I'd just crash on the floor the nights she was there.

Amelia's face popped accusingly into my mind. I didn't want to hurt her, but I was sure this attempted reconciliation would only be temporary. It was the best way I could think of to satisfy my wife's new desire to do right by us, yet also urge her further along the path toward accepting the inevitable: that our marriage was over. Mel wouldn't love me going away with Laura, but if it was the means to get to the end we both wanted, she would just have to understand.

Amelia

I was *not* in a good mood. I'd made a stupid mistake, and unfortunately Marilyn Silver had brought it to Diana's attention, which resulted in me spending the better part of my lunch hour in her office getting raked over the coals. Somehow I managed to bite my tongue and politely assure her I'd fix the problem posthaste. If she'd been spoiling for a fight, I left her disappointed.

I spent a good chunk of my afternoon backtracking my calculations, re-entering data, printing off revised copies of the proposal, and sending out apologetic e-mails. All the while, my stomach growled and my head throbbed in time with the clacking of my keyboard. When Declan called at 3:30 and asked if I could swing by his office on my way out, I was more than happy to oblige.

I paused in his doorway until he looked up from the file he was studying. Flashing me a grin, he motioned to one of the guest chairs, and as I sat down, he rose and closed the door.

"How was your weekend?" I asked.

For a moment, his smile vanished, and when it reappeared it seemed just a bit less genuine. With a slight shrug he replied, "Laura's back." This was no surprise—I already knew when she was returning, and he knew I knew.

He didn't say anything else, just glanced out the window, so I pressed on. "And?"

"And…and I have to tell you something." His eyes shifted to mine again and I saw uncertainty there. My gut dropped.

"What's that?" I asked, dread seeping in where none had been before. My fingers unconsciously began to twist my ring pendant.

"You might not like it."

Uh oh. Was that guilt I detected in his tone? I squared my shoulders, bracing myself. "Just tell me, Declan."

"I'm heading to Vegas for a conference this weekend."

Confused, I said, "Yes, I remember. What about it?"

"Laura's coming with me." He picked up a pen and began to spin it.

I sucked in a breath. I don't know what I'd been expecting him to say, but that sure wasn't it. "What? Why?"

"Don't get upset. It's really no big deal."

"It's not?" My last word came out a bit squeaky.

"It's not. She wants…" He paused like he was trying to figure out how best to explain this to me. "She wants to try to fix things. Taking her with me this weekend seemed like a good opportunity to prove they aren't fixable. I figure once she gets it through her head that we no longer work, she'll ask me for a divorce."

I stared at him.

"It's only one weekend, Mel. Can you try to understand?" His eyes implored me.

Chewing on my lower lip, I mulled it over. I didn't want him to see how unhappy I was about this. Green had never been my best color.

Finally, I sighed, standing to go. "You do what you have to do."

"Wait." Declan rose as well, reaching for my arm. I turned to look at him, and his hand fell back to his side. His posture was tense, worried. "It's two days. Just so she'll get the hint. You have nothing to worry about."

Staring into his expressive blue eyes, my irritation subsided little. "I'm not," I lied.

"Yes, you are. And I get it—I do. If our roles were reversed, I wouldn't be real thrilled either. But I have to do this. Don't be upset. Please?"

"Okay," I said with a shrug, forcing a small smile.

He visibly relaxed. Leaning close to my ear, he whispered, "You look sexy as hell in that little blue dress. I wish I could kiss you."

My smile became genuine. "Me too." Brushing my fingers along his jaw, I said, "Have fun in Las Vegas, Declan. But not *too* much fun, okay?"

He chuckled. "I promise to have the worst possible time for a guy to have in Vegas that doesn't include getting an STD or losing a shit-ton of cash. Deal?"

Laughing, I agreed, "Deal."

As I walked to my car, the reality of the situation hit me hard. Declan and Laura were going to be spending two nights together in a hotel room in a city that thrived on adult entertainment. On *sex*. A hotel room with just one bed in it, presumably. I believed that he loved me. And I wanted to believe he wouldn't have sex with her. But she was still his wife. She was gorgeous, she was charming, and now she was actively trying to repair their marriage. He'd been in love with her—probably a part of him still was. How hard would it be for her to remind him of what they used to share? How hard would it be for her to seduce him in a place like that?

I couldn't shake a sick feeling of foreboding.

Declan

The flight to Las Vegas took six and a half hours, including a transfer in Charlotte. As we waited on the tarmac, I scrolled through e-mails on my Phone as Laura read her magazine. All the work messages reminded me of Amelia, and I wondered how she was. I *so* wished she was sitting beside me instead of my wife. Glancing at Laura to ensure she was distracted, I dashed off a quick text to Mel asking what was up, just so she'd know I was thinking of her. Then I put my phone on Flight Mode and stuffed it inside my jacket.

We left home at two on Friday and finally checked in at New York, New York at 8:30 in the evening, Nevada time. The lobby desk was tucked into a corner of the very loud, very busy casino, and after waiting through a long line-up, I managed to score our room key cards. It was a bit of a challenge finding the right elevator bank and then navigating the maze of hallways, but eventually we found our room.

A queen-sized bed dominated the small space. The simplistic décor was predominantly black and white: white bedding, mahogany furniture, a modern geometrical print framed in black above the bed. Beyond the desk and chair, a narrow window overlooked the Strip, and I could see part of the red track of the roller coaster that crowned our hotel's rooftop.

I tossed our bags to the floor as Laura began to strip off her clothes. Flopping onto the bed, I flicked on the television. Much as I tried, I couldn't resist sneaking a few peeks her way. She still had a magnificent body, and I'd be lying if I said I didn't appreciate the view. When she was down to her black lace bra and panties, she glanced up and noticed me noticing.

With a grin, she turned and wiggled her ass. "You still like what you see?" she teased, looking at me over her shoulder.

I couldn't hold back a smirk. "I'd have to be blind not to."

"Don't get too excited now—I'm just getting changed." Pulling out a black dress from her suitcase, she stepped into it. "I'm starving, aren't you? Let's go find some food." She presented her back to me. "Can you help me with my zipper?"

I sucked in a sharp breath and got up. Old habits die hard they say, and Laura was a very sexy woman. It might be more difficult than I'd thought to avoid temptation this weekend. I needed to remember that my plan was for her to realize we're weren't compatible anymore. And here I was, already failing.

I pulled the long zipper up quickly, managing to resist the urge to run my fingers over her smooth exposed skin, resist the urge to push the straps off her shoulders so the dress puddled on the floor instead, like I probably would've not so many months ago. Resist the urge to slide my hand around…

Get a grip, Kavanaugh! Eyes on the prize.

I stepped back, nearly stumbling in my hurry to get away. "Food sounds great. And a drink or several." Grabbing my own bag, I headed to the bathroom to change.

Thirty minutes later, we were sitting at a table for two on the 'patio' of Il Fornaio, an Italian restaurant along the edge of the huge casino floor. We weren't really outdoors, but the whole row of restaurants was designed to look like a street in New York, hence the pseudo-patio. It even had big white umbrellas and a hip-high decorative brick fence around it.

"So, how authentic does it feel?" I joked to Laura, sweeping my arm toward the fake city setting.

She laughed. "About as authentic as anything in Vegas."

"Do you miss it?" I asked before taking a sip of my pinot.

"New York?"

I met her eyes. "Yeah."

Laura was quiet for a few seconds. "In some ways, yes. I mean, the vibe there is so different from home. That city is a like a living, breathing thing. It's constantly on, constantly *going*—you know?"

"Not really," I chuckled, shaking my head. "I barely remember why I used to like big cities. Just not my scene anymore."

Her lips curved into a rueful grin. "Yeah, I know."

"Are you sure you're gonna be happy back in small town Virginia? Won't you miss it?" I already knew she would. I just needed her to admit it to herself.

She reached across the tablecloth and gave my fingers a squeeze. "It doesn't matter. I'm committed to you guys. I'll be happy wherever you are."

I swallowed nervously and pulled my hand away. Steeling my resolve, I said, "What if it's just too little, too late, Laura?"

Instead of taking offence, she gave me a tight smile. "That's what we need to figure out, isn't it?" She raised her glass to her lips. "For now, let's relax and see where this weekend takes us. We're here to have a good time, right?"

Holding her gaze for a moment, I considered whether to toss out another snarky comment or just leave it for now. "Right," I agreed.

We enjoyed an amazing meal, and steered further conversation away from anything heavy. Afterward we headed out onto the noisy casino floor and spent the next few hours drinking whiskey and moving between the roulette and blackjack tables. Laura's luck held, but I lost a couple hundred bucks, which I wasn't real thrilled about. By two AM, I was done watching my cash disappear and ready to go upstairs. A bit tipsy, she clung to my arm as we made our way to the elevators.

After closing the door to our room, I turned to find Laura standing close to me, her floral perfume filling my senses. She slid her arms around my neck and pressed her lips to mine. At first I reacted like any other slightly drunk hot-blooded male would when a beautiful woman kissed them—I pulled her against me and kissed her right back. But then a flash of a memory of making out with a different beautiful woman, in a different hotel, in a different part of the country popped into my head. I remembered pressing Amelia up against a different door, and it was like a dash of ice water over me. Pushing Laura away, I shook my head and turned my back.

"What's wrong?" she asked, confused. It sure as hell wasn't normal for me to reject her advances, and she knew it.

"Sorry. Just tired," I sighed. "It's been a long day."

She gave me an odd look before disappearing into the bathroom. I stripped to my boxer-briefs and fell into bed. I was almost out when the mattress dipped as she got in beside me. Cool fingers touched my shoulder, and I felt a kiss on my cheek.

"Good night, Declan," she whispered. "Thank you for this."

I mumbled goodnight and fell into a sleep plagued by tormented dreams.

We both slept late. Laura felt a little rough around the edges at first, but seemed better after her shower, and we decided to walk across the road to the MGM Grand to indulge in their extravagant breakfast buffet.

Once we left the restaurant, she told me there used to be an exhibit of African lions on display in the huge lobby, but it had closed in early 2012. I shook my head, chuckling at the excess. I'd never been to Las Vegas before, but from what I'd seen so far, I wasn't surprised. If she'd told me they'd had a damn tank of mermaids to greet guests, I might have believed it.

We left the air conditioned comfort for the baking concrete of the Strip and began to make our way along the sidewalk. As we approached one of the ubiquitous Tix 4 Tonight booths, Laura grabbed my arm.

"Let's see if we can get tickets for one of the Cirque shows tonight! How much fun would that be?"

She dragged me in front of the corded-off line-up so we could check out the offerings. As she scanned through the various Cirque du Soleil choices, a poster in a plastic frame on the counter caught my eye and I broke into a massive grin. I couldn't believe my luck— Pearl Jam was playing tonight. The venue was located inside Mandalay Bay, which was only three hotels down from New York, New York. I was nearly giddy with excitement at the thought of seeing one of my lifelong favorite bands.

There was a tug on my elbow. "Declan, check this out! Let's try for *O* at the Bellagio. Or *KA* at the MGM Grand if that's sold out. What d'ya think?"

I suddenly saw an opportunity to further my 'get Laura to come to her senses' mission. "Fuck seeing bendy guys in tights—Pearl Jam's at the House of Blues tonight! That's where I'm gonna be."

Her face fell, and I felt a momentary twinge of guilt. In the past, I would have given in and bought the Cirque tickets anyway, just because it would make her happy. But I needed her to realize I wasn't that guy anymore.

"Are you kidding me?" She sounded petulant.

Pointing to the poster, I moved to the back of the line. Laura followed me in silence. As we stood waiting, I deliberately didn't look at her, keeping my eyes on the crowd and the plethora of advertisements vying for our attention.

I heard a sigh behind me. "Fine, Declan. If that's what you want to do, then Pearl Jam it is."

Surprised, I turned to examine her face. There was disappointment there, but I saw she meant it. Laura was not really a Pearl Jam fan, but she was willing to put up with seeing them to prove her commitment to fixing our relationship. If I wanted my plan to succeed, I was clearly going to have my work cut out for me.

Lady Luck seemed to be on my side at last as I managed to snag two tickets to the nearly sold-out concert. In theory, I could have asked the guy for Cirque tickets to an earlier show that would finish in time to still make it to the gig. But I didn't inquire about earlier shows. And if Laura thought of it, she kept silent.

We continued walking along the Strip, stopping every now and then to check out shops and a few of the amazing hotel lobbies—not just for some respite from the heat, but also to marvel at the extravagance. Paris was gorgeous, and Bellagio blew my mind. I couldn't help but hope I'd be able to come back someday with Amelia and spoil her rotten at one of these incredible places.

The smoldering heat grew worse as the afternoon wore on. I was happy to spot an outdoor bar near one of the fountains in front of Caesar's Palace. We stopped for drinks and a rest at a table in the shade of a grove of strategically placed palm trees.

"So…I have a question for you, Declan," Laura said coyly as she sipped her daiquiri.

"Shoot."

"While we were separated the past three months, did you date anyone?"

My beer thumped against the tabletop harder than I'd intended as I looked up at her, startled. Did she know something?

"Are you fucking serious?" I asked with my best righteous indignation. "When the hell would I have had time to do that between working and taking care of Lex?"

She shrugged. "I heard one of the girls from Accounting has a little crush on you."

What the hell? Shit.

Frowning, I rolled my eyes. "And who would *that* be, exactly? You know as well as I do all the snooty bitches in Accounting can't stand me."

Exhaling a little chuckle, she said, "That one you golfed with last summer—the girl who went to high school with me. What was her name? Emily?"

My pulse throbbed so goddamn loud it echoed inside my skull. Bristling, I replied, "Her name is Amelia. She's not as bad as the others, and yeah, we're sort of friends. But nothing more. And she's married. Who told you that bullshit?"

Laura arched one of her perfectly tweezed eyebrows. "Have I hit a nerve? *Fine*, she's your *friend*. Doesn't matter. Technically, since we were separated, you could've dated whoever you liked."

It would've been so easy to just own up to it right then. And, no matter what she'd just said, it probably would have propelled Laura that much quicker down the path to divorce-filing. But there was no way I could tell her the truth. Not when Alexis' well-being was at stake.

Angling my shoulders to mirror hers, I looked her right in the eyes. "I didn't. But since you brought it up—did you?" A sick feeling spread in my gut when I lied to her face. It didn't feel good at all. In fact, I felt like a massive piece of shit.

She laughed—actually laughed—at my question. "I could have. On more than one occasion. But I didn't. It just…didn't feel right."

I had to ask. "You got hit on?" Yeah, I'm a hypocritical asshole.

"Several times." She shrugged again.

"And you turned them down?"

"I just said that. Why? Would you be jealous?" There went that inquisitive eyebrow again. Sometimes I felt like she'd known me so long she could see right through me.

It was a valid question. Would I be upset if she'd been with another guy while we were apart? Honestly, yes. The idea made me nauseous, not that I'd ever admit it.

I shook my head. "Nope. You're the one who walked away from our family. You made your choice months ago. In the meantime, I've learned to live with it. We both have." With those words, I turned the accusatory direction of our conversation back onto her.

She flushed. "You're right. I did. But I'm back now, and that's why we're here. I've said I'm sorry. Are you ever going to be able to forgive me?"

After a moment, I sighed. "I can try. I *am* trying." Picking up my beer, I took a long draught. Then I changed the subject to marveling about Vegas' lax drinking rules and legal, right-in-your-face prostitution. I think Laura was relieved.

Later we had a light dinner, more to offset our buzz from drinking most of the afternoon than from hunger. We returned to our room to change before walking next door to the castle Excalibur and jumping on the shuttle train, which passed through the giant pyramid of Luxor on its way to the huge Mandalay Bay property. New York, New York had seemed gigantic to me at first, but I soon came to realize just what big really meant in Sin City.

By the time we made it to the House of Blues, it was later than I'd planned. We were both pretty tipsy and definitely weren't efficiently hurrying. Once our tickets were verified, we carefully climbed up the stairs to the last two empty seats along the front row of the balcony. A blues trio was on stage warming up the crowd. From the corner of my eye, I noticed Laura retrieve earplugs from her handbag, stuff them into her ears, and fluff her hair over them. I just smiled.

I went down to the bar to grab us drinks, and by the time I forced my way through the crowd back to my seat, the stage was being set up by Pearl Jam's roadies. The big room rang with cheers when the band came on about twenty minutes later.

They put on a seriously incredible show. I don't know if Laura enjoyed it—probably not, to be honest—but I stopped paying attention to her around the time Eddie Vedder sang the first lines of "Daughter". When the final note of the final encore died away, the applause was thunderous, and I was standing and hooting right along with them.

We headed back to our hotel and stopped at one of the bars along the edge of the casino floor for more drinks. Laura decided to play some slots nearby, but I elected to remain on my comfy barstool. I was feeling a bit unsteady on my feet, and sitting seemed vastly preferable to standing. She was wearing a low-cut white top that showed off her chest, and when she bent over the machine, even more luscious cleavage spilled out. As I watched, a tall blond guy approached and began to chat her up. She flashed him her mega-watt television personality smile, and I could tell by his reaction that he wanted her. He couldn't keep his eyes on her face for long; every time she glanced back to see where the scrolling fruit would land, they darted down to her tits.

I observed them for a while as I sipped my whiskey. At first, I was amused, but as time passed, I started to get more and more annoyed. When he put his hand on Laura's shoulder, that was it. Abandoning my glass on the bar, I slid off my stool and walked unsteadily over to them.

"Babe? Ready to head up?" I asked her, leering. As soon as he saw me, the guy's fingers dropped back to his side. Apparently, he was smarter than he looked. I gave him a quick once-over, just for show, and then ignored him. "C'mon," I persisted. My words were beginning to slur.

"I'm nearly done," she informed me, her attention on the screen as she hit the 'Play' button again.

Grabbing her elbow, I raised my voice a little. "I *said*, c'mon! It's time to go."

She shot me an irritated look. "Don't be a dick, Declan." But she stood, shouldering her purse.

As we made our way to the elevators, her arm slid around my waist and mine clutched her across her shoulders. Just to keep us both from stumbling, I told myself.

But once we were inside the room, she turned to me and pulled off that sexy shirt, giving me a spectacular view of her boobs nearly overflowing out of a white push-up bra. Right about then, my brain ceased to be in command of my body.

I pulled her to me and kissed her.

The next morning I woke up with a jackhammer drilling into my skull, my mouth as dry as the Nevada desert that surrounded us, and my bladder about ready to explode. I tried to remember what went down last night, but after the concert and coming back to the casino for drinks, everything got pretty fuzzy.

I pushed the covers back and stumbled out of bed. The cool air hit me, and I realized I was naked. Looking over my shoulder at Laura still asleep on her side, I saw that she was, too.

Squeezing my eyes shut, I groaned.
Fuck.

Chapter 31

Amelia

Though I usually liked Mondays as they often brought with them a chance to see Declan, April 21st was not a good day. In fact, it turned out to be fairly awful.

Around ten, I got a call from him asking if we could meet in one of our usual spots over lunch. He told me he couldn't wait until after work, which made me smile as I assumed he was just as eager for some face time as I was.

"How was Vegas?" I asked after sliding into his car and greeting him with kiss.

He looked uncomfortable. "About that..."

A sick feeling tightened my chest. I pictured a hotel room with a huge messy bed in the middle, and I became suddenly sure he was about to tell me we were over.

"I take it your plan to convince her to divorce you didn't go as well as you expected?"

Was that a flash of guilt I saw in his eyes? He whisked it away so fast I couldn't be sure. His frown deepened. "Not exactly. But don't worry; I'm still working on it. She'll see the light—I know she will."

Relieved he wasn't about to dump me, I gave him a tight smile and slipped my hand into his. "Okay. Then what's making you look so unhappy?"

Declan swallowed and squeezed my fingers, his gaze holding mine. "Laura asked me about you."

And there it was. My stomach dropped through the floorboards, and tears welled up in the corners of my eyes. Though I rarely swore, the first word from my mouth was, "Fuck."

"Yeah."

"What…" I stopped in an attempt regain my composure. "What did she say?"

"Someone from work told her they think you have a crush on me."

"Crap," I sighed. "Who?"

"She wouldn't tell me."

My throat was tightening. Taking a deep breath, I asked, "How did you respond?"

He rolled his eyes. "I said she was being ridiculous, of course, that everyone in Accounting hates me. She knows it's true. Besides, she didn't act like she was too bothered about it. According to her, since we were separated, I was allowed to date whoever I wanted." Blowing out a bitter laugh, he added, "Yeah, right."

"Yeah, right? You don't believe her?"

"Nope. She'd mind." His mouth was set in a grim line as he stared out the windshield. "We'll have to be extra careful at work now. Probably best to dial back our interactions."

My stupid tears were itching away, threatening to spill over. "Oh. Right. Okay. So we keep our distance for a while, until she asks you for a divorce? Is that what you want?"

Declan turned back to me and examined my face. Then he pulled me into his arms. Pushing a loose strand of hair behind my ear, he brought his mouth close to it. "No. That is *not* what I want at all. But it might be a good idea, at least for now."

I pulled away so I could look into his concerned eyes and laid my palm against his cheek. "I wish we knew who told her."

"A lot of people don't like me in that office. Quite a few would be more than happy to fuck me over. It could be anyone."

"I know, but…I didn't realize *I* had any enemies there." Silent tears finally overflowed, and I fumbled in the pocket of my jacket for a tissue.

"Hey, hey, don't cry." He stroked his thumbs through my tears, swiping them away. "It's not you they hate, Mel, it's me. You're just collateral damage. I'm really sorry, baby. I'll try to speed up the process at home so we can move past this, okay?"

I nodded, but inside I was panicking. If someone had said something to Laura, chances were they'd said it to other people as well. My reputation was at stake. And if it somehow got back to Scott…

Burying my face into the crook of Declan's neck, I sobbed my frustration. I knew every time we'd talked in his office with the door closed we were risking rumors. We both knew it, but we'd done it many times over the past eight months anyway. Long before we'd ever even acknowledged what we had between us, we'd been acting like giddy teenagers, so eager to spend time together.

So careless. So idiotic.

We'd hadn't been cautious enough, and it had finally come back to bite us.

The rest of the afternoon I stayed in my cubicle as much as possible, burying my nose in work. I kept my ears perked to other conversations around me, just waiting to hear a snippet that included Declan's name or my own. Predictably, I heard nothing of interest. When four arrived, I almost ran to my car, anxious to get out of that building that felt like it was closing in on me, suffocating me.

My heart raced the entire drive home. All I could think about was that someone at work had seen something suspicious and told others. My co-workers in Accounting would find out. Diana would find out. Laura and Scott would find out.

Declan and I were in big trouble.

He didn't seem all that worried, though he actually had even more to lose than I did. Maybe he was just pretending to be calm so I wouldn't freak out. If that was his intention, he'd failed. I was absolutely freaking out, and had been since the second he'd told me.

As I walked into the house, Scott greeted me from the kitchen and asked what I wanted for dinner. The thought of food made my stomach clench, but I didn't want to tell him that, yet again, I wasn't hungry. Instead, I suggested he order pizza. Then I went upstairs, changed into comfy clothes and curled up under the covers.

Those stupid tears, which had been on the verge of making another appearance all day, began to flow again. Soon I was sobbing in earnest, coiled in a tight ball, trying in vain to hold myself together.

"Ames? What's wrong?"

Crap. I'd thought he'd already left for Pizza Palace. The mattress dipped as Scott sat on the edge. Rolling over, I looked up at him through bleary eyes. "Just had a…a bad day."

He examined my face, brows narrowed. "Your moods have been up and down, mostly down, since not long after you started there. The meds seem to be helping a bit, but yet here you are, upset again about something that happened at work." He paused and sighed, taking one of my hands in his. "What was it today? Diana again?"

I shook my head, sniffling, "N-not this time."

Scott was silent for a few moments, frowning. "You want *my* opinion?"

Shifting up against the pillows, I swiped my face with a tissue and nodded.

"BWK doesn't seem very healthy for you. I can't remember you ever coming home from Bellmore in tears. Maybe it's time to start looking elsewhere?"

My eyes widened. Was he really suggesting I should resign? Looking down, I mumbled, "It's not that bad."

He put his other hand on my shoulder. "Amelia, listen to me. You're obviously miserable. I'd thought it was…well, I'd thought it was something to do with me, with us, but maybe I was wrong. Maybe it's just that you're unhappy with your job right now."

I raised my eyes to his, but didn't reply. He'd thought it was him. Guilty tears welled up again. What kind of torture had I been putting my poor husband through? Here he was, trying to help me fix my problem, wanting only what he thought was best for me, and how was I treating him in return? Like crap, that's how. If there was a Hell, I surely had a one-way elevator ride straight down awaiting me.

"It's not right that you're so upset at work all the time. You're very qualified—you can find something else." He took a deep breath. "I think you should quit."

My eyes widened. "You do? You know we can't afford that." But inside I was turning the idea over. And it definitely had its appeal.

"You've got your dad's inheritance in the bank now. We can manage in the short term while you look for something better." He squeezed my hand. "I hate that you're always crying because of that place. Life's too short to be down all the time."

Biting my lip, I gave a small shrug. "I'll think about it."

"Good." He rose and went to the door, turning to look at me before he left. "Don't stress about our cash flow. We'll be fine. You're great at what you do and have excellent references. If you take a few weeks or a month off in-between, it might be good for you."

I blinked, feeling those ever-present tears about to make yet another appearance. "Thanks, Scotty."

"You're welcome. I'm off to get the pizza, in case you have any appetite."

Much to my surprise, after a few minutes of mental regrouping, I did.

As I ate, I pondered the idea more. Maybe Scott was right. Maybe moving on from BWK really would be the best thing for me at this point. Now that I knew at least one person had suspicions, continuing to work at the same company as Declan seemed like a recipe for disaster.

I'd miss seeing him regularly of course—so much that the very thought hurt my heart. And I'd miss Josh and Kaitlyn and Sam. But would I really miss the job? I sure wouldn't miss working for Diana. She'd removed nearly all our empowerment to make important decisions, insisting now that anything more than simple pricing be reviewed by either herself or Josh before it went back to Sales. When I'd started I'd hoped to get on the fast track to becoming a Senior Accountant, but with her as my manager, that didn't seem like it would happen anytime soon. If ever.

If Declan and I were found out, our lives as we knew them would be over. I might get fired, and there would go my reference. I'd have a black mark on my employment record. Our personal lives would also suffer. If Laura learned the truth, Declan could lose Alexis. If Scott did…well I didn't even want to think about that.

No, the more I thought about it, the more I realized my husband was right. It was time to hand in my notice and look for something more challenging elsewhere.

Once the dishes were put away, I opened my laptop and typed up a letter of resignation. I saved it, recalling a recruiter who had contacted me a month or so ago. I thought I'd check with him first to see if he still had anything. Then I looked online for accounting job postings in the area. I found two: one way too advanced for my skill level, and another I was pretty sure I was over-qualified for. Closing the lid with a sigh, I idly wondered how much it would cost to start my own business doing accounting for individuals and small companies. That had always been my long-term dream.

Again, I buried myself with work, skipping lunch with the girls in favor of staying at my desk. I searched my email folders until I found the one from the recruiter and sent him a message from my phone asking to let me know if he had any relevant openings.

He called me a few hours later, but he didn't have anything useful. The only accounting position he knew of was over in Norfolk, which was too far away for me to commute.

I went home and added a line to my resignation letter stating my final day. It was two weeks and three days away. My heart pounded with nervous excitement as I printed out three copies and folded two of them into envelopes: one for my records, one to give to Diana, and one to send to Human Resources.

This decision felt massive. I'd never been unemployed before, not since high school. The idea of not earning any income for a few weeks—or maybe even a few months—terrified me. Since I'd moved away from home, I'd always been able to pay my share. I'd always been responsible. I had some money socked aside from my dad's will, but I didn't want to put too much of a dent in that. Scott and I would have to live frugally for the next while. We weren't big spenders anyway, so it wouldn't be that difficult, but the whole thing still made me apprehensive.

When I got to work on Wednesday, I tucked the envelopes into a drawer, deciding to sit on them for one more day. Ignoring my protests, Kaitlyn dragged me to the cafeteria at lunch. I prayed I wouldn't run into Declan. Though they tried to get me involved in their conversations, I was reticent. Sam whispered, "What's wrong?" into my ear, but I just shrugged. She flashed me a sympathetic smile, but didn't press for more.

Thursday morning, I came in extra early and distracted myself by diving into the list of requests in our departmental inbox. I'd gotten through three of them by the time Diana breezed past heading for her office.

Okay, I told myself. *It's time.*

A tense lump lodged in my throat as I retrieved an envelope from my drawer with shaking fingers. Before I could lose my nerve, I went straight over and knocked on the edge of her open door.

When she looked up questioningly, I asked, "Can I speak with you for a minute?"

Diana frowned as if anticipating something annoying. Then she beckoned me forward. I shut the door and took a seat opposite her cluttered desk.

"What is it, Amelia? I have a management meeting in ten minutes."

"I'm handing in my letter of resignation," I told her, laying the envelope on her desk blotter.

One of her eyebrows arched in curiosity. "Oh really?" She pulled the letter out and scanned it over. "Hmm. What's this about? Did you get an offer somewhere else?"

I briefly debated lying before realizing how easily she could check out any false claims. "Not yet, no. But I'm confident I will soon." I forced a smile.

She narrowed her eyes. "Why would you quit without another job to go to? Is there a problem with someone here?"

I hoped she hadn't heard any gossip about Declan and me. "No," I replied. "Everyone's great. I just don't feel challenged enough anymore. And I want to find something closer to home so I don't have to commute."

"Really?" She sounded skeptical.

I nodded. "Really. Is everything covered in the letter, or do I need to revise it? Does May 9th work for my last day? I can be flexible on that if you need me to."

Diana gave my letter another cursory glance. "It's fine. We'll be sorry to see you go, Amelia. You're going to just miss your one-year anniversary."

"Thanks," I said. Inside I thought, *Liar. You won't be sorry at all.*

I stood, assured her I'd send a copy to Human Resources, and made my way on somewhat shaky legs back to my desk.

There. It was done.

But that had probably been the easy part. I still had to figure out how I was going to break my news to Declan.

I was a bundle of nervous energy as I sat at my desk and tried to prioritize e-mail requests. I'd actually done it. I'd resigned. In a little over two weeks I'd be finished at BWK. Me, unemployed—I couldn't wrap my brain around it.

Last year about this time, I'd been offered the position here. So much had changed in the past twelve months. Nearly *everything* had changed in my life, and most of it not for the better.

Sighing, I decided there was one person I could tell before I'd have to suck it up and go see Declan. When I got to Josh's office, I closed his door and sat down across from him.

He raised a curious eyebrow when I didn't speak. "What's up, Amelia?"

"I…um…I just…I just quit."

"You *what*?" Now both brows shot up to his hairline and his eyes flared.

"I just handed my letter of resignation in to Diana," I said with a shrug. "My last day is two weeks from tomorrow."

"Seriously?"

I nodded.

"Did you get a better offer someplace else?"

"Not yet," I replied. "I'm still in the process of looking."

"Then why? Why up and quit right now?" He frowned. "Unless? Did something happen?"

Heat flooded my face. I should've known he'd assume it was connected to Declan. And of course he was right.

My eyes dropped to my twisting fingers. "Just some people asking questions."

"Some people? Or Laura?"

354

"Both, from what I understand." I looked back at him. "But it's not just that. You know better than anyone I haven't been feeling very challenged here. And working for Diana's no picnic. The time's come for me to move on. You understand, right?"

Josh's forehead wrinkled as he examined my face, no doubt trying to see if I was being honest. Then he sighed. "Yeah. I get it. But we're gonna miss you around here."

"I'll miss you, too. But we'll still see each other socially. And I really think it's for the best."

His expression grew more serious. "Does he know yet?"

I shook my head. "Not yet. But I'll tell him soon. Today, if I can."

"He's not gonna be happy."

"I know. But when I said it's for the best, I guess I meant for both of us." I stood to go.

"Hey Amelia? If you need a reference, you know you can use me."

With a smile I said, "You're the best."

Josh laughed. "Don't you forget it."

Two down, one to go. The first two had gone better than I'd feared. Maybe telling Declan would be okay, too.

My hands clenched into clammy fists at my sides as I stood in front of Declan's office door. He was staring at his monitor and hadn't seen me yet. Scanning the room, I realized he'd replaced the hinged photo frames on his desk with a new one which just held a recent shot of Alexis. His wedding portrait was no longer on display. I wondered how long ago he'd taken it down, and if I'd been too distracted to notice. Its removal pleased me.

Taking a deep breath, I rapped on the doorframe. When he turned, his face broke into the wide smile he always had just for me. My heart clenched at the sight of it. God, I was going to miss seeing that smile every week.

"Hey," he greeted me. "What brings you over this morning?"

I tried to grin back, but it faltered. Closing the door behind me, I sat down and clutched the file folder I'd brought against my chest. How to even start?

"Baby, you look stressed," he said softly, standing and coming over. "What's going on?"

As he dropped into the other chair beside me, I raised my eyes to his. "I have to tell you something. And you're probably not going to like it much."

He took my fingers in his. "I don't like the sound of that one bit. Is this a conversation we should be having elsewhere?"

"Probably," I sighed, "but I couldn't wait that long. I have to tell you now. Please go back to your chair, just in case Colleen or someone walks in."

He frowned, but retreated behind his desk again. "You're worrying me, Mel. What's going on? Are you…have you…changed your mind?"

I shook my head. Then, steeling myself against his reaction, I blurted, "I handed in my letter of resignation this morning."

Declan's jaw dropped. "*What*? Why the *hell* would you do that?" Then his brows narrowed as he processed the news further. "Was this because of what I told you the other day? What Laura said?"

Pressing my lips together, I nodded.

"It's just a stupid rumor! It'll pass. Someone's just trying to fuck me over. When they see it didn't work, they'll move on. You don't have to up and quit over it!"

I sighed. "It's not just that. I mean, yeah, that's a big part of it. I was really freaked out after you told me. It's not good for either of us if we keep trying to juggle our working relationship and our…personal stuff. But honestly, I don't feel like this place is a good fit for me anymore. I want more challenges, more authority. A boss who respects me and who'll help me succeed. It might be better for me professionally if I move on."

He exhaled a wry chuckle. "Guess I can't argue with that last bit."

We looked at each other for a long moment. "I'm sorry," I murmured.

"For what? For abandoning me to the wolves? Hey, no problem." He turned to the side and braced an elbow on his knee, lowering his head and pinching the bridge of his nose in his fingers. With chagrin, I realized he was fighting to regain control. He was on the verge of tears.

"Oh, Declan," I breathed. "I'll miss you like crazy. But you know it's better for us both if I go."

He gave his head a quick shake and straightened to look at me. "Speak for yourself. I'm better with you here." His eyes widened as he thought of something else. "Is this the last time...?"

Shaking my head wildly, I replied, "No! I just handed in my notice. My last day is two weeks from tomorrow. I'm sure we'll see each other before then. And hopefully we'll be able to make time to get together once in a while after. Right?"

He nodded without smiling. "Yeah, of course." Then he sighed. "I'm sorry—I'm just really floored by this. I'll miss working with you. It was nice to have another ally over there in the shark tank." A tight, bitter grin surfaced.

I opened his office door, ever conscious of what passers-by might think.

"I'd better go. I'm glad you were here so I could tell you in person. I'd hate for you to have heard it from someone else."

Declan stood and came toward me, his face etched with pain. "Yeah." His voice dropped to barely a whisper. "I wish I could touch you right now."

For his sake, I attempted a smile, but couldn't quite manage it. I mouthed the words, "Me, too."

Declan

Vegas was a bust. Well, the conference had gone pretty well, but my plan to convince my wife the two of us weren't compatible anymore had failed.

Spectacularly failed, to be more accurate.

I'd tried my best to be a selfish, cold asshole, which shouldn't have been all that difficult for me. But when it came right down to it, I just couldn't keep up the ruse. Every time I let my aloof facade slip, I realized the two of us were actually having a great time. Laura did a remarkable job of reminding me of the woman I'd fallen in love with six years ago. She was thoughtful, she was in the moment with me instead of distracted, and most of all, she was fun. We hadn't truly relaxed and had fun together in a very long time. Much as I tried not to, we ended up laughing far more often than arguing. The distance between us gradually and naturally fell away without me even really being aware of it. And after drinking more than I probably should've on Saturday night, the green-eyed monster jumped out at seeing some dude flirt with her—old habits die hard—and though I'd sworn it wouldn't happen, we'd stumbled back up to the room and ended up in bed.

Naked.

Yeah.

Don't get me wrong—I hadn't changed my mind about the future of my marriage. Even after waking up the next morning together and realizing what we'd done, I still had every intention of carrying on with my plan. I still wanted shared, if not full, custody of Alexis, and Laura and I to try our best to remain friends and co-parents. And I still hoped for a chance at a future that included Amelia.

I was disappointed as fuck in myself for losing control, for being weak. For giving Laura the wrong idea. For still being attracted to her. For not wanting any other man to touch her. For still caring about her more than I wanted to.

For betraying Amelia's trust.

I felt like a massive piece of shit.

So I went back to acting distant with Laura, and pretended the previous night's activities never happened. Her eyes flashed with pain when she realized my walls were back up, but only for a moment. Then she replaced it with that firm determination I knew so well. Laura was a woman very used to getting what she wanted. Helping her come to terms with the fact that we were unfixable without revealing I was in love with someone else was going to be a lot harder than I'd originally anticipated.

Much as I loved Amelia, I realized, after thinking things over long and hard after Laura left for the airport, that a part of me still loved my wife as well. It wasn't the same type of all-consuming love as it had been before, but vestiges of it still remained. She'd changed a lot over the past six years, but some of the old Laura was still in there. I didn't want to hurt her, and I sure as hell didn't want to hurt Alexis. I also hated knowing that my choices could end up hurting Amelia.

Everything was just so motherfucking complicated.

The following week at work I'd told Amelia the gossip Laura had revealed to me. And Amelia had freaked the fuck out. Her reaction didn't surprise me all that much, but what I didn't expect was for her to up and quit over it.

When she told me she'd resigned, I damn near lost it. That old familiar feeling of abandonment flooded over me, though I tried to fight it off. I think I managed to disguise the intensity of my reaction from her, but after she left, I sat there for a long time behind that closed door, head in hands, trying desperately to get my shit together.

My emotions were floundering. It felt like my entire life was spiraling out of control and I didn't have a single fucking clue how to dispel the vertigo. All these decisions were being made that affected me, and I had no goddamn say in any of them.

And as it turned out, I didn't even know the half of it yet.

Chapter 32

Amelia

The weekend after I resigned, Scott and I drove down to visit his dad in Greensboro, North Carolina. All those long hours in the car and hanging out in my father-in-law's cramped house gave me plenty of time to think.

I didn't know what I would do with so much free time looming, but I wondered if this little hiatus from the workforce might be just what I needed. I'd keep up the job search. I'd go to my weekly therapy sessions with Debbie Westwood. I'd go visit Indira for a few days. Maybe I'd even look for work in Richmond while I was there, although an hour's drive was kind of far from Declan for my liking.

In less than two months, Scott would be on summer break. He'd said he'd be cool with me not going back to work until September, as that way we'd have the entire summer off together. During the long ride home from Greensboro, he even suggested we could drive across the country to California in July, sightseeing roadside attractions along the way. He seemed to be in great spirits about it all.

I was less thrilled, but I tried to hide my discomfort. Because the other big thing on my to-do list was to ramp-up my search for a suitable place to live. And once I found one, I was going to have to break it to my sweet, loving husband that I was moving out.

The following workweek flew by as I scrambled to get stuff done while surreptitiously scoping for apartments during any free moments. I even went to look at one not far from the office, but it turned out to be dingy and cramped. I began to wonder if I'd need to get a roommate to afford someplace decent. The idea did not thrill me.

When I got to work on May 5th, I realized it was my last Monday at BWK. Only five more days until I'd have to reevaluate my career and my life, and start both down new paths. I had no idea where those paths would lead, or who might join me along their possibly treacherous twists.

Near the end of the day, Declan called. "So? How's it feel to be in the home stretch?"

"Weird," I replied. "I keep thinking about what needs to get done next week, and by the end of the month, and then I remember I won't be here to do it."

"You have a lot to finish up still?"

"Nah, it's not too bad. I've got a handle on things. Josh's already been delegating my caseload."

"Cool. You wanna have lunch on Friday?"

I laughed. "I'm pretty sure I can swing that."

"Any chance of skipping out for the afternoon again? Or is that asking too much? I have to take James to a follow-up appointment in Charlottesville, but we don't need to hit the road until 4:30."

Visions of us entwined naked in a hotel room bed danced in my head, and I smiled. Lowering my voice, I said, "I still have a few hours plus time left. I'm sure I can convince Diana to let me use them on Friday—she'd be more than happy to see me gone earlier. I'll let you know."

"Perfect. Not sure if I'll see you around before then or not. My schedule's nuts this week."

"Okay, well Friday for sure then."

After confirming with Diana that it was okay to leave at noon on my last day, I texted Declan that we were on.

Suddenly I couldn't wait for my time at Baker, Wright and Kavanaugh to come to an end.

And so my final day arrived.

Friday morning, I plunked my purse and coffee onto my desk, flicked on my monitor and slid into my chair sporting an insuppressible grin. This lasted for a little over an hour.

Shortly after nine, I heard my cell phone ping inside my bag. It was a text from Declan telling me we couldn't have lunch after all, that James' appointment had been moved up, and he now had to leave at 12:30. He apologized and promised we'd reschedule soon, suggesting next Tuesday.

To say I was disappointed was a vast understatement, but I didn't guilt-trip him. Instead, I replied that I understood, and asked him to please not head out without saying goodbye.

My mood switched from giddy anticipation to jumpy edginess. I couldn't get past a nagging feeling that something unpleasant was going to happen.

Since I was no longer in a hurry to get everything cleaned up so I could leave early, I gave in to my restlessness and took frequent breaks away from my desk. Any little excuse had me bouncing up: a page waiting for pick-up at the printer, a smudge on my wrist needing washing, returning desk supplies to the cabinet, anything.

At one point, I went around the building saying my goodbyes to those I had gotten to know over the past eleven months. Ryan was on his way out when we bumped into each other by Sam's desk. He gave me a big hug and told me how much he'd miss seeing my smiling face in the hallways.

Once 11:30 slid past and I still hadn't heard from Declan, I grew a little anxious. I'd finished all the work I had left and was sorting through my notebooks and binders, packing things in an empty paper box.

11:45 came and went, and nothing. My nails drummed restlessly against the edge of my desk.

When noon arrived, I couldn't stand it any longer and strode over to the Sales department. As I walked, I felt my heart pounding in my chest, heard its relentless throbbing in my ears. My fingers curled and uncurled into sweaty palms.

The area was deserted. I guessed everyone had gone for lunch. Declan's office was empty, but his monitor was on and his jacket still sat folded on his credenza.

Spinning on my heels, I hurried back to my cubicle, just in case. No new messages awaited me. My own department was also nearly cleared out. Other than the distant sound of a phone ringing in one of the manager's offices, everything was quiet. Kaitlyn and Sam had gone outside to eat. Josh's office door stood wide open. Diana seemed to be the only one at her desk, but I didn't really feel like chatting with her.

I went back to the file room annex. Peeking out the window, I saw every table on the deck was occupied. One of the cafeteria ladies stood flipping patties on the grill. I'd forgotten today was Backyard Barbecue Friday. Scanning the faces, I spotted Declan at last in the back corner eating with Josh.

Irritation surged through me. He'd told me he needed to leave at 12:30. It was currently 12:12, and, instead of finding time for me on my last day, he was outside gabbing with Josh, wasting away the precious minutes he could have been spending with me.

Gritting my teeth, I returned to my desk. All I could hear was my pulse throbbing in my veins. I packed a few more things. Checked my inbox. Examined my cell phone for new texts. Glared at my desk phone, willing it to ring.

My anxiety skyrocketed as the minutes crawled by. At 12:18, I jumped up and stalked back over to Sales. He wasn't there. I darted to the file room and looked outside again. Sure enough, there he still sat, laughing at something Josh was saying, not looking at all like he was in any rush to go anywhere.

Or to see me.

I was nearly vibrating with anger. Heading into the washroom, I splashed water on my burning face. My heartbeat was still on overdrive. I realized I was having another panic attack, but curling into a fetal position on the floor didn't seem like a viable option.

When I returned to my desk and found there was still no message from Declan, I pulled open my drawer and glared at my purse, tempted to just grab it and leave. It'd serve him right if he didn't get to see me today. Even when he did get back to his office, I knew he'd have to head straight out to drive his father to Charlottesville. He'd had all morning to find a few minutes for me, and instead he'd chosen to have lunch with Josh. Maybe he was avoiding me on purpose.

Slamming the drawer shut, I checked my inbox for the hundredth time. Nothing.

By the time my phone rang at 12:27, I was so livid I could barely see straight.

"Hey," Declan said. He sounded easy and relaxed. He sounded like he was smiling.

I wanted to kill him.

"Hey," I replied, unable to mask the edge in my voice. "I take it you're heading out?"

"I've got a few minutes. Have time to pop by before you leave?"

A few different responses flashed through my mind:

I'm not leaving. I was only taking off early to spend time with you, so there's no point now.

Nope, sorry, gotta go.

Considering you've only spared 3 whole minutes to say goodbye to me, I think I'll pass, thanks.

What I ended up saying, rather stupidly in hindsight, was: "Sure."

My palms were no longer sweaty; they were cold and dry. In fact, my entire body felt cold. Foreign, even. Like I was a robot walking around on autopilot.

When I got to his office, I went straight in and sat down without knocking or saying hello. He smiled at me, rising to close the door.

It was the first time I'd seen Declan in person since the morning I'd told him I'd quit. He wore a pale blue button-up, open at the neck, cuffs rolled up to his elbows revealing his shiny silver Tag Heuer watch. He looked happy to see me. My anxiety dropped a notch, but I was still at about DEFCON 4.

"So, how was your last day?"

"Fine. Just packing up my stuff now." My icy fingers came up as if they had a mind of their own and began to twist my ring pendant. Instead of focusing on Declan's face, my gaze flicked to various objects around the room.

"You're not heading out yet?"

"Not for a while." God, this was all so awkward. I really didn't want to be here.

"Ah." His hands fidgeted on top of his desk. He seemed at a loss for words.

"Don't *you* need to get going?"

He glanced at the time on his monitor. "Yeah. In a few minutes."

Sighing, I muttered, "I was sort of hoping you might allocate more than just a couple minutes for me today."

Declan's eyes widened. "It's not like we're never gonna see each other again. What's the big deal?"

My barely-suppressed rage boiled up again. "Oh, I'm sorry. I thought us no longer working together might actually be sort of a big deal! I thought, since we met here, that my last day might hold some significance to you. It certainly does to me." I was fighting back tears. The last thing I wanted to do right now was cry.

He looked at me in shock, clearly not expecting this reaction. "I'm here now, aren't I?"

"Yep. I'm so glad you found a spare minute to call me over. So glad I was just waiting there, able to jump right up the second you were ready for me. So glad I'm worth that much to you." I knew I was overreacting, but I couldn't help it. Maybe it was a side effect of the ongoing panic attack, but my fury had taken me over, and I knew those damn tears were imminent. But I was bound and determined I would not weep in front of him this time.

Standing abruptly, I pulled open his office door. "I won't take up any more of your precious time today. Have a good afternoon."

His eyes narrowed as he took in my anger. "O...kay." Getting to his feet, he spread his arms to me. "A goodbye hug then?"

I just stared at him. I knew if I hugged him, I'd lose it. I was hanging on by only the tiniest wisp of self-control as it was. Shaking my head, I backed up a step.

His face fell, and his arms dropped back to his sides. He swallowed nervously. "Not even a hug?"

"I can't," I murmured, my voice cracking.

Obviously noticing my struggle, he tried to offer me a reassuring smile. "Just remember: Every new beginning starts with the ending of something else."

My throat, which had been harboring a large lump already, closed up tight. A dank feeling of dread came over me. This felt like more than just saying goodbye to us working together. Looking at him right now, it felt like goodbye forever. Like I'd never see him again. Like we were over.

"Goodbye," I choked out.

I spun on my heels and nearly ran to the nearest washroom, only just making it before I fell apart.

Monday at home whizzed by. I kept busy all day with laundry, cleaning, and sorting through drawers and cabinets I hadn't paid much attention to in years. By the time Scott got home, I had a box of items to donate and a garbage bag at least half-full of junk.

"Spring cleaning?" he wondered with an approving smile. I knew once I moved out, the house would rarely be cleaned, so I'd decided to try to be useful with my free time.

After dinner, I searched online for jobs while Scott did paperwork in front of the baseball game. I ended up forwarding my resume to one company in Lynchburg, but that was it.

I hadn't heard from Declan at all since I'd walked away from him the previous Friday. He'd mentioned when he'd cancelled our lunch plans that maybe Tuesday would work to reschedule, so I hoped he'd contact me soon.

The next day felt weird. With not as many make-work projects to do, I spent part of the morning researching apartments in Lynchburg, but found nothing I liked enough to contact the management. Once again, I was restless with anticipation. Every ten minutes or so, I checked my e-mail, my cell phone, and Facebook to see if I'd gotten a message from Declan. I wondered in passing if I might be developing a mild case of OCD.

By mid-afternoon, I arrived at the disappointing conclusion that I wasn't going to see him. Maybe he'd forgotten he'd even suggested it. Laura's recent questions about me, and knowing someone at the office was suspicious were probably why he was keeping his distance. Perhaps he assumed I needed some space after my emotional outburst last time we spoke. Logically, I understood these reasons were probably why he hadn't been in touch. But it still hurt.

I also didn't hear from Declan on Wednesday, nor did I try to message him. I was anxious all day long, moving around my house with nervous energy, constantly on edge, constantly feeling like I was on the verge of tears. I met with Debbie Westwood and confessed all my anxieties about quitting my job and being unemployed. But I still didn't tell her about my relationship with Declan. To be honest, I wasn't sure if I still had one or not. Things between us felt bleak.

Thursday, I slept late. I just couldn't find the energy to get up and face my computer or phone with no message from him on it, so I stayed in bed curled up under the covers until past noon.

When at last I hauled myself downstairs to make coffee, I sat at the kitchen table and reluctantly opened my laptop. My inbox icon showed I had one unread message waiting. Probably just spam, I told myself. My heart jumped when I clicked it—it was from Declan.

How's your first week off going? We miss you around here.

Since he'd used his work e-mail, he'd kept it general and friendly, but I understood. I knew this was his way of telling me *he* missed me. A relieved smile broke over my face.

Hitting reply, I typed, *Are we still on for lunch soon? And me, too.* I hoped he'd get the double meaning in those last two words.

He didn't respond until Friday afternoon. *I'll let you know.*

As I read it, a dull ache formed in the pit of my stomach and that old familiar despair rose up to smother me. He may not have meant anything by it, but all I could think was that he was pushing me away. And I remembered that insistent feeling I got when I left him on my last day—the certainty that it was the final time we were going to see each other, the final time things between us were ever going to be even remotely okay.

I slid off my chair and fell in a heap on the floor. Pressing my face into the soft pile, tears coursed hot and fast as I sobbed all my fear and anxiety into the carpet, digging my fingernails in hard and raking it in frustration. I was sure he was about to end things with me. I was losing him. He was slipping away, and there wasn't a single thing I could do about it.

A tiny voice in my head piped up that I was being ridiculous, that he loved me and I *knew* it, that I had no reason to worry, that I was being an over-emotional fool. It warned me that if I didn't smarten up, I would scare him away myself with these crazy outbursts.

I wasn't very good at listening to that voice though; I cried myself out on the floor, waking up an hour later stiff and sore with sticky tear-tracks on my cheeks.

I was a mess.

That was a bad day. There were others. There were also some good days in-between the bad ones, days when I felt productive and like I might actually be able to pull my life back together.

On Sunday night, I drove to Richmond to visit Dee—for real this time. I spent two nights with her in her two-bedroom apartment on the west side of the city. And I poured my entire heart, soul, and messy story out to her.

Dee had always been a good friend. We didn't see each other anywhere near as much as we would've liked, but she'd often been there for me in times when I'd really needed someone. She didn't judge me or tell me what a horrible person I was, she just listened and tried to understand why I'd made the choices I had. She either brought me tea or poured me wine, depending on the time of day and my mood. We talked and cried and laughed and made pancake messes in her kitchen.

All in all, it was a cathartic and much-needed escape. When I returned to Swann's Landing, I felt better.

Until I checked my e-mail, which I'd purposely avoided while away, and found no replies about the three job applications I'd sent, no replies about the single apartment query I'd submitted last week, and to top it all off, not a single message from Declan.

Declan

Things at home were still strained as Laura tried her damnedest to prove she could be the perfect wife and mother. I did my best to keep my walls up without making it noticeable to Alexis. I continued to sleep in the spare room, although Laura had attemped to coax me back into our bed several times since we'd returned from Las Vegas. I knew she was confused and frustrated with my change of attitude since we'd slept together, but so far she hadn't brought it up. I guess she figured she just had to work even harder to earn my forgiveness.

James and Miriam flew in for Memorial Day weekend, and as such, both spare rooms were occupied and I had no choice but to re-join my wife in the master bedroom. Though it was only for three nights, it made me uncomfortable. I didn't want her to get any wrong ideas about us sharing a bed again.

My father and sister arrived on Friday afternoon. Once Alexis finally went to bed, the four of us stayed up chatting over drinks. Laura was oddly quiet, mostly just listening to our conversation. In hindsight, I probably should've paid more attention to the little changes, but in my state of near-constant unease, I suppose it's not that surprising I didn't notice anything out of the ordinary.

I felt a little light-headed, but definitely not drunk when I came upstairs, only about five or six minutes after Laura. As I was changing into an old t-shirt and pajama bottoms, I saw a small black box lying on my pillow. A tiny white bow was stuck on top.

I frowned. *What the hell?*

Sitting, I picked it up and looked at it curiously. Laura came in from the en suite bathroom and dropped onto the bed across from me.

"What's this?" I asked, turning to her and holding up the box.

She smiled at me, a sort of crooked, nervous smile. "Just open it."

My eyes narrowed in confusion. There was no reason I could think of for her to give me a gift. I pulled the top off and looked inside.

Within was something white and satiny, and at first I didn't understand what I was seeing. I pulled it out and held it up in front of my face. When it finally clicked what was dangling from my fingers, I froze, lifting shocked eyes to Laura.

It was a little baby bootie.

"What...?" I whispered. Then I fell silent.

She put her hand on top of mine on the mattress. "I went to the doctor today. I didn't want to say anything until I was sure."

I just gaped at her, immobile.

She added, "I'm six weeks along."

I remained unresponsive, my mind flat-out refusing to process.

"Declan?" She chuckled. "I'm pregnant, in case you need a smack from Captain Obvious."

Blinking a few times, I managed to say one word. One rather stupid word, but it was all my brain could produce. "How?"

Laura's smile fell away. "Don't tell me you don't remember."

"Vegas?" I croaked, my throat bone dry.

She nodded.

"You...you weren't...on the Pill?"

369

She nodded again. "I was. I guess we're just part of that fabled point-five percent. Obviously this was meant to be."

Her former nervously excited expression now morphed into lines of worry. "I know it's a bit of a shock. It was for me, too, believe me. You probably need some time to get used to the idea. But you've always said you wanted another child. I hope you're glad about this?"

She was right—I had said many times in the past that I wanted us to try for a second baby, and she'd always put me off for one reason or another. I'd stopped even bringing it up a long time ago, assuming it just wasn't in the cards for us.

And now…now… *Holy shit.* I was going to be a dad again.

An irrepressible smile broke over my face as it finally hit me, and in response, I saw relief flood hers. She put her arms around my waist and hugged me.

"We're going to have a baby," Laura whispered.

I held her tight. My tongue felt too thick to speak.

Pulling back, she asked tentatively, "So you're happy?"

"I am," I admitted in a rasp.

And I was.

The many implications of this pounded me full force the minute the lights went out. I stared at the ceiling listening to Laura's breathing deepen and realized all the complications this surprise pregnancy brought with it.

Did knowing Laura was carrying our child change my mind about wanting a divorce? I sighed as I thought it over. Part of me said, *Yes, of course! This changes everything!* The other part argued, *No! You love Amelia. You want a life with her. You need to stay on the path you're already on.*

I was happy. I was heartbroken. My mind was jumbled and flailing.

What the fuck was I supposed to do?

Tossing and turning in frustration, I eventually got so fed up I slipped out of bed and went downstairs, ending up on the couch in the living room watching old black and white movies until the rising sun painted the room with gold.

Chapter 33

Declan

The next day we didn't share our unexpected—to put it mildly—news with Miriam and James, or anyone else for that matter. Laura'd had a miscarriage about a year after Alexis was born and she'd already told her mother she was pregnant. She didn't want to take the risk it might happen again after we told people, so on Sunday morning she made me promise to wait until the Fourth of July to announce it to our friends and family. I was pretty sure I wouldn't be able to keep my end of *that* bargain, at least in one specific case.

I felt guilty as hell that the idea had darted across my mind that a miscarriage would actually simplify things. Following hot on its heels was the knowledge that I was a massive selfish asshole for even thinking it. This was my child too, and no matter how much of a curveball it was, I didn't wish it gone.

That night, I stayed up late with James after my sister and Laura went to bed. There was a west coast playoff game on, and though the Sabres were already out for the year, my father was cheering on Detroit to crush the Kings.

During the first intermission, I rose to refill our glasses. As I handed James his whiskey, he turned to me. "So how are you and Laura these days? If you don't mind me asking."

I swallowed. That was a very good question, one I didn't have a clear answer to. Shrugging, I replied, "Undecided at the moment."

James gave me an odd look. "What does that mean? She seems happier than I've ever seen her." He paused, studying me. "But you don't. I mean, I can tell you're still feeling…conflicted. Feel like talking about it?"

I took a large swig and held my glass before me, examining the television light through the amber liquid swirling against the crystal. Did I feel like talking about it?

I sighed. Why the hell not? "You know we had a trial separation while she was in New York."

"Yes. From the looks of it I assume you guys are trying to work things out?"

My eyes lost focus, no longer seeing the glass swiveling in front of me. I was silent for a while. Dropping my voice, I confessed, "I wanted to end it. I wanted a divorce. But now…"

"Now, what?"

"She's pregnant." I whispered.

I darted a glance his way and saw his mouth fall open in surprise before a big grin appeared. "I guess congratulations are in order!" Then he paused, his smile vanishing. "Or are they? You're not happy about it?"

I grimaced. "I'm not…unhappy. Just, as you said, conflicted."

"Why? Because you'd already accepted you guys were through? And now the idea of having another child changes all that?"

"I just found out last night. I'm honestly still processing. And yeah. It changes *everything*."

"A baby won't fix a broken marriage, Declan. Only you two can decide if you want to raise your children together or apart."

I sighed again, re-examining the tumbler. "It's more complicated than just that."

"Why?"

Frowning, I didn't reply. I didn't know if I could admit the truth out loud to anyone, even James.

"You can tell me," he pressed. "I won't judge."

My lips became into a hard line. This was *so* not a conversation I was comfortable having. With anyone. I cleared my throat. At last, I admitted, "I might have...um...been seeing someone while we were separated."

"Ah."

I glanced at him, brows drawn in tight. "Ah?"

"That explains everything."

"It does?"

"You're in love with her." He stated it so matter-of-fact, like he was almost expecting it. How could he read me so goddamn well?

Closing my eyes, I exhaled in a rush. "You can't tell anyone."

"Of course not."

I was silent again for a few moments. Then I sighed, "So what do I do?"

"That, my son, is the million-dollar question, isn't it?" James patted my knee. "What tangled webs we weave. No matter what you decide, it affects other people, and someone ends up getting hurt. You've got a lot to think about."

"No shit," I laughed bitterly.

"Whatever you choose, just remember I'm here if you need me. I'll always be on your side."

I looked him in the eyes—eyes the same as mine, the same as Alexis', maybe the same as the new baby growing in my wife's belly. We were all connected. We were family. And I wouldn't walk away from my family.

"Thanks...Dad." The second word just kind of slipped out. Since we'd met, I'd always referred to him as James. He reacted the same way I did as soon as it left my mouth. We broke eye contact and refocused on the television, both understanding nothing more needed to be said.

Amelia

My second week at home wasn't a whole lot better than the first one. I kept myself busy with long walks in the mornings and searching online for jobs and apartments in the afternoons, but my emotions were still pretty volatile. And other than one short text postponing our lunch for another week, I hadn't been in contact with Declan.

I kept reminding myself that maintaining some distance was the right choice right now. Someone at work had suspicions about us, for one. And more importantly, we both needed to get our personal lives straightened out before we could really spend time together again. The logical part of me understood why he'd barely been in contact, but I still hated it.

Some days I missed him so much that any random thought of him would bring tears of longing. I finally understood what the phrase 'to yearn for someone' meant. I yearned for him. I could only hope he felt the same.

Dee called on Wednesday to tell me she was going to be in Swann's Landing visiting her parents this weekend, and that we were going out to Finnegan's for a Girls' Night on Friday. She claimed it was because I needed it, but I could tell from her tone that she needed it just as much. A series of texts to Liv later and we became a threesome.

When Friday rolled around, I actually felt excited for the first time in a while. I got off my butt and took the time to curl my hair, apply a bit of makeup and choose a cute blue top to wear with my jeans. Eying the three pairs of high heels in my closet, I opted instead to just wear sneakers. I didn't feeling like risking sore feet in the name of sexy. It would just be us girls tonight, so why bother?

By the time Dee rang my doorbell, I'd already finished a glass of wine, and my mood was decidedly upbeat. On our way to pick up Liv, I cranked up the music in her car and we sang along.

When we got to Finnegan's, the three of us found seats at the end of the bar and ordered drinks. We relaxed and got caught up on each other's lives. For me it was just what the doctor ordered.

Since my medication tended to amplify the effects of alcohol, by the time I'd finished my martini I was feeling rather fuzzy. I clutched Liv's arm as we slid off our barstools to head to the restroom. I was raving about how much I loved the song playing, not paying any attention to the people around us.

"Oh, hi!" I heard Liv exclaim. Looking up, blood drained from my cheeks as I saw two women we'd gone to high school with standing in front of us. One of them was Laura Logan.

"Hey Liv! Long time no see." Laura turned her attention to me. "And it's…Amelia, right?" She looked immaculate, as always. A low-cut, lilac blouse showcased her full breasts and tight dark jeans accentuated the curves of her hips. She wore black stilettos, had flawless makeup and perfectly curled hair. She was stunning. I bet every guy in the place was drooling.

Suddenly, I wished I'd worn my heels after all. And maybe a touch more mascara. I glanced down at my meager cleavage and couldn't help but wonder if Declan preferred larger assets. He was clearly used to more than just a handful. Flushing, I lifted my eyes to meet her curious ones again.

"Nice to see you again, Laura," I said, painting on a too-wide smile, although I couldn't imagine it looked any less sincere than her own toothy grin. I forced my facial muscles to dial it down a notch. I needed to remember she had no idea we were rivals for the same man's affections. And it was imperative it stayed that way.

Laura introduced the woman beside her as Heather Long, and when she said the name it clicked. Heather was tall, blonde, and willowy, and she'd been on the cheerleading squad with me in eleventh grade. We hadn't exactly been friends, but we'd known each other enough to say hi. Heather also greeted me with a disingenuous smile. Or maybe I was just being paranoid. Bumping into Declan's wife had me a little freaked out, and my brain wasn't functioning at full capacity.

Liv had known Heather better back in the day, and as they chatted, I realized Laura and I were both here for the same reason: a night out with our girlfriends. It figured we would both pick the same date and place. Just my dumb luck.

"Declan tells me you've left BWK?" Laura asked me with casual indifference. I concealed a grimace. If she wanted to chit-chat, I had to play along.

"Yeah, my last day was a couple weeks ago." I was surprised he'd even told her. Then I remembered she had other friends at the company who kept her informed.

"So where are you working now?"

I was beginning to dread that question. "I'm still in the process of looking"

"Really? Why would you quit before you had another offer?"

Oh, just because you were getting suspicious about your husband and me. No big deal really. We're definitely not having an affair or anything.

"I decided to take some time off in between," I said, forcing my tone to remain light. Making small talk with Declan's wife was the last thing I thought I'd be doing tonight.

She arched a skeptical eyebrow and chuckled. "Lucky you. Most people can't just walk away from a well-paying job without someplace else to go. You're married, right?"

I swept a hand through my hair, wondering where she was going with this turn of conversation. "Yes, I married Scott Templeton. Remember him?"

Her eyes widened. "Scotty Templeton, the all-star quarterback with the deep blue eyes? Of *course* I remember him! He's your husband? Huh. What does he think about you quitting?"

"Actually, it was his idea. He's a teacher at the high school now, and he thinks it'd be cool if we had some time off together this summer to travel and stuff."

"Scotty's a teacher? I never would've guessed. Good for him! Please tell him I said hello."

Something about hearing Laura Logan call my husband "Scotty" made me cringe. That was what *I* called him, and his mother and sister, but as far as I knew, no one else. I was certain Scott and Laura had never dated, as he surely would have mentioned it. Still, her use of the familiar name irked me.

"Will do," I assured her. Then I got an idea. "Hey, so do you know a lot of people who work at BWK?"

Shrugging, she replied, "Sure. Loads."

"Like who? Just curious." I flashed my big smile again, trying to look both casual and interested.

Laura laughed. "Too many to list them all. How long were you even there, Amelia? Six months?"

"Almost a year," I corrected. "Doesn't seem like long, but I made some great friends there. I already miss them."

"Like my husband?" Again, she raised that perfectly tweezed brow.

My cheeks got hot. Sweat broke out on my palms. With no thought to what I was doing, I reached for the ring pendant at my throat and began to fiddle with it. "Like lots of people. But yeah, Declan's a friend. I was disappointed we didn't get to have lunch together on my last day, but his schedule's been just so nuts lately." I snorted, quirking the corner of my mouth up as if to say, *As I'm sure you know.*

"Yes. Well, I'm sure he'll miss having another ally in Accounting."

With a giggle, I replied, "That's exactly what he told me!"

Laura stared at me, narrowing her eyes for a split second, before plastering on that big fake smile again. "Well, it was nice running into you. We'd better get back to our friends." She took the crook of Heather's arm and lead her away, both fluttering their fingers our direction in goodbye. Liv and I looked at each other in surprise at their abrupt departure. Then we laughed and continued to the restroom.

I really didn't give a whole lot of thought to that conversation afterward. And after I had my third drink of the evening, I pretty much forgot about it.

Declan

Alexis and I cooked up a big bacon and eggs breakfast Saturday morning, while we let Laura sleep in. Lex was in charge of the toast, buttering each slice with care before piling them neatly on a plate. When she finished, she ran upstairs to call her mother down.

She returned alone. "Mommy's still not feeling well," she said sadly. "She says she's not hungry."

We still hadn't told Alexis the big news. Considering how often Laura had been sick so far with this second pregnancy, I was of the opinion it was high time we just let the proverbial cat out of the bag. I couldn't wait to see the look on my daughter's face when she found out she was going to be a big sister.

Laura trudged down the steps a few minutes later looking tired and pale.

"Rough morning?" I asked, greeting her with a sardonic grin.

"Yeah." She ran her fingers through her hair and sighed. "You'd think I was hung-over or something."

I chuckled. "No such luck. Hope you still had fun, even sober. You feel up for breakfast?"

She came into the kitchen and sat with us, reaching for a slice of toast. After a tentative bite and swallow, she said, "You'll never guess who I ran into last night."

"No idea. Where'd you gals end up?"

"Heather wanted to be close to home as her dog's about to give birth, so we just stayed in Swann's Landing and went to Finnegan's."

My eyes shot up to meet hers. I had a sick feeling I knew exactly who she'd seen.

Laura's voice dropped as she leaned close to me. "Oh, and I had to let her in on our little secret. She wasn't buying the DD excuse for me not having even a single glass of wine."

"What secret, Mommy?" Alexis piped up. She had a smear of strawberry jam on her cheek, and I reflexively reached across to wipe it off.

Looking back at Laura I muttered, "Since you already told Heather, I think maybe it's time we just spill the beans." I darted my eyes toward our daughter as I took a sip of my coffee.

With a barely perceptible shake of her head, Laura murmured, "Not yet."

"She deserves to know." I gave her a hard look before turning to Alexis. "Mommy and I have a surprise for you. But you have to keep it a secret for a little while until we say you can talk about it with other people. Think you can do that?"

Alexis grinned. "Yes! I bet I know what it is, too! Are we getting a puppy?"

I laughed. "Nope. Even better." Glancing at Laura again, I raised an eyebrow. She pursed her lips, hesitating. At last, she nodded with a reluctant sigh. We both turned to face Alexis.

"You're gonna be a big sister, Lex," I told her in my most serious tone.

Her face went still for a few seconds as she processed my words. Then she broke into a huge smile, looking to her mom. Laura opened her arms and Alexis flew into them, squealing with joy.

A tight knot closed my throat as I watched them embrace. Alexis put her palms against Laura's stomach. "There's a baby in there?" she wondered in awe.

"There is," Laura confirmed. "A very tiny baby, who will grow and grow until they come out to live with us sometime in early

January. How's that for an exciting way to welcome in the New Year, sweetie?"

"Awesome! Is it a baby boy or a baby girl?" Alexis looked to me, as if I might somehow know the answer.

"We don't know, yet," I said, smiling. "But we can find out in about three months or so."

Laura explained the concept of ultrasounds to her as I cleared the dishes from the table. She still hadn't told me who she'd run into at Finnegan's, but it didn't take a genius to figure out it had probably been Amelia. The big question was: what had they talked about? I assumed Laura would fill me in as soon as we had a chance to speak privately.

Once Alexis had settled onto the couch to watch cartoons, I went upstairs for a shower. I was getting dressed when Laura came in and sat on the bed.

"We need to talk."

My gut dropped. No conversation starting with the words "we need to talk" was ever good. I sat beside her and looked at her expectantly, all my muscles tense. "About what?"

"I bumped into your friend Amelia last night." She stared at me, examining my face to see my response to this.

No shit. "Oh yeah? How's she doing?" I was a salesman; I knew how to control my reactions.

"Frazzled, from the look of her." She paused. "She told me she was looking for work, which means she didn't quit her job because she got a better offer elsewhere. She claimed she wanted to take time off to spend with her husband, but she tried a little too hard to sell it, and I definitely wasn't buying. So tell me, Declan—why did she *really* leave BWK?" Laura leaned back on the mattress, bracing herself on both hands.

Exhaling a sharp puff of air, I said, "How the hell should I know?"

"Oh, I thought you two were friends?"

"We are."

"*Just* friends?" She looked skeptical.

I rolled my eyes. "Yes, *just* friends!"

"Are you sure?"

"Yes, I'm fucking sure! Why? Did she say something that made you think otherwise?"

Laura laughed, but there was no humor in it. "She said she misses you. And that she was sad you guys didn't get to have lunch on her last day, but you were too busy." She straightened and looked me in the eyes again. "I'm not an idiot. Call it woman's intuition or whatever, but I can pick up on these things. And that girl has it bad for you. It was written all over her face."

I sighed heavily, in as much of a put-upon manner as I could. "You're seeing things that aren't there, just 'cause you believe the gossip that so-called friend of yours told you. Amelia York is happily married. She does *not* have a thing for me!" I stood and went to the window, pressing my palms against the sill and staring into the back yard.

"If you really believe that, you're being awfully naïve, Declan. And you're normally anything but naïve." Laura rose and came over, resting a hand on my shoulder. "I know what I saw."

I snorted, shaking her off. "You're wrong," I insisted.

"I'm not."

Spinning to look at her, my whole body went rigid. Through clenched teeth I asked, "So what do you want me to do about it?"

"Are you committed to our family? To our unborn child? To me? Because if the answer's yes, then I think you know *exactly* what you need to do about it."

I didn't like being pushed into a corner. When I was cornered, my hackles rose. I would protect and defend at any cost.

"Are you giving me an ultimatum?" I demanded, my voice low, icy, dangerous.

"Am I?" Laura chuckled bitterly. "Hmm. Yes, I think I am. Whatever you did while we were separated is yesterday's news—I don't care about any of that. But now, as far as I understand anyway, we're a family again. In order to go forward as a family, I need to know you're dedicated to us and us alone. End things with her. If you don't, you'll lose us."

It's not like I wasn't expecting this reaction from her—had been all along really—but hearing her say it out loud only pissed me off further. My hands were shaking. I had to struggle to maintain my even tone. "Let me see if I get this straight: either I tell Amelia we can't be friends anymore or you're leaving? Is that what you're threatening me with?"

"Tell her you never want to see her again or I'm taking Alexis and moving back to New York. I'll divorce your ass and take half of everything you've got, and you can fight me in court for visitation rights for both your children. And I'll draw it out for a long, long time. And your attorney fees will be so huge you won't even be able to afford the plane ticket to visit them." Her green eyes were seriously cold. I knew she meant every word.

I'd been waiting for months for her to tell me she wanted a divorce, anticipating it like some great solution to all my problems. And now, when she finally warned me she'd do exactly what I'd wanted for so long, the very idea made me nauseous. Everything had changed, and her threats affected not one, but two little lives.

I thought about spending months, or possibly years, battling a vindictive Laura in court for the right to see Alexis and the baby. I thought about how little time I'd get to spend with them in the meantime, how they would grow up without their dad around, and how they'd hear all kinds of horrible things that Laura, and probably her parents, too, would say about me. The baby might never even know me before starting to hate me. And in New York, they'd likely end up being raised by a nanny most of the time instead of either of their parents.

Laura was also a bitch to be reckoned with when she was backed into a corner. And right now she felt like she had to fight dirty to protect what was hers. I understood it, because it was exactly what I would have done if our roles were reversed.

At that realization, I crumbled.

"Alright," I whispered, dropping back onto the edge of the bed.

"Alright?"

"I'll tell her Monday," I sighed. "I still think you're making a big deal out of nothing, but I'll end my friendship with her if it means that much to you. You're right, my family comes first."

Laura squared her shoulders and smiled. "I doubt you two being *friends* is very healthy for her marriage, either. You'll be doing her a favor. You'll see—it's for the best. She needs to get over her little crush on you and get on with her life."

Then she went downstairs, pleased with herself for destroying the competition, no doubt.

I fell backward. Spineless. Broken. Staring at the ceiling with empty eyes.

I imagined Amelia's face, her expressive brown eyes filled with tears as I told her we couldn't be a part of each other's lives anymore. After the first time we'd made love, I'd watched her sleep and swore to protect her from all the hurt the world could ever fling at her, all the while knowing, of course, that I was the biggest threat of all.

A massive lump blocked my throat at the idea of never seeing her again. My eyes clouded with tears, and I roughly swiped them away. My chest ached. I rolled over, pressing my face into the pillow to muffle my labored breathing. Those goddamn tears refused to be contained, soaking into the cotton, and I prayed Laura wouldn't return.

Fuck my life.

I didn't know if I could go through with this. There had to be some other way to fix this mess. There just had to be.

But then James' calming voice echoed through my mind, telling me how much he regretted walking out on my mom when she was pregnant with me, how sorry he was that he'd missed knowing me and being a part of my life, being my dad.

I couldn't make the same mistake he'd made. I wouldn't walk away from my pregnant wife, wouldn't risk losing Alexis, letting her feel abandoned as I had, having her grow to hate me for my choices. My kids needed to know I'd always put them first. I had to be there for them. I, of all people, understood how much a child needed both parents.

I loved Amelia. So fucking much. More than I'd ever thought I possibly could. I would always love her. But I had to let her go.

So I took those feelings and I balled them up tight, and I pushed them down, and I buried them. I locked them away so deep within me that it felt like I'd splintered off a part of myself, like a piece of my very being was now missing.

I would honor my promise to Laura, even though breaking Amelia's heart might be the worst thing I'd ever have to do in my entire life. My own heart was already shattered at the thought. And no matter how hard telling her was going to be, afterward would come the hardest part of all.

I'd have to live without her.

Chapter 34

Amelia

Mondays suck. It's like a universally known fact, right? But while I worked at BWK I'd looked so forward to Mondays I'd forgotten just how much they were capable of sucking.

Monday, June 10th, however, reminded me. In fact, it ended up being the worst Monday of my entire life.

And it was nearly the last one.

It started off pretty normal, as the future-titled worst days of your life often do. I woke when Scott came in to kiss me goodbye before he left for work, and a few minutes later trotted downstairs to pour myself some coffee, as he'd made enough for two. I popped a slice of bread into the toaster, and sat at the table, opening my laptop while I waited for it to crisp. Smiling, I saw I had an e-mail from Declan, and warmth unrelated to the coffee spread through me. It wasn't a huge surprise, as we were supposed to have lunch the next day. I figured he was just confirming things.

I couldn't have been more wrong.

The message was titled, *Important.*

*Lunch tomorrow isn't going to work. I need to speak with
you about what happened at Finnegan's on Friday. I'm in
meetings today, but can talk tomorrow. Let me know what
time works for you.*

I went still. A wave of icy fear expanded outward from the
epicenter of my heart. I remembered running into Laura Friday night
and chatting with her for a bit, but not the specific details of our
conversation. Obviously, I must have said or done something that
bugged her enough to go home and complain to Declan about it, but
what, I had no idea.

From the tone of his e-mail, it was not good.

There was no way I could wait until tomorrow to find out what
was going on. I'd spend every single second freaking out and
imaging the worst. No matter how much I dreaded the fallout from
our talk, I had to know the truth.

With trembling fingers, I hit Reply and typed, *Please call me today
and tell me what this is about.* After sending my plea, I stared blankly
at the screen. Nothing about this felt right. Nothing. What had she
told him? What did he need to say to me?

Panic mode switched on.

I jumped to my feet, sending my chair to the tiles with a
resounding crash. I barely noticed. The sound of the toast popping up
vaguely registered, but I ignored that, too, instead going straight to
the cupboard where we kept the alcohol. Breakfast was now the
furthest thing from my mind.

Waiting for the phone to ring was like simultaneously anticipating
the most important event in the world, and also the most horrible.
Every nerve ending vibrated as I wandered from room to room,
sipping my vodka, my mind grasping to recall my conversation with
Laura.

I grabbed the cordless phone and went into the backyard. Scott had
strung a hammock between our big tree and a fence post, and I
climbed carefully into it, lying down and tucking the phone against
my side. Bracing one foot on the ground for leverage, I rocked back
and forth and tried to make myself relax.

I tried—I really did. I imagined what my future life might be like.
Maybe a year from now, Future Me would look back on this day and

laugh at how silly I'd been. Maybe all this worry was for nothing. Maybe I'd be living with Declan, both of us divorced from our past and joyfully committed to each other. Maybe Alexis would be living with us, and I'd be a step-mom of sorts. Maybe we'd make love every night and wake up every morning in each other's arms, like we'd both confessed we wished for. I could just picture us racing each other for first dibs on the shower, taunting the loser for being too slow before laughing and diving under the spray together. Afterward, we'd bounce down the stairs to make breakfast for Alexis and see her off to school. Together.

A little smile surfaced at the thought of that perfect life, just waiting for me to come and live it.

Then my phone buzzed against my stomach. Adrenaline surged, my grin evaporating as all that heavy, heavy dread descended and smothered me once again.

I held the phone in my hands for a few seconds, just staring at it. At last, I forced my finger to press the Talk button.

"Hello?" I said tentatively.

"Hey." He didn't sound happy. The dread tightened.

"Declan," I breathed. My brain was a little cloudy from the alcohol, but hearing his voice forced some of the fog away. In hindsight, drinking probably wasn't the smartest idea I'd ever had, but I was stressed, and I chose to combat it with vodka, and it was what it was.

"Heard you ran into Laura on Friday." The only word to describe his tone was *grim*. Grim, grim, grim.

"Yes. Why? Is something wrong?"

"What did you say to her?"

"Nothing!" I protested. "Nothing bad, anyway. I didn't, I swear! We just chatted casually...about why I quit, and how she remembered Scott from high school, and...and..." I paused as I realized what it must have been. "You, a bit. Oh God, I don't remember saying anything suspicious!"

Crap! What had I said about him? Did I tell her I missed him? Was that it?

"Me. Yeah. Well, whatever you said, she knows something's up."

My heartbeat throbbed in my ears. "What did she tell you?"

"She said you obviously had a crush on me, said she could tell, that it was her women's intuition or some such shit. What exactly did you say about me?"

"I…I don't know! I'd had a few drinks—I can't recall it all very well. But I'm sure I didn't say anything incriminating! I would never, ever, do that!" Clear panic radiated off me, lacing my words as I fought for control.

He sighed, a long regretful sound that scared the hell out of me.

"I know you didn't do it on purpose. I know you, and I know that. But nevertheless, stuff was said. And now we have unfortunately reached an impasse."

I went still. "What does that mean?" My voice was a thread.

"I won't lose my kids."

"She threatened you? Told you…" I gasped. "Told you what? To never see me again or she'd take Alexis away from you? Is that it?"

"Basically. But…there's more.

"More? Isn't that enough?" Then something hit me. Hard. "Wait. Wait, wait, wait, wait, wait. You just said *kids*. Plural." Any semblance of hope I'd been clinging to fell away, and the tears I'd had on lock-down burst forth like a broken water-pipe, flooding my cheeks with hot rivulets.

There was a long pause, and then I heard a sigh. "I'm so sorry, Mel. I really didn't want you to find out like this, but…yeah. Laura's pregnant."

Searing pain travelled from my chest up to my throat. I winced, sucking in a sharp breath. That meant… *Oh God*. He'd slept with her after she got back. I knew I had no right to assume he wouldn't—I knew it—but the thought he'd…after all we… *Ugh*. Nausea swept over me, and I squeezed my eyes shut, a flimsy barrier against it all. I was the other woman here. So why did it feel like he'd cheated on me with his own wife?

Like the fool I clearly was, I had to ask. "Wh…when?"

He didn't reply.

"When, Declan?" I demanded hoarsely. "It was Vegas, wasn't it?"

"Yeah." A long exhalation. "None of this was supposed to happen. It just…did."

"You said I had nothing to worry about! That it was no big deal! You promised!"

386

"Mel..."

I choked back a half-laugh, half-sob. "Am I supposed to say congratulations?" My voice got higher, more frantic. "Should I send flowers? A gift card for Toys R Us? I don't know what to do in this situation. Tell me what I'm supposed to do!" I began to weep harder.

Again, he was silent for a few beats. "I'm sorry," he sighed. "I never meant to hurt you. I never meant for things to go down like this. But they have, and I have no choice now. I have to protect my family. I won't abandon them. I hope one day you'll be able to understand."

My tears were flowing so hard and so fast I couldn't speak. Labored sniffling filled the silence between us as I tried fruitlessly to pull myself together.

I heard another soft sigh. "I have to go, Amelia. I have a client meeting."

Choking back my breakdown, I forced out the most important question. "So you don't want...to be...in contact with me anymore? This...is it, then?"

He didn't answer immediately. Then, with a quiet, firm voice, he said, "I think it's for the best. For now, anyway. Maybe someday..."

I barked out a bitter laugh. "Someday, yeah. Right. So that's it? You're just done with me? None of it really mattered to you? None of the things you said? We'll just forget the whole thing—that's what you want?"

His carefully controlled demeanor fractured. "No! It's not what I want at all! Of course it mattered! I love-"

"Don't! Don't even say it. You don't get to say those words to me anymore. You've made your choice, and while I do get why, it still sucks. God, I'm *such* an idiot! I should have known. All your talk of abandonment..." I snorted. "Ironic, isn't it?"

"Mel..."

I heard his voice crack and could stand this no longer.

"Goodbye, Declan."

I ended the call and rolled out of the hammock, landing on my hands and knees in the grass. The phone hit the ground in front me. I shoved it away. My mouth opened wide, but nothing happened.

I couldn't breathe.

I couldn't make a sound.

The world around me seemed to stop and hold its own breath, watching me as I struggled. Waiting with idle curiosity to see if I survived.

God, the agony was too much.

At long last I managed to drag in some much-needed air. With its exhalation, everything that had been locked up so tight just let go.

And I began to wail.

After what seemed like an eternity, but was probably less than a minute, I clapped a hand over my mouth and stumbled upright, still gasping. With watery vision, I staggered back inside, heading first for the kitchen to get more vodka, then, clutching my glass tight in my fist, upstairs.

I stared at my pitiful reflection in the bathroom mirror. Silent tears streamed down the sides of my nose, dripped off my chin. I felt hollow, like some vital part of me was missing, like a black hole had opened up in my chest and swallowed up everything good and right.

Crumpling to the floor, I wrapped my arms around my knees, pressing my face into the soft cotton of my jeans. It just wouldn't compute, refused to make any sense.

Declan had slept with Laura.

Laura was pregnant.

And he never wanted to see me again.

He'd said he loved me. But if he did, it wasn't enough. *I* wasn't enough.

I was a fool, a complete and utter fool, for ever believing in him, in us. Maybe it had all been a lie. Maybe all I'd ever been to him was a sexual diversion while his wife was away. I'd been ready to give up everything for him, and he didn't even want me. He'd tossed me to the curb like yesterday's garbage.

With one phone call, he'd taken away the only thing I had left to look forward to. Now I had nothing. I *was* nothing.

I stood up so fast my head spun, and I had to clutch the edge of the counter to steady myself. Opening the medicine cabinet, I pulled out my little bottle of anti-depressants and examined it. The directions said to take one pill a day, and I was in the habit of taking it before bed. I stared at the bottle for a while, thinking about pain.

Anti-depressants were really painkillers of sorts—painkillers for mental anguish rather than physical, but still, painkillers just the same. And I was in so much pain. It was eating me alive.

I popped off the top and shook some onto my palm. Four little white pills glared up at me, daring me, taunting me. Promising me in lithe whispers that they could take the hurt away.

Idle promises, just like his had been. Idiot me for believing.

Picking up my glass, I downed them in one gulp. As I left the bathroom, I avoided glancing into the mirror. I had no urge to see that pathetic girl.

Once again, I didn't know what to do with myself. I drifted around the living room touching objects, picking up photos and putting them back, pulling books off the shelf, reading a few passages, then putting them away. Nothing held my interest for long.

Noticing my glass was empty, I headed to the kitchen to refill it. On the way, I became distracted by the glaring sun out the front window. It illuminated the lawn, making the grass seem an absurdly vivid shade of green. The car parked across the street wasn't just red, it was violently red. Did cars really come in such intense, brain-blinding colors? And the sky above was *so* blue, so very, very blue. It reminded me of his eyes…

No.

I refused to allow my thoughts to wander in that direction. He never wanted to lay those incredible blue eyes on me again, so I would not think about them.

Dragging my gaze from the window, I changed direction, heading to the front hallway and crammed my feet into my sneakers. In a daze, I went outside, somehow managing to find the wherewithal to lock the door behind me. Moments later, I realized I'd left my cell phone up on the bathroom counter. I no longer cared.

I moved as if on autopilot down the deserted sidewalk. A gentle breeze blew against my bare skin, raising goose bumps. Stopping in my tracks, I marveled with fascination at all the little nubs on my forearm, wondering if I could smooth my skin out again through sheer force of will.

At the corner of my street and the next, I came across a mess of broken cone and spilled strawberry ice cream on the pavement. What used to be a delicious treat was now just a sticky puddle. Eventually the hot sun would bake it to a pink stain. Then the rain would come and wash it away, like it had never even existed at all. Once it was desired; now it lay abandoned.

My heart went out to that ice cream. I *was* that ice cream. Discarded. Forgotten. Slowly melting away to nothingness.

Wrenching my eyes away, I forced myself to move. Instead of looking where I was going, I watched my shoes step along the pavement. I just kept walking, turning left here, right there, until my purposeful feet brought me to where it seemed inevitable I'd end up: Morningside Cemetery.

Soon I stood in front of my dad's newly erected headstone. Its polished granite top reflected the beams of sunlight pushing through the leaves of the oak tree nearby. I dropped to my knees before the stone, reaching out a shaky finger to trace the grooves of the engraving.

William York
1953 – 2013
Beloved Husband and Father

My mother's name was carved to the right, with her birth year only. I shuddered as I thought of the empty space beside my father in the earth below, waiting for my mom to come join him. Even in death, they would be together. Forever.

I realized I was once again twisting the pendant at my throat. Josh's words about the symbolism of the ring popped into my mind, and I ripped the chain from my neck and threw it to the ground.

The sun glinted off the silver band, reflecting its glare into my eyes, accusing me. *You're so gullible*, it said. *You believed his lies. You're a fool.*

I nodded at the ring as if it had spoken aloud. "I know," I whispered to it. "Stupid girl."

Then I looked up at my father's name again. "I'm so sorry, Daddy. I've done an awful thing. I've become a terrible person, and you'd be so disappointed in me." My voice was rough, nearly unrecognizable. A fresh volley of tears escaped to retrace their well-worn path.

With a sob, I rolled onto my back in the grass. The earth below me spun on its axis, and I could feel my body spinning along with it. I dashed the wetness from my cheeks and stretched out my arms, palms pressing against the ground in an attempt to steady my vertigo.

The late spring sun beat down on me. My skin grew hot beneath my jeans. Still, I shivered. I was baking, yet had the chills. Eventually, like the dizziness, they too subsided.

For a long time, I watched the clouds move slowly, oh so damn slowly across the afternoon sky. I became one with the ground, as immobile as the massive oak overhead, as still as the headstones surrounding me. My eyelids grew heavy, so I let them slip closed. And I wondered what it would be like to die.

Would I feel it, as the life ebbed out of me? Would I know when my last seconds were almost up? Or would it be more like a light switch—one moment lucid, the next flicked off into absolute nothingness? Would it hurt? Or would it just be sweet, sweet oblivion?

Birds chirping overhead were my only response.

I lay there for a while, until I heard voices in the distance. It was time to go, before someone saw me and wondered what was wrong. *Everything* was wrong, but that secret was just between me and the silent dead.

As I stood, I again caught a flash of sunlight off the discarded ring. With a sigh I retrieved it, stuffing it into my jeans. Though I refused to put it back in its place, I couldn't quite bring myself to leave it behind.

He left you behind, the voice in my head reminded me, but I shoved that thought away as roughly as I'd shoved the necklace inside my pocket.

A few minutes later, I found myself on a swing in a deserted playground a couple streets over, lazily swaying back and forth. Pumping my knees, I soon soared higher, higher. I stretched out my toes with every forward motion, yearning to touch the fluffy clouds, needing to find out if they were soft as cotton.

Suddenly my stomach lurched. I leapt off the swing and landed clumsily, pushing myself upright to stumble to the nearest tree. Bracing myself against the trunk with both hands, I vomited a thin stream down the bark. I groaned, closing my eyes as I wiped my mouth with my forearm.

Disgusting. I was truly disgusting. No wonder he didn't want me anymore. I didn't blame him. Even my sweet, patient Scotty wouldn't want me if he knew the truth. The tears started up again, as if they'd never stopped.

I went home.

I don't remember the walk back, but once inside, I clutched the walls of the stairwell and dragged myself up to the bathroom again. After a deep drink of water, I collapsed to the floor.

I fumbled on the counter for my phone and called Dee, but got her voice mail. I tried Josh, but he didn't answer either. I left no messages. Panic crept over me, constricting my chest. I had no one else I could call. Neither Scott nor my mom were viable choices, and Liv's friendship with Scott made her too risky. I couldn't call Sam or Kaitlyn because they couldn't know my secret. Before today, before a few hours ago, I would have instinctively reached out to Declan, but now he was no longer an option.

Or was he? Would he really forsake me so completely, when I was drowning and desperate? Did he really not care anymore? In a moment of weakness, I dialed his cell phone. After two rings, it went to voice mail. He'd seen it was me and hit Ignore.

"I'm the ice cream," I mumbled. "Forgotten, like the strawberry ice cream." Just a careless stain, waiting for the rain to come wash me away. I needed it, would have welcomed it, but I knew there was no cleansing me. I remembered all we'd said and done when I'd believed he'd loved me, and I knew it wouldn't be enough, could never be enough. I was filthy. My stupid choices had destroyed everything.

Clutching my knees to my chest, I hung on for dear life. The pain inside, it battered me, threatened to extinguish me.

I sat there for a long time. My cloudy mind was stuck on an endless loop of *We have unfortunately reached an impasse* and *Laura's pregnant* and *I think it's for the best*.

I didn't think I'd ever missed my dad more. He would have been there for me, whether to give me advice or just tell me he loved me no matter what. But my father was dead and gone, and now Declan was as good as dead and gone from my life, too.

I had no one.

And I had never felt so alone.

My anguished shriek reverberated off the narrow walls. I was a stupid, idiotic girl for believing in Declan, for betraying my husband, for letting my ridiculous emotions ruin a great job and destroy my marriage. I hated myself, hated this weak and pathetic person I'd become.

Self-disgust overwhelmed me. What right did I even have to take up space anymore?

I just wanted to die.

Pulling open the cabinet door below the sink, I looked over toilet paper rolls, feminine hygiene products, rags, sponges, and various cleaning solutions. At random I grabbed a blue bottle of toilet bowl cleaner. Near the bottom of the label was the familiar poison symbol: the black-framed white hexagon with a black skull inside, its toothy grin full of lethal promises.

I stared at it for maybe two seconds before twisting off the cap and raising it to my lips.

"Fuck you, Declan Kavanaugh. And fuck you, too, Amelia York," I whispered to nothing and no one.

Then I drank a large swallow.

It smelled repulsive and tasted even worse. And oh, how it burned. My body's reaction to the bleach in my throat was instantaneous. I had just enough time to fling up the toilet lid before vomiting. It hurt almost as much coming back up as it had going down. The fumes burned the hairs on the insides of my nostrils as I gagged and coughed and gagged again. When I finally stopped convulsing, I dragged myself up to the sink to gulp down a glass of water. My stomach, however, had different ideas. The water came right back up, too.

My entire body was drenched in sweat and humiliation. My esophagus felt like it was on fire, and I fleetingly wondered if I'd done any permanent damage. I realized I didn't really care.

Seems I can't even do that right, I thought with a bitter laugh. The sound of it was so empty, so utterly alien that I looked around, confused and frightened.

Then I remembered I was alone. All alone.

Hauling myself upright, I was shocked by my reflection in the mirror. I barely knew who that bedraggled, bleary-eyed, and pale woman was who stared back at me. She looked…hollow. Eerie. Like a ghost.

I felt as frail and ethereal as a ghost, too. After forcing myself to brush my teeth and rinse out my mouth several times, I lurched to the bedroom, curled up under the covers and surrendered to sleep.

When Scott got home later that afternoon, I was still out. His hand on my shoulder startled me.

"Hey," he whispered. "Got a headache?"

"I don't feel well," I rasped in a foreign voice. Talking hurt. My throat felt raw. As what I'd done sifted back to me, I realized it actually was.

"You need me to get you anything? Something to eat?" he asked with concern—concern I absolutely did not deserve.

I shook my head and let my heavy eyelids drift shut.

"Go back to sleep, Ames. Hope you feel better soon." There was little chance of that. I didn't think I'd ever feel better again.

It turned out my brutalized body was not yet done punishing me for the indignity I'd placed upon it. Around one AM an intense surge of nausea woke me. I whipped off the blankets and stumbled to the bathroom in the dark, barely making it to the toilet in time.

Convulsions again shook me as I violently retched over and over. There was nothing left inside me, but my offended stomach didn't seem to care—it just kept on trying to turn itself inside out.

When my spasms subsided at last, I stumbled weakly back to bed, sweaty, in pain, but so exhausted I passed right out.

But my penance was far from over. That nasty process repeated five more times.

The next day I slept until past noon. When I forced myself upright, my lungs hurt with every inhalation, only allowing shallow breaths. I felt feeble, like I was eighty years old, staggering downstairs to get coffee, clutching the walls for support the whole way.

I knew I should probably drag my sorry self to the emergency room to see what kind of damage I'd inflicted. I knew it. But I wasn't about to do it. If I did, I was fully aware I'd have to field too many questions I didn't want to answer. If what I'd stupidly attempted was discovered, I'd likely end up spending a night or two in the Psych ward. How on earth would I explain *that* to Scott?

Oh God. What had I almost done to Scott?

I didn't want to die anymore. I realized what a stupid move it had been, and I was ashamed. But something needed to change, and it needed to change now. I could not continue living this version of my life any longer, or soon enough I would end up in the Psych ward after all.

So I called Dee. Without going into all the gory details, I confessed what had happened. "I can't go on like this. I need to tell Scott we're over. It's time to reboot my life."

"Here's what you're going to do," she instructed firmly. "Go upstairs and take a shower. Next, grab a bag, pack about a week's worth of stuff, and put it in your car. When Scott gets home, sit him down and have that hard conversation you've been avoiding. Then I want you to get in the car and come here."

I started to protest, "I can't just-"

"Yes, you *can*, Amelia. Tell him you're going to stay with me for now. You need to get away from your life, or you might not have one anymore."

"But-"

"I'm not taking no for an answer. See you tonight. Wine will be waiting." She hung up.

So I did what I was told. I loaded up my car with a bunch of my stuff, far more than just one bag. It felt terrifying, but also kind of a relief when I slammed the trunk and went back inside.

It was 2:55. It wouldn't be long now.

I brewed a pot of coffee, poured two cups, and went into the living room to wait for my husband.

Chapter 35

Amelia

Scott walked in the door around 3:15 and found me resting on the couch waiting for him. He looked tired, like he'd had a crappy day. Guilt prickled me. It was about to get much worse.

"How you feeling?"

"Better," I replied, though it was only true by the thinnest margin. "I made coffee. Please come sit down, Scotty."

Dropping his satchel, he came into the living room and lifted my legs to plop down beside me. "What's going on?" His face looked so open, so trusting. For a moment my resolve wavered.

I sighed. How to even start? "I have something I need to talk to you about." I paused. "Something I need to tell you," I corrected.

His brows drew together. "What's that?"

Be brave, Amelia. For Scott. He deserves for you to set him free.

Retracting my legs from his lap, I shifted and sat up, clutching my hands in front of me. "I don't know how best to do this, so I'm just going to say it. I'm…" I paused again, taking a deep breath. I had to force the words from my mouth. "I'm moving out. I'm going to live with Dee for a while."

He stared at me in confusion. Then his eyes widened as comprehension dawned. For a long time he didn't speak. The ticking of the clock on the mantel reverberated in my ears; it filled the room, seeming to grow louder with every passing second.

I was just about to break the unbearable silence myself when Scott asked the question I'd been dreading. "Why?"

Biting my lower lip, I mumbled, "I'm not…happy." Surely the understatement of the century.

"I realize that, Amelia; I'm not an idiot. But *why* aren't you happy? The truth this time." He stared into my eyes, willing me to not look away.

I had to, though. I couldn't stand it. Staring down at my fingers twisting in my lap, I said, "I love you. I do. Please don't ever think I don't love you anymore. It's just…not the same."

He was quiet again. Finally he sighed. "I've had a long, crazy day. I wish you'd stop talking in circles and just spit it out. You only love me like a friend now, not like a lover—is that what you're trying to say?"

My face grew hot with shame. I darted a glance his way and nodded.

"Why didn't you tell me this sooner?"

I looked back up. My throat constricted at the sadness I saw in those familiar eyes I'd loved for as long as I could remember. "I wanted to—I did. But I couldn't stand the thought of hurting you."

Scott snorted. "But now you're okay with it?"

"No!" I assured him, my decibels rising. "I hate this!" My voice dropped again. "I…I just need to make some changes. And moving out is the first one."

"Tell me something." His tone was firm.

"What?" I asked with apprehension.

"Is there another guy?" He held my gaze, trying to see the truth in my eyes.

I flushed deeper, shaking my head. "No. Honest to God there's no one else." My heart clenched as the words left my mouth. It was true, there wasn't. Not anymore. And now I was letting go of the one who did still want me.

Scott examined my face. Then he gave a little nod. "It's not like I didn't kinda see this coming. I kept telling myself you were depressed about your dad and your job, and that things would get better if I gave you enough space and time. But I get now that no amount of space or time from me was gonna fix what was wrong. You just don't want to be married to me anymore."

His voice cracked on the last few words, betraying the emotion he was trying to hide behind his calm façade, and I felt tears itch at the corners of my eyes. I'd known Scott for nearly half my life, knew him probably better than anyone, and I could feel his pain. I hated that it was because of me.

"It's not your fault," I choked out.

He shook his head, exhaling incredulously. "You're not gonna pull the ole 'it's not you, it's me' shit, are you? Is that what you were about to say? Well you're right, Amelia—it *is* you. And you're right about something else, too—you *should* move out. I think maybe I need some space, too." He shot to his feet, stepping away from the couch.

"Oh, Scotty. I am so sorry," I whispered.

"I know you are. I'm sorry, too." Striding into the hall, he announced, "I'm heading to my mom's. You'll be gone when I get back?"

Those old familiar tears overflowed, cascading down my cheeks. I nodded, covering my face with my hands.

The door slammed, shaking the entire house, shaking me to my very soul.

For a few minutes, I sat frozen in the deafening silence, staring into space, stunned by what had just happened. Then I got up and walked, weeping, around the house. I sat on the queen-sized bed I'd shared with Scott for the past seven years. I glanced into the spare room where his grandmother's quilt lay folded on the futon. I even took a look into the refrigerator at all the food we'd bought together only a few days before as we'd planned out the week's meals—meals he would now be eating alone.

Ending my tour at the entranceway, I put on my sneakers, grabbed my purse, and walked outside, locking the door behind me for the final time.

I wept not only for saying goodbye to my home, not only because I'd broken the heart of the first man I'd ever loved, but for at long last leaving the old me behind for good. I wept for the Amelia I once was, the girl who had been so naively happy with her life, who'd never wanted for anything more than the love she already had.

I knew I could never return. And though it hurt to let go, I understood maybe that was okay.

Declan

On Monday, July 7th, I found myself in a coffee shop in Charlottesville with James, killing time before we had to head over to the brain cancer center for his monthly check-up. We sat on cracked vinyl benches across from each other, nursing lukewarm cups of joe. Narrow strips of sunlight sliced through the gaps in the blinds, illuminating twirling dust motes hanging in the air between us. It was eerily reminiscent of the first time we met.

Laura and I had told our families the news of our impending little bundle of joy over the Fourth of July weekend, so everything was now out in the open. James had feigned his surprise well. Alexis had, with her mother's help, made herself an "I'm a Big Sister" t-shirt for the occasion, and as expected, everyone was pretty excited. Patrick had even clapped me on the back and offered me a cigar. I still found it vaguely disconcerting when he treated me like a real son, but, hey, I wasn't about to complain. Even Diana seemed genuinely pleased for us, which made me wonder if she and Ryan ever talked about having kids. My brother had never mentioned anything to me about wanting to be a dad, but then again, he probably wouldn't.

All in all, it had been a great weekend. I'd been distracted enough by all the goings-on that I barely even had time to focus on that hollowed out place deep inside me which throbbed dully every second of every day, refusing to let me forget what I'd given up.

"I have a little favor to ask you," I said to James after the waitress had brought our coffee.

"What's that?"

Reaching inside my jacket, I withdrew a fat envelope. It was sealed. "Can you take this, hold onto it for me?" I slid it across the table.

He looked curious. "Sure thing. What is it?"

"Just some papers I don't wanna lose, but can't keep around the house." The envelope actually contained my attempt at getting all my memories of Amelia out of my head. I thought—hoped—that maybe if I put them down on paper I could purge them out, banish them away somehow.

Arching an eyebrow, he said, "Meaning, don't ask?"

I sighed. "Something like that. Thanks. It's just some…personal stuff I needed to document. I may never ask for it back, but just in case…"

"Got it." James grimaced down a swallow of the brown swill masquerading as coffee. "On what I'm sure is a totally unrelated note, how you doing these days?"

My eyes flicked back to his. "Fine."

"How did your conversation with… How did it go?'

Through clenched teeth I tersely said, "It's done."

James held my gaze over the top of his mug, silently studying me. "You're hurting," he observed in a low voice.

"I said I'm fine."

He was silent for a while. I could tell he was waging an internal battle with himself over whether to let this drop or not. Then he sighed. With obvious determination he said, "Declan, I missed out on almost thirty-five years with you, not to mention eight additional years I could've spent with the love of my life before she died. Not a day goes by I don't regret my choice. I don't want you to have similar regrets."

"I know," I muttered.

"Do you?"

"Do I what? Have regrets? Fuck, yeah! So goddamned many. But it is what it is. This is for the best." My tone declared the subject closed.

Proving once more how very alike we were, he chose to ignore it. "You sure?"

With a sigh, I said, "It has to be this way. I love my family and I *will* be there for them. That's the bottom line."

"Okay. I respect that. You made a very difficult decision and you're sticking by it. Good for you." He reached across the table and touched the back of my hand. "I know I should have got in touch years earlier, but I finally got my second chance with you. I'm so glad I'm part of your life now."

I offered him a tight but genuine smile. "I'm glad you're around, too. You know that."

"I do. I just want you to be happy, Declan. I truly hope someday you can have the life you really want, with the woman you really want to be with. You deserve it." He picked up his cup and took another sip.

My throat tightened, and I shifted my gaze out the window to the parking lot and the busy street beyond. We were both quiet for a while, drinking our lackluster coffee, lost in our thoughts.

When it was time to go we got up, but before we could move toward the door I stopped him.

"Thanks. I hope so, too," I admitted, looking him in those oh-so-familiar eyes.

My father, who in the mere ten months since I'd known him I'd grown to love like he'd always been around, smiled.

Amelia

Nearly two months had passed since I'd packed up my car and driven to Richmond to stay with Dee. Two months of trying—and more often than not, failing—to pick up the shattered remnants of my life and see if any of them still fit.

I'd love to boast about how strong I was, how I pulled myself together using a reserve of inner strength I didn't even know I had, and got on with the getting on with it.

But in reality, it didn't go quite like that.

Frequent nightmares plagued me. Sides of me that didn't exist in real life came out in those awful dreams—violent, nasty sides. Sometimes I dreamed I was yelling at Declan. More often, I was searching for him, desperate, frantic and unable to find him anywhere. But the ones that unnerved me the most were the dreams of punching Laura right in her perfect, fake-smiling face. I would wake up covered in sweat, clenching my fists so tight my fingernails left little crescents in my palms. The fierce woman I turned into in those dreams freaked me out. I often ended up in the corner of Dee's small living room rocking back and forth in her rocking chair in the dead of night, fingers clutching the wooden arm rests, knowing I would not be falling back asleep.

There were far more bad days than good for a long, long time, days when I didn't even leave my bed unless I absolutely couldn't avoid it. I cried too often, drank too much, and ate far too little. Time seemed to pass in miniscule increments, all too often holding me frozen in its grip, unable to see further ahead than the next glass of wine. Dee was the best friend a girl could want, but I tried even her stalwart patience sometimes.

Gradually those rare good moments began to stretch into good hours, and even, once in a while, almost entire days. They'd sneak up on me. I'd find myself enjoying simple things like an upbeat song on the radio, or the taste of a particularly delicious meal. I felt guilty sometimes, when I realized with a start that I felt okay. I wasn't sure I really deserved to feel okay.

Slowly those better days began happening more often. And bit by bit the crushing guilt started to subside. It didn't go away—I wasn't sure it ever really would—but it wasn't always at the forefront of my thoughts, gnawing away at me until I wanted to rip out my hair and claw off my skin. It lessened, a bit. And things sometimes…didn't suck.

I paid my share of the rent from the money I had socked aside. Dee suggested I do the accounting for her salon, and she discounted my fees from my portion of the expenses. We began to build a life together, simple as it was.

Scott and I had talked a little, when I'd gone back to retrieve more of my things. He was spending a lot of time with Liv, who had been acting kind of cool toward me—not that I blamed her. I hoped she was able to give him the comfort he needed. He seemed to be doing better, and I wasn't too worried about him anymore. I was confident he was going to be fine.

I even saw Declan once, a few weeks ago. I'd gone into BWK to meet Josh and the girls for lunch. In some bizarre coincidence, Sam picked that day to inform us all that Ryan was going to be an uncle again. It was new information only to Kaitlyn, but Josh's eyes had lifted to mine with sympathy. As we sat in the cafeteria chatting, my heart leapt when I saw Declan pop in to grab a sandwich. We didn't speak, but as our eyes met, he flashed me a tight grin. It wasn't much, but it was something. Better than a scowl, I guess.

It hurt to see him and not be able to talk to him. Flashes of the pain I'd felt that horrible Monday so many weeks before hit me, but I did my best to conceal it. I just kept telling myself that if it hurt *me* this bad, then he couldn't possibly be unaffected himself. No matter what

I'd thought the last time we spoke, I knew deep down he'd truly cared about me. There was no way he'd faked it. I'd seen in his eyes the depth of his feelings—they were real. And you can't just turn off loving someone, no matter how much you might wish you could.

God knows I knew that.

One of the last things Declan had said to me was, "Maybe someday." I didn't want to put any faith in those words. I knew it was just an empty phrase he'd tossed out to lessen the blow. But still. Someday. I had a lot of somedays ahead of me yet. If we really were meant to be together, then someday, somehow, somewhen, we would find our way back to each other.

And if we weren't, which I knew was probable, then this was for the best.

I was ready to accept it.

Life went on.

I continued to meet with Debbie Westwood, although not as often as before with my restricted financial situation. She knew about my separation from Scott and how I was trying to rebuild my life, but I still hadn't revealed the Declan-shaped catalyst to those events. To be honest, I wasn't sure I ever would. I think she realized I wasn't telling her the whole story, though. Last month she suggested I consider writing everything down somewhere, on paper, or in an anonymous blog, just to purge it all out away from judging eyes. She said it could be helpful in sorting out all my complex feelings without having to confess them out loud to anyone. I agreed to think about it, but didn't, really. Not until a few days after I saw Declan again, anyway.

I was wandering through Walgreen's after renewing my prescription when something purple on a bottom shelf caught my eye. It was a stack of fake-leather bound journals. When I was a teenager I used to write in a diary almost every night. I'd packed it away when I'd gone off to college, and hadn't really written anything that wasn't part of an assignment since. In high school I'd loved my senior Creative Writing class. My teacher had been inspiring, and at the time I'd been proud of the short stories and poems I'd written for her. Smiling to myself, I wondered where they'd ended up. At the bottom of a box in my mother's attic, no doubt. I bet if I dug them out and read them, they'd sound childish and embarrassing. It had been so long since I'd written anything just for me.

On impulse, I bought one.

Before bed, I pulled the journal out of the bag and propped it up on my pillow. I grabbed a pen off my night table and opened it to the first crisp, white page, smoothing it down with my fingertips. The familiar smell of new paper washed over me like some long forgotten memory, and as I inhaled, a strange calm descended. I had no idea what I wanted to say. I didn't have some grand intention to cathartically purge the tale of what I'd gone through. I just began to write:

My name is Amelia York and this is the story of the last year of my life.

Let me make one thing clear right off the bat. This is not a story about two people who met and fell in love, and of course had hurdles to overcome, but they loved each other enough that nothing was insurmountable. You know the ones—the kind where in the end true love always conquers all. This is a story about real life, and real love, and it may not be a fairytale, but it is ours.

THE END

About the Author:

J.S. Eades lives in southwestern Ontario, Canada, with her family. An avid traveler and scuba enthusiast, she can often be found under the warm waters of the Caribbean.

She's currently working on the *Forever Twenty-One* supernatural series.

Connect with me
Website: www.jseades.com
Facebook: AuthorJSEades
Twitter: @JS_Eades
Instagram: @jseadesauthor

Dear Readers
Thank you so much for reading my novel. If you enjoyed it, would you please take a moment to write an honest review on Amazon or Goodreads.com so other readers can find and hopefully enjoy it, too? Even just a few sentences would mean a lot to me.

Thank you!
J.S. Eades

Other Books by J.S. Eades

THE FINE ART OF FORGIVENESS
(Amelia and Declan book 2)

You don't always get what you want.

Amelia York knows this all too well. Her entire life has been torn apart and she's lost nearly everything that matters: her job, two of her closest friends, her father, and most devastating of all, the man she loves. Though she's gotten good at pretending she's fine, inside she's still shattered. All she wants is to move on and rebuild. She never thought it would be easy, but she didn't expect it to be this hard. And an impulsive decision at a friend's wedding throws a surprise wrench into her life that makes it even harder.

Declan Kavanaugh considers himself a damn good salesman, but he's got no pitch capable of convincing himself the choice he made was the right one. He promised to be there for his family, but he's hurting. And he misses *her* more than he's willing to admit. Can a miracle give him the second chance at happiness he craves? Or is he doomed to always destroy everything he cares about?

Things never turn out quite the way you think they will. But sometimes you might just get what you need

AGAINST ALL ADVICE

Giving advice is easy; taking it, on the other hand...

Evie Colville has one goal: earn a college scholarship to escape from small-town Sutterton. Between studying and working in her dad's coffee shop, she doesn't have much free time. None for a boyfriend, that's for sure.

Then she meets Alistair.

Alistair fled to his uncle's after the woman he loved brutally betrayed him with his own brother. The last thing he wants is another relationship. And after what he's gone through, he has zero tolerance for lies.

Evie, however, is keeping a big secret, not just from Alistair, but from everyone in town. Along with her other responsibilities, she's also the clandestine author of the local paper's Miss Lonely Love advice column. And recently she's been corresponding with a frustrated young man who has sworn off women for good.

Falling for each other is the *last* thing either wants. There's no possible way they could make this work.

Is there?

DEATH DEFYING
(Forever Twenty-One book 1)

What happens when you discover nothing you'd believed about yourself is true?

All Genny Dupont wants for her 21st birthday is to sleep in, eat a great breakfast, and go out dancing with her best friend. At first, it seems like her day goes exactly to plan. She even meets a cute guy at the club. But when they get together for coffee the next afternoon, she realizes she's made a huge mistake.

Because the story JP tells her, that she and her sister are the only remaining descendants of a family of immortal vampire slayers, is completely insane. He's obviously a lunatic. Disappointed, she walks out, but Genny can't quite shake the idea he's planted. Could he possibly have been telling the truth?

Learning about her family and how they died opens the door to a world she'd thought only existed in fiction. Sure, this world includes enemies that want her dead, but it's not all doom and gloom. As Genny starts to embrace her legacy, she and JP grow closer.

She's a slayer. JP insists vampires are evil. But when she strikes up an unlikely friendship with Quinn, a vampire who risked his own life to save her, she comes to understand that not everything—or everyone—is how it seems.

Books available at most online retailers.

www.ingramcontent.com/pod-product-compliance
Lightning Source LLC
Chambersburg PA
CBHW050900250626
47155CB00001B/42